HUNTED BY FAE

The Last Battle of Moytura Book I

MOLLY J STANTON

FREE BOOK

You're about to meet some unforgettable characters inside this book! I don't know about you, but even as a kid I always loved the villain. Luke Skywalker was cool and all, but Darth Vader was the best.

The villain in *Hunted by Fae* started her life as a goddess on the side of the light. But villains aren't born. They're made.

Download your copy of *Badb Catha: Betrayal of the Tuatha* today.

https://www.mollyjstanton.com/badbcatha.html

CHAPTER 1

PROLOGUE

25 years ago

The white-hot flame of raw power seared through every vein and nerve in her body, but nothing could be hot enough to purify her soul of the horror she was committing. Tears of pain and regret evaporated from her cheeks in wisps of steam. If they had only heeded her warnings. Seen the threat. They could have battled the forces of destruction together, preserved this precious Green World, and they wouldn't be dying at her feet.

Badb Catha looked down at her sisters' faces twisted in silent screams. Anand and Macha lay side by side, backs arched in torture. Once the siblings had been so close, referred to by a single name, the Morrigna, the Great Queens. For thousands of years, the Morrigna fought to protect this new world against forces of evil and destruction. Whether they battled against men, or the evil Fomorians whose power rivaled their own; they kept the balance. Now she was draining them of their magical essence. For the world to be preserved, her family had to die.

Part of her wished it wasn't so, but the power she required had to be like her own. Another's magic wouldn't bend to her will as easily. Another Tuatha's chaotic sea magic, for instance, would spread and squirm, rather than lance through obstruction.

A choked gurgle percolated through the grimace her youngest sister, Macha, wore. Macha, whose only mistake had been her inability to pick a side between her warring siblings.

Mother Danu, what have I done? She prayed to the creator of her people, the Tuatha. The torment written in her sister's sad blue eyes, the blood caking her strawberry hair, painted Badb Catha as a monster. For a fleeting second, Badb allowed her hands to dip, the torrent of magical power surging into them slowing to a trickle.

Flashbacks of the prophecy she'd spoken at the end of the second Great War thousands of years ago replayed visions of rivers aflame, leagues of forests reduced to stubble, and skies choked with poison. That instant at Moytura, on that ancient Plain of Towers, her life had changed. The night she left her people forever, she'd made a sacred pledge to be the blade for the voiceless. She gritted her teeth and the bright filaments of magic she was draining from her kin flared. *They made me betray them. Only I speak for this world now.*

"I'm sorry, my sisters. It's the only way." The words came out as a ragged gasp. "We're all lost if I fail." Her last word ended in a scream. One body, even that of a Tuatha, could only contain so much elemental power. This was akin to swallowing lightning. The strength drained from her legs. Her knees crashed to the earth, and her shoulders slumped.

Macha and Anand shrieked and writhed. Crackling white energy snapped and hissed along their bodies, on its way to their red-haired sister's outstretched arms.

Anand's hand, contorted into a claw, clutched the hem of Badb's black cloak. In her prime, Anand had led armies and mentored the greatest heroes of Inisfáil, now called Ireland.

Cuchulain, Arthur, and many more owed their skill in battle to her. Rattling sounds tore from her chest, brown eyes rolled back, and she fell still. The Phantom Queen was dead.

A sob, wretched and thick with self-loathing, shook Badb. Unbidden memories flowed once more. This time, the two of them flapped over battlefields in the guise of great ravens, war frenzy coursing through their veins while their enemies fled before them. No army prevailed against the Morrigna. The last of Anand's life force jabbed into Badb's muscles like a million hot needles. She howled.

Macha flailed and smacked her palms against the ground. Badb turned her face away. She couldn't bear to look at her. Macha was the gentlest of the three of them, and the most level-headed. She played war like a chess match. Analytical and cold but no less deadly.

It would seem Macha had one last surprise in her. She swept her leg and knocked Badb the rest of the way flat on the earth, facing her. Her hands spasmed involuntarily, clutching handfuls of dirt. She dragged herself along on her stomach closer to Badb and seized her shoulder.

"Look. At. Me." Macha rasped, every word squeezed through her clenched jaw. "Face what you have done."

Badb wrenched her head up. Blood poured from Macha's nose and mouth, her strawberry head trembling with the effort of skewering Badb with her glare. Pangs of sadness wrapped Badb's heart in an iron grip, squeezing a single sob that sent a wave along her entire body. *It'll all be worth it. It has to be.*

"Sister, I—" No words could explain or offer comfort.

Macha only pulled her lips from her teeth and released a long groan. When it ended, the irises disappeared from Macha's eyes while an invisible hand plucked her into the air. Arms and legs dangled beneath her cloak like a rag doll. Strawberry hair and dark blue cloth whipped around Macha as though blown by a vortex.

Badb Catha was no stranger to the force seizing her dying sibling. A similar experience had set her on the path that led to this moment. An oracle gripped her sister. Soon, the Great Mother Danu would speak through Macha's voice, portending what would come to pass. Would it foretell the success of Badb's attempt to rescue the world from its oppressors, or would she be condemned? She dreaded the prophecy, yet it pumped more magical energy into her sister. More power to drain from Macha now increased her chances for success.

Macha's limbs jerked and stiffened, empty eyes fixated on Badb, and her full ruby lips drew into a slow smile. Despite her waning life, Macha's voice carried through the entire Underworld and across the seas to the Undying Lands.

"The prophecies of the Morrigna stand incomplete, sister. But two of the three were spoken at the close of the Second Battle of Moytura. One by Anand. One by you. The final echoes from my own lips today." Macha paused and searched the skies. "Hear my words, Nuada my husband, wherever you are. Carry my oracle in your heart and stop this madness."

———

"THE LINE OF THE HIGH KINGS OF INNISFAIL,
    An unbroken chain.
The blood of Niall runs true.
A great shield in the West.
Between a ring of fire and a grey sea,
Where rivers meet stands a new Plain of Towers.
There, the last heir rises.
Sleeping giants wake.
When ancient enemies unite
 against the gathering storm,
Worlds split asunder,

THE IRISES FLICKERED BACK TO MACHA'S EYES AND HER voice was now her own, soft and ragged. "And now I claim my right to lay a geis upon you. Badb Catha, Betrayer of the Tuatha, if this gateway opens, you will be blind to the line of kings. Even if the heir stands before you, you will not see them. With my last breath, I deny you the rest of my power and I send it to the heir of Niall. May you fall in battle."

Badb felt the flow of magical energy from her sister cease like a door slammed shut. The air around Macha fell calm, and she plummeted to the earth with a dull thud.

Dead.

Badb's face contorted in rage. She threw her head back and howled. Balled fists pummeled a nearby tree. Sharp pain lanced up her wrists and hot, sticky blood flowed from her knuckles. She let gravity carry her sliding down the trunk. How dare she! Spite had never been a quality of her youngest sister. Her little power play might ruin everything.

Badb staggered back to her feet. Time was growing short. If she didn't work the sorcery her sisters had paid for with their lives, she would have to choose between allowing the magic of all three Morrigna to burn away her life, or release it back to their inert forms. Her body spasmed, struggling to contain nearly the power of three in one vessel. Her anger felt as wild as the magic boiling beneath her skin. If she couldn't stop this heir to Niall, murdering her sisters would count for nothing. Worse than that, both the Underworld and the Green World would die.

Badb bent forward, stamping the ground with her booted feet, pounding her fists against her thighs. With the outcome now uncertain, she could end this now. Pick up the bodies of Anand

and Macha and take them to the Undying Lands. As long as Badb didn't use their magical life force, they could be lowered into the Cauldron of Rebirth and wake with the new dawn. Her sisters would live again, and she could return to her exile.

Badb braced herself against a tree and scanned the Underworld landscape. This forest she stood in was once lush and bursting with color. Filled with chattering pixies and capering satyrs. Now the trees grew too far apart, twisted and leafless in a landscape painted in greyscale. Nothing more than the listless vegetation lived here anymore, yet nothing here died either. Everything just wound down and rotted without its connection to the Green World, and it was too damaged to sustain the connection that kept both vital. Two worlds depended on her.

Macha's geis might slow Badb down. Now her attention would have to be divided between bringing the Fae to their new home and putting an end to this heir. She promised herself that hope remained. She would merely need more allies to hunt down and kill every last descendant of Niall in this new Plain of Towers, since she, herself, would be unable to discover them.

The Fomorians ruled the human world now, pulling the levers of power in secrecy. The sour taste of disgust painted the back of her throat. In the past, she'd worked with one in particular, and he owed her. And there were other, even less savory allies she could draw upon. Some dark Fae, some even worse. Once she discovered where this new Plain of Towers lay, she'd summon them to purge it of every descendant of Niall.

Her plan had to move forward and fast. Her body was failing under the strain of her forbidden sorcery. *I must make the gateway,* she told herself, *geis be damned.*

Badb reached a shaking hand into the deep inner pocket of her black cloak and drew out a gleaming golden branch with metallic silver leaves. How she obtained it, perhaps an even bigger crime than murdering her family, for there was but a single Alheimurinn tree in all existence, and she held the last vestige of it. The magical tree had grown in the Dragon's Spine mountain range in the Underworld but formed connections to all times and places, the only thing powerful enough for reestablishing travel between the worlds.

She levered herself to the earth on one knee, worked the little branch into the dry, cracked soil, and poured her stolen magic into it. All that energy draining from her felt like deflating a waterskin, the flames and pressure raging through her body calming as the branch soaked it up, growing to a towering height in seconds.

The tree pulsed with light, bark rippling. The trunk rocketed skyward, its flailing branches whistled. When the tree could stretch no more, it coiled itself into a circle.

She sent her mind slithering down the roots of the tree. The jagged tips of roots wormed through stony soil. Deeper and deeper they grew and then whacked into a barrier.

Badb felt the wall between worlds thickened, like the stone of a castle. Long ago, there were places in the Veil so thin even humans with no magical blood could pass through. Their folklore brimmed with stories of such travelers. But the Green World was too damaged for that now. The barrier had thickened like a callous everywhere. Not even one of the Tuatha had the strength to cut through it. But in this moment, Badb Catha was not one of the Tuatha. She was three.

She propelled all her powers, stolen and her own, along the roots against the barrier. Her teeth clenched with the effort. Sweat poured down her face. The harder she pushed, the more unyielding the wall became. She dug down, scraped up as much magic as she could, and hurled it full force down the roots like a battering ram. She staggered forward when the barrier broke. Too exhausted to catch herself, she tumbled to the ground and lifted her green eyes to drink in the beauty.

A surface appeared in the center of the tree, shimmering like a lake in the sun. Beyond it, tall pine trees and the full moon visible even through drizzle. The smile on her lips felt foreign. It had been long since she had experienced such joy. A blast of energy blew in from the Green World side, a cool breeze on a stifling day. All around her prone form, tiny blue flowers sprouted. The first new thing that had grown in the Underworld in decades.

She lay for a moment, feeling life seep into the Underworld once more. She clambered into a crouch. Her knees shook and her head felt like it would split apart, but she had to step through, see the other side. It had been too long.

Badb rested a pale hand on the warm golden bark. Its living energy pulsed as though a heart beat within it. With a deep breath, she lifted her black boot and emerged on the other side to a warm summer night. The beach of an island glistened in the moonlight where two great rivers flowed on either side.

Badb laughed. Fortune had smiled on her, for she already stood in the place Macha's prophecy foretold. A new Plain of Towers nestled in the shadow of a long-dormant volcano. Ring of fire. She'd bet a sea lapped a sandy shore to the west.

The twinkling orange lights in the distance would be beautiful if they didn't signify a human city. She thought of the forest that gave its life in order for that place to exist. Razed to the ground. Nothing left. But this island had escaped that fate. It looked pristine. If humans lived here, they were far enough away they wouldn't find her until it was too late. The perfect place to carve out a new home for her people.

With the last of her magic, she inhaled. Cool air flooded her lungs until she could draw no more and she released it. Breath poured out as a thick mist. It crawled and spread along the ground, thickening as it went. Thousands of years ago, the Tuatha had arrived at Innisfail in a mist with the goal to shape the world for the coming humans. Now Badb created a mist to form a new homeland for the Fae. A base from where they would annihilate humanity and reclaim what was theirs.

Badb looked back through the portal at a winged form flapping toward her. She held up her arm, and the crow flew through the portal to land. She ruffled the bird's feathers. He croaked and ran his beak along her arm. His red eyes glittered.

"Fiach, my pet, our war begins."

CHAPTER 2

Harper O'Neill chewed absently on the fleshy pink eraser at the end of her pencil and smoothed a stray brown lock back into the end of her braid. Lukewarm air wafted from the vent above her desk, never hot enough to take the chill from an autumn day nor cool enough to wring the swelter from the swampy air in summer. For the fifth time in the same hour she checked the clock. Forty-five minutes and the tedium of her receptionist job would end and the guessing game she'd played every day for nearly ten years would begin. Which mother would greet her when she walked through the door at home. Would Eileen O'Neill be drunk and hopeless, drunk and obsessed, or drunk and frenetic?

Sandwiched between the mind-numbing boredom of office work and the gut-wrenching misery of her home life was Emilio. The cramped, smelly bus ride home every day marked a liminal state where she could lose herself in his bubbly optimism and life would feel a little less pointless. It had been the same way since they'd met in middle school.

She rubbed a weary hand across her round face and balanced on tiptoes to check the waiting room for new patients to check in.

This time of day, the office normally brimmed with the miserable and the indigent uncomfortably shifting around on the beige waiting room chairs that she swore only existed to motivate people never to be early for their appointments. Her brows edged closer to each other over her hazel eyes as she plopped back down to her seat. The past few weeks' attendance in the mental health clinic had slowed to a trickle, something that hadn't happened in the four years she'd worked here.

The rat-tat-tat of steady rain assaulted windows tiny enough to belong to a prison. Her thin lips pressed to an even thinner line. *Nice work, Harper, left your umbrella again. How long have you lived in Portland?* She resigned herself to a soaked mad dash to the bus stop. Her head dropped back against the back of her chair and she spun in a lazy circle. Dull white ceiling tiles wheeled over her head.

Halfway around her second circle, Harper spotted Candace behind her rifling through the filing cabinet while returning a client record, her pink lips silently mouthing letters of the alphabet while matching pink acrylic nails scrambled across rows of manila folders. Harper whipped the chair back around and organized the highlighters and papers on her desk. The click-clack of stilettos on tile announced the therapist's arrival at the reception desk.

"That's the third no-show today. Guess everything's more important than taking care of your mental health," Candace mused as she arrived at Harper's desk. Her perfume cloyed. Like spicy cotton candy and Candace Brown marinated in it. "Before you go, can you call these three patients for me and reschedule them?"

"Sure thing." Harper pulled the paper over next to the phone and a familiar name leapt out at her. Dull as it may be, her job had reunited her with her childhood friend, Abraham, and for that, she was thankful. He was due for therapy every Friday; she'd hoped she just missed him while downstairs filing. Her hand drifted to the jacket pocket where she kept the protein bars she had brought for him today. "It's not like Abraham to miss."

"I bet it's Dust. One of Tim's clients got hooked on that junk. It took him out fast."

"Took him out? Like he's dead?"

"No one knows. He was living in the tent city over off Burnside. Tim said he came in one day raving about weird black-haired teenagers. He left his jacket in the waiting room. There was a vial of Dust in his pocket. No one's seen him since."

"And you think Abraham's on drugs." Harper's voice was flat. She couldn't imagine her friend using drugs, much less a new and dangerous one.

"Dunno. Either way it means a tiny paycheck for me." Candace shrugged and minced back to her office.

Right. Like your paycheck is the most important thing when people might be missing.

Harper pulled the end of her nut-brown braid across her shoulder and twined the end around her fingers. The homeless may not have homes, but most of them had cell phones. She dialed Abraham's first. No answer. None of the patients picked up and her concern grew. What were the odds of all five people missing her calls?

The clock announced the end of her shift, and she forced the niggling worries back down. They had plenty of company in there. She tucked the bars meant for Abraham into her olive drab backpack, slung it over her shoulders, and stepped out of the building. Grey sidewalk matched the grey sky. The rain paused, but in its wake, the air hung around the city like a wet blanket. Leaves in shades of orange and brown slicked the sidewalk, and a steady stream of cars marked the start of rush hour.

Throngs of pedestrians glued to the comforting glow of their phones herded by, oblivious to the cluster of homeless huddled under an awning. That was the problem with the city. No one saw or cared about the suffering around them. Most people bumbled mindlessly through the day-to-day blissfully unaware of how close most probably were from sleeping in an alley themselves. Perhaps selective blindness brought a sense of safety. But Harper knew full well how fragile stability was.

After Harper's father was murdered and her mom went on an involuntary trip to the psychiatric hospital, her mother had lost their house and they'd landed on the cold streets. Six months they slept on a concrete bed that seeped every ounce of warmth from Harper's body while hunger coiled in her stomach like a wild beast.

That was when she first met Abraham. Abraham had protected them, showed them the ropes, taught them the rules of the street. Like a high school basketball coach, he stayed near, correcting their behavior play by play so they wouldn't be victimized.

He'd say things to Harper like 'Keep your head down, don't get noticed, and never, ever stick your nose in stuff that ain't your business. But if trouble comes your way, be ready to fight like hell.' Wisdom she lived by with rare exception.

Child protective services put an end to their life on the streets and gave Harper an opportunity to put every one of Abraham's lessons into action. After being passed around from foster home to foster home for thirteen months, she applied the 'fight like hell' part when her mother stabilized just enough for a trial run at reuniting. From that moment on, Harper managed her mother. She dumped the alcohol in the house before home visits, did well in school, kept the home clean herself, and CPS backed out of their lives.

Still today, she applied the 'keep your head down and not be noticed' part. Harper was already quite average in many ways. Average height. Average build. Average looks. She was easy not to notice, and she strove to never make waves. Waves, good or bad, brought the system, and Harper had had enough of the system. On the streets with her unlikely mentor, Harper grew up early. She owed him, but more than that, she cared for him.

Abraham was a good man. Fought a war no one wanted to fight but, despite his service, life had thrown him to the gutter. The horrors of war in that distant jungle left him shattered. He could have become bitter or numb, but he hadn't. Instead, Sergeant Wilkes defended a new country: the ranks of the down and out. Even though almost no one in this city noticed him, he was a hero to Harper.

She drifted to a group of people she recognized as patients of the office, each of them wearing the same bone-weary sag to their eyes. They smiled gap-toothed grins at her approach. With a shimmy, the backpack slid from her shoulders. Harper scrabbled around the front pocket for the protein bars and sandwich she'd not eaten at lunch.

"Here, guys. Stay safe out here tonight."

A small Hispanic woman bobbed her head and smiled, passing some bars to each of her friends. "Thank you, sweetheart, and god bless."

Harper grinned. God hadn't seen fit to bless any of these people for a very long time. Grubby fingers tore open wrappers while Harper loped toward Burnside Avenue to catch the bus home.

A familiar shape leaned against the bus shelter, flipping through his smartphone. Emilio's black slacks and tailored wool jacket clashed horribly with the blue streaks in his black hair. His usual electric blue mesh shirt and purple Dr. Martens boots better matched both his sweeping hair and his flamboyant personality. Even a paid internship at Erimus Pharmaceutical couldn't tame him completely. In addition to his colorful hair, he sported a shiny bright purple tie no serious businessman would wear.

She raised her hand and waved to her best—well, only—friend.

Emilio slipped his phone into his pocket and beamed so wide Harper couldn't help but smile back despite the anxiety souring her stomach. While she had to hide under the cloak of being average in as many ways as she could, Emilio was a live wire. She lived vicariously through his harmless misadventures.

"How's working for the man?" Harper asked.

"You'll never believe what I scored from the marketing department!" Emilio's eyes bugged above his grin and the words tumbled out of him, accompanied with exaggerated sweeps of his hands.

"Free samples?"

"Oh. Ha. Ha." Emilio waggled his head. Undeterred by her dry response, he pulled two brightly colored strips of fabric from his pocket. Smiling ear to ear, he handed the strips to her.

Harper turned the pair of nylon admission bracelets in her hand and read aloud. "Mystic Island Admission. What's this?"

"Only the hottest ticket in town. Been sold out since they released tickets. Turns out Erimus is the main event sponsor. Marketing gave them to all the new interns! I bought us some matching accessories at lunch." He jammed his hand into the messenger bag at his side. His massive collection of pins and buttons clacked together, another stubborn vestige of a less corporate life. He dug a crinkly purple bag out of the front pocket and ripped the contents free of tissue paper.

Harper wrung her hands and studied the constellation of ancient chewing gum dotting the sidewalk. She bit her bottom lip while her friend shoved the wrapping into a trash can.

"Check these out." Emilio held up two intricate headbands, one black, one red. Each sported a single horn protruding from the middle flanked by soft velvety ears. Gems and flowers wove around the ears and horn and sparkled even in the overcast Pacific Northwest light.

He thrust the red horn into Harper's hand. The bauble

dangled limply by her side while she watched Emilio slide the black headband over his blue-streaked hair. His fingers fumbled around by his left ear, eventually flipping a tiny switch along the edge. The horn sprang to life with pulsating multicolored lights.

"These are so freaking cool. Watch," he said as he gyrated and whirled around on the sidewalk to a beat only he could hear. He wheeled his arms and spun around like a wild man. The horn's rainbow of lights blinked and swirled in time to his movements.

"It changes the pattern as you move. Put yours on. Imagine, the entire island covered in gnomes, fairies, and vampires. But we will be fabulous unicorns." Emilio swept his hand across himself like Vanna White revealing the solution to a word puzzle. The horn's lights pulsated a slow blue like a heartbeat.

Harper glanced down at the glitzy contraption in her hands and sighed. Emilio's dancing wound down like a mechanical toy and the joy melted from his face.

"This is where you bail on me."

"I don't know, Emilio. It's not really a good time. Mom's a train wreck right now." The bus announced its arrival with a squeal of brakes and flung its doors wide.

Emilio swept the headband from his head and let his hand flop to his side. "Eileen's always a train wreck. One night. She can take care of herself for one night." His head hung as he stepped onto the bus and dropped into a seat. Harper slid in next to him. The usual mix of students, commuters, and the unfortunate packed the bus. All wore the same hunched back and tired droop to their features.

"It's easy for you to just bop off to a party with a day's notice. I've got responsibilities at home, you know that." Harper's words carried an edge. "You know how we both get this time of year." Roughly a week would mark the tenth anniversary of her father's murder. It had happened right in their old home. Her eyes focused on her scuffed black loafers, unable to bear the look of disappointment Emilio no doubt wore. She felt the pull of protecting her mother dragging her in one direction and the force of not disappointing Emilio jerking her in the other.

"When do you get to live your own life?"

"I know, but she needs me." Harper placed a hand on Emilio's shoulder and finally meet his deep brown eyes. She managed a weak smile she hoped was reassuring. His lips were slightly down-turned, and he focused on the back of the seat in front of them.

"I love your mom, too. But she's smothering you."

Harper hated the look on her friend's face. "Let me see how she's doing tonight and I'll FaceTime you after dinner. I really do want to go."

And she did. It had been months since she'd been able to just turn off her mind and cut loose, something she rarely allowed herself the freedom to do.

The change in Emilio was immediate. He clapped his hands and lifted his spine straight. "Awesome!" he said in a sing-song voice. "We can plan our outfits. I'll help you with yours. This is the event of the season. You can't just wear any old thing." He waved his hand up and down, mock assessing her rather bland government job outfit, but his face tilted toward an unruly passenger.

A man in filthy, torn canvas pants staggered backward, almost running into Harper's shoulder.

"Hey! Watch—" Harper's rebuke died on her lips. His mouth hung in an expression of blissful surprise matching the low bubbling laugh percolating from his chest while he pointed at an invisible something near the ceiling of the bus. A string of drool threatened to fall on Harper's shoulder, so she nudged him with her foot across the aisle toward the rear steps.

Other riders muttered to themselves and shifted in their seats to avoid eye contact. As the man clapped his hands in glee, Harper noticed a pale lavender powder around his nose.

Next to her, Emilio let out a hiss. "Dust head. Everyone knows if you do too much you go completely loopy." He spiraled his hand around his ear and rolled his eyes.

"You do Dust? Don't be stupid." She knew Emilio dabbled in various substances, but Dust was raging through this city. No one knew what it did long term.

"You're just hypersensitive because your mom's a drunk," he shot back with a dramatic shrug.

Harper's eyes flashed. A hundred scathing retorts ran a race to her tongue. No one knew what they'd endured, not even her best friend. Not everyone came through adversity whole. Before she could respond, Emilio spread his hands.

"I'm sorry. I shouldn't have said that."

A lump formed in Harper's throat. "I shouldn't have called you stupid." She rested a hand on his knee just as the bus jerked to a stop where he usually exited. "Please, just stay away from Dust. I think it might kill people. A lot of clients at my job are missing."

Emilio nodded and slid past her. "I promise I won't become a hopeless drug addict. Talk to you after dinner." With that, he bounded off the bus.

Harper's phone chimed. A text from her mom. The screen full of manic ramblings told her it would be a rough night. Harper clicked her phone off without reading it and focused her gaze where the intoxicated man had been. He must have got off the bus with Emilio. Seeing his bizarre behavior made her worry even more about Abraham. If he was on this stuff too, there was no telling what trouble he might stagger into.

The tent city where he lived most of the time was near the next stop. She decided to check on him. At least it would give her another hour before she had to go home. If she waited a little longer, her mother's mania and the alcohol might make her pass out. Then there'd be no chance of any fireworks.

CHAPTER 3

Nuada pulled his long black coat tight around him. The damp chill went straight for his bones, especially where the silver arm attached to his shoulder. He wondered why the cauldron revived him with it rather than the arm of flesh and blood the brilliant healer Miach had grown for him before their war with the Fomorians. Probably a sign he would not be High King for a third time, for no one blemished could sit on the throne.

He feared at this point no one would take that throne ever again, Tuatha or human. Gazing out at the throngs of people bustling about the city hypnotized by tiny screens they clutched in their hands offered little hope of a savior. He found it impossible to imagine the heir of Niall he sought could be among them. They all acted like automata wound by an unseen hand, repeating the same motions over and over each day with no real thought behind their actions. All of them were shadows of the humanity he knew in Inisfáil, or as it was known now, Ireland.

Macha had always told him he judged them too harshly. She had loved to call him a curmudgeon, pointing out the artists and visionaries among them. A familiar ache pulled his heart low. He missed her. With no throne and the Tuatha scattered through the three worlds, hope grew slim. Her entreaty to him, carried on the wings of a magical prophetic storm, was the sole reason he clung to this world. *Protect the heir of Niall,* and he dragged himself from lead to lead making good on his promise to grant her dying wish, but it got harder every year because, without Macha, life felt meaningless.

Over a quarter-century had passed since her prophecy echoed in his mind on the night she died. Oracle or not, she'd want him to battle tyranny no matter who perpetrated it. Long ago he wouldn't have needed her urging for that battle, but tens of thousands of years of the same repeating fight wore him thin. Perhaps he, too, was an automaton now.

Deeper than honoring his lost wife, the simmering desire for vengeance kept him dragging one foot in front of the next, plodding on this path searching for Badb Catha. And when he found her, she would pay for murdering his wife. Her own sister. He would relish every delicious moment of her death. Perhaps the silver arm wasn't the only sign he was no longer fit for High Kingship.

He kept his head down against the putrid air of the city and walked swiftly up the street labeled 'Burnside.' The sun had slipped behind the clusters of square towers the humans jammed together and called a city. Years walking the earth in these times never took the shock out of seeing modern cities. They were like an unforgiving desert of flat stone. And they reeked of poison and rot.

Over a decade of false starts made him think the lead that brought him to this street would be just another dead end to add to his growing collection. That the information came from a phooka heightened the probability of a wild goose chase. Still, he had worked with this particular phooka before. The Fae had more or less delivered, and he'd mentioned seeing an all too familiar red-eyed crow in the tent city for three consecutive nights. Phooka are Fae. Fae cannot lie. In the tens of thousands of years Nuada walked the Green World, he had known only two red-eyed corvids. Both of them Badb's pets.

As if on cue, the squawk and din of a flock of crows swarmed overhead. Nuada craned his neck to peer into the sky. His long silver hair slipped from beneath his black coat and carpeted his back. There must have been hundreds of dark birds. Great clouds of them wheeled across the skies, banking and turning as though of a singular mind. Most were too small to be crows. Curiouser and curiouser. Crows, even Badb's flock, didn't play nice with other birds, and these, he decided, looked a little off.

A furry black shape bouncing toward him interrupted Nuada's observations. A jet-black dog, roughly shaped like a German Shepherd, sauntered up the sidewalk. Quick intelligence emanated from the canine's striking yellow eyes. The Phooka.

Nuada nodded toward him and they both meandered into the alley. Once out of sight of the pedestrians, the Phooka padded close to Nuada.

"You see the birds?" The Phooka swiveled his head side to side, likely in surveillance of the alley. A talking dog would definitely raise a few eyebrows in the human world.

"They were quite obvious."

"They're worse than birds. Sluagh. And they arrive first every night. After that, others come."

Nuada narrowed his eyes at the Phooka. "Fae trapped here when the Veil between the worlds thickened and closed do visit human cities from time to time. Present company included. What's so unusual about this?"

"Look, Silver Hand, I'm doing you a favor. There's something happening here that shouldn't be. You wanted to be alerted to strange goings on, consider yourself alerted."

Nuada rested the flat of his boot against the grimy brick wall and leaned backward against it. Almost all phooka were aligned with the Unseelie Courts. While the Bright Court had no love of humanity, the Night Court loathed them. If anyone was in league with Badb, it would be the Unseelie. They'd helped her in the past. Yet here was the Phooka blowing the proverbial whistle. That is, if his intel panned out.

"Strange goings on, as you so eloquently put it, are hardly evidence it involves Badb Catha. Yet you seem certain it's her. Just how do you know that, I wonder?"

"You got pants under that dress?"

"It's a coat," Nuada said. "Meant to conceal this." He pulled the hem aside to reveal an intricately carved scabbard with the radiant grip of a magical sword peeking out the top.

"Is that—"

"Ready to cut the malarkey?"

"You got any?"

"Any what?"

"Malarkey." The Phooka licked his lips.

Nuada's hand hovered over the sword and he leveled his gaze at the Phooka.

The Fae reared up on his haunches and held his paws in front of him. "Great former king, I am but a lowly Fae unused to the highfalutin' ways of the Tuatha. I'm merely here to humbly report my concerns. I leave any assessment of who is behind these nefarious goings on to your superior kingly awesomeness and lofty intellect." The Phooka dropped back down, placed one paw in front of the next, and bowed his head to the ground, pointy ears brushing the concrete. His jaws pulled into a sideways dog smile while his yellow eyes narrowed to slits.

Classic Fae non-answer. They may not be able to lie, but they were still slippery. Phooka in particular. Nuada lacked the patience for Fae nonsense; he was here, he'd just have to keep one eye on the Phooka and the other on whatever came to this place tonight.

"Just what are we expecting to see in this den of human misery?" Nuada asked.

"Oh, I wouldn't want to ruin the surprise. You'll be on the edge of your seat." Black paws hovered at face level, framing the scene of tents at the end of the brick-lined alley. His voice dropped deep and garrulous. "In a world where the downtrodden languish in forgotten alleys. Where the earth has turned to stone and the air to poison. Where no one believes in monsters anymore. Something wakes. Shadows stir. A creature rare and dark from another world waits to strike. A shapeshifter and his sidekick are the only hope for—"

"After all these years—"

"All right, all right. You can have top billing." The Phooka dropped his voice low again. "A musty has-been demigod needs the help of his wondrous, swashbuckling sidekick to remove the stick from his—"

Nuada sighed and rolled his eyes. "Just lead the way."

"You're right. We should grab front row seats and see for ourselves how this gripping horror show plays out." A grey satchel appeared at the dog's side. He reached a paw in and pulled out a bag of popcorn.

Nuada pushed off from the wall and swept a hand up the alleyway, inclining his head toward the tent city. The Phooka gripped the popcorn bag in his jaws and sauntered up the alley, bushy black tail bobbing merrily from side to side. Nuada had the sinking feeling he would regret granting this trickster an audience.

CHAPTER 4

Harper's black loafers clomped along the sidewalk toward the homeless encampment, splashing grimy water onto the hems of her plain navy slacks. The clammy autumn mist draped over her skin like a mask, pasting the wispy escapees of her braid to her cheeks. Rush-hour traffic filled the street with a cacophony of bleating horns and revving engines. People stuck in metal boxes going nowhere fast.

Despite the clammy air, Harper loved fall. The trees lit the world on fire with a final passionate display before pulling on a snowy blanket where life paused and dreamed fertile spring fantasies.

It was a time of year Harper's own aspirations surfaced. Distant hopes of traveling the world away from the only city she'd called home beckoned. But Portland closed in around her like a cage. This was where her life crumbled beneath her feet and where year after year she barely hung on. The romantic idea of fleeing to a sunny beach in Cancun, spending a month in an ashram in Mumbai, or hitchhiking across Europe made her wonder who she would be in those wondrous places. Certainly not the exhausted, boring woman she was now.

Reality dashed plans of adventure and discovery fast. Who would look after her mom while she chased dreams never meant for people like her?

Her shoulders ached from the weight of the backpack. She made a little hop and hoisted it into a higher position, feeling instant relief. Emilio always poked fun at her for the sheer amount of stuff she kept in there. He'd dramatically mime weightlifting moves whenever he handed her the bag. For added effect he'd belt out his best weightlifter grunt. She always laughed him off. Better to be prepared than up a creek without a paddle.

On their own, Harper's feet slowed their rhythmic march toward her indigent friend's home. A quick check of the seventeen more texts her mother had sent gave time for her mind to catch up with the growing sense of wrongness permeating the area.

The shadowy maw of the back alley straddled two neatly defined worlds. Behind her a glimmering city of artsy prosperity. Ahead lay its shadow: a pocket of desperation where the forgotten languished in squalor. All the world had to offer them was a walking death.

She peered down the alleyway. She'd visited this camp plenty of times. Her office managed several outreach services to the homeless, and Harper always volunteered her time to attend. This time, though, the encampment felt off in a way she couldn't quite verbalize, but her heart shifted up a gear in response to the nebulous sense of discord.

The stench of hot garbage assaulted her nose with its acrid mix of sour and rancid. Harper picked her way around some discarded chairs with her sleeve pulled over her mouth and nose. Nearly a hundred lost souls bivouacked among these buildings under tents, boxes, and tarps. That many people always made a fair amount of noise at dusk, bustling about, conversing, and cooking food over metal fire barrels.

The rasp of dry brick scraped under her hand resting on the corner of a red building. She turned her ear toward the camp. The only sounds she could discern came from the river of rush-hour traffic in the street behind. The tent city was as quiet as a graveyard. Not only that, but almost no one milled around the rows of improvised quarters. A thousand spiders raced up her spine. This was wrong. Very wrong.

Harper stepped to the edge of the alleyway, keeping her shoulder pressed tight to the building. An exit back the way she'd come, one to the left to another alleyway, and plenty of cover to her right with rows of hulking dumpsters hugging the walls promised options should her expedition go sideways.

The blood rushing in her ears sounded like it was actually whispering 'run, run, run' with every thump of her heart. Right now, listening to her heart seemed like the wisest plan, but she had to find out if Abraham needed help.

I'll just do a quick walk-through and see if he's here. Get out before it's dark. She reached her arm around to the front pouch of her backpack. Short fingers scrabbled over the edges, seeking the zipper. Tooth by tooth, she dragged the zipper open, attempting to muffle the sound while she sought a weapon.

In the wake of her family tragedy, self-defense became a warm blanket; she always carried something with her to fend off an attacker if escape failed. All part of the 'fight like hell' piece of Abraham's sage advice all those years ago.

She chose a short black collapsible baton from the compartment stuffed with an assortment of small-scale weapons. Something she picked up after one of her self-defense classes that had quickly become a favorite. Easier to sneak into venues than a knife and less likely to backfire on you than pepper spray. Her fingers gripped the handle until her knuckles turned white.

A torrent of black wings and furious squawking erupted from a dumpster. She staggered back, yelping. The baton extended with a flick. The reflex that came from training coiled her in a defensive crouch, ready to strike out in any direction. Flapping wings fluttered at the corner of her eye. Crows. And something smaller, but just as inky black. They scattered upward to the tops of the building, their sharp squawks cursing her for the intrusion.

Just a bunch of birds. You interrupted their fine dining at Chez Dumpster. Holy hell, Harper, you gotta chill. Or not. It's too quiet. Wait, doesn't the crap always hit the fan when someone says that in movies?

A single black bird refused to join its cackling brethren. It perched on the dumpster rim, muttering and clacking its beak. Then the bird took two bounding hops around the rusty lip, twisting and cocking its head from side to side. She felt studied under scarlet eyes.

Crows don't have red eyes, do they?

An icy wave washed over her. She whacked the side of the container with the baton. The clank made the bird take flight. "Go on. Get the hell out of here." The crow ascended to the top of the building to join its brothers, oddly silent.

Harper tore her eyes from the murder of crows and stepped around the corner. A colorful group of tents and tarps fluttered in the breeze. The garish colors would have looked festive if the place wasn't the last stop of the ones society had cast off.

Plastic shopping bags blew like tumbleweeds across this societal desert. A handful stuck to the shopping carts full of junk parked by some tents. Barrels usually simmering with cooking fires stood cold under scrubby trees. Only one cooked tonight. A single metal cylinder crackled and popped with flame.

"That you making all that racket?" a deep and raspy voice said.

Harper started, pivoting toward the speaker. A tall, thin black man emerged from the tent next to the lit barrel.

"Yeah, it was me. The crows scared the crap out of me. Sorry." She gave a nervous laugh.

The man scanned her up and down. His hand swept over her sky-blue wool sweater and pressed slacks. "What you doing here, young miss?"

"Looking for a friend." Harper sidled over to stand across the barrel from the man. He looked to be in his fifties with short, tightly curled grey hair. He wore a filthy orange sweatshirt, tattered jeans, and sneakers that appeared composed of duct tape.

"You don't look like you got friends from 'round here."

"Do you know a guy named Abraham, a little taller than me, grey hair and a beard?" Harper's hand hovered a couple inches over her head.

"Yeah, young miss, I know Abraham."

"Is he here? Is he OK? I'm Harper, by the way." She stuck out her hand.

"Dante." He gripped her hand. "I seen him earlier today. Might still be in his tent. The green one on the far right along the back row. As for him bein' OK, no, Harper, I don't think he is."

Harper's stomach plummeted to her knees. "What happened to him?"

"Best you just turn 'round and take yourself outta here. It's not safe in these parts."

"Please. He's my friend. Just tell me."

Dante drew his head back like he needed that extra inch of distance to size her up. "Easier to show you. Follow me."

He motioned her forward with a finger pressed to his lips. Harper fell into step behind him. The pair wove between a row of empty tents. The gravel crunched underfoot, too loud for the peculiar quiet. In moments, a grassy patch opened out between scrubby trees that clawed their way toward what little light fell between the buildings.

Harper stifled a yelp at the scene before her. The handful of people in the clearing were each behaving very strangely.

A young woman with red hair and unfocused eyes stroked the side of a small tree. Her mouth hung open, head tilting to the side. She bent forward from the waist and kissed the rough bark. Across from her, an old man slumped on the ground, rocking back and forth and laughing. He stuffed his face with handfuls of grass he yanked from the ground and smiled as though it were a lavish banquet. A group of younger people stood in a circle, admiring something that wasn't there. Looks of complete awe made their grubby faces radiant. Harper and Dante hovered at the threshold of a magical world. Only they couldn't behold the miracles.

"What the hell are they doing?" Harper stepped back and something crunched beneath her feet. She lifted her shoe and peered at the ground beneath. Shards of glass from a small vial sparkled in the light. A purple residue with an opalescent sheen clung to the broken bits. Harper bent down to inspect and saw several empty vials scattered around the edges of the path.

"Dust," Dante said and pointed at the pieces. "You breathe that junk in and go on a hell of a trip." He jerked his thumb toward the clearing. "Been spreadin' like wildfire 'round here."

"How long do they stay like that?"

"First few times, two hours, maybe three. Each time gets longer and longer until one day they go wandering off. Never come back."

"Wandering off? Where?"

"Dunno. All I know is they use that junk long enough, when the Dark Boys come, they follow 'em. We don't see 'em again."

Harper swallowed hard. "Dark Boys?" A tremor in her voice.

"You don't wanna know, Harper. This ain't your fight."

"But it is. I lived near here when I was homeless. Abraham helped me, and I have to help him now if he's in trouble. Just tell me about the Dark Boys."

Dante pursed his lips and shrugged his shoulders. "Bunch of teen boys. They ain't right. All of 'em got jet-black hair, look like brothers. They bring the Dust. About time for them now. Always show up as the sun's goin' down. Never speak, just smile and hand out vials. Then some of 'em follow the music." Dante pointed at a cluster of hallucinating people.

Music. Drugs. Odd boys. Questions chased each other around and around. "If they end up disappearing, why does anyone take this stuff?" Harper asked.

Dante chuckled. "Look around." His hand swept over the camp. "For a few hours they bliss out and the world is beautiful. They forget they live here. For just a bit they ain't worried about being too cold. Or wet. Or hungry. Don't notice the rock that jabs into their back when they sleep. And the Dark Boys never ask for anything in return. For just a while, it's a way out of this hell."

They walked back toward Dante's shelter. Looked like her arrival had interrupted his packing. He had a shopping cart filled with his possessions parked to the side of the burning barrel.

"I'm gettin' out of here tonight. I don't want no part of them Dark Boys." He tossed a pair of boots into the cart.

Harper unslung her backpack and reached into the front pocket. She pulled out the last couple of protein bars and all the cash she had. She held it out to Dante. "It's not much," she said, "but it should get you out of the city."

"I may be poor, but I don't need no charity, Harper."

"It's not charity. You've been a wonderful tour guide."

Dante smiled and accepted the gift. "This ain't no place for you. You should leave before them Dark Boys come."

Harper smiled at him and nodded. "I'll be leaving soon. I need to find my friend. Be safe, Dante, this is no place for you either."

With that, Dante pushed his cart up the alleyway. Harper watched him go for a moment and waved at him when he neared the mouth of the alley. He waved back and disappeared from sight behind the dumpster.

Hues of deep orange and yellow seeped into the horizon. *They always show up as the sun's going down.* If she could find Abraham before she ran into danger, she'd need to hurry. She held the baton in front of her like a shield and sidled toward her friend's green tent.

A tall man with long, straight silver hair leaned against the next building. He looked like he belonged here even less than she did. Long black coat hung all the way to the middle of his black motorcycle boots. Too new to mark him as a resident. A voluminous hood occluded most of his face.

At his feet sat a jet-black dog. Not in itself unusual, but most dogs didn't have bright yellow eyes. And most dogs didn't drill into you with their eyes unless you had food, and she was fresh out. A crow fluttered overhead and she reflexively tracked it for a half second. When her eyes returned to the black dog, those unblinking golden eyes were still laser-focused on her. The hairs on the back of Harper's neck prickled to attention.

I don't like the look of that guy or his creepy mutt. He might be the boss of the Dark Boys; he certainly dressed goth enough, and drug dealers often had vicious dogs as protection. *Back the way you came. You don't want to tangle with that creepy dog or his master.*

Harper slunk back the way she came to circle around to Abraham's tent the long way. She shot one more glance toward the man and his dog. It hadn't moved. Still it sat. Golden eyes almost glowing in the twilight. She shuddered and slipped between a row of tents.

There was Abraham. He stumbled around and around the base of a tree with his arms outstretched. Filthy overalls hung unbuckled around his waist. His long white beard hung crusted with Dust and vomit.

"Abraham!" Harper called to him. He laughed like a delighted child and continued his doddering revolution around the tree. She slid her baton into her front pocket and ran to him.

"Abraham. It's me, Harper." She stepped in front of him, placed her hands on his shoulders, and turned him toward her. "Abraham, remember me?" He looked right through her and kept reaching for the base of the tree. She gently shook his shoulders and looked into his brown eyes. "Abraham. Abraham. Snap out of it." But it was useless. Abraham's body was there, but his mind was in Neverland.

Harper gripped his sleeve and pulled him toward the exit. To her surprise, he shuffled along beside her, all the while reaching back for the base of the tree. If she could just get him to the street, she could call for help. That plan evaporated as soon as it formed.

Abraham jerked violently from her grip while a low moan oozed from his slack jaw. She caught his hand again. He wrenched it away and uttered another wavering moan. Abraham staggered away from Harper but not back to the tree that contained his invisible friend; instead, toward the back of the camp. The entire area sprang to a shambling kind of life. Streams of shuffling feet from every direction flowed in the same direction like a river of moaning bodies. Harper pursued, hoping to catch Abraham again.

As she emerged from between two of the tents at the outer edge of the camp, her blood ran cold. She stopped in her tracks, grabbed her baton, and darted behind a red tent.

Several pale forms with stringy black hair melted out of the opposite end of the alley. They didn't walk so much as glide like they were on an invisible conveyor belt.

The Dark Boys. She clapped her other hand over her mouth to stifle a terrified scream. Her breath came in shallow, shuddering gasps between her fingers. The strength drained from her legs, and she slid to the ground.

CHAPTER 5

The settlement the Phooka had guided him to stretched through the entire clearing between the towering buildings. A tent shanty made of cardboard, remnants of plastic tarps, and bits of anything that would keep out the rain or offer the slightest barrier against the cold. Row upon row of them crammed together as tight as possible. Nuada had never witnessed the level of debasement that stretched before him. What High King would allow so many of his subjects to descend to this hopeless condition?

The squalor saddened him, but so did the behavior of the residents. Most of them wore the empty bliss and unfocused stare of the glamoured. Each bopped along in their own little world, seeing and feeling things that were never physically there. That took a lot of energy. Whatever Fae or group of Fae who maintained it must have power to rival a Tuatha.

He swiveled his head, silver hair slipping like mercury over his shoulders. Blue eyes probed every hidden crevice, each patch of shadow, revealing nothing. He expected to find some of the Fae gentry, elves, perhaps, weaving their glamour over these poor folk. But why? No gentry would ever deign to waste their abilities on the ill and broken. And yet the glamoured humans stumbled about, all the same victims of an age-old Fae spell. Could the gentry have developed the skill to hide themselves from him in his long absence?

He let his eyes drift shut and sent filaments of awareness winding through the clearing. Wisps of magic curled around corners and slithered along branches, seeking the jolt of electricity that would reveal the Fae casting the glamour. But all he felt was the flat pulse of human life. Other than himself and the Phooka, there were no other magical beings here, and that made absolutely no sense.

The Phooka was right. Something nefarious was happening in this sad, forgotten alley.

While the shapeshifter sniffed the ground around a blue tarp, Nuada spent several minutes observing the glamoured people. They mooned about, gaping and laughing at nothing as all humans under this enchantment did.

He was about to suggest there was nothing more to see in this place when, out of the corner of his eye, Nuada spotted something out of place. He watched the girl sneak between rows of tents. She was a little short with an athletic build. She moved with the efficiency of a martial artist, but Nuada was certain she'd seen no war. Simple clean clothes in shades of blue told him she was no resident. The young woman had chosen the wrong time and place to go wandering.

Humans were like that. Even when the first of their kind arrived at Inisfáil, they'd blundered along. The Milesians stuck their nose in the negotiations of Tuatha kings, arrogantly rebuffed the requests of sovereign goddesses, and picked a fight with Badb Catha that set humanity on a trajectory to face her in battle at some point in the future. If the Phooka was correct, that time may be upon them.

Under the golden boughs of apple trees in the Undying Lands, he'd heard Macha's prophecy spoken. Nuada had spent every waking moment since seeking the heir she spoke of and listening for tides of war. His last promise to his love had brought him to this desolate place and to the new low of having to place his trust in a trickster.

From across the sea of shabby tents, the Phooka stared, transfixed by a brown-haired human. Amber eyes bored into the girl in a very un-doglike manner, almost like he knew her. *That will be our next topic of discussion once this little diversion ends. I don't trust that beast.*

When the girl disappeared from his line of sight, the Phooka ducked behind piles of refuse, nose to the ground. Nuada continued his surveillance of the alley. Row upon row of avian shapes of the Sluagh with their crow friends dotted every building and treetop. They unsettled him. The Sluagh burgeoned when the Veil between worlds thickened and they collected where large quantities of humans lived: cities.

Nuada shuddered. The sound of paws beating the earth pulled his eyes back from the skyscrapers. The Phooka galloped toward him. His shaggy fur bounced in time to his flying feet and he skidded to a halt in front of Nuada.

"They're here." He panted with wide eyes. The Phooka spun on his back legs and rocketed back the way he had come. Droplets of drool flew off his lolling pink tongue.

Nuada loped after him, dropping to a crouch where the dog had stopped behind a large orange tent. A prickle on the back of his neck confirmed the Fae had arrived. They peered around the edge of the tent. A group of dark-haired boys drifted through the hallucinating residents of the encampment. Droplets of water coursed over their wiry bodies even though the rain had stopped minutes ago. "Kelpies," Nuada whispered with a shudder.

Kelpies lived in riparian waterways where few humans lived. They avoided cities this large. Whatever they were here for had to be big to make them endure the urban pollution. Nuada hoped to spy on the Fae, but the innocent girl's arrival meant divided attention. Duty commanded him to protect her. She hid behind a row of tents. Safe. At least for now.

Nuada's foot tapped the shaggy dog on the flank. "If you are going to wear the shape of a dog, at least have the skill to act the part," he whispered.

His companion ignored the remark. He leaned forward over his lanky front legs, tail bobbing side to side like a metronome. The Phooka's attention locked on to the brown-haired girl again. Nuada kicked his flank a little harder.

The Phooka narrowed his eyes and let out a low rumble. "I'm behaving precisely like a proper canine. Have you ever been a dog, great and glorious former king?"

"No."

The Phooka sat on one of his haunches with his leg slung over his head and licked his bottom to make a point about his expertise. He offered a canine smile and licked his lips. "Then don't criticize."

Nuada wrinkled the bridge of his nose and drew back. "Care to explain why you are acting like a besotted fool?" He inclined his head toward the woman.

"Just looking out for someone who clearly straggled into the wrong situation."

Evasive as ever. Answers from the Phooka would prove elusive, and they had bigger problems. "Let's not forget why you called me here." Nuada gestured toward the kelpies. Their grisly ear-to-ear smiles never dropped or increased. The Fae nodded their dripping heads while surrounded by the slack jaws and reaching arms of desperate people.

"That's right! On the case." The dog put his nose to the ground and walked in circles, sniffing the earth.

Nuada ignored the Phooka's antics. He wanted to get a closer look at the Fae. He motioned the Phooka to follow. The pair slid around the tents toward where the girl still hid. The golden eyes of the dog wandered to her.

Two rows of tents separated them from the kelpies. Nuada squinted to make out their actions. They pressed vials of something into outstretched hands. Kelpies shouldn't be interested in these sad souls, and they never handed out gifts. The Phooka was right; something deeply strange was underway here. He needed to get one of those vials if he had any chance of figuring out if this had anything to do with Macha's dying words.

"Bloody kelpies. Awful blighters. I can take them. You get to handle what's coming behind them," the dog whispered.

Nuada made silent accounts of terrain, exits, and sight lines. This was a terrible place for a battle. Too many obstacles and innocents. "Now is not the time," he said, laying a hand on the Phooka's neck to stop his advance. "A clash could harm these people. Besides, if you think Badb has something to do with this, we need to discover their destination."

"You never let me have any fun. Can't we kill four and persuade the fifth to share some information with us? I can be very motivational." The Phooka made an approximate fist with one paw and slammed it against the pad of the other.

Nuada pointed at the lines of black birds perched overhead in the trees and buildings. "We have other company. Sluagh."

A ripple moved through the dog's shiny fur. "Ugh. Bloody scavengers. They're probably just here to drain the kelpies' rejects."

"Of that, you cannot be sure. Regardless, a fight may not end in our favor. For now, we observe and follow. Nothing more."

The Phooka didn't answer. He prowled closer to where the girl crouched. Eyes like saucers and a shaking hand signified her terror at seeing Fae for the first time. The kelpies hadn't bothered to glamour themselves, but he supposed they wanted to be seen handing out their treasures. *Poor girl. Today she learned monsters existed.*

Nuada crouched low and crept up next to his friend, grabbing his bushy tail. "Sit. Stay," he whispered.

The Phooka's lips curled, showing a row of sharp white teeth. A low growl rumbled, but he sat. And stayed, even if his tail lashed from side to side and his muscles tensed, ready to spring into action. Pointed ears twitched rapidly in all directions.

"You know something, Phooka." Nuada jerked his chin toward the young woman. "Does she have something to do with all this? You've obviously seen her before."

The Phooka didn't answer and Nuada had no more time to press him about the issue because the 'something rare and dark from another world' the Phooka spoke of entered. The ethereal strains of a harp emanated from the back of the camp, playing a song that was old when humanity cowered in caves from the dark outside. Soft and melodic notes created a counterpoint to the jagged honking horns in the distance.

Only one creature played that exquisitely or knew such songs from eons past. From where the kelpies had emerged, an impossible creature stepped into view. Hunched and black, it towered over both Fae and human. Where eyes should be, balls of fire flickered and sent tongues of flame licking the top of its forehead. One thick clawed hand braced a golden harp to a hairy shoulder while the other plucked the strings with a softness at odds with its grotesque appearance.

Nuada traced symbols in the air, flicking his fingers first toward his ears, then to the Phooka, and finally across the asphalt to the girl. The simple air spell would cancel out some of the effects of the Aillen's tune, at least for a few minutes. He felt a pang of regret it wouldn't work on the already glamoured.

The Aillen lived only in the Underworld. He could walk in the Green World for only three nights of the year, and tonight wasn't one of them. The ancient monster had slain kings and heroes, and the music it played turned the mind to a slave, especially if the mind was already weakened by glamour. Yet here it was, in the Green World. Precisely where it was impossible to be.

CHAPTER 6

Harper registered five of them. At first glance they might be a pack of teen boys, common for the city, but they were far from normal. Each looked to be around thirteen years old, clothed in identical dingy grey clothes, and all with the same shoulder-length jet-black hair. Their dress and hairstyle weren't the only similarities. Each of the boys had nearly identical features.

Their creepiness didn't end there. October in Portland meant the chill closed in even before the sun sank, yet none of them wore shoes. The glass, stones, and other detritus should be slicing through their skin, yet they remained uninjured. But, Harper thought, the most disturbing thing of all were the eyes. No pupil. No iris. Just inky black pools stretching corner to corner, with a dull grey glint, almost like a cataract but more metallic, floating like a haze across each malevolent stare.

They're just teenagers. Contacts. Their eyes look like that because of those ridiculous contact lenses that make your eyes look red or glow. These just happen to be black. And cover the whites of their eyes, too. They make those, right?

Her body contradicted the narrative her mind brewed up.

Quaking hands and palpitating heart banished any hope of convincing herself these were normal children. And some nebulous terror simmered below the membrane between her conscious thoughts and the vast unconscious, building pressure with each passing second.

Wait. Didn't the rain end a couple hours ago? Why are they wet?

The Dark Boys weren't merely damp. No. Every single one of them dripped, soaking wet, complete with tangles of aquatic weed twined in their locks, like they'd gone for a dip in the icy Willamette River only seconds before. Fully clothed. On a cloudy fifty-two-degree day.

Another shove from her unconscious mind sent a wave of dizziness rippling through her. "They'll have pointed teeth," Harper whispered under her breath.

At the appearance of the Dark Boys, the Dust affected had shambled toward them. Now they arrived, moaning, with upturned palms. The boys passed wicked smiles between them. Each curved grin revealed a line of yellowing, pointed teeth, almost more than should fit in a child's mouth. Harper recoiled.

How did I know they'd have pointed teeth? No fucking way I could know that. I'm just hyped up. Imagining things. No. I know that's not true. I knew about the teeth before I saw them. Gotta be a lucky guess. Or I'm going nuts and will end up in the funny farm like Mom.

Harper shook all over and her vision narrowed, darkening around the edges so only the Dark Boys registered, retreating down the long tunnel of her fading vision. She dropped her head between her knees, partly to remain out of the sight of the boys and partly because she was sliding into unconsciousness. A familiar terror she still couldn't place sent icy tentacles through her thoughts.

A pair of the boys were visible from her vantage point near the ground. In unison, they each lifted a hand and slowly gestured the people forward. Their pointy smiles never slipped and did not reach their eyes.

That was when the music started. The dulcet tones of a harp came from behind the Dark Boys. She could only see the shadow of the musician hunched over his harp. He stretched tall with a bald head, but it was the claws at the end of his thick fingers that dried her throat. A handful of the residents harkened to the song. Heads floated up, jaws hung, and eyes fixed on the harpist. The others remained riveted on the Dark Boys.

The shadow turned and moved away from the camp. The gentle thrum of the harp receded with him. About a dozen of the homeless lurched along in the musician's wake as though he were the Pied Piper. Abraham was among them. Harper's mind screamed at her to stop them, leap between the people and the musician and save them all. But her feet had grown roots. She froze in terror, just the way she had on the night her father died.

As the harpist and his procession exited the area, the Dark Boys drew out more handfuls of tiny glass vials and glided through the camp. They said nothing, their frozen smiles never slipping as watery hands dropped corked bottles into outstretched fingers.

They were almost on her. She forced her immobility to break, something years of self-defense classes had drilled into her, and scrambled to her feet. Her toe caught the edge of a tent and tore up a stake. The fabric shook and one side collapsed when it dragged behind her while she hopped and staggered into the open. A pair of crows lit on the ground in front of her, cawing and flapping their wings.

"Shhhh!" Harper flailed the baton at the birds. That only made them hop back and squawk louder.

The commotion drew the attention of the visitors. Gleaming grey eyes shot her direction, the first quick movement the teens had made. Two of them broke toward her, as fast as a striking snake, while the crows fluttered out of the way.

Oh crap. Crap. Crap. What the hell do I do?

Her arm shot out in an involuntary move of protection as the Dark Boys dripped in front of her. A cold, wet hand pressed a glass vial into her hand. Her fingers closed around it in reflex. The Dark Boy inclined his smiling head and glided past.

He took just two steps, then paused. His head swiveled back toward her. She gazed into the dull glint of his eyes and a magnetism lured her, promising the obliteration of all fear and pain. So beautiful. So full of joy. She couldn't help but dive into those black pools.

Harper's body warmed and a sensation of buoyancy surrounded every limb, like floating in a bubbling hot tub. For the first time since her dad died, all her cares melted away, replaced by a soporific peacefulness. Gone was the emptiness Gerald O'Neill left with his passing. Gone were the scars of her tumultuous childhood. Gone was her guilt at her daily failure to save her mother. In its place, feelings of a joy so deep she wanted to weep, and the euphoric sense that everything was perfect just the way it was.

Why was I so scared? They're here to help me. Take away all my pain.

She stood and held her hand out to the boy. She'd follow him anywhere if only she could keep the tranquility of this moment.

"Niall," the dark boy hissed. Rivulets of water coursed down the hand reaching for her.

It sounded like he said 'knee all' to Harper. She giggled. Knee all was a very odd thing to say. *Knee all. Kneel?* Was the beautiful boy wanting her to kneel? She dropped to the ground to comply. *Wait. That's not it at all. My name. He said my name.*

"My name's O'Neill," Harper heard herself say in a dreamy voice. They knew her by name and wanted her to go with them.

Profound joy flooded her at the thought. Her fingertips hovered inches from the bone-white hand of the Dark Boy. Inches away from everlasting happiness.

And then the slavering jaws of the black dog snapped closed, but he missed the outstretched hand of the boy. The Dark Boy's pale fingers whipped back, and he fled toward his companions.

"No!" Harper shouted. The goddamned mutt had ruined her only chance for happiness.

The golden-eyed dog gnashed its teeth and snarled. The Dark Boys ran, and the dog bounded after. He caught up with them in a flash and tore into the nearest one. The boy didn't even have time to scream before he lay scattered in pieces. His friends streaked away, following the strange musician. Strings of dog drool spattered the ground behind the retreating teens.

With their departure, the gut-wrenching sense of fear roared back into Harper's mind. She staggered back, clutching her chest. In the elation's shadow, her grief felt as deep as a canyon.

The black dog pursued its prey, followed by the silver-haired man. She swore she saw him draw a sword.

Harper teetered close to a mental breaking point. The yearning for escape expanded like a balloon, crowding out any other thought. She dropped the vial and sprinted back down the alleyway. At full speed, she burst out onto the sidewalk on Burnside and didn't stop running until she got to the bus stop.

CHAPTER 7

Nuada drew the shorter of the two swords hidden beneath his long coat, cursing silently to himself. This was supposed to be a mission to simply observe and discover. The girl's rash move had changed all that, so he raced to aid the Phooka whose jaws were clamped around one of the kelpies.

Blood dripped down the shapeshifter's maw while he planted his canine paws and lashed his head from side to side. The kelpie's face creased with pain, but he scraped up the strength to lift his free hand and blast a ball of shining energy at his attacker. The Phooka's jaw snapped open when the magic slammed into his chest. End over end, he tumbled from the force of the blast. The impact of his rump smacking the ground elicited a cry, half yelp, half whine.

The motion sent the cloud of black birds rocketing from their perches like they shared a single mind. The cawing of crows mixed with the guttural sounds from the Sluagh.

The black avian cloud dove toward the ground and banked up between Nuada and the injured kelpie. The birds sliced the air above him, blowing his hood back and revealing his shining silver hair. He snatched the hood back down over his face. If Badb truly was behind this, she could see through the eyes of her crow minions, and he needed to keep his return a secret.

The distraction from the flock gave the injured kelpie just enough time to limp toward his departing friends. Just like them to leave one of their own to face death alone. The creature cradled his right arm and disappeared up the alley toward the fading tones of the harp. Odd that the usually bellicose kelpies and the usually murderous Aillen chose not to fight. Either they had orders, or they'd wandered the city long enough to be weakened from the iron that surrounded them. The Phooka must have lived here long indeed if he could tolerate his surroundings this well.

The Phooka pulled himself to his feet and shook his head. With a baying howl, he leveled his head and charged for the retreating Fae.

"Heel!" Nuada sheathed his sword and scanned the ground where the girl had fallen under the glamour. The shapeshifter might not be ready to let his quarry escape, but now was not the time to bring any further attention to themselves. They were two against an untold number of foes. Light on information and devoid of allies.

The dog careened to a halt and growled. The Phooka lifted one paw and used the other to mash it into a good approximation of a middle finger. But he did saunter back to where Nuada crouched, turning the vial of opalescent power over in his gloved, clockwork hand.

Nuada craned his neck up at the sky. In wartime, clouds of crows and Sluagh swarmed battlefields. Both were scavengers. The crows came for the meat; the Sluagh, the souls. He scowled. The Fae, even kelpies, viewed the Sluagh as something akin to maggots. Necessary, but repugnant. On their end, the Sluagh believed the Fae to be hedonistic fools. Both gave the other a wide berth, and yet what Nuada had just seen was a coordinated intervention.

To force groups who despised each other under normal circumstances to join was no minor feat. For that to happen, someone powerful held the reins. Someone strong enough to summon the Aillen across an impermeable Veil.

The former king's eyes slid to the shapeshifter and narrowed. Where did the Phooka's allegiance lie? Yes, he'd attacked the kelpies, presumably to rescue the young woman. He'd recognized her. Nuada was sure of it.

"Why did you let them get away?" The Phooka rolled his eyes like a grounded teenager.

"You were right. There are indeed things here that shouldn't be."

"Say that again?"

"There are—"

"Not that part. The first bit about me being right. It's my favorite song." A black paw cupped the Fae's pointed ear.

Nuada sighed. "Battling the Aillen would only result in collateral damage to these wretched souls, and thanks to your guardian angel routine, we probably lost any hope of remaining undetected from whoever is pulling its strings."

"I'm just here to protect and serve." A shining halo materialized over the Phooka's head while his lips pulled into a beatific smile. "Wait. That's the police." The Phooka shuddered.

The Fae played the Good Samaritan, but Nuada knew it was disingenuous. He hadn't lifted a finger to save the unfortunate, just the girl. Nuada wanted to know why. But getting the truth out of the Phooka was about as likely as a troll dancing the ballet.

"There's something you're hiding from me, Phooka. Like why you're so sure Badb Catha is behind this." Nuada studied the glass tube of purple Dust the girl had dropped in her retreat. "And you knew that girl, but I have not the time to torture an answer out of you tonight." He gestured toward where the kelpies disappeared with their victims. "We need to follow them. Hopefully, they will lead us to whoever made this stuff." Nuada held the vial up to his face and peered at it while he strode toward the retreating party of Fae and humans.

"Well. Um. You see, I have another engagement tonight." The Phooka's yellow eyes drifted in the direction the girl had fled and his paw tips tapped together.

"You are going to follow her."

"That kelpie seemed pretty interested in her. With you gallivanting off to tilt at windmills, I think I'd best follow her and ensure her safety. It's my civic duty as a long-time resident of this city."

"This discussion is far from over." Nuada had great reservations about placing the young woman's fate in the hands of the likely duplicitous Fae, but something terrible was happening here, and he had to stop it. Besides, he reasoned, if the Phooka had any intent to harm the girl he could have done so already.

"Your kelpies are escaping you." The Phooka flicked his furry head.

"If that girl comes to any harm . . ."

"Yeah, yeah. You'll chop off my head with your fancy sword. I want her in one piece as much as you do."

The dog shape shimmered and rippled until only a transparent cloud remained. The shapeless mist roiled and shrank. As it thickened, it pulled into the shape of a black raven. The amber-eyed bird hovered at eye level to Nuada. "You know how to find me." With that, the Phooka shot up high over the alley.

The sun had sunk behind the mountains around the city a half hour before. The sky held soupy clouds painted in the deep reds and oranges of the last slivers of the day. Just enough light remained to show the shadowy silhouette of the retreating kelpies. Like an otherworld parade, their motley crew of indigent shuffled along in tow, slowing their supernatural shepherds. With a resigned sigh, Nuada jogged forward. His black boots made no sound on the ground.

Nuada closed his eyes for an instant and felt the warm glow of his magic flowing over him. He brought his cupped hands over his head as though dousing himself with water. They continued their path along the back of his head and by the time they dropped to his sides he was invisible from human and kelpie alike. Tuatha magic was stronger than Fae magic; he was certain they couldn't see through the spell. He sprinted to catch up.

He pursued the kelpies through the city, keeping a safe distance. He was invisible but not undetectable to the Aillen. Better to be cautious. Kelpies had a keen sense of smell, and he was sure he smelled very different than the dozen indigent humans they herded through the streets.

The group headed straight for the Willamette River where the dripping boys resumed their large black horse shape and slipped into the water. The humans scrambled onto their backs, two or three on each one. The hulking Aillen slipped into the water beside the horses, the water steaming and bubbling where it touched his skin.

Once in the water, the kelpies swam impossibly fast. Nuada sprinted at supernatural speed along the banks of the river, barely keeping pace with the creatures. Soon the kelpies joined a stream of other leathery-skinned water horses returning from their own kidnapping missions. Dozens of them churned the water. Each carried a burden of slack-jawed humans.

After a few minutes, the creatures banked and swam across the water, heading straight toward a vast, mist-shrouded island. Across the water, Nuada could just make out the kelpies melting back into teen boys.

They guided their shuffling prey into the mist. A mist so thick and unmoving that he knew immediately magic had spun it up.

He closed his eyes and projected his senses. The mist had the silky feel of Tuatha magic. As it existed in a between state—not quite water, not quite air—mist magic was the best way to hide something as huge as an entire island. And to change it as the Tuatha had done to Ireland eons ago. Within the Phooka's web of deception might lie a grain of truth, because only a handful of his people possessed this sorcery, and Badb Catha was one of them.

Even from across the river, magic whispered to Nuada's unconscious that he really didn't want to be here right now. The warding spells pushed a sense of unease outward in waves. Probably enough to keep any humans from even thinking about visiting that island. He could likely force his way past the wards and enter anyway, but every Fae or Tuatha in a hundred miles would know he was there. For tonight at least, this was the end of the road.

His fist clenched at his side. Frustration simmered in his heart, though at least he knew more than he did weeks ago. They were bringing the addicted to this island, but for what purpose? And how did this drug work without the proximity of a powerful Fae to hold the glamour? Every answer led to more questions. None of this made the tiniest bit of sense. He inhaled a bone-weary sigh.

"Macha, my love, we should be walking beneath the golden trees and smelling the honey-sweet air of the Undying Lands together. For eternity. You set me on this path to save humanity, but, Mother Danu, I am just so tired." This world felt tired too, threadbare souls in a threadbare land. His throat felt achy and raw. Self-pity was new to him. Perhaps it was the natural result of ages of loss grinding down the best parts of him, like waves wear down the very rocks.

Another deep sigh anchored him in the present. Nuada's fingers found the vial of Dust the brown-haired girl had dropped in the homeless camp. Pursuit was a dead end for now, but the contents of the tiny bottle might present a fresh lead. He would discover what the Phooka knew about the woman later, but the kelpies had led him close to an old acquaintance. One who might know something about the iridescent lavender powder.

When the gateways to the Underworld had closed because of the environmental devastation of the industrial age, a handful of its denizens had been trapped in the human world. Some adjusted better than others. None thrived like Heironymous. And he had eyes everywhere.

CHAPTER 8

Harper hunkered down in the back of the bus, shoulders braced almost to her ears and her olive drab backpack clutched to her chest like it could shield her from the nightmare she had just witnessed. She felt fuzzy and disconnected, like the few times she had woken with a hangover. Broken images, some banal, others surreal, scattered through her mind as though her memory of the events had been smashed by a hurricane. Try as she might, she couldn't arrange them into a coherent narrative.

Wide hazel eyes flicked over the packed bus, searching for Dark Boys or anything else out of the ordinary. Her shoulders dropped two notches when her surveillance revealed merely the usual gaggle of commuters and students. The side-to-side sway of the bus and the familiar rumble of its engines soothed her like pulling on a favorite sweatshirt and enjoying a mug of hot chocolate.

Her body may have cancelled the defcon five, but her mind fast forwarded through fragments of events in the alley over and over, desperately searching for an escape hatch to normalcy. Pale fingers fiddled with the zipper on the front of the pack and her muddy loafers tapped out a fast beat against the wall of the bus.

She shifted in her seat and rested her forehead against the smooth, cool window. *How did I know they'd have pointed teeth?* The bit of foreknowledge pinched like a splinter, becoming ever more insistent as it worked its way down under the skin. The deeper it burrowed, the more her mind picked at it.

She lifted her head from the window, scanned the passengers again, and rubbed her face with the flats of her hands. *Stress. That had to be it. I psyched myself out back there. Like when I was a kid and thought monsters lived in the closet, but only when the lights were out.*

She shifted her legs so one ankle rested on a knee, and her foot jounced up and down. *Didn't I watch an episode of 20/20 with Mom that said a lot of drug cartels were family businesses?* Harper let out a sigh that skimmed part of the muscle tension from the surface. That had to be it. She repeated the story to herself like praying the rosary. Stress and seeing twins, well, quintuplets, helping in the family drug business. That was the ticket. Sure.

But they were wringing wet. Not just a little moist but soaked through and they never dried. She dropped her leg back down, resuming her previous posture and leaning her head back on the window so the streetlights streaked by. *They probably just got way wetter in the rain than I did. That had to be it. That was why I thought they dripped.* Her skittish brain was close to buying the improbable drenched quintuplet theory until she remembered the pointed teeth. Her shoulders rose and her heart hammered once more.

Because the world had shifted under her feet so many times in her brief life, Harper had developed a few tools for coping. By far the one she was best at and used most frequently was stuffing. As a kid she envisioned a giant Mickey Mouse hand grabbing whatever she couldn't or wouldn't deal with and cramming it deep down an unconscious well. When it got full and the contents threatened to pour out the top, the hand just shoved harder and snapped the lid back on real fast. Once the lid was on, it trapped all those nasty things safe and sound and away from everyday thoughts. But this time the nasty things had actual pointy teeth, and the lid had peeled back for just a moment. Pandora's box had been opened, demons had rushed out, and they refused to climb back in.

The clatter of the bus grinding to a halt a block from her house pulled her out of rumination. She scurried off the bus and into the brisk night air. Icy fingers found her defense baton in her pocket while she scanned the street for evidence they had followed her. Only streetlamps, cars, and the strip mall where the bus stopped occupied the night. Two other passengers exited with her, the same ones every day.

Satisfied the sidewalk was safe, she yanked the hem of her sweatshirt back over her waistband and hustled for home. Drizzle quickly soaked through the thin pants. She increased her pace despite her dread of the condition she would find her mother in. Out of the frying pan and into the fire.

Gresham brimmed with rows of modest suburban homes like any other lower middle–class neighborhood in the country. Harper and her mother lived on the corner in the shabbiest house. The single-level ranch home had been unceremoniously plopped too close to the sidewalk by someone Harper swore was intoxicated. Instead of the front door opening up to either cross street, the house faced the corner.

Staff at the agency that child welfare had referred them to when they closed their case helped the O'Neill family first rent the structure, then get a mortgage once it seemed like her mom was healthy enough to return to her lucrative marketing career. That hadn't happened and her mother's meager disability payments weren't enough to pay for their home. So, at fourteen, Abraham helped Harper buy a fake ID listing her age as the sixteen required to work without parental permission. Within a week she found two part-time jobs, one pumping gas, the other at a Subway, to pay for what she jokingly referred to as Castle O'Neill.

Originally white, years of neglect left the little building with marbled gray streaks. Lawn more weed than grass and wet leaves gave the yard a sickly yellow hue. Working full time, household chores, and managing her mother left no time for home improvements.

Harper ignored the buckling sidewalk that led to the front door in favor of tromping through the grass to the side entrance. Damp earth squelched beneath her loafers, mud caking the edges around the soles. A flutter of movement from the skeletal tree on the corner caught her eye and she flicked the baton. Just a crow settling in for the night.

Harper dragged the bottoms of her shoes across the concrete step and vigorously wiped her feet on the doormat. She slid her key into the lock and paused. She took in a deep breath, thrust her anxiety back down in her interior well, and steeled herself.

The door creaked open to reveal a cramped living room that no home decorator had touched since 1976. A mustard-yellow couch, far too big for the space, perched on rust-colored shag carpet. Wooden shelves crammed with useless knickknacks loomed from all four walls.

Eileen O'Neill had spent thousands of dollars over the years on her resin treasures. When in the grip of mania, she convinced herself the tacky collectibles would be worth a fortune someday and Harper could use them for college money. They came from the illustrious Franklin Mint, after all. Her mom had the same idea about the small army of Beanie Babies locked in their acrylic prisons lining the bathroom shelves. Their worthless, beady black eyes ogled Harper every time she took a shower. Daily, the tie-dyed peace bear reminded her that finishing college was probably forever off the table.

When her mania flowered, Eileen O'Neill spent money like she had when she made six figures. That meant Harper had to get creative. Before she was old enough for her own bank account, she had hidden the money from her jobs in a Tupperware container she buried in the yard. When a bill was due, she dug up the container, took the cash to the post office, and bought a money order. Let her mom spend her tiny disability check on kitsch if it made her happy for a minute; Harper would make sure they were never homeless again.

She dropped her bag on the couch and padded into the tiny eat-in kitchen. No sign of her mom, but the bottle of Nikolai vodka half full on the counter told her what to expect. She felt heavy. No matter how good she thought she was at finding the hiding places and dumping the contents down the drain, there always seemed to be another. It was like an endless, demented Easter egg hunt.

"Mom, I'm home," Harper called and tipped the contents of a little plastic pill box labelled 'Friday evening' into her hand. No answer, but scraping and rustling emanated from the spare room. Harper groaned and rolled her eyes. She referred to this room as her mother's war room. With a shrug and a sigh, she marched down the hall toward another probable battle. Avoidance may have served better, but Eileen had to take her medications. Retreat was not an option.

The door creaked open on an all too familiar scene. Just like *Seinfeld* reruns, it had replayed frequently through the fifteen years since her father's murder.

Her mother bent over a spray of photographs and post-it notes. One hand scanned down the long tail of a printed newspaper article while the other scribbled across a page like she was fencing with it, not writing on it. Tongue clamped between her lips as if it had tried to escape. Her bottle-blonde head snapped back and forth between pages, pausing just long enough to take a drink of the glass of clear liquid Harper presumed to be vodka.

Eileen O'Neill had never accepted that her husband's murder remained unsolved. Harper had been very young when Eileen resolved to crack the case on her own. Bumbling cops be damned. Her extensive research spilled over every wall of the room, even the closet door. Newspaper clippings, photographs, and scrawled messages caught in a web of colored string and rainbow push pins. Harper tried to make sense of it years ago, but she'd need a Rosetta Stone to interpret the secret language of connections plastered to these walls.

Her back to the door, Eileen lurched, swaying, to her feet with a picture and sticky note in one hand. Her other hand reached out to steady herself against the heavy oak table. She added the picture to a cluster of newspaper clippings. She was out of space on the giant corkboard she'd hung over the previous layer of evidence, so she just pressed it into the only millimeter of putrid green wall peeking out between pictures. Harper set the handful of pills on the table. "Mom . . ."

When you imprisoned all your internal demons in a well, there was just one problem. They reached the top when the well got too full and organized a rebellion against the lid. A little help from the outside would be all they needed to take out the exhausted guard and mount a full-scale attack against the cap on the well. Eventually, they always won. The lid clattered under the strain of the day. Harper drew in a deep breath and shoved against it with all her remaining internal strength.

"Harper! You're home. I've made a breakthrough. There was a similar case in Vancouver five years ago, only it was the wife who went missing. They found her in a cult up there in Canada. Police hit all the same roadblocks—"

"Mom. Please, not again. You have to let this go." She reached a reassuring hand forward. If she couldn't get this under control now, her mother would be in here for days feeding her conspiracy theories, not eating, not sleeping. Without a fast course correction,

Mystic Island was out. The ensuing guilt stung. It was selfish to want to attend a party while her only family needed her.

"You sound just like the useless police today!" she slurred.

"God, Mom, why did you go to the police again?"

The hall was rented. The music queued. And they began a well-rehearsed dance.

Eileen took a drink, slamming the empty glass on the table. Droplets of vodka soaked into a pile of adjacent newspaper clippings. "Damn straight I went to the cops. This is a new direction for the investigation. I found fresh evidence in places they'd never dream of looking! And how did those donut-swilling fat pigs react?! Told me I should let it go. You're just as bad as they are!"

Harper's head bowed, and she rubbed her forehead with her hand. Her spine slumped. Years of pressure managing the alcoholism and delusions. The surreal fear of the tent city. Emilio's words about living her life. All of it kindling to the rage that surged beneath her skin. She was on fire. The lid blew off, and her demons rampaged.

"Yes, Mom. Let it go. Let it the hell go. He's dead, and he's not coming back. He's not in goddamn Canada. He doesn't have amnesia in Iowa. He's not working for the bloody secret service. He was just murdered and we'll never know who or why."

"How dare—"

She jabbed her hand around the room. "This. This is fucking crazy. The police know it, and I know it too!"

Her mother's bright red face shifted toward purple. "What's fucking crazy is how easily you forgot about him!" she shrieked and hurled the empty glass straight at Harper's face. It exploded against the doorframe. At the same time broken glass showered her daughter, Mrs. O'Neill toppled to the brown carpet and sobbed.

The storm was past. Harper should go comfort her mother. But that's not what those neglected parts of her wanted. Mean and horrible thoughts vied for expression. Monstrous accusations clambered up from the bottom of the well. The shattered glass in her hair shredded the rest of the filter between those darkest thoughts and her voice. She surrendered to the tempest and reveled in the sensation of being powerful.

"Forgot him?! I think about him every damn day. And you know what else I think every miserable day in this hell you created for me? The wrong fucking parent died."

Her mother's face froze in an expression half pain, half shock, head shaking from side to side in slow motion. Silent sobs hitched in her chest and a single tear rolled down her cheek below wide eyes. Harper had screamed at her mother plenty over the years, but she rarely said anything terrible, and this went far past terrible. Seconds ticked by with the two of them frozen in place just staring at each other. The adrenaline-soaked strength and vicious words that went for the jugular demanded a heavy price. Guilt and regret joined the cadre of inner demons every time, stealing from the happiness of each subsequent moment.

"I—I didn't mean that, Mom." Harper's voice now small. Tears of her own ran down her cheeks.

"I know, honey, but I need you to leave now." Eileen ran a shaking hand through her tangled hair.

"Mom, I—"

"Get out! Get out! Get out!" Eileen pounded the carpet with her fist.

Harper turned on her heels and half ran, half stumbled down the hallway. Tears streamed behind her. She clomped down the stairs to her basement bedroom. Her back crashed up against the slammed door, sending her sliding to the floor. Her head fell onto her knees. Harper spent several minutes hugging her legs while sobs rocked her body. She felt small and helpless, like when she was a child trying to save them both from the abyss.

Her stomach twisted and a burning sensation filled the back of her throat. She raced for her tiny bathroom, bent her head over cold porcelain, and vomited. She reminded herself again that her mother had been right next to him when he died.

How do you come back from that? *God, I'm a terrible daughter.* Pretty bad friend too. She'd failed to help Abraham, and Emilio would be crushed when she told him she'd have to manage her mother all weekend.

CHAPTER 9

At the far side of her basement room, Harper kicked, punched, and body-slammed the heavy bag dangling from the rafters. She practiced roundhouse kicks until her legs solidified like concrete. Only when her muscles spasmed and her untaped hands felt tender did she drop into the purple beanbag chair on the other side of the room.

She practiced pain as a tool to stuff her feelings like ancient philosophers practiced alchemy. In sufficient quantity, pain short-circuited her brain, and for a few blissful hours her inner demons slept. Physical suffering, after all, was simpler. Some ibuprofen and time provided a predictable, well-defined end to physical aches. In contrast, mental anguish dragged on and on for months. Years. Therapy. Medication. Distraction. Nothing gave reliable relief, but the sharp slice of scissors always did.

She ran a hand along the neat parallel scars on her upper thighs. Before she enrolled in self-defense classes, she'd used less healthy methods to summon enough hurt to keep the lid on all the things she had no solutions for.

Harper felt drained. With every surrender to rage came a

hangover. Not the kind her mother used to have, but a crash, nonetheless. Listless, she draped across her beanbag chair like it was a life raft and she drifted on a black sea. She rested there for several minutes, enjoying the temporary relief. The vinyl creaked when she levered herself upright.

Harper rubbed her face between her hands. She felt lighter. That was the only silver lining when the internal dam crumbled and unwanted feelings rampaged. The pressure disappeared when the well was empty. At least for a while. Her stomach growled. It was empty too.

Leaden legs levered her up the basement steps. At the top, she paused and listened like a deer stilling itself to scan for danger. Silence. Her mom had probably passed out. Harper slinked lightly through the living room. Eileen sprawled unconscious over the couch, half on and half off, her pink robe crumpled underneath her.

Guilt flooded Harper. The first new resident of the internal well. It would have company soon, because it was almost time to disappoint her best friend. After tonight, now was not the time to be away from the house any more than necessary.

Harper smiled at her slumbering mother, eased her leg back onto the couch, slid a pillow underneath her head, and pulled a colorful crocheted blanket up to her chin. She made some sandwiches in the kitchen and left one for her mom on the coffee table along with a small dish containing her night meds.

Harper slipped off her loafers and pulled on navy blue sweatpants and a black T-shirt with the *Stranger Things* cast drawn as cats emblazoned on the front. Sandwiches in hand, Harper flopped back on her bed and flicked on the tiny TV perched on a ramshackle chest of drawers.

KATU's plug for their nighttime news promised the heartwarming story of a local woman turning one hundred. Terrible things were happening in this city, and the anchors covered an elderly woman's party. People were missing, but no one cared because they were the wrong people. The thought rebooted her replay of the evening's events. Her toes wormed into the cream-colored shag carpet.

The chime of her laptop saved her from the reruns of her harrowing evening. She closed her eyes and furrowed her brow. Best break the news fast. She flipped the laptop open and moved into a more comfortable position on her bed. The screen filled with Emilio decked out in his fabulous black unicorn horn. Furry boots, mesh shirts, and other elements of rave clothing lay haphazardly over the closet door in the background. The slightly auto-tuned voice of Kylie Minogue warbled in the background.

"Hey Emilio," Harper said. She clicked the remote to silence the TV.

"Hey girl. So I think I'll go with a moody emo look for my unicorn costume. Maybe a saddle that shouts 'I'm up for anything.' How much is a saddle?" Stream of consciousness babbling betrayed his excitement about the festival. Harper's feet continued to worry the carpet filaments.

"I don't think unicorns have saddles and do you really want to be ridden by a virgin, anyway?"

Emilio laughed. "Fair point. Nix the saddle. I'm thinking fiery beast unicorn for you. We can get some red hair extensions." He ducked out of view for a split second, popping back up with something red and fuzzy clutched in his hand. "I have these fur leg warmers you can borrow that match your red vinyl skirt. Saddle for you. Virgins are definitely more your speed."

Harper dropped her head. "I don't know, Emilio. She's worse than I thought. She threw a glass at me this time."

"Shit. You need me to come over?" Emilio's joyful expression melted, replaced by the creased brow of concern.

"No, but you have to find someone else for tomorrow. After

the day I just had . . ." She forced herself to look at the screen and absorb Emilio's crestfallen face.

He picked up his laptop and stretched out on his bed. In the background she heard the rolling music of his roommates chatting in Spanish. Emilio's artwork lay strewn over the nightstand. Howling werewolves and bloody vampires drawn in heavy black lines. He was good but had chosen the sensible route of a degree in biochemistry rather than walk the starving artist's path.

"It's one evening," he said and threw up his hands. "You cancel everything."

"I want to go. I do. What if something happens to her while I'm gone?" Harper didn't mention her fears about the other events of the evening.

"You can't babysit her all the time. You have to start living your own life. Just dump out all her booze. She'll be safe for a few hours if she's not drunk."

"You really don't get it, do you? She went through hell—"

"And so have you. You'll be forty and still working a shit job and saving her from herself. I've stood by you too. Don't you owe me?"

Tears threatened to well up again, so she closed her eyes.

"You know there will be a lot of drugs there," Emilio said. "Who will make sure I get home OK?" Emilio's face pulled into a grin and he winked.

He was playing dirty. He may act coy, but he knew which buttons to push. Besides, Mystic Island sounded amazing, and after today she needed to cut loose a little, even if part of her said the safest place to be was locked down in her house away from alleyways and strange dogs.

"Ok. You win. I'll go." She threw up her hands in mock surrender.

Emilio let out a loud whoop and chattered on and on about

outfits and bands. Harper's mind drifted back to her experience in the tent city earlier.

"Just promise me, no Dust."

Emilio opened his mouth, and judging by the know-it-all look on his face, he was about to protest. Harper didn't give him the chance.

"I saw some strange things today." Harper spent the next several minutes telling Emilio about the events at the homeless camp. Although she shared that the Dark Boys were odd and the man and his dog looked out of place, she left out the more supernatural bits. No need to make Emilio certain she was just as crazy as her mother.

When she finished, Emilio paused. His normally flamboyant gestures and speech became very serious. "What's wrong with you? You can't just walk into these places by yourself."

"I had to find out what happened to Abraham."

"Call the police then, but don't go gallivanting around back alleys alone. You could be killed."

"Cops don't give two craps about Abraham. Or my dad." A little jab of anger made her pulse quicken.

Emilio sighed. "Promise me you won't go in there alone again. It's reckless."

Harper didn't think she'd have the courage to go back there again, regardless of Emilio's protests. She thought of Abraham and her throat constricted. "I'll be careful."

"Sure you will. Anyhoo, I have a shift at the bookshop in the morning. We can head to Mystic after that. We'll miss a few of the early events but beat the rush." He blew her a dramatic kiss.

Harper smiled, wished Emilio a goodnight, and closed her laptop. She let her head fall back against her headboard. She was still wired, and a torrent of emotions warred for supremacy in her heart, including guilt about fleeing, leaving Abraham to his fate. She was sure he'd left with the teenagers, but the rest of the memory remained stubbornly just out of reach. She dialed her work's hotline number to get him some help and felt only a little relieved when they agreed to send someone to check for him in the morning. She vowed to as well, once she got her mother stable again.

She completed her nightly routine and crept silently up into the living room to check on her mother again. With relief, she noted her mother had eaten the sandwich and swallowed her pills. Eileen snored softly on the couch.

As Harper rinsed her dish in the sink, the bottle of vodka beckoned from its seat on the counter. There was enough in it to get her to sleep more easily tonight. The bottle felt heavy and cold in her hand. She tipped it to her lips and took a few quick gulps. Fire flamed down her throat. She bent over the sink and stifled her coughing. A couple more quick pulls and she hid the bottle behind the refrigerator, just in case she needed more to fall asleep.

Is this how Mom started?

CHAPTER 10

With his speed-enchanted feet, it took Nuada just a few minutes to arrive at Heironymous's home in Forest Park. He slowed to a walk as he neared the old stone ruins that marked the entrance to the establishment the eccentric Fae ran. The humans called it the Witch's Castle; to them, it looked like the ancient ruins of a stone house with no roof.

Every day, herds of them walked the path from the parking area to the ruin. They'd snap a few pictures and then move on to the next thing. A handful lingered longer to make a more lasting impression, evidenced by painted names, mushrooms, and other bright splashes of color coexisting with thick carpets of moss on the walls.

Nuada circled around the back of the structure where a flight of cold rock steps ascended, blocked by a fallen tree. The magical entrance nestled just beyond the trunk. He reached to his side to keep the longest of his swords from hitting the stone while he crouched and slid under the trunk.

An unremarkable arched doorway spread before him, spattered with the lacy shadows of trees. With his silver hand he tugged on the end of each finger of his glove. When it was free, he stuffed it into his pocket. He drew out a long dagger and jabbed the tip of his finger. A pair of crimson drops splattered on the threshold of the door, spreading out quickly on the drizzle-dampened stone.

The building accepted the offering. Within moments, a blinding light filled the arched gateway and coalesced into a shining blue door with a golden doorknob. Nuada stepped through into a vestibule, the roar of a crowded inn emanating from beneath. The acrid scent of alcohol and the warm smells of cooking wafted out. His stomach growled. Lively strains of fiddle accompanied by the pounding feet of dancers promised a bustling night at the lodge.

Two hulking river trolls jostled into his path. They towered over him, greasy black hair hanging down over long pointed noses.

"Good evening, gentlemen. I seek an audience with the proprietor."

"Give weapons. None allowed inside." The heaviest of the two thrust out a grubby grey hand. Nuada dutifully handed over a pair of long daggers, his everyday sword, several throwing knives, and a slingshot. He smiled, inclined his head, and stepped forward, heading past the pair.

Rough hands seized his shoulders. "Must give all weapons." Nuada's eyes dropped to the long sword in the ornate scabbard at his hip. The very one the trolls were staring at. "You get back when leave."

Nuada pulled his head back to put a little distance between himself and the fetid rotting fish smell roiling from the trolls' open mouths.

"I am sorry, gentlemen, but this particular sword stays with me. Rest assured, it has not left the scabbard in a thousand years."

"No go in then. Bye." Rough hands swung him halfway round.

He felt a powerful shove on the small of his back. He dug his heels in, swung around, and dove between the bowed legs of the smaller troll, then felt a calloused hand pluck him up by the scruff of his neck. Black boots swung a foot from the landing. This was going to escalate quickly. Nuada's silver hand clamped over his captor's wrist and squeezed. The grey-skinned lummox let out a yelp and released him.

"This weapon is far too dangerous to be left anywhere but at my side. I promise to use it against none inside." His reasoning fell on deaf ears. Both trolls clenched their fists and bared their teeth. Slimy dollops of green spittle dangled from thick lips, whipping toward Nuada with every labored breath.

"Glawd. Brax. That's enough. Let him keep the sword. He will not be drawing the Sword of Light against anyone in my humble lodge tonight." The voice was resonant with a slightly arrogant edge. Glawd and Brax lowered their eyes to the floor and stepped aside to allow their master up the stairs.

"Hello, Heironymous." Nuada greeted his old acquaintance, sliding gingerly past the strings of drool. The trolls screwed up their mouths to the side and scratched their low, sloping foreheads, confused by their master breaking the only rule they enforced in this place.

"Nuada Silver Hand, I thought you'd decided not to return from the Undying Lands." Heironymous clapped Nuada on the back with a fur-tufted brown hand. "Brax, Glawd, you should be bowing before the king of the Tuatha de Danann." The troll brothers made a sloppy bow and resumed their slumped postures at the door. Heironymous beckoned Nuada to follow him down the stairs. "To what do I owe the honor?"

"Former king. I have sought you out because I believe you are the only one who can help me with this." He paused and drew out the glass vial with the lavender powder. It shimmered with an opalescent sheen in the light of the torches dotting the stairwell's walls. He placed it into Heironymous's outstretched hand. The ogre's lace cuffs framed the vial in his wide palm.

Great twisting horns swept along neatly combed hair. Heironymous was small for an ogre, barely eight feet tall. What he lacked in size he more than made up for in his passion for knowledge. Deep below the pub, the ogre hoarded a collection of tomes vast enough to make the best Green World universities seem like the Lower Po-Dunk Public Library.

"You managed to procure a sample of Dust." Heironymous slipped on a monocle with his free hand and held the vial up to his large red eyes. "How did you swipe it from the kelpies without being noticed? You don't exactly scream human."

"Mostly blind luck. Someone dropped it. I'm guessing you have a Fae in your employ who can help me figure out what the substance is and where it came from."

"That I do." A slow smile spread across Heironymous's broad mouth, revealing the full length of the two tusks that jutted upward between his lips. Nuada prepared himself for the ogre's next move. Nothing came free in Fae society. Even the simple human custom of showing gratitude could trigger a debt. "We merely need to settle on a price for my assistance." Heironymous leaned in to Nuada so he could hear his words above the growing din of the nightly revels.

"That discussion is best held in private. It would be unfortunate for your patrons to discover just how you acquired this magnificent lodge. Some of them might use that knowledge in a most unsavory manner." Nuada's blue eyes sparkled.

"I see. So that's how you're going to be." Heironymous's hand snapped around the vial and he drew himself up straight. The smile slid from his face. It was immediately replaced with another: the practiced smile of a welcoming host. Thick claws on each furred finger contradicted the rich embroidered purple velvet of his sleeve. A thick oak door flew open to reveal the bacchanalian revels within. "I'll have a room prepared for us." He bellowed over the roar of music and crowd. "Until then, please enjoy the pleasures of Fogradh Lodge."

With a curt bow, Heironymous disappeared into the throng. Nuada scanned the majestic hall with wonder. The last time he was a guest, this lodge of exiles was new. Barely a stage and a few tables. Banishment served Heironymous well. He had channeled his longing for home into a glimmering inn that rivaled the best of the Faerie Courts. Nuada felt the tightness in his heart easing with the dizzying fiddle reels, the refined scent of Faerie food, and the twilight glow of the lodge.

He wove his way through Fae of all shapes and sizes. Tiny sprites with gossamer wings tittered at the bawdy jokes of wiry goblins. A pair of ethereal sylphs draped in diaphanous spidersilk gowns were bent in concentration over a game of fidchell with a tall, blond elven man.

Nuada found a place at the sweeping mahogany bar. Rows of brightly colored liquor bottles were lit from beneath by banks of glowing shelf mushrooms. He raised his slim-fingered hand to the white-furred faun working the bar.

"What'll it be, elf?" the faun said. Nuada did not correct him.

"Honeysuckle mead and whatever the special is." He dug into his pocket and sprinkled a handful of gold coins into the upturned palm of the Fae. "If my meal arrives in less than five minutes, keep the change."

"Coming right up, my lord." The little faun beamed at the pile of gold. It was at least twice what the meal was worth and repayment of the boon simple enough. His mead had already arrived by the time the faun had minced off to the kitchen, placed onto the bar by a swarthy redcap. He took a sip. It was sweet and warm on his tongue. He savored the syrupy drink and swiveled the stool to survey the club.

Species who would not normally get along, some from warring

Courts, chattered and laughed together, tapping claw and hoof to the reel drifting from the next room. Nuada smiled and took a long sip of his mead. Heironymous had achieved what even the Tuatha could not; he'd created a place of peace.

Nuada supposed the task was easy given their circumstances, trapped here with no way back to the Underworld, eager for a slice of home. Many were solitary Fae who preferred the Green World to the ephemeral lands of the Underworld. But some appeared to be Underworld dwellers long trapped here with the thickening of the Veil between the worlds. From their lack of scarring, these had been here before the Veil became unstable. Their brethren who chose to stay in the Underworld, on the other hand, were prisoners of a world winding down. Nuada wondered if any of them would be recognizable as Fae anymore.

"The special, my lord." The faun spread out three plates of food before him. Pancakes that smelled of lavender, drizzled with honey, piled high on the biggest plate, heaped with exotic fruits and nuts that spilled over into a sweet custard. A plate of salted meats completed his meal.

"Thank you, more mead when you have the chance." He slid coins across the smooth bar to the faun then swiveled partway around on the stool and continued to enjoy the beauty of the place. Macha would have loved this lodge with its blend of the wild and the sophisticated.

Instead of pillars, vast living ginkgo trees supported the lodge. Their golden leaves caught the warm reddish light of the teardrop lanterns dangling from every branch. Treasures Heironymous, as the former leader of the Elven Elysium, smuggled from the Unseelie Court crammed rows of ornate silver shelves, no doubt stolen from the nobility before Heironymous fled for his life. Paintings of the Underworld, goblets, small sculptures, and more adorned the longest wall. Nuada understood why Fogradh had grown so; to many, this was a museum filled with the lost treasures of the Sidhe.

He felt certain Badb Catha was on that misty island planning an assault on humanity. On which side would the patrons of the Fogradh Lodge fight in the coming war? Would they unite under Heironymous or splinter into factions, each choosing their own allegiance?

Nuada had just finished his meal when a frog-legged nixie sloshed to his side. "Heironymous sent me," she croaked. "Twitch has discovered something." Thin membranes flickered across her green eyes. She beckoned Nuada to follow her.

The green-haired nixie's feet slapped along ahead of him. She guided him to the back of the farthest kitchen through rows of gnomes baking and marinating every kind of delectable Faerie food imaginable. Rows of torches and glowing shelf mushrooms lit the stairwell that wound deeper and deeper down into the earth.

A long hallway emptied them out into another room supported by more golden-leaved trees and lanterns. Nuada grinned. He was tens of thousands of years old and had seen wonders in all three worlds. These ornately carved shelves filled with books were a marvel to rival the forests of the Undying Lands. The rows of volumes stretched as far as the eye could see. Puffy quilted leather chairs flanked oblong tables with woodland scenes carved around the edges. Tiny green-skinned pixies flitted here and there, replacing and reorganizing books, straightening mahogany-toned furniture, and tittering between themselves.

The nixie opened another oak door and flipped a webbed hand to usher Nuada inside. He stepped into a wide laboratory. Heironymous bent over a broad table next to a wiry brown goblin with a puff of black hair that made his head look like a perfect sphere. Glass bulbs of liquid in every color bubbled under flames. Golden instruments, potion bottles, and books littered the rest of the table. One element stuck out. To Nuada's surprise, several pieces of human electronic lab equipment plugged into a wall of batteries lined a long shelf. He suspected the purpose of this lab was to create chemical ways of comforting the vagabonds and exiles who frequented his establishment. Even a Fomorian would be envious of the possibility of profit.

"Twitch has already made some fascinating discoveries about the Dust you brought us."

Nuada stepped around the table to join the pair. The goblin fiddled with rows of tubes in silver frames. Wide yellow eyes blinked rapidly while he furiously stirred some Dust dissolved in a clear liquid. Like a hummingbird, Twitch squeezed a single droplet of the mixture into each tube. The goblin kept screwing up his face and rubbing his long nose. He certainly earned his name.

"What did you find?" Nuada asked.

"Before we come to that, the information I can reveal to you is of surpassing value. We must revisit the unfortunate ugliness of settling on a price," Heironymous said. His voice was unctuous.

Nuada lifted a gloved silver hand toward the ogre and wagged his finger back and forth. "I don't think there will be any price for this little favor. I always heard ogre memories were famously long, but it seems your memory matches your stature. How quickly you forget your debt to me."

Heironymous arched a shaggy eyebrow. "I had hoped you forgot about that."

"Forgot rescuing you from the King of Air and Darkness all those years ago? No. I still have a scar as a souvenir. Give me the full information I seek about the Dust and I consider us even."

Heironymous sighed. "Done. Twitch, tell him what you've discovered. All of it."

"Many things. Curious. Terrible. Yes, terribly curious and curiously terrible." The words tumbled out in a high cracking falsetto. Long fingers flew across the vials, administering different colored drops into them. Some changed color, or a tiny billow of smoke burst up. Others did nothing at all.

"I need specifics. What does this drug do, and can you tell me how it was made?" Nuada said.

"Clever, clever, clever." Twitch skittered over to a microscope with a dropper filled with the smoking mixture. A single drop dripped onto a slide. He pulled on a pair of gloves and whipped the knobs back and forth, muttering to himself. "The binding agent is human design."

"Are you saying that Dust is a human drug?" Nuada said.

"Oh no. Glamour. Sparkly purple. Bends the will. Brings the visions." He dipped a claw into the remaining residue of the glass vial. He brought it up to a long nostril, inhaled sharply, and wiped his hands on the gray apron he wore. "Highly addictive." The goblin tittered and scampered back to a second row of vials. His tongue pinched between his lips while he dropped more samples of Dust into the vials. "Incomplete. Spell not done. Couldn't be done. Need a better binder. Still need Fae close by to make user do things. See what you want them to."

"Incomplete?" Heironymous asked. He bent forward to look at the tubes, hands clasped behind his back.

"When the kelpies came they brought the Aillen. His music drew many of the people in the tent city. Would that possibly complete the effect?"

"The Aillen? Here?" Heironymous's eyes were wide. Nuada nodded and held up a hand to pause his friend's next question.

"Fae music like glamour. Possible. Can't say for sure." Twitch dipped his claw back in the vial and snorted more up his pointy nose.

Nuada turned toward the goblin. "You said it is of human origin."

"Yes and no. Some human, some Fae. Both."

"How can that be?"

"Humans make chemicals. Make potent and long lasting. Chemicals in this the best of the best. Only one place for that."

"Erimus Pharmaceutical," Heironymous said. The goblin tapped his nose and nodded.

"Breas. The Phooka may be on to something," Nuada said. His silver hand clenched and he ground his teeth. He had never forgiven Breas for the torture he put the Tuatha through during his brief reign as king. He felt the gears and springs working his clenching fist. If he hadn't lost his flesh and blood hand in the First Battle of Moytura, he would have remained High King, and the half-Fomorian would have never taken the throne. Years of suffering and pain avoided, for Breas proved himself a tyrant.

Nuada's mind drifted to the young girl. Badb. Breas. What promised to be a dead end turned out to be big. He needed to get back to the Phooka and extricate the girl from the mess she'd stumbled into. After that, he had a date with Erimus Pharmaceutical. If it involved Breas, things had just gone pear-shaped.

"Be careful who you call friend, Silver Hand," Heironymous said as though reading Nuada's mind. "I've had dealings with the Phooka. He is not to be trusted."

"He led me to this city, right when this all started."

"Yes. But how did he procure that knowledge?"

Nuada recalled how the Phooka had responded to the young woman in the alley. Heironymous was right. The Phooka may be useful, but untrustworthy. What did the Phooka want with that girl?

CHAPTER 11

Once the alcohol took effect, sleep grabbed hold of Harper and dragged her into the blackness like sinking into the sea with pockets full of stones. But, like all alcohol-induced rest, the peace was short lived. All too soon, she drifted from the delicious self-obliteration she sought and into that strange land where past terrors mixed with the day's struggles and long-repressed moments stepped into the light.

She screamed and slammed into an upright position. Her breath came in sharp pants. Flailing legs pushed her back against the headboard in a vain attempt at escaping the monsters that had stalked the edges of her awareness since Gerald O'Neill's murder. The events of the day had flung open the gates and let them flood back into her well-worn nightmares, where they threatened to escape permanently into her daily life.

Harper pressed her hands to her eyes as though the action would stop the internal dream movie from playing again for her waking mind. It didn't.

She was a child again, creeping from her bed at the sound of baying hunting dogs outside her window. At the top of the stairs, with her little face pressed between rails, the scene unfolded for the thousandth time. A lady with fiery hair and a black horned headdress pulled a sword from her father's chest while a tall man in an antlered deer skull mask backhanded her mother to the floor. Young Harper clapped her hands over her mouth to stifle a scream. Spectral white dogs with red ears and monsters of every shape slipped into the room behind the dark lady.

The dreamtime scene morphed into the moment she hid under her bed. That was new. Her father bleeding to death on the floor and the still form of her mother were usually the instant she awoke, heart pounding and tears streaming. She hadn't thought about what happened after that moment since she was still a child. A tiny piece of her stood guard at the door leading to those memories fighting around the clock to keep them from roaring to consciousness.

No. No. No. Not this. Anything but this. It's not real. It's just a dream. I couldn't have known they'd be wet and have pointed teeth.

She was lashing her head from side to side, shoulders at her ears, hands gripping her scalp. It was to no avail. The end of the dream played out for her waking mind.

Young Harper felt the wall press against her back as she huddled under the bed listening to the sounds outside. Her Harry Potter nightgown was pulled over her knees as she hunched in its familiar warmth. She heard the bitter laughter of the black-clad lady, followed by light footfalls padding up the stairs. They paused at the top. Harper's ears strained to discern the hissing whispers the intruders shared. She risked leaning over to glance at the bedroom door. The door hung half open and her heart pounded so loud she heard it in her own ears, certain the invaders in the hallway heard it too.

Two sets of bare children's feet appeared in the doorway and paused. Harper squeezed her eyes shut and pushed the pooling tears down her cheeks. A low creak signaled the door yawning all the way open. She opened her eyes and stifled a whimper. Both sets of feet dripped with water, then one pair of feet turned and faced the bed, then the other. Slowly they stepped forward. One dripping foot after the next left wet footprints darkening in the carpet behind them.

The only movement Harper was capable of was pushing against the wall like she could fade through it and escape to safety. Her head buzzed and her entire body quaked. They were right next to her now. She could reach out and touch the white wet feet. When tiny, pale fingers wound around the dust ruffle, a tiny rivulet of water soaked the carpet inches away. She choked back a scream that had been fighting its way out as a small face peered down at her. That horrible face had jet-black eyes that shone with a dull gray shine. Smiling blue-tinged lips revealed rows of yellowing pointed teeth.

How did I know they'd have pointed teeth? Harper's mind contorted to avoid the implications of that thought. It slipped past her defenses anyway. *Because I've seen them before. No. No. No. That's impossible. Monsters aren't real, and Dad's killers didn't wear antlers.*

The events in the tent city contradicted years of disavowing the truth, and she knew the dream was a replaying of the events of the worst night of her life, just as they'd happened ten years ago. Those monsters were there the night they murdered her father. And now they were back.

She looked frantically around her room, her eyes stretched wide and her breath jetting from her throat in rapid pants. She could just make out her Muse posters and some of Emilio's artwork. At that moment she wished his usual subjects weren't fantasy creatures.

Coiled energy forced her to move, so she threw back the blue floral comforter and climbed out of bed. The carpet felt rough on the bottom of her feet. She flipped on every light she owned to banish the demons, then paced, her footfalls keeping time with the parade of thoughts trying to make it all not real, to get it all back in the box.

Her basement room had windows, the tiny kind that appeared at ground level from the outside. She walked toward the desk, cupped her hands against the glass, and peered into the night.

The backyard, illuminated by the patchy glow of the streetlights, revealed nothing out of the ordinary. She made out the silhouette of overgrown and shapeless hedges and the small pine tree. The grass was high. Harper had hoped winter would come before she had to go out and mow it. The quiet darkness of the yard and the drift of her thoughts to the mundane offered her a lifeline back to the borrowed sanity of denial.

From the corner of her eye, a shadow darted across the yard. Her head snapped toward it and she squinted at the spot where the movement had been. The hairs on the back of her neck stood on end. Years of martial arts and self-defense classes taught her to trust the feeling of being watched, because instinct was usually right. *You're just rattled, jumping at shadows. There's nothing out there.* A crow fluttered its wings in the branches of the pine tree. *See. Just a stupid bird.*

She convinced herself that thought was true and the other, darker ones were the delusions borne of the impending anniversary. Rubbing the back of her neck, she took a step back from the window just as a black shape trotted across the back perimeter, shaggy tail bouncing along behind it. The dog from Burnside. Impossible. There was no way that dog was here now, miles from the tent city. It had to be a neighborhood stray.

She ran her hand through her hair and barked out a single laugh. *Harper, you're losing it. They'll lock you in the nut hatch in your mom's old room if you don't get your poop in a group.*

Harper checked that the locks were secure on both her windows and made a quick circuit through the rest of the house.

Three times. Satisfied nothing could breach the ranch home, she pulled the blinds down and crawled back into bed, but not before a couple more pulls from the bottle of vodka. Covers brushing the bottom of her chin, she repeated the story she had created about the Dark Boys in her dream. They hadn't been there that night; they got edited into the illogical dreamscape because of her fear in the tent city, and a black dog was definitely not following her.

CHAPTER 12

Nuada slipped silently into the O'Neill family's backyard while still trying to fit the puzzle pieces together. Dust extended the effects of Fae glamour over both time and numbers of individuals affected so Fae could more easily abduct a handful of Portland's most unfortunate souls. And that was where logic shipwrecked on the rocky shores of why-the-hell-bother. Fae often enchanted humans they took as midwives or other servants, but Seelie and Unseelie alike favored young, beautiful, and talented humans to enthrall, not the broken and indigent. Even then, they barely tolerated their human slaves, frequently objecting to their smell. And why so many? The resources spent to manage the usual servants loomed large. Nuada couldn't fathom the power needed to maintain glamour on large groups of people.

The fact that Erimus Pharmaceutical crafted the extended release component of Dust made sense for two reasons. First, Breas had allied with Badb in the wake of the Second Battle of Moytura, assisting her in cultivating her deep obsession with the apocalyptic visions she endured while delivering a prophecy at the end of the Second Battle of Moytura. Those visions drove her mad, ultimately resulting in the death of Nuada's wife at her own sister's hand. Second, a longer-lasting glamour spell would be beneficial for large numbers of human prisoners. But why did Breas and Badb need human prisoners?

Soggy grass squelched underfoot. He scanned the weathered exterior and the fir trees in the backyard. Then his thoughts turned to the island where the Aillen and kelpies hailed from. That mist was an ancient Tuatha enchantment meant to conceal and transform. That, too, pointed to Badb and would probably be the thornier stop along the journey he planned to begin at dawn.

Nuada might have more questions than answers, but he was certain the girl was in significant danger. Ensuring her safety was his remaining task tonight. With Heironymous's warning ricocheting in his mind, he decided the first step in that task was wrangling information out of the Phooka.

The Fae crouched behind an overgrown juniper bush in his dog shape. Nuada released his invisibility glamour right beside his friend. Raised hackles and bared teeth welcomed him.

"Jumpy. What's gotten into you?" Nuada said with his hands raised in mock surrender.

The Phooka held a paw first to his lips, then to the row of pine trees lining the border to the next house. The tops of the trees held a handful of avian forms.

"My Spidey sense is tingling."

"Sluagh." Nuada shrugged. The Sluagh were abominations loathed and feared by Fae and human alike. Most of them were human once. A handful used to be Fae, now fallen to such a low state they fed on the energies of the newly dead, occasionally the living if they could get away with it.

The ranks of the Sluagh had burgeoned when the Veil thickened, since human souls could no longer make their journey across the Underworld to the Undying Lands for rebirth. Their presence was hardly surprising, yet concerning now given the flock of them following the red-eyed crow. If the Sluagh host had joined with Badb, she might already have amassed an insurmountable force. Perhaps the Phooka was right to be concerned.

The Phooka's eyes slipped closed, and he muttered a spell as his furred paws swept a wide circle over his head. Nuada felt a membrane form around the shabby house. The cloaking spell made them invisible to the Sluagh. If their enemies worked with the avian horde, the spell would block their ability to eavesdrop.

"They arrived right after I did," the Phooka said.

"For now, your spell should protect us and the girl."

"Forty years I've lived in the city and I've never seen so many of these abominations skulking around as I have in the past few weeks."

"They're like rats. You're bound to find them anywhere humans gather, and for the same reasons."

The Phooka's dog shape lost its focus at the edges. In seconds the Phooka stood before Nuada in his own three-foot-tall form. He was still jet black, but he looked composed of assorted bits from several other animals. The back legs of a goat gave way to an overall body shape like a lanky monkey. The monkey resemblance carried up to his arms and hands, which ended in long black fingers. His head and face appeared as though a sheep and a rabbit had a love child that sported tall black horns.

"Is the young woman safe, Phooka?"

"Safe, yes, but rattled, and I think a wee bit drunk." His hands fidgeted along a tail that looked stolen from a cow while long velvet years swiveled like satellite dishes in search of a signal.

Satisfied nothing had befallen the woman, Nuada decided to uncover what he could about his Fae acquaintance, since they'd be working together for the near future. He and the Phooka had known each other for a few years now, yet Nuada knew little about him. Not that trickster Fae were ever an open book, but this Phooka's behavior stood out. His brethren living in the British Isles preferred mountains and forests. Strangely, this one had taken up residence in a bustling city. There must be a compelling reason.

Nuada scraped mud off his boots against a stout rock. "Why do you live in this city?" Nuada tried to make his voice sound conversational.

The Phooka ran his fingers through his lush neck ruff. "I just love all the glorious hipster beards."

"That is not an answer."

"It's an answer. Only not what you were fishing for."

Nuada's furry friend smiled a toothy grin and rubbed his hands together. He plopped down on the rock and rummaged around in a dark grey satchel that had appeared at his side. The bag was beautifully adorned with stones and stitched spirals.

"Look, Phooka, if you know something that can help us—"

"Distrust of your friends is not a good look for you." The Phooka didn't look up. His face hovered over his satchel.

"Friends? Really?"

The Phooka's mouth pulled into a wide grin. He yanked free a bag of cheese curls too large to have ever fit inside the small shoulder sack. Fur-tufted fingers scrabbled over the crinkly plastic, teasing it open. "Now you've got me stress eating." The Phooka crammed a handful of the snacks into his mouth. Golden eyes rolled back and a shuddering sigh sent orange bits spraying. "Divine ambrosia. The food of the gods."

Nuada took a step away from the Phooka and wrinkled his nose. He wandered toward the corner of the house. Just then, waves of warmth bloomed in his breast pocket. His fingers crept beneath his coat and drew out a small, jagged stone the size of a baby's fist. His eyes widened when it pulsed with a bright glow. "It can't be," he whispered. "She killed them all." The final prophecy of the Morrigna, of his wife Macha, foretold the line of Niall would be the end of Badb. Before Badb Catha had gone into hiding, she'd gathered her staunchest supporters and spent many years locating and purging the descendants of Niall, the last of the High Kings.

Nuada waggled the bright shard in front of the Phooka's orange-stained face. "Care to explain this?" he said.

The Phooka stopped in mid-chew to fish something out of his bag once more. He held out his hand to Nuada and wiggled his fingers. Nuada passed him the shard. An orange-crusted tongue squirmed out of the corner of the Fae's mouth while he fidgeted with the stone. "There! Now your pet rock looks more like an actual pet."

The Phooka passed the stone back to Nuada, who scowled at the pair of cartoon eyes he'd affixed. "Phooka—"

"They're googly eyes. Who's a good pet rock? Sit. Stay. You've really trained it—"

"Do not toy with me, shapeshifter."

"Oh. So now it's 'shapeshifter,' not friend. I see how it is."

Nuada's face darkened, and he thrust the glowing shard right under the Phooka's long nose, googly eyes wiggling. "This is a piece of the Lia Fail. You know full well what it does."

"Duh. Were it in a single piece, it cries out when a worthy High King stands upon it." The Phooka rolled his eyes.

"Let us try this again. You summoned me to that alley where you clearly recognized a woman with the blood of kings in her veins. Following Badb's purging of the line, a small miracle. Probably the last. Your timing is suspect. Tell me—"

"Timing, my resurrected friend, is the hallmark of the trickster." The Phooka regarded Nuada with innocent wide eyes as cheese curl after cheese curl popped into his mouth in rapid succession, like bramble through a woodchipper. He grinned. Cheesy orange residue caked his teeth, and orange sawdust peppered the long fur ruff carpeting his neck.

"You are avoiding the question. You recognized her before the Lia Fail did."

The Phooka turned to Nuada and held up a long black and orange-crusted finger. The crunching didn't stop. "Technically, you made a statement, but I will answer part of your implied question, Your Former Majesty. The bit about my phenomenal timing. Is it timing, or merely time? I've made my home in this wondrous city for forty years. I am, in point of fact, the very thing that keeps Portland weird. It's a huge responsibility but I think I bear it well."

"Pretty certain that guy in the pink Darth Vader costume who plays the bagpipes while riding a unicycle might lead that procession." Nuada gave up at getting any more answers from the Phooka, peeled the google eyes from the shard, and slipped the stone back into his pocket.

"And who do you think whispered that delightfully bizarre notion into his ear as he slept?" The Phooka looked dejectedly at the empty bag in his hands. "It's true." His long ears drooped. "You really can't eat just one. Oh wait, that's potato chips. Never mind." He rummaged through his small bag again. "Oh tragedy! That was my last bag."

Nuada ignored his friend's diversionary antics. "Someday, Phooka, I will demand an answer for your unlikely foreknowledge, but for now we need to focus on the task at hand. I am going to pay a visit to Erimus Pharmaceutical."

"Why would you want to go there? It's so. Corporate." The Phooka wrinkled his nose and stuck out a long tongue covered in orange goo.

Nuada gave the Phooka the quick version of what his visit with Twitch and Heironymous revealed.

"Why would Badb collect a bunch of malodorous homeless? She loathes humans, so whatever it is must be zombie apocalypse level bad."

"That I do not know just yet, but I do know where they are going and that Breas made the hybrid drug."

The Phooka clapped his hands and danced a little circle on his tiny goat hooves. "See! I told you! This entire thing is Badb's plan. This is where you go back to telling me what an awesome friend I am and what a service I—"

"If you are right about Badb, it is obvious she has an alliance with the Unseelie. That would be very good for you, given your allegiance to the King of Air and Darkness."

The Phooka's ears drooped and his tail twitched. "About that. Let's just say I'm one of the solitary Fae now and leave it at that."

That was as close to factual truth as Nuada was likely to get. The Phooka's presence in the human world made a little more sense. His residence in this vast city still did not; his race normally loathed cities. Was he there to hand the girl over to Badb and collect a reward? That the young woman remained tucked away in her home lent the Phooka a sliver of credibility. Still, Nuada didn't fully trust the shapeshifter.

Nuada's silver hair swept forward as he reached into his breast pocket and retrieved the stone. It lay in his black gloved hand and glowed faintly. He shook his head. Badb easily worked around the geis Macha had laid on her. If Badb Catha herself couldn't detect the heir, the Sidhe or her other allies could. How this girl had avoided the slaughter baffled him.

Nuada sat down and rested his head in his hand. "She's so young and inexperienced." He imagined this wisp of a human standing on a mended Lia Fail. The glow of its shard told him it would cry out for her as long she took right action. Regardless, he couldn't see the Tuatha following her to the mead hall, much less to war, High Queen or not.

"Don't let her appearance fool you. There is great power in her," the Phooka said in an uncharacteristically contemplative tone.

Nuada was confident the Phooka was powerful enough to protect the girl from kelpies and Sluagh. But their very presence meant they weren't the only ones who knew she existed. The Phooka was right. This is where Badb would make her stand. This was also where he would make her pay for Macha's death.

"You keep watch on this girl, protect her with your mangy life. She may be the only person alive with the bloodline to unite the magical races under a single banner. I will drop in at Erimus and pay Breas a visit."

"You know once you do that, we're out in the open. She'll move against us."

"Her crows were in the tent city earlier. It is a good bet she knows by now both we and an heir are here. If they come for her, get her out of here."

"You mean when—"

Nuada's scowl stopped the Phooka from finishing.

"You can count on me, captain." The Phooka stood full upright and gave Nuada a mock salute.

"Just keep her safe, Phooka." With that, Nuada turned and disappeared into the overgrown greenery of the yard.

CHAPTER 13

The shrill, electronic scream of the alarm jolted Harper awake. She groaned and smacked the clock to stop the torture. She always forgot to turn the damned thing off on Friday night. The insistent beeping made her head feel like a thousand angry hornets were buzzing inside her skull. Slivers of warm daylight crept through the blinds, burning away the fears of the night much like flipping on a light made fear of the resident closet monster seem silly.

Every muscle in her body ached and throbbed with the slightest movement. A night of dancing at the Mystic Island festival seemed unlikely, but at least she could listen to the music. The smell of hot coffee wafted down to her room. Her mom was already up. Guilt over last night's exchange made her contemplate pulling the covers back over her head and staying in bed. Eventually the relief promised by the coffee overpowered her reluctance and she swung her feet out of bed, pulled on a tattered red Roxy sweatshirt, and dragged herself up the stairs.

Eileen O'Neill hunched over their small, round dining room table. Like all the furniture in the cramped house, it was secondhand and covered in scratches and dents. One hand cradled a cup of coffee, the other her forehead poised over a bowl of Rice Krispies. The cereal appeared to have lost its snap, crackle, and even its pop, several minutes prior. She didn't notice Harper.

"Morning, Mom," Harper said as she slipped behind the kitchen island and poured her own cup of coffee. She eyed her mother carefully, trying to assess what kind of day this would be and whether a hasty retreat would be the best policy. Sensing which way her mother's moods blew was a skill developed for emotional self-preservation and honed to a fine art over the past fifteen years.

"Hey." Eileen gave her cereal a half stir. Internally, Harper breathed a sigh of relief. The crash to depression meant another screaming match was unlikely.

"Mom, about last night—"

Eileen held up her hand and shook her head. Her bleach-blonde hair slid over one of her eyes.

"Let's not. It's a bad time for both of us. I know you didn't mean anything you said."

"No, I didn't, Mom. I just had the most bizarre day before I got home." She grabbed a banana to go with her coffee and slid into the wooden chair across from her mom.

"I heard you scream last night. The nightmares have been bad for me too." Eileen's fingers traced the stitched outlines of the green placemat beneath her cereal.

Harper paused, silent for a moment, trying to judge whether she should talk about what occupied her mind. She opted to risk it. "Mom, can I ask you a question about that night?"

"Honey, I don't like to think about it."

"I know, Mom, me neither . . ." Harper's mind scrambled for a line of questioning that would neither shut down her mother completely nor end in a blowup. "Well, it's just like you said, you heard me in my sleep . . ."

Her mother looked up from the placemat. Years of suffering

and alcoholism had prematurely gouged deep lines in her beautiful face. She nodded once slowly and focused her green eyes back down at the placemat.

"Do you remember anything odd?"

"What do you mean?"

Harper's mind scrambled to come up with a question that would get her the answers she sought without making her sound like a whacko. "Like dark-haired teen boys. Or water all over the floor." She held her breath and scrunched her toes deeper into her slippers.

"Water? No. That night's always been hazy for me, but no water. I remember a woman's voice, two, maybe three men, no boys. Why the sudden interest?"

Harper feigned a nonchalance she didn't really feel. "That was what was in my dream. Dad's loss, water on the floors, some dark-haired teenagers, and a man in an antlered mask."

Her mom's reaction was fleeting, but Harper caught it. For a split second, Eileen's eyes widened and an intake of breath made her torso jerk up ever so slightly. As soon as it happened, she melted back into the slumped posture of sadness and shook her head.

There was something her mother was hiding, probably from herself as much as her daughter. Harper quickly changed the subject. She didn't want to consider the implications of that spark of recognition just now.

"Just a weird dream, no biggie." Harper focused on her own coffee. The spoon clinked around the edges of the mug and a tiny vortex formed in the center. "So I'm going out tonight with Emilio. There's a big concert over on Government Island. I'll probably be home pretty late."

Eileen looked up from her soggy cereal. The smile she flashed didn't reach her eyes. "That's good. You need to get out more. I didn't sleep so well last night either. I'm going back to bed. Have fun at your party." Her voice sounded faraway, almost robotic. Eileen shuffled out of the room with her eyes half focused. Harper was relieved. After one of her manic episodes, her mother slept sometimes for days. At least she wouldn't be needing her daughter's help tonight and Harper could go to the party guilt free.

Harper wolfed down breakfast, then got ready for the day. She crammed her red unicorn headband in her backpack along with makeup and other essentials. She stepped out into the crisp morning air of Oregon in fall. The trees greeted her in hues of orange and yellow. The musty smell of leaf mold saturated the still air.

She buttoned her red plaid jacket a little tighter against the chill. The brightness of the day forced her eyes to flutter rapidly and she paused for them to adjust. Turning back to lock the door brought a warning prickle to her skin. The featherlight weight of an unwanted gaze danced on the back of her neck. Her pulse quickened and she froze, listening while a tingle scuttled up her spine. She was being watched. *My overactive imagination working overtime again. There's nothing there, just like there wasn't really a zombie living in the bathtub drain when I was eight.* She fired a glance over her shoulder. The street was empty except for a mopey-looking teen pedaling a bike. The lush maple tree in the neighbor's yard contained a half dozen roosting crows. The base of the tree cradled a jet-black cat with yellow eyes. The way the cat was staring at her made beads of sweat break out along her lip. The dog in the alley yesterday had eyeballed her in precisely the same way. Harper shuddered. She was losing her marbles if she thought domestic animals were ogling her. It was just a cat. She turned on her heel and almost jogged to the bus stop.

Harper spent the bumpy, swaying bus ride focused on playing games on her iPhone. Twenty minutes later she slung the backpack onto her back and loped up the winding sidewalk toward Powell's World of Books to meet Emilio. She scrolled through her Facebook while she walked. That kept her from noticing the golden-eyed raven flitting from perch to perch behind her.

CHAPTER 14

Nuada realized the flaw in his plan the instant he craned his neck to scan the top of the enormous glass tower of Erimus Pharmaceutical's corporate offices. He had absolutely no idea how to find what he was looking for. The world of business suits and corporations was the realm of the humans and the Fomorians who controlled the vast majority of this society's wealth. He regretted not trying to convince Twitch to come with him. He didn't trust the goblin, but Twitch knew his way around human society.

Nuada perched on a bench near the main entrance and wracked his mind for a plan. He snorted. Everywhere he looked in this concrete plaza, dramatic fountains and statues vied for attention, each more ostentatious than the last. Waves of winged horses and women clothed in flowing gowns flanked a soaring bank of revolving doors.

Breas hadn't changed in the thousands of years since his short-lived kingship; only his victims had. Instead of secret alliances with his Fomorian relatives to tax the Tuatha to the bone, he made secret alliances with corrupt human governments to place his boot on the necks of people like the unfortunate souls scratching out subsistence in the alleys. All so he could erect these soaring monuments to his own perpetually adolescent ego. It had taken the Second Battle of Moytura to end Fomorian tyranny. What would it take now?

Dead end. This is no longer my world. I am the Master of the Elements, not a Green World businessman. I have no idea how to work their technology. Even if I did, I would never know what to look for. Nuada's back hunched, his long exhale like a slow leak of hope.

How could I be so blind? I may not know how to find what I need in there, but the people inside would. A vague plan formed. A little glamour first, to make Nuada appear like a mortal wrapped in a dull suit and tie, then force someone to give him information. Simple. Solid enough. And all he had.

He kindled the sorcery that always waited inside; a simple glamour barely drained his personal energy. The little spell tingled like static electricity, and in seconds he blended in perfectly with upper management. A fitted gray suit and cerulean tie that made his blue eyes appear incandescent, his silver hair bound at the base of his neck. As for the sword, camouflaged as a long silver cane. He drew himself up and raised his head in the haughty comportment he observed in the men who swaggered into the building.

The rotating glass doors swept him into an expansive white marble lobby. Two paintings of Breas flanked a row of golden elevators. They had to be twenty feet tall and revealed every detail of his sweeping, short golden hair and heavy eyes. The portraits captured his arrogance with perfection. A round information kiosk held a pen of security guards and clerical staff. There was no option but to pass by the station. Its gilded dignity was marred by psychedelic posters advertising Erimus Pharmaceutical as the main sponsor for the Mystic Island festival taking place tonight on another island, not far from the one cloaked in mist.

"Identification?"

Nuada's eyes scanned to the plastic badges the employees wore. They flashed them at the spectacled woman and continued into the building. He didn't have one of those and couldn't get a close enough look to use glamour and fake one. "I don't work here. I'm here to see Mr. . . ." He dropped his head and pinched the bridge of his nose with a gloved hand.

"Mr. who?"

"This is embarrassing, but I can't seem to recall. I'm here to interview someone about your ncw drug for a story." He made a show of patting down his pockets, half smiling, half wincing.

"Oh, that's OK, sweetheart. It happens all the time." The woman smiled. "You're going to head up to the third floor, hang a right, and you'll see the Public Relations office. They're all super helpful. Here." The perky blonde handed him a card with a black strip running along the back. "This will get you through the main doors and elevator up to the third floor. The upper floors are all research, we allow no guests past the fifth."

"Thank you." Nuada inclined his head, accepted the card, and strode toward the elevators.

He had no intention of speaking to the Public Relations department. The doors slid shut, and he slid his card into the slot to make the door close. The directory announced that floor fifteen housed the Research and Development offices. It was a good bet the fifteenth floor would hold some answers.

Yet his key card had him stuck at the third floor. He looked around the top of the elevator, seeing no cameras. Another surge of magical energy broke over him like a warm wave and he faded from sight. He may be forced to ride the contraption for quite a while before it finally landed on the fifteenth floor. Better to be invisible to human eyes.

Nuada acquainted himself with the elevator for several minutes before someone finally exited at the fifteenth floor. He couldn't smell any iron at all in its walls, unusual for a human building. That meant this structure could host human and Fae alike. Twitch had discovered both human tech and Fae magic melded together to create Dust. That fact and this unusual building was suited to Fae habitation confirmed for certain Erimus was the source of the drug.

A soft chime ended the smooth ride of the metal box, and a man in a white coat stepped out with Nuada close behind. Long hallways stretched from either side of the lift. White marble tiles reflected the cool light from filigreed wall sconces. His unwitting companion turned left and started up the hallway. The brown-haired man took a few steps, paused, and cast a glance over his shoulder right at the place Nuada stood. Instinct froze him to the spot. Magic crackled just beneath his skin, ready to strike out. But as quickly as he had looked back, the man turned his head forward and strode up the hallway.

Nuada exhaled. The guy probably feared he forgot something, but Nuada couldn't shake the sensation he'd somehow been seen.

Within moments of his arrival, a woman with auburn hair and a lavender pencil skirt exited an office with a balding man in a wrinkled blue shirt. He fell into step behind them, his footfalls making no sound.

"Dr. Jones better have the next round of serum ready for testing or there'll be hell to pay." The woman clipped along on stilettos.

"We've got far bigger problems right here." The rotund man's face turned a darker shade of red. "The new batch of Dust is twice as powerful as we thought, but I'm having a hell of a time getting it to bond to a substrate light enough to cover a sizable area, and the concert is ten hours away."

The woman barked a harsh laugh. "Without Jones's Abraxas serum, more subjects won't matter. He keeps saying he's close, but I think he's dead in the water. Maybe literally when Badb realizes he's failed."

And there it was. Badb. The Phooka was right. Nuada had no time to ponder just how the Phooka had uncovered her presence because his quarry was changing course.

"Let's just hope the new batch of serum performs more predictably than the last batch. Jesus, that was a mess." The man's hand reached out and held the door for his companion. Nuada slipped between them and into the room before either of them collided with their invisible shadow.

"Have you seen the animals they were testing it on? They say they're from some Asian jungle somewhere. If you ask me, they look like Martians." The woman's fingers raked the underside of her neck, strands of her bobbed hair slipping between her fingers.

"Have you seen the reeking street filth they're planning to test it on now? I guess that's what the Dust is for. Bait to trap better human animals." The bald man waved while the lean woman strode into her office.

"See you at the meeting, Andy." The woman nodded and nudged the door wider.

Luck had smiled on Nuada. Either of these two likely knew at least something he could take back to Heironymous and Twitch. The little bald man continued his waddle up the hall while the woman veered into a small office. The nameplate announced her as Jennifer Galloway, Project Director. He followed so closely behind he could smell the gardenia shampoo she used. She busied herself rummaging in her desk. While her attention was focused on the drawer, Nuada waved a hand slowly down. Magic lowered the blinds over the glass window that offered a constant view of the hallway. They were alone and unseen. He toggled the lock shut just as the woman looked up from her desk.

He didn't give her a chance to wonder about the blinds. His invisibility glamour slid from him like a veil of cobwebs. The woman yelped and pressed herself against the back wall.

"I will not harm you, Jennifer." Nuada made his voice silken and laden with glamour. Jennifer's eyes lost their focus and her face softened. Nuada motioned her into her chair. "Sit."

She sank into her seat like she was in slow motion, every movement exaggerated. Once she was settled, she leaned toward Nuada as though trying to be as close to him as possible. "You're so beautiful." Her words were barely a breath.

Nuada seated himself across the desk and laid his camouflaged sword across his knees. "Jennifer, I need some information about one substance this company manufactures."

"OK." Her elbows rested on the desk. Her chin fell into her open palms.

"Does this company have any involvement in actually making Dust, or are they buying it from someone else?"

"Yes, we make it. It's a test for our new market, a drug that transports you to a wondrous place so you won't have to experience painful procedures like chemotherapy."

"Erimus is testing this on indigent humans? Why?" Nuada leaned back in his chair. He was still missing something.

"There were too many new compounds in the drug. He couldn't explain what they were to the FDA, so we started our own trials. He'll just buy their approval later, once we know the drug is safe." Jennifer reached out a hand to caress Nuada, but her fingertips fell short.

"I overheard you talking to your coworker about testing a serum. Is that the same thing as Dust?"

The woman was leaning toward Nuada so forcefully the desk was digging into her ribcage. "No, that one is for the military, something about super—"

The door flying off its hinges halted Jennifer's answer. Nuada's glamour shattered along with the rest of the glass wall to the hallway. The woman shot to her feet and screamed.

A cluster of men wearing black cargo pants and shirts burst into the room with guns drawn. There were at least five of them cutting off the only escape from the room. Nuada's hand clamped on to his sword but then he looked at the guns in the men's hands. He lifted his own arms in surrender. He struggled to grasp how he'd been noticed. Maybe the man from the elevator. No. Humans were too weak to notice the spike of magic. Even a Fae would have to be unusually powerful to pierce it.

The woman slid down the wall to the floor in the room's corner. She watched wide-eyed while the security guards yanked the sword from Nuada's hands and patted him down. Not satisfied he had no other weapons to conceal, they spun him around and rough hands shoved him into the hallway.

"Are you OK, Ms. Galloway?" a man with skin the color of rich chocolate asked. He twisted Nuada around and pushed him against the wall, kicking his legs wide. He confiscated the pair of swords and all the knives.

"I think so. He didn't hurt me." Nuada saw the confusion on her face. He felt compassion for her. One minute she was enamored of a tall stranger, the next her office was teeming with armed guards.

"HR will want to brief you. They'll be expecting you now."

The woman nodded and stepped into the hallway, pushing her back as tight as she could to the wall and side-stepping past Nuada. Her head swiveled to look at him over her shoulder. Her stilettos clicked up the hallway in the opposite direction.

Nuada felt the last vestige of his glamour torn from him like someone whipped off a blanket. His head was wrestled along the wall to face the other direction. A slender man with hair the color of night sneered at him. The crimson fabric of a silken tunic spilled from under gunmetal armor.

The guards clenched him face to face with a Sidhe elf from the Unseelie Court.

CHAPTER 15

"Your Highness." The elf sneered and dropped an exaggerated bow.

Nuada stared at the man. When the Veil began to thicken, the gentry were the first to return to the Underworld, preferring the majesty of their forests and halls to the shrinking woodlands and iron cities above. The Unseelie especially preferred their fading world to contact with humanity. However unlikely, Nuada supposed it was possible that a handful had been trapped here. Given the Unseelies' loathing of humans, the fact they were working hand in hand with this human company was unheard of.

He'd expected to discover solitary Fae and creatures like the Aillen so malevolent they killed indiscriminately, but not the gentry of any Court. Then he noticed the crisscross of dark, leathery scar tissue covering the pale hand and peeking out of the neckline of his tunic. The elf was lucky. His perfect face and pointed ears remained unmarred.

Scarring raised questions Nuada had no answers for. The scars this elf bore marked him as a definite resident of the fading

Underworld. A blight that slowly wore down everything in that land began with the Industrial Revolution in the Green World, causing all the gateways between them to fall. Was there still a place where the Veil was thin enough for passage? Not likely, he thought. He had searched everywhere for a gate, when he sought to save his wife from her own sister. They were most definitely closed. And yet he had seen the Aillen the night before.

A rough hand closing around his wrist broke him from the winding pathways of his thoughts.

"Did you really think we wouldn't have safeguards in place to alert us to the use of magic?" The elf's voice was light and musical. "I'll take the prisoner from here." He waved a hand and looked down his long nose at the uniformed men. They inclined their heads and stepped away from Nuada, dropping his wrist.

The black gentleman passed his sword to the Sidhe. He turned it over slowly and held it up to his eyes for appraisal. The single braid he wore to the side of his long hair swung forward. "So this is the legendary Claimh Solais. I never dreamed I would see it."

"Do not become attached to it."

The elf smiled, his eyes glittering, and motioned Nuada to join him. They walked side by side halfway up the hallway. Gold-framed pictures of waterfalls and forests flanked the hall at regular intervals between glass-walled entrances to offices and conference rooms. Their human occupants didn't look up as the pair walked past. Either by familiarity or by glamour, none seemed concerned to see the elf.

Inside a small alcove sat a gold-leafed table with claw feet holding up an outrageous display of flowers of every shape and size. Breas had always loved the pointlessly decorative. Nuada's captor walked up to a blank wall and pressed his hand on a small framed mirror. Instantly the wall rippled, replaced by what appeared to be the surface of a pond. The Sidhe grasped Nuada's elbow and ushered him through before stepping over the threshold himself.

Nuada emerged into a gilded suite of rooms that must have taken up most of the wing. Gently cascading water endlessly circulating into a stone pond below covered an entire wall. Long green hair twined with blooming lily pads flowed around a pair of yellow eyes hovering at the surface of the water. Thin membranes flicked across the eyes before they sank beneath the surface. The room flaunted a bank of windows that revealed a 180-degree view of the city. Elaborate furniture and baroque paintings of glorious battles covered the walls.

"Welcome to my little company." Breas's voice sounded unctuous. "You could have just asked for a tour instead of glamouring one of my employees." Several more Sidhe slipped into the room, men and women alike clad in red tunics and dark armor. The elf handed Breas the sword and fell into line next to one of his female compatriots. Breas ran his hand along the carved scabbard and laid his prize on a long table. His blond hair framed his perfect face.

Nuada knew his time here would be short. Breas might make good sport of grinding him under his heel for a bit but would soon tire of his company. He needed to get out of here and fast, yet he doubted he could fight his way out either by magic or sword. The building probably contained a small army of Fae within its ironless walls. The instant he drew on his internal power, a throng of enemies would swarm him in these close quarters.

The Master of the Elements was not about to be brought down by corporate security. Magical or not. He decided to test the sensitivity of their magic detection systems. Ever so slowly, Nuada stretched out his fingertips and tugged just a little on the surrounding air. A tiny prickle of elemental energy flowed into his hand. Scanning the eyes of the still immobile Sidhe, he knew they hadn't felt the disturbance. He just had to keep them talking long enough.

A tiny brown satyr ambled toward Breas and Nuada, hoisting a silver tray laden with fragrant cakes and drinks above his head. "Appears as though you finally learned the basics of hospitality." Nuada waved the satyr away.

Breas's smile widened. He swirled an amber liquid in his glass and took a sip. He must have recalled the lack of hospitality that sparked the war with the Fomorians, yet his face betrayed no hint of indignation at the cutting remark. The Second Battle of Moytura ended with Breas dethroned and Nuada High King for a second time. Perhaps Breas had matured a bit in the past couple thousand years.

"Since our last meeting, I learned more effective ways to amass power." Breas swept his hand around the extravagant room. "Crowns mean little when one has the wealth to own the kings."

"You never wanted to get your own hands dirty. Coward."

"That's what the Tuatha were for."

Nuada's fist clenched and he stepped toward Breas, eyes focused on his sword. The Sword of Light should never be drawn for mere vengeance, but slaughtering this false king tempted him, nonetheless. Breas had treated his own people like slaves for his sole benefit. It was dishonorable, and also the Fomorian way. The ring of a half dozen swords leaping from their scabbards forced a momentary retreat.

"King Balor is long dead, and yet his scorching gaze still afflicts your people," Nuada said.

His nemesis perched on the end of the table, cool blue eyes dancing with amusement. "Oh, not just my people. The humans have become our equals in that regard. They may lack strength and wisdom, but the gnawing void in their souls gave them complete power over this world. They've nearly used up Earth and still it isn't enough. More is their prayer, consumption their king, and we Fomorians their gods."

"False king to false god. At least you're moving up in the world. You know what they say, the bigger they are the harder they fall."

"In the United States, we have another saying. 'Too big to fail.'"

"Humanity will wake up to Fomorian usury just like we did."

"And who will wake them? The Tuatha? You abandoned them to hide under the hills. I suppose that ended up in their collective favor. They shape the world instead of being imprisoned by it."

It galled him, but Nuada had to admit Breas was right. His people's withdrawal from this world had left a void. Humans were a young race in need of guidance. When their teachers left, they found others offering appealing lessons. Lessons that salved the fears mortality brings. Both dying worlds were his people's fault for abandoning their stewardship.

"Even you cannot be this ignorant. What will your people do when the land is all used up? Human greed has already closed the Veil. The Underworld withers. The fate of the Green World is the fate of all. When it falls, the other worlds die, even Fomorian cities under the oceans. I never thought of your people as fools. Evil, yes, but not fools."

Breas brought the glass to his full lips and took a long pull. Nuada could see by the flash of his eyes that he was more angered by the insults than he wanted to reveal. Good.

"Aren't we lucky you're here to save us all. Walk us back into the light."

"You couldn't find the light if the sun was up your ass." Nuada inclined his head with a smile.

Breas inhaled sharply through flared nostrils. Nuada felt a little thrill of satisfaction.

"You know something big is coming. It's why you crawled back here. To avenge your wife. The day comes when we will reassess who the fools are." Breas reached beside him and picked up the sword. "This little trinket should make our work much easier."

He had slipped. He may be half-Tuatha, but his Fomorian blood forbade his use of the weapon. Only someone of Tuatha blood could free it from the scabbard. Only one Tuatha had formed an alliance with Breas during the Milesian invasion of Ireland. Badb. The presence of the Unseelie Sidhe was double confirmation. The King of Air and Darkness had aided her too. There were more questions, but Nuada doubted he would find any more answers today. He needed just a few more moments. The little ball of air energy he'd been winding was almost ready.

"That sword will never draw for you. I knew there was a Tuatha master holding your leash. Badb Catha, isn't it?" Nuada was stalling.

"I tire of this conversation. Callon. Leander. Take our esteemed guest to the pit and prepare him for transport to Sauvie Island. I want to keep him alive, to witness the destruction of everything he holds dear."

He was out of time. He could only hope now he had enough power to break through. Two raven-haired elves gripped his arms. Both of them bore the telltale scars of the Underworld on their faces and hands. Nuada planted his feet and looked up at Breas and a smile spread across his face.

Nuada twisted free of the Sidhe, darted forward two steps, and dropped to the ground. Momentum carried him sliding past Breas to snatch his sword from the desk. Before the half-Fomorian even had time to react, Nuada brought the pommel up under his jaw. Breas's head snapped back and he crumpled to the floor. A life of privilege had made him slow.

The Sidhe were on him in a flash, but the furnishings left little room to maneuver. He feinted to the side of the nearest one. She brought her sword up toward his face, exposing her entire left side.

Nuada's leg swept her feet from under her and she slammed to the floor, shattering a glass table on her way down.

The desk and statues impeded the rest of his attackers. For a second, the way was clear. He turned on his heel and sprinted from the approaching Sidhe. The tip of the sheathed sword directed toward the quickly approaching glass. He leapt with all his strength straight at the window, ready to smash through and cushion his fall with the air energy he'd collected.

The first part of the plan went as expected. His shoulders jarred when the sword tip shattered the glass, making a shimmering cloud around him. He thought for an instant he'd lost consciousness, tumbled through the air, and splattered on the concrete. The impact on his ribcage sent the air in his lungs erupting from his mouth. Pain shot from his chest and neck and his legs hung limp.

His mind raced to catch up to the physics of the situation. *I'm not falling. Why aren't I falling?*

His vision danced with tiny lights and flared too bright, giving the sidewalk below a hazy, overexposed look. He realized he was losing consciousness fast.

With the last of his fading strength, Nuada pulled his face to the side to see the clawed feet circling his waist. Above them, broad wings flapped. A small black dragon suspended him only a few feet from the window he had leapt from.

Breas appeared in the window, a broad smile stretching across his face despite the blooming bruise under his chin.

Nuada's vision was a tunnel narrowing fast. The Sidhe warriors joined the half-Fomorian.

"You didn't think we'd be prepared for that little move? All those statues aren't really statues," Breas shouted.

Nuada was too weak to respond.

"Shall I tell Badb to prepare a welcome fit for the king?" Callon wore the same mocking smile.

"Oh yes. And tell the good doctor he will have some powerful new blood to experiment with. Tuatha blood."

Nuada clung to awareness, but he was too exhausted by his impact with the dragon to struggle. He clenched the Cliamh Solais in his hand and let the dragon fly him across the sky.

CHAPTER 16

Harper stepped into Powell's World of Books and caught Emilio's eye as he finished helping a customer locate the Spirituality section. He waved enthusiastically and sauntered over to her. Tight black jeans clung like a second skin to his thin legs. A belt serving no useful purpose hung loosely about his waist. The three rows of metal studs would have looked badass if they weren't every color of the rainbow. His usual bright purple Doc Martens harmonized with the electric blue of both his shirt and his highlights. The dull nametag stuck out like a sore thumb against all the fabulous.

"What's up?" He embraced Harper, planting a kiss on her right cheek, then her left. "You look like you've seen a ghost."

She pulled from his amicable embrace and focused on a pile of lint on the carpet. "Still suffering from the overdose of weird from last night."

"Weird is Portland's primary export."

Harper nodded and glanced over her shoulder at the street outside. *Relax. You checked. No Dark Boys or staring yellow-eyed dogs.*

"Five minutes and I'm done with my shift. We can change in the bathroom." He draped an arm across her shoulders. "I'm so excited you're coming, it's going to be off the hook!" If he beamed any wider, the corners of his mouth would meet at the back of his head.

"Yeah." Harper nodded. She tried to imitate his smile, but it failed halfway to a grin. "I'll go back and start changing now."

Emilio's hand on her shoulder brought her more fully into the present moment, just as she turned to slouch off toward the back. Deep brown eyes were softened with concern.

"Are you sure you're OK? You know you can tell me anything."

Harper wanted to tell him, but this was the kind of thing no one believed. "I'm all right. Family stuff." The knitted eyebrows and thin line of his lips told her Emilio wasn't buying it. "All right, girl, we'll talk about all your morose secrets later." With a nod, he wandered off to wrap up his shift.

She crammed herself into the bathroom stall and peeled off her street clothes. Going to the party, knocking back a few drinks, and dancing promised to push all the weirdness and pain right out of her life for a few hours. *Emilio's right. This will be awesome.* Besides, he was the single bright spot in the pressure cooker that was her life; she supposed she owed him his night of fun.

What did my high school counselor say? 'Your focus determines your reality.' I'm going to focus on having fun for Emilio and not on being a horrible daughter, or black animals with yellow eyes. And I absolutely, positively am super-ultra sure I will not think at all about Dark Boys.

Of course, she was wrong. All the things she wanted to bury in the deepest graves of her thoughts just kept popping up like daisies because in willing herself to not think about them she thought about them more.

It was a relief when Emilio joined her. They found a quiet

place in the storage room to get ready. Shelves full of boxed books awaiting transfer to the storefront made perfect tables for the array of glittery cosmetics and hair falls Emilio dumped out. Emilio, as promised, did Harper's makeup and wove shiny red hair falls deftly into her warm brown hair. When he finished, she had a fiery mane that tumbled down her back.

In the summer, Emilio often used his artistic skills to do face painting at art shows and other events in the city. He was a Picasso of his craft. Emilio avoided any lengthy conversation while he worked, and he expected Harper to do the same and remain statue still; the artist demanded silence while crafting his masterpieces. In the mirror, Harper studied the doe's eyes he'd painted for them both. Some trick of shading made them look bigger than normal. Wisps of glitter-laced color trailed around their hairlines and ended in glittery lips.

"All done, you magical beast." He stepped back with his arms crossed and motioned with a finger for her to spin around. His infectious enthusiasm melted away the last of her tension for now. She laughed, tossed her mane, turned, and winked at him over her shoulder.

"I look like a goth My Little Pony."

Her entire costume shone in shades of blood red. A shiny vinyl miniskirt slid over soft velour leggings that ended in shaggy fur leg warmers. Red patent leather Doc Martens looked like shiny hooves beneath long fur. She swiveled back to face Emilio and blew him a kiss from hands wrapped in velour gloves that peeked out under the centerpiece of her outfit, a crimson fitted knee-length coat. The faux fur trim promised to keep out the cold. Emilio crowned her with the red-lighted horn.

"Girl, you crushed it!" Emilio said as he snapped his fingers.

"But all the boys will look at you!"

"You're not wrong." Emilio pursed his lips in a dramatic pout.

Emilio's ensemble looked like a moody goth had collided with a majestic black unicorn. Shiny skintight pants covered in buckles and zippers, oversized black fur leg warmers up to his knees. Somehow, he had found glittery black hooves to cover his boots. The coat with tails brought in an element of cyberpunk conductor. A headdress of jet-black feathers and light nylon tubes cascaded down his back. He walked a pretend catwalk and spun around in front of Harper so she could admire every angle.

"Where did you find that coat?"

"Isn't it amazing? Goodwill." He slipped his horn off and tucked it into his matching messenger bag.

No one gave them a passing glance as they walked the few blocks up to Emilio's car. This was Portland, after all. Harper spotted several other party-goers heading for mass transit. A cluster of white-lace and black-clad Victorian vampires chatted with a green goblin on stilts. Seething throngs of frilly flower fairies drowning in tulle scampered, giggling, up the sidewalk.

"Your carriage, m'lady." Emilio patted his jet-black Smart Car, which Harper referred to as the goth golf cart.

"You better not hitch us up to that thing, although I guess if you did it would go faster."

Emilio responded with his middle finger.

Harper returned fire and chucked her backpack against the seat, transferring the essentials into a smaller red shoulder bag. She left her pepper spray and self-defense weapons in the backpack, sure security would confiscate them. She felt vulnerable and naked without them.

Emilio's goth golf cart soon rolled up Route 405 toward Vancouver, Washington, where he told Harper catching the boats from the Washington side to the Government Island dock would be faster. Psychedelic trance music laced with fiddle and guitar thumped from the stereo. He grooved to the beat, moving his shoulders side to side and bobbing his head up and down. Seeing

Harper look down at his phone, he said, "Aural Nocturna. They're headlining tonight."

A few seconds of harp sent a twinge of anxiety bubbling up her spine. "I like it," she said and shoved the feeling back down.

"So when are you going to tell me about whatever it is you've been hiding?"

"You promise not to think I'm crazy."

Emilio made the scout's honor sign with his right hand. "Solemnly swear."

Harper took a deep breath. At the risk of sounding like a lunatic, she told him everything, only leaving out the part where one of the Dark Boys almost knew her by name. That little detail deserved to stay buried as deep as possible for as long as it could.

When she finished her story, Harper's hands twisted in her lap and her foot tapped a rapid beat against the door panel. "I'm having trouble believing it myself. Probably just a plain old nervous breakdown. No fairytale creatures at all." She peeked out of the corner of her eye at Emilio, trying to determine how crazy he thought she was. To her surprise, he was calm and focused on the road ahead.

"I don't think you're crazy. My gran told me about the monsters that lived in the forests in Mexico."

"Yeah. But didn't you think those were just stories once you weren't a kid anymore?" She felt a thousand pounds lighter, and yet the sense of a sword hanging above her head, ready to drop, failed to recede under the bright light of Emilio's belief. If Emilio trusted her account, the possibility increased it was real.

"I never saw them, but my gran wasn't someone who made stuff up. Even as a kid's story."

Harper nodded. "I guess not." She knew Emilio's grandma. Leticia Soliz was an intense and serious woman, not at all prone to flights of fancy. She believed in the Catholic God and all the saints. Alongside, she worshiped several of the old Mayan gods from her homeland for good measure.

"She told me many stories, just like yours, of spirits. She even encountered them when she was young. I don't think my gran is insane and neither are you. You should share this with her tomorrow. Her insight may help you understand what you saw."

Harper sighed with relief, her chest and throat constricting with oncoming tears. She choked them back because she didn't want to streak the makeup Emilio had so meticulously applied. Chilly hands twisted the soft tails of her admission bracelet. "I'm scared, Emilio. I don't think going to this festival is the safest thing to do, considering."

"There'll be hundreds of people there. It'll be the safest place around. Magical creatures avoid crowds of humans. If any do show up, guess you'll keep us both safe like you always do."

"Somehow I don't think I have what it takes to fight one of those things."

"There are two people I'd bet on in a fight with, well, anything. You and my gran. Both of you defended me through all my inner and outer battles."

"Like in ninth grade when Miles Roberts called you racist names and broke your phone, so I kicked his ass so he'd leave you alone."

"And your mother had to sober up and come to school to keep you from getting expelled."

Harper laughed, the burden of keeping her nightmare story to herself completely evaporated, and she felt free. "And all she did was tell Principal Reed the little poop deserved it and he should be fired if a fourteen-year-old girl had to stop a bully for him."

Emilio laughed. "Your mom's profanity-laced logic was sound. Miles was terrified of you after that."

CHAPTER 17

A sense of dread felt like a rope dragging Nuada toward consciousness. His heart pounded the rhythm of retreat in his chest, commanding his legs to run anywhere but where he was. But they refused his command. He didn't move, yet the landscape still slid past like he walked the path himself.

He instantly regretted his sharp intake of breath. Pain lanced from his chest; it wrenched him back to full awareness. Blue eyes opened to slits, confirming the absence of the dragon. Two of the black-and-red-clad Sidhe from Erimus strode in front of him. The almost inaudible crunch of footfalls announced one more behind him.

Coils of lightly glowing magical energy wound along his body, binding his limbs tight. He drifted along behind the leader, Callon, like a balloon. A flash of irritation at the sight of his sword slung over the elf's shoulder drove away the last of the haze.

A mild anxiety tugged at the back of his mind, a nebulous fear he couldn't name. The longer he bobbed along behind the elves, the greater the sense of dread grew. The invisible force pressed him on all sides, urging him to turn back, insisting he really didn't want to be here. Powerful warding spells, the same ones he had felt the previous night, betrayed his location. He neared the mist-filled Sauvie Island.

Even though he knew precisely what stirred his emotions, the feelings rolled over him anyway. With each passing moment, mild repulsion became anxiety, and anxiety ratcheted up to terror. He centered himself, willed his heart to slow and his muscles to unwind.

Anxiety vanquished for the moment, he risked twisting his head to the side just a millimeter or two. Out of the corner of his eye, the river ambled along beside him. The water churned seconds before a slippery scaled tail reared up and slid back into the water. At least the spell that floated him along had spared him a dip in the river on the back of the serpent that had ferried them here.

"I still cannot see the harm in allowing us to fly to the tower. I'll be smelling that beast's foul odor for days." The warrior behind him flicked water from his sleeves, splattering Nuada with a cold shower.

"We can't afford to be discovered by the humans until we're strong enough to begin the battle." Callon's voice carried a note of condescension.

"Those fools couldn't find us if they tried."

"A few can. And there are still traitors like this one who will try to save them. Your place is not to question." Callon picked up the pace.

His captors turned away from the shoreline and marched steadily toward the mist-soaked line of trees. Nuada doubted they meant him to be conscious as he was dragged across the magical barrier that now separated this island from the rest of the world. He bit his tongue to keep from groaning with the pain. The palpable magical shove, like the hand of an invisible titan, pushed against his already sore chest. Another warding curse. The spell gripped him like quicksand and drained his strength to the brink of unconsciousness again.

His quick battle with Breas and his minions had left him weakened, lacking the strength to fully block the magic crowding him from all sides. Time for some help from Mother Earth. He focused on the ground beneath him. Tendrils of his consciousness stretched out through his fingertips, seeking the energy of the earth to draw up and buttress his own. He waited for the reassuring tingle of the world's life pulse, but nothing was there. *No. That is impossible. The earth's energy could not just be gone.*

He squeezed his eyes shut and pushed his consciousness harder and farther down. Instead of the warm, bubbling energies of the earth, he felt cold, like a dead spot festered there. He looked back up to the late day sun, just to remind himself he was still in the Green World. It hung like a pale disc behind a thick patch of clouds. He hadn't crossed into the Underworld where celestial bodies didn't create the light and the Green World's pulse didn't beat. All the same, the island was out of place, wrong.

A sensation of intense pressure throbbed inside his skull. He clamped his teeth to prevent the scream of pain. Veins popped out on his forehead with the effort. Just as the resistance became more than he could bear, he burst, sweating, beyond the barrier. His body sagged with relief against his invisible bonds.

"I wonder how far the journey will be this time," the female warrior said.

"Hopefully quite far, for that would mean the island has grown enough so the humans in the labs would have served their purpose. We could finally kill them," Callon said.

"And all our people will join us here."

"This world will soon be ours once more, but not yet. It has grown, though. From here I should be able to see the lights from the tower in the distance, and I cannot."

The conversation confirmed Nuada's worst fears. The scarred

Fae at Erimus were not a small group of Sidhe who had escaped the decaying Underworld before the last gate fell. They were recent arrivals. That meant Badb really had reopened a gateway between worlds and throngs of angry Fae were poised on the other side.

All the same, he felt a pang of sadness for the Underworld Fae. Immortals trapped in a dying land with no escape. It had to be hell without end. Enough to drive them all mad. They didn't deserve their fate, but if Badb won, did the humans deserve theirs? Either way, too many would die if the Fae and humanity clashed. He'd have to convince Niall's heir to help stop them.

Their little party traversed the island at a brisk pace. His escorts shared conversation, but Nuada no longer focused on that. Instead, he let his head loll to the side and strained to see as much as he could from the corners of his eyes without betraying his wakeful state.

Everything about this place seemed wrong. The trees were too black and too tall. On the other side of the barrier, the mist clung to the ground and visibility improved. Every step his captors took stirred up eddies that twirled and drifted, eventually winding themselves out. The mist was all too familiar. Not only did it have the satiny subtlety of Tuatha magic, it also had the grain of a specific sorcery. If Callon and his friend were right that distance in this place was no longer fixed, Badb used its power now to sculpt the fabric of reality for permanent habitation by Fae.

The discordant landscape slid by. Nuada estimated they had been walking for over two hours at a pace far faster than a human could move. Still, they hadn't encountered the other shore or much of anything but more mist, even more trees, and the occasional pixie. He'd visited this island decades before. He figured, at their current pace, the journey from one shore to the other should take an hour. Maybe less. But, like the Underworld, the island expanded and folded in on itself, like creasing an enormous sheet of paper to fit inside an envelope. From the outside, the island's footprint would appear much as it always did, but past the barrier, it was becoming literally its own expanding world. It was the only explanation for this place, and it was very bad news for humanity.

Not even Morfesa, the greatest sorcerer of the Tuatha, could manage this level of magic alone, especially not now. Fury set Nuada's mind on fire when the last piece of the puzzle fell into place. Badb hadn't accomplished this alone. This was why his beloved was dead. Badb hadn't murdered her sisters in revenge for their abandonment or because the prophecy she spoke so long ago had driven her insane. No. It was far worse than that. She had slaughtered her own family for power. The power to make this place.

He let his head droop farther toward his chest to hide the hot tears leaking from his eyes. To steal her power, Macha's death would not have been quick. She would have died in agony, feeling her immortal life and magic being torn from her. The Tuatha valued the more refined feelings—love, honor, duty. They spent eons cultivating these and rooting out the baser emotions from their souls. The basest of all feelings sprang to life within him now. He hated Badb Catha. He would make her pay for the pain she brought to his wife. What Macha had endured would seem utterly relaxing compared to what he would make Badb experience.

He risked a glance up to assess the ease of access to his sword. The elves hadn't bothered to focus much attention on him, overconfident in their magical skill. His weapon bobbed side to side at his enemy's hip like a metronome keeping time with each step. He could break free, slaughter these elves, find Badb, and slay her with it. It was the nature of the Claimh Solais that, once drawn, it prevailed against its enemy. Never in his immortal life had he even entertained drawing the holy weapon for vengeance, let alone personal vengeance, but the betrayer deserved worse.

That thought drained the fury from his heart. He flexed his

silver hand and stifled a laugh. Perhaps the Dagdha's cauldron was the wisest one of all, the silver hand a reminder how far he'd fallen from the perfection of a High King. He felt his blemish ran deeper than the cosmetics of his wondrous mechanical arm.

"I'll never get used to seeing those disgusting things." Callon's words pulled Nuada from his rumination.

"The trolls?"

"No. Those."

Nuada couldn't see what the elf was referring to without lifting his head.

"I suppose they are another necessary evil. Trust Badb's plan."

Nuada let his head roll to his other shoulder and caught sight of their destination. A pale gray citadel rose over the trees. Next to it, an ostentatious sign read 'Erimus Pharmaceutical.' Nuada rolled his eyes. Arrogant little bastard. Who would see that monument to his massive ego out here?

The building must have had about thirty floors. It was all smooth stone edges with a massive arched top. The only visible windows ran like a strip up through the very center of the inverted U that formed the central spire, flanked by two broader flat sides that gave way to a massive plaza. A small set of stairs descended toward what was either a large pond or a small lake.

Countless species of Fae milled about the plaza. Many of the Folk bore the marred flesh of their time in the Underworld. One of the lumbering trolls had a face almost covered in scars and a missing eye, and the beautiful pale sylphs bore a webwork of thin blemishes. High in the trees dangled dozens of white ovals. Each was nearly six feet long and composed of dense mist. They swirled and plumes erupted and fell all along the surface. A few bubbled as though they boiled.

Streams of Fae of multiple species herded human prisoners in and out of the swinging glass doors. The captors poked, prodded, and shoved along their charges. The humans' blank eyes registered none of the abuse.

Questions rose again. Why did Badb need all these people? She must have collected a couple hundred by now. Had so many Fae come through the thin spot in the Veil she'd created that they needed a sizable service population? If that were the case, it was possible the drug could be a way to quickly gather human servants to the island. Depending on how wide the gateway was, they might need a lot of servants, midwives, and handmaids quickly and all at once. He supposed stealing away those that no one would miss was the most expedient way to accomplish the goal. A poor way, but less risky than the alternative.

All the same, something about that theory didn't set right. The missing pieces were locked away inside that tower, but Nuada had all the answers this unpleasant side trip was likely to provide. There would be no way he could fight his way back out of that building with a battalion of Fae now living on this island, and Badb herself to contend with. He needed to escape now, while the trio of elves were still far enough from reinforcements no one would hear a scuffle. Besides, he had a party to attend. The Mystic Island festival promised more information.

A great clanging and grinding noise startled Nuada. He strained his eyes as far to the side as he could to witness two massive central doors several floors up drag open.

The baying of hunting hounds and the clarion call of a horn pierced the air. The Wild Hunt and its leader, Gwyn ap Nudd, streamed out and swept toward the ground. Clouds of crows and Fae rose from all sides to join the Hunt, dragging clouds of mist behind them.

Nuada pulled on the last shreds of energy he'd saved from his botched escape from Breas, hoping it would be enough. With a yell, he blasted through his bonds. Callon had no time to react before Nuada tore his sword from the elf's shoulder.

The other elf and his female friend stood wide-eyed with shock. "Jian. Keep him occupied, we'll get reinforcements."

Callon and the woman sped toward the tower. Jian's sword flew from its scabbard. The elf's rapid breathing betrayed his fear. Nuada placed a hand on his own sword and the elf's lips formed a thin line. Nuada had no intention of drawing the blade on a single Sidhe warrior, but the distraction was just enough to give him an opening.

Nuada rushed at the man while throwing his arm across his chest. When he had enough momentum, he lashed his arm out, slamming the scabbard into Jian's neck. He yelped and fell to the ground. Nuada was on him in an instant, landing a blow with his fist to the elf's face.

Jian slumped, out cold. Nuada grabbed the warrior's sword and spent a few valuable seconds relieving him of another short sword and two knives.

The baying of Gwyn's hounds sounded too close. Off to his right, the Columbia River roared, he guessed a couple minutes' away. He'd have more than the Wild Hunt to worry about in moments. The faster he got to the water, the greater chance he had to pull off his escape. The Hunt had banked and headed due south, and he saw no sign of his other pursuers. First lucky break all evening. Now to catch a ride.

Within minutes, Nuada stood on the banks of the river. The wind played with his hair under a sliver of sun that dipped beneath the horizon. He drew out a small blade, wrapped his hand around the sharp edges, and squeezed. Crimson drops fell into the water from his outstretched hand. Immediately, the water roiled and a large reptilian head broke the surface. The scaled creature skewered him with round green eyes. When Nuada motioned it to his side, the serpent bellowed and thrashed its finned tail.

"Don't resist. I will release you from service quickly."

Beneath the lapping waves of the Columbia River, long coils

lashed. It tried to pull its horned head away, but an instant debt to Nuada snared the creature. The blood of a Tuatha was a handsome gift, and the serpent had gulped it down. In the end, the creature acquiesced and Nuada climbed on its wet, green-brown back. Overhead, the Wild Hunt undulated through low hanging clouds, on a trajectory for the Mystic Island Festival.

"Southwest, follow the Wild Hunt," he commanded. The monster lurched to life beneath him. Its massive length propelled by a powerful winding action, the pair flew along the river. Government Island came into view in a few minutes.

Nuada leapt from its slippery back onto the shoreline. "Your service to me has ended."

The monster's reply was a long low rumble deep in its throat, no doubt serpent tongue for 'piss off.' It dipped beneath the surface of the water and hovered there. Great scaled coils wound and unwound while the pale green eyes hovered just above the surface, glittering with malice.

The thump-thump of awful music in the distance assaulted Nuada's ears. He hoped the Phooka still kept the young heir safe; he had no idea how long it would take to uncover the answers he needed to get at this infernal gathering. With a long sigh, he started trudging up the beach.

Stepping off the boat into the festival truly felt like leaving the mundane world behind and entering a land of myth and magic. The ethereal decorations fully transformed Government Island into Mystic Island. Paths studded with hundreds of tiny globe lights, colorful giant mushroom sculptures, and gossamer banners mingled with the natural beauty of the island, the perfect backdrop to the throngs of costumed people milling about.

Costumes ranged from the cheap nylon Tinkerbell outfits offered by the Halloween store to movie-quality latex-and-foam cosplay creations that looked all too real. Any other time Harper would have delighted in the lights and smiled at the stunning costumes, but she scanned the crowd for anyone with wet black hair and tracked the movements of the more realistic costumed revelers.

The Portland weather smiled on the venue, rain expected to creep in well after the close of ceremonies. Regardless of the lack of moisture, the bite of the chill raised goosebumps on Harper's skin. The rapidly dropping sun promised to send temperatures even lower. She shivered and pulled the faux fur–lined coat tighter.

"Let's get some food before the lines are ree-diculous," Emilio said.

Harper startled, but she didn't think Emilio noticed. A deep breath banished her jitters, at least for now.

"I've heard goblins make the best tacos," she said, pointing to the 'Goblin Market' sign towering over clusters of lighted toadstools studding the food and vendor clearing.

"I think I'm going to try the fish and chips. Or is it mermaid and chips?"

"Would that be cannibalism? I can't quite tell." She forced a smile.

While Emilio lined up across the clearing for his fish and chips, Harper collected her tacos and crossed the Goblin Market just as a group of performers—nine-foot trolls—strolled through the venue delighting a cluster of young women with iridescent wings and long flowing gowns. One troll juggled a trio of yellow glowing balls and the other two belched fire over the heads of the admiring crowd. The absence of any obvious stilts sent a shudder up her spine. *What if they're real like the Dark Boys turned out to be real?*

"Ooh churros!" Emilio smiled as he plopped an enormous basket of fish and chips down next to Harper. A smile stretched from ear to ear. He was clearly loving everything about this. "Did you see the trolls?"

Harper nodded in acknowledgment, her mouth too full of taco to reply. "Mmmmmhh."

"Selfie time." Emilio slid over to Harper's side of the table. She swallowed her bite of taco while he arranged their feast artfully before them. She smiled. His enthusiasm left no room for misery.

Emilio leaned in next to Harper with his phone held high at arm's length. He turned the device so Harper could see the picture. The face staring back at her was missing any sign of the strain of the past couple of days. She looked happy for the first time in months.

"Send me that," Harper said, sipping her soda.

"You glad you came?"

"Yeah. The theme is a touch ironic, though." She flicked her gaze around the venue, noting the location of the troll costumes.

"True. I doubt the real kind would want to be around this many people." Emilio smiled. "What do you want to do next?"

"Well, we've got an hour before Aural Nocturna's first set. We could check out the vendors then get a good spot by the stage."

"Want to get some official swag?"

"No. I'm going to grab a drink and check out the artsy stuff."

"You? A drink?" Emilio's hand flew to his heart in mock surprise.

"Didn't you tell me I needed to unwind?"

"Cut loose, I'll be the designated driver."

Harper didn't miss the look of concern on his backward glance when he slipped over to the souvenir booth.

The unexpectedly potent fruity rum slush burned the back of her throat. Festivals like these usually watered the drinks down. She sipped through the bright red straw while scanning the row of vendors selling creative clothing, mystic jewelry, and other usual event wares. The first one hosted a plump woman in a Romani costume offering an array of herbs, stones, and jewelry fanned out on tables and hanging from the canopy frame. Harper inhaled the rich scents of jasmine and vanilla candles and found running her hands through the bins of smooth tumbled stones oddly pleasant.

"You have the look of one haunted by Fae," the woman said. Harper couldn't quite place her thick Eastern European accent, but it made her sound exotic and look the part.

"We're surrounded." Harper cast a hand around the festival and smiled at the woman.

"Not people in costumes, my sweet. The authentic kind leaves a mark." She flipped a ring-crusted hand across her face. "It's in the eyes."

Harper's eyebrows pinched together. She turned and stepped away from the tent. This was probably part of her schtick; no way the woman knew. All the same, she didn't want any reminders of her previous encounters. A hand strayed to her bag, unconsciously seeking the comfort of a weapon as she turned to leave.

"Once they are interested in you, there will be no place you can hide," the woman called to Harper's back. "You need protection."

"Look, lady, I'm not—"

"You fell under their spell, didn't you?"

The string of bells the woman wore around her waist jingled as she got up and reached over her head where long necklaces dangled. Harper returned to the edge of the table, convinced she'd later regret it, yet captivated all the same. The Romani woman drew down a very primitive-looking necklace. A nondescript twig on a black silk cord. A closer look revealed a collar of iron wire wound in the center several times and ending in a spiral. The tiny amber bead at the center was tied on with a bit of red fringe.

"That's very, um, rustic." Harper turned the pendant over in her hands. "A stick will save me from the monsters?"

The woman barked out a belly laugh, black curls bouncing around under a red headscarf. She gestured to much fancier pieces in cast silver and gemstones nestled in glass cases. "These are what the dilettantes take for a magical item. But that bit of rowan wood and iron is the real deal. It's not showy, but people who'd buy showy are seldom of interest to the Fae."

Harper scanned the sixty- and seventy-dollar price tags of the jewelry in the case, comparing it to the twenty-dollar piece she held in her hand. If the woman was trying to bamboozle her, she'd certainly attempt to unload a more expensive item.

"What's this thing supposed to do?" Harper asked. Considering the past day's strange events, she'd take any comfort she could find. Even if it was probably hippy-dippy bunk.

"I made that myself. Every element is a protection against the glamour of the Fae."

"So it protects me from fairy spells?"

"Shh!" The woman ducked her head low, eyes darting side to side while she flapped her hand. "Don't call them *fairies*. They take offense! They are Fae, Good Neighbors, Fair Folk, but never by that word, unless you want more trouble than you can handle," she whispered.

"What's glamour? Other than that." Harper flicked her head to the side indicating Emilio who was still adding festival souvenirs to his collection.

"The Fae glamour is a spell they cast, often only by their presence, to bewitch and make you see what they want you to see. A splendid feast materializes from nowhere when only rotten fruit and empty plates fill the table. Under their spell, you love them, want only to meet their every whim. The Fae can't hurt a human directly, but through a glamour they can make you do or believe almost anything. And that makes them dangerous."

Harper knew that sensation, and now she had a name for it. Glamoured. The Dark Boys had glamoured her last night before the strange dog shattered their spell. None of the details would surface, only the feelings echoed. She would have crawled in the mud, debased herself in any way if it would have made the black-haired boy with the pointy teeth happy. She loathed them for it, and loathed herself a little too, for being so weak.

The possibility that this woman was more than a mere performer seemed real, and she may be able to help Harper make sense of what happened in the alley. Protect herself from them so she never again fell under their spell and get the hell off this island before the real Fae discovered her. She wiped her suddenly sweaty palm on her coat.

"How did you know I'd been touched by the Fae?"

"Like I told you. It's a look about the eyes, hard to explain, but if you've been where I've traveled, you know it when you see it. Judging by the look of you, they've been in your life for many years."

Harper jerked straight and almost dropped the pendant. Her pulse quickened. The old and new memories she had banished to the depths blew off the lid and muscled their way forward.

The woman reached out a reassuring hand, a sympathetic smile spread across her face. But when her fingers rested on Harper's upper arm, her expression shifted. The smile melted from her round face, the corners of her mouth sagged, and her forehead creased. Her dark, almost black eyes met Harper's. "I fear your destiny is bound to the realms of Fae. Oh, sweet, this is going to be a painful road, but there is hope. You are stronger than you know, Harper O'Neill."

Harper whipped her hand back, breath coming in pants. "How? How do you know my name?"

"Don't be afraid, sweet." She tapped a finger to her head. "I've been touched by the Good Neighbors myself. Most of my divination is the usual telling people what they want to hear over a spread of tarot cards. But sometimes, with certain people, I just know things. Past, present, even some future events. Sometimes I see flashes of images, but more often, I simply know what I didn't before."

"What did you see? Are the Fae going to kill me? My mom? Emilio?"

"I didn't see anything about anyone's death, but the Fae had a hand in a great loss you suffered. I think you know that. As for the future, less clear. It's certain you are central to what's coming. The third of the Great Wars is upon us and you are the fulcrum on which all will turn."

"The fulcrum?" Harper's rational mind was screaming this was all hocus pocus nonsense, but in her bones she knew the truth. The shopkeep was psychic.

The woman's hand lifted and touched Harper's chest just above her racing heart. "There is great power here. Whether that power is used for good or for ill will be determined by whether or not you can keep it soft. Take the talisman. You will soon need all the protection you can muster, and the magic is stronger if it is a gift."

Harper closed her fingers over the necklace in her palm. If her new friend didn't emanate peace and comfort, she'd be freaking out. *It can't be true. I'm nobody. Not a magician. Psychic. Warrior. And I'm most definitely not some 'chosen one.'* She may be a nobody, but the Fae had ruined her life anyway. It wasn't fair.

Her lip trembled and she pulled hazel eyes up into the warmth of the woman's gaze. "But I don't want to be involved in any of this. I just want my life the way it was," she whispered.

"Ah, sweet, so do all those whom the Fates have chosen, but you can no more choose to ignore this path than you could choose whether you were born. From what I can see, the Fates have chosen well." She motioned for the necklace. Harper passed it back to her, and the large woman looped it around her neck.

Harper's eyes misted over and threatened to rain down her cheeks and streak her makeup. She swallowed the lump in her throat.

"I don't even know your name," Harper said.

"Selina, my sweet. Selina Leanabel. My heart tells me we will meet again, but for now, wear that talisman. There are more than just costume Fae on this island tonight. Trust the silver-haired man. He can protect you."

Harper used her sleeve to dab the tears from the corners of her eyes. "Silver-haired man?" Across the semicircle of vendors, Emilio still shopped.

"You'll know him when you see him, Harper."

"Thank you, Selina."

Harper turned to intercept Emilio. Her head flicked from side to side, scanning the crowd for Dark Boys, costumes that looked too good, anything that would betray one of the Fae. Escape routes were all around her, leading into the forest or to the water. If she had to, the trees offered cover, but she'd need somehow to get them to the dock and then hope for a boat. The island suddenly felt very small.

She paused long enough to chug the rest of her drink while her other hand gripped the little protective talisman. Protection or not, she needed to get Emilio and leave this island.

That was when she saw the black dog trot across the ring of canopies into the trees and her blood ran cold.

Nuada flicked the last of the water from his sleeve just as the Phooka bounded toward him through a semicircle of merchants hocking their wares. The dog-shaped Fae's ears pressed flat against his head and his golden eyes were wide. The shapeshifter cantered to Nuada's feet.

Nuada's eyebrows shot up. "I told you to watch the young woman. Why are you here?"

"The girl's here. Underworld Fae here." The Phooka choked out the words between pants. "Badb here. Everyone here. That's bad."

The Phooka didn't know the half of it. Outnumbered and far behind the learning curve, Niall's heir popping up in the same place as Badb threatened unmitigated disaster.

"We have to collect the girl and get off this island." Nuada felt a pang of guilt. Over two thousand years ago, he would have charged in to save the unwitting guests of the event, odds be damned. But the Green World had changed them all. Macha labeled it pragmatic. To Nuada, it seemed akin to surrender. He raised the silver hand to his eyes and flexed his fingers.

"There's a surprise you need to see first." The Phooka had regained his breath and was more capable of complete sentences. "The girl is safe at the moment. Besides, she's not going anywhere for a while."

"What is it, Phooka?"

"Oh no. A phooka never ruins a surprise. They'd revoke my trickster license. Follow me." Bushy tail high, the Phooka trotted through a copse of trees toward the side of the stage, where a horrible thumping blanketed the island with the sounds of monotony.

Nuada brought the Phooka up to speed about his trip to Sauvie Island while they wove their way through the woods. Once he got to the part about his leap from the Erimus building, the Phooka fell to the ground, clutching his sides and rolling. Great donkey brays of laughter competed with the droning music from the stage.

"The great king of the Tuatha de Danann captured by a baby dragon. A *baby* dragon. Oh, to have the video for my TikTok!" Tears streamed from the dog's eyes while he whooped until the only sound he could make was a dry wheeze.

"You done?"

"Yes. Yes." The Phooka, still flat on his back, pressed his lips in a tight line, but a peal of laughter forced its way out, like the sour note of a trumpet. "Ok, no," he confessed. Black feet jiggled in time with each giggle.

"You laugh at my—"

"A baby dragon!" The Phooka cracked up again. His shape shimmered and coalesced into a dragon with a pacifier. He lunged at Nuada. "Boo." The Phooka erupted into more laughter.

"As usual, your self-indulgent focus on your own amusement has caused you to miss the point."

The Phooka returned to his dog shape. "You are simply the worst. Sidekick. Ever. I thought a straight man might be good for my act. Give me someone to set up all my best sarcastic remarks. Really make this epic quest sizzle with witty banter. But you, sir, are a straight up buzzkill."

"Badb opened a gateway between the worlds on that island. I think she is—"

"A weapons-grade party-pooper."

Nuada grabbed the Phooka by the scruff and pressed his face close to the shapeshifter. "I think Badb is luring humans to the island with the drug, to use them as servants or some darker purpose. And they're planning something bigger here tonight."

"Duh. I already figured that bit out. Always ten steps behind. That's why you're the sidekick." The Phooka jerked free and trotted back toward the stage.

Nuada shook his head and followed. When they arrived at the tree line, they peered toward the back of the stage. A group of small goblins lugged a glass canister bigger than the Phooka himself. Several more pushed and pulled similar containers into place while an elven warrior screwed long tubes into their lids.

Even thirty feet away, hidden in the underbrush, the purple tint of the jug's contents swirled inside. Dust. Heaps of it.

"What are they hooking those tubes up to?" Nuada whispered.

The Phooka pointed to a contraption containing the Dust and powder in every color. "Those dispersal tanks look like they could blast that junk half a mile. This crowd will be technicolor and tripping balls. Awesome!" The Phooka rubbed paws together and smiled.

Nuada ignored his friend's enthusiasm. He had no grasp of why anyone would find a rainbow coating appealing; it was the Dust that concerned him. All of this fit with the overheard conversation from Erimus's downtown headquarters. "The same thing we witnessed last night is about to happen right here."

"Crazy talk. If they nick a crowd this big, too many loved ones will search for their missing family. Too risky. Even for Badb. Not to mention the gargantuan magical power needed to keep this many people glamoured when all crammed together on a teeny island. I know a good shrink, Silver Hand. She really helped—"

"I think that entire building on Sauvie Island is devoted to solving all those problems. And the island isn't so tiny anymore. I heard them talking about a new experiment, maybe that's what they plan to do with this batch."

The Phooka's ears drooped. "We just ran out of time."

"It's worse than that. The Wild Hunt is on the way, probably waiting for nightfall to attack."

"The Hunt?" The Phooka's amber eyes were circles. Chewing a paw like he was chomping corn on the cob, he pointed the other at the sun sinking below the western horizon.

Once the sun was down, the Wild Hunt would be at their full power, and no human on this island could escape them. Nuada's mind raced. He and the Phooka alone could not stand against the Wild Hunt and also prevent the Dust from afflicting the crowd. They had to find the girl, escape, then raise an army and develop a proper plan. The Tuatha were unused to thinking in terms of collateral damage, but being late to the game, outclassed, and outmaneuvered forced the adoption of the long game. He peered around the edge of the stage at clusters of people. They laughed. They danced. They drank. None of them were aware that Nuada was leaving them to a grim fate, but alternate options failed to present themselves.

Nuada sighed and dragged his flesh hand down his face. "Where did you leave the young woman? We need to escape. Now."

"Back near the food tent double-fisting Southern Comfort slushies." The Phooka was already racing toward the crowd.

Nuada caught up to him, pacing around the little circle of people selling food and trinkets with his nose to the ground.

"Nuada Silver Hand, as I live and breathe. Things must have

gone to shit to pull you back to this world." A resonant woman's voice spun Nuada around.

"Selina Leanabel. I would say this is the last place I would expect to find you, but this is just the sort of soiree you would be drawn to."

"Smack dab in the middle of Fae trouble, right where I belong." Selina was already around her table and clasping Nuada in a crushing embrace.

The Phooka sidled up to them.

"Did you find her, Phooka?" Nuada asked.

Before the Phooka could respond, Selina traced a hex with her hands. "You with that?" She snorted and shook her head. "Better watch your back."

"Selina." The Phooka's voice was flat. He looked away from the Romani woman. "You're not still sore about our tiny incident, are you?"

"Betrayal has a way of sticking with you." Selina tore her eyes from the Phooka, who studiously avoided her gaze. "You looking for a young woman. About my height. Nut-brown hair. Noble blood?"

Nuada nodded. "How did y—"

"Her name's Harper O'Neill." Selina tapped her head. "I really thought she'd killed them all. The young woman and her friend went to the stage to hear the music. I told her to trust you, for what it's worth. Just you." Her nose wrinkled when she looked at the Phooka.

"Gypsy."

"Fairy." Selina spat the word like a curse.

The Phooka's hackles raised. Nuada laid his hand on the shapeshifter's head.

"Selina, I do not have to tell you things are about to get dicey here, and my forces number exactly two. The Phooka and I will barely be able to rescue this Harper O'Neill, so saving all these people will have to wait. You should leave now. We may need you for what is coming. Find a place to weather the storm. I am sure Heironymous—"

"Doesn't want to see his ex-wife." Selina laughed. "Sometimes, Silver Hand, you find yourself exactly where the Great Song wants you to be."

Nuada rested a hand on his friend's shoulder. The Romani woman laid her tanned hand over his and nodded. "May we meet again," Nuada said.

She looked wistful and dropped her eyes to her feet. "May it be."

Selina was more than capable of taking care of herself; the young woman was not. Time grew short. Nuada nodded farewell to his old friend and followed the Phooka toward the music.

They made slow progress dodging wire-framed plastic wings and plastic bits of fantasy clothing on their way to the stage. The black dog padded silently in front of him, weaving in and out of a sea of legs. They had an easier time avoiding most of the revelers by sidling along the edge of the stage.

As the pair pushed past the first stack of speakers, Nuada caught sight of flaming red hair cascading from beneath a black horned headdress. She hovered in the opposite backstage area and ushered a group of Sidhe musicians into the wings. Nuada grabbed the Phooka by the scruff and hauled him back.

The dog's mouth was open, ready to protest. Nuada held a finger to his lips and inclined his head toward a slight gap in the curtains at the side of the stage. Badb Catha loomed, and at her side stood Breas draped in his fine grey suit, absently picking at his fingernails. Here to see their own handiwork. They both took a colossal risk leaving the cover of the island. Then again, Badb never could stand to be very far from battle, and Breas was too arrogant to think he'd ever get caught.

Every muscle in Nuada's body leapt to attention, tuned and

ready to cut her down where she stood. The silver hand slid to the scabbard at his hip. Tiny gears whirred and metal joints slid across one another. In a heartbeat he was ready to draw the Sword of Light and drive it through her black heart. The image brought a wintry smile to his lips. The sword edged a couple inches from the scabbard and he dropped into a crouch.

The Phooka must have guessed his intent, because he had already adopted another shape. A deep-brown hand gripped his shoulder and spun him around. Before him stood a tall black man with waist-long dreads. The only sign the man was, in fact, the Phooka were his amber eyes."Of all people, I know what it is to crave vengeance. Desire it so deep you'd sacrifice your very life to get it, but now is not the time. Revenge can come later. We have to save Harper now." His voice was deep and had a hint of an island accent.

The suddenly level-headed Phooka behaving with uncharacteristic empathy. And he was right. Nuada pushed the blade back down and pinched the bridge of his nose. Finding Harper took priority. Vengeance had to wait. Both Badb and Breas would immediately sense his presence if he used magic. They'd have to find Harper the hard way. The lip of the stage offered both the fastest passage and the best vantage point, but they might as well put a spotlight on themselves. With the sun setting, it was still their best option.

Nuada pointed to Badb and then to the stage. The Phooka nodded. They didn't have long to wait before she turned her attention to the sumptuous fiddle music flowing from the stage. The group of Sidhe musicians had replaced the last act. They were hooking up their instruments to the sound rig and playing a few test notes. It surprised Nuada he hadn't noticed the end of the hideous noise from the last act. He motioned the Phooka forward. The two men hunched as low as they could and ran for the front edge of the stage.

The clearing teemed with dancers grooving to the beat of the music playing between acts. They twisted and jumped, sometimes in place. This would be like finding a needle in a haystack. Nuada leaned over to the Phooka and had to yell into his ear to be heard.

"What costume is Harper wearing?"

The Phooka pressed his lips to Nuada's ear and bellowed back. "Long red coat, red shoes, red hair weave, and a light-up unicorn horn."

A lot of revelers wore light-up items, but looking for them narrowed the search. It wasn't the costume that picked Harper out of the crowd. It was the fact that she was the only one in the throng not dancing. She and her friend approached the stage from near the center. The black-haired boyish man with her bobbed along and bopped to the music as he bounced toward the edge of the stage. Harper's eyes darted in every direction as she walked, heading for the front row.

Nuada tugged at the Phooka's black sleeve and pointed.

The Phooka's golden eyes met his, and he nodded vigorously.

Badb Catha and a handful of Sidhe waited in the wings of the stage. The very monster who was hunting Harper was about to walk out on that stage and stand but a few feet away from her. all while her behavior and the magical blood she carried were about to light her up like a bonfire at midnight.

The Phooka was already muscling his way through the crowd.

CHAPTER 20

The sun had slipped below the horizon. The darkening twilight made the light-up pieces of the costumes look like winking stars. A light breeze blew the red hair extensions across Harper's face. She swept them out of the way, grabbed Emilio's elbow, and pulled their backs to the milling crowd whose movement ushered them closer and closer toward center stage where Aural Nocturna performed their sound check.

"We need to get out of here now." Harper's eyes were wide, her voice raised to be heard above the buzz of the crowd.

Emilio lifted her hand off his elbow and held it in his own for a moment, his eyes soft with kindness. "We just got here. I promise it'll be OK."

Her words fell over each other. She knew she sounded just like her mom when she was in a manic phase, but she needed to convince him to leave, for both their sakes. She described her encounter with the woman who seemed to know her name and that there were real Fae there. Emilio's face scrunched with concern, but he was adamant about staying.

"Harper, you're keyed up from your mom and the alleyway.

The woman's a fraud. You know how those fortune-teller types work. They make some vague ominous prediction and then gauge your reaction. She's not magic. Just a talented reader of people."

"But how did she know my name? Emilio, she *knew my name.*" *And that Fae had murdered my father.* There was no way she could have guessed that.

"I bet she has a confederate. Did you pay for your tacos with your bank card?"

Harper nodded.

"There you have it. That's how she got your name. Someone saw it over your shoulder and told her when they saw you walking toward her booth. Harper, relax. All I see here are people in costumes. No Dark Boys. No harp-playing monsters. It's just a party. The boats don't start back for a couple hours, so it looks like you'll have to stick around and protect me from the likes of those." Emilio smiled and pointed at a group of vampire costumes. "You're safe. I promise."

His words did nothing to quiet the maelstrom of worry swirling in her skull. Nor did they slow her racing heart or stop the acid burn in her stomach. Selina's sight was not an act. She'd asked for nothing. Instinct told her something bad was here, to flee and not look back. All the same, without a boat, she was stranded. Her hand rooted around in her bag for her baton or a small knife. Then she remembered they were all in the car, left behind so they could pass the security checkpoint. She felt exposed. Like a rabbit in a snare.

"Look what I got." Emilio held up a brightly colored Mystic Island tank top, effectively changing the subject. "Did you get anything?"

"This." Harper showed him the talisman while her eyes roved over the crowd. Costumes formed a wall of polyester and tulle, and none looked as real as the fire-breathing trolls had.

Emilio wrinkled his nose. "That's actually a stick. She sure saw you coming."

"It's protection against the Fae. Iron, rowan, and some other stuff. She gave this to me. She wasn't a crank fortune-teller, Emilio." She shifted from foot to foot, hands toying with the strap of her bag. She needed another drink. Now.

"Well, at least tuck it into your shirt. It ruins the ensemble." He laughed and winked at her.

"I'm going to get another rum slush." Harper almost jogged to the alcohol booth at the edge of the performance area before Emilio could protest. She hoped he was right, that she was overreacting. She rejoined him in moments as the next band finished tuning their instruments and retreated into the wings.

Selina's words echoed in her mind. She scanned the crowd and tree line again, rehearsing their escape paths if things went sideways. The dancers moved around so fast she couldn't see well enough to guess whether any of them were more than met the eye.

"Might as well dance our way closer to the stage." Emilio grasped Harper's hand in his and pulled her into the pulsing crowd.

Emilio was an excellent dancer. His lighted horn flashed in time to the intricate patterns his feet wove. He posed and spun and slipped around the other dancers until they were two rows back from the stage. It was impossible to carry on a conversation over the driving beat and the whining of electronic melody, so the pair danced in place. Try as she might, Harper couldn't will her leaden feet to dance. She bobbed in place half-heartedly, finished her drink, and made sure she knew the fastest way to the exit.

The recorded music faded and the crowd fell silent. Aural Nocturna strode out onto the stage and took their places. Red velvet and white lace poured out under metallic black corsets, and knee-length jackets clung to their lithe frames. Every one of them was perfect. Jet-black hair framed pale faces that would make supermodels appear plain. The pointed ears of their costumes accentuated sculpted features and full lips. Harper had difficulty tearing her eyes off them, but fear kept her continuously checking the crowd for signs of the Dark Boys. Behind her, rows of slack-jawed, starry-eyed faces tilted up, mesmerized by the perfection before them.

The band started a soaring, airy tune that was mostly fiddle. Harper had never heard anyone coax such glorious sounds out of a fiddle. Beside her, Emilio stared, open mouthed and transfixed by the gorgeous musician.

"Your new crush!" Harper said. He only tilted his head toward her and smiled a little, never taking his gaze off the compelling fiddle player. "Sheesh, you got it bad." She elbowed him gently. Emilio payed her no heed and started swaying gently in place to the slow, lilting strains of the fiddle solo.

Something about his empty look set her on edge even more than she already was. *He's acting just like the homeless last night. I have to get us out of here.*

Harper turned toward her planned exit point and froze. Every single soul in the crowd swayed just as Emilio did. A sea of bodies moved in perfect timing, like wheat stalks caressed by a gentle breeze. She was the solitary point of stillness. The black eyes of the fiddle player met hers and narrowed. He rested a knee-high black boot on his monitor, bending forward toward her. The fiddle deepened to a series of mournful low tones.

The black glittering eyes of a beautiful predator bored into her, and she felt as small and terrified as a mouse. The rough point of the rowan amulet jabbed into her clenched hand.

There are more than costume Fae on this island tonight.

Under the burning attention of the musician, she swayed with the others, adopting the unfocused eyes and loose jaw Emilio wore. A reptilian smile played across the musician's face, then he retreated from his monitor to join the guitar player with the hourglass figure. She softly strummed an intertwining melody.

A sharp breath rushed from Harper's mouth. "Emilio, snap out of it." The firm stamp of her foot on his failed to rouse him from the stuporous effects of the music. She grasped his shoulder and gently shook, but he remained focused on the musicians. Swaying and swaying.

Then things went sideways, just as she feared. The band launched into a song with a driving beat so forceful the bass line rumbled through her chest. Haunting notes of the fiddle chased the wail of the electric guitar. The dancers roared to life in a hurricane of limbs.

Harper seized Emilio's arm to keep him from being swept away. He pulled against her.

"Harper. You need to dance with me." His voice was hollow and flat, eyes unfocused.

"Let's take a break and get a drink. I'll buy. Please. Let's just get a drink," she shouted over the music.

"Later. You go. I'm dancing." His feet pedaled in place as she held him. He didn't even look at her. A man in a goblin costume slammed into Harper, took no notice, and charged past. The impact tore Emilio from her grip. He careened off with his feet flying, following the arc of the orbiting crowd. Harper flung her hand out in vain and screamed. Wham! Another frenzied body crashed into her back, knocking her staggering forward.

"Emilio!" she shouted. The impact of another dancer against her back threw her into the lip of the stage.

A river of stamping feet and flailing limbs threatened to pummel her senseless. With a cry, she clawed her way along the edge of the crowd, using the edge of the stage to drag herself along, and slipped into the tree line. The drink she had mentioned to Emilio seemed like a brilliant idea. Her nerves were shot, and she needed to calm down to figure out how to pull him out of the revels.

With everyone entranced by the Fae music, not a single guest stood between her and the rum slushy booth. When she arrived, it was empty. Its owners were probably in the crowd. She plopped a few bucks into the tip cup and grabbed one of the fresh drinks abandoned next to the cash register.

Drink in hand, she crept back to the tree line, still out of sight of the band members. Her hand strayed back to the amulet. It must work; the music wasn't affecting her. Her fingers tangled and rolled the stick while in front of her dervishes whirled, feet stamped, arms flailed, and heads lashed from side to side.

She sank down to a cold, uncomfortable seat on a rock, trying to relieve the feeling of a vice clamped around her chest. Stories her gran had told her as a child bubbled up from the past. *Never step into a ring of mushrooms. For once you're in the center of the fairy ring, you'll dance until your shoes wear through and you die of exhaustion.* In Gran's stories, only the lucky ever escaped by being pulled out by another or by turning their coat inside out. So furious now was the spiraling dance, Harper had lost sight of Emilio. Even if she were to glimpse him, breaking through the throng and getting him back out again was impossible.

The flutter of wings ratcheted her eyes to the sky. Clouds of black birds soared overhead and perched in the treetops, their squawks muffled by the music. Harper swallowed a lump in her throat and chased it down with a long swig of her drink. The same thing had happened in the tent city. First the birds, then the Dark Boys. Would the hulking shape of the harpist step out onto the stage next?

Her head swam, and she felt like she'd fall off her rock. Head down between her knees, she waited for the dizzy feeling to pass, then she did the only thing she could think of. She finished her drink.

The last of the sugary brew slid down her throat and an idea hit her like a flash of lightning. If the music stopped, the dancing might stop too. Then she could find Emilio, maybe make him turn his coat inside out, and they could somehow get back to the car. If she could creep backstage and find the electric drop, she could stop the musical enchantment.

It was now or never. She pulled herself to her feet and nearly toppled to the ground when her head swam. That last drink had probably been an awful idea, but without it, she'd be a gibbering moron right now.

Step by step she slipped, listing a bit, through the trees toward the backstage area. Her head swiveled toward the stage when the last airy quaver of the fiddle died away. An eerie silence followed. No applause, no whoops. Just an abrupt halt to all movement and unfocused eyes turned toward the musicians.

Harper stood on her tiptoes, using the shadow of the stage for cover, scanning the audience for Emilio. A small sound escaped her throat when she couldn't find him. High above the thunder of beating wings and a motley chorus of cries and squawks heralded the arrival of a black-clad woman with hair the color of flame. An elaborate headdress tapered into branching horns, like a stag's but black. The members of Aural Nocturna bowed their heads and took several steps backward to allow the woman to claim the stage. Harper felt waves of power emanating from her, and she seemed familiar, but viewed in profile, Harper couldn't place her.

She was escorted by a tall blond man in a grey suit. He had full sensuous lips drawn in a moody pout. His blue, deep-set eyes reminded Harper of Steve Buscemi if he were young and attractive. The man stepped up to the microphone at center stage.

"Welcome to Mystic Island, my esteemed guests. Are you having the time of your lives?" Crowd and crows alike erupted into a din of caws and whoops, the first signs of life the guests had shown since the music stopped.

The woman leaned close to the microphone. "Can I get some applause for Aural Nocturna?" The crowd went wild, and the band nodded elegantly.

That voice. That smooth, haughty voice echoed across fifteen long years. Harper had definitely heard it before, lately in her dreams with the kelpies. As a child, she'd only glimpsed the red-haired woman the voice belonged to. This same woman with the flaming hair had murdered her father.

Selina's words echoed in her mind again. The Fae had been in her life for a long time. Since the night her world had ended. The Fae, led by the black-clad woman on the stage, had been the one to end it.

She squeezed her eyes shut to hold back tears. If she couldn't get to Emilio, he'd suffer the same fate as her father.

The red-haired woman looked out over the crowd and smiled the smile a wolf makes at the door of the sheepfold. The long, wispy tails of her black sleeves fluttered in the chill breeze. Behind her, fog machines were wheeled into place.

"Our goal for tonight is to bring the magic of this event to a new height," the blond man continued. Applause roared.

"Well then, let's have some color to match this gorgeous music." The red-haired woman held her hand high. Behind her, the band poised to play. Lances of stage lights swept over the crowd and pulsed in every color, bathing the band in a kaleidoscope of shifting light. The transfixed masses pressed close to the stage.

The woman brought her hand slashing toward the ground and explosions of colored powder arced over the crowd. A glittering opalescent mist drifted down like technicolor snow. It was the exact color of Dust. Right on cue, the band began a raucous tune and the crowd wheeled and twirled once more while the drug rained down.

It was then that Harper felt hands grab her from behind, one clamped down tightly over her mouth. She kicked backward with her booted foot, then pushed off the ground with all her might to knock her attacker down. But he only gripped her tighter.

Harper did what every self-defense class she'd ever taken told her not to. She panicked. Her limbs became an uncoordinated storm of flailing and kicking. Moderate intoxication only magnified her lack of coordination. Who, or more likely, whatever gripped her was impossibly strong. Her adrenaline-fueled thrashing only exhausted her.

In desperation, she bit down on the gloved hand. Both the hand and the music muffled her howl. Her teeth throbbed. She wasn't entirely sure she hadn't broken a couple. It had been like biting down on a leather-covered rock, and the hand didn't budge.

She was past the edge of the stage now and being dragged deeper into the tree line where her attacker would probably kill her. Another storm of half-intoxicated bucking and kicking failed to budge his grip, but he stopped dragging her. She cursed herself for allowing someone to get the jump on her. Years of training and she'd screwed it up.

The same black dog from the tent city, the one with yellow eyes, trotted around from behind her, sat down, and said, "Relax.

We're trying to help. Your apparent seizure is only drawing attention to us."

Harper stopped struggling, mostly from shock. The desire to flee in terror warred with the revelation that a dog had spoken to her. In English. She went limp and drew a steadying breath.

"You're a dog," Harper said, but the hand over her mouth made her words sound like a string of grunts.

"Promise not to scream?" the smooth voice of her captor sounded in her ear.

Harper nodded. Even if she yelled, she'd probably be swarmed by worse than these two. The hands holding her came away.

She stumbled and whirled to see the same silver-haired man from the alley readjusting the glove on the hand she had tried to bite. A metallic gleam shone through a hole in the glove.

"Talking dog." Harper's head moved between the silver-haired man and the dog like she was watching a tennis match. "And you were there too."

"Quickly now, back farther into the tree line, and don't inhale any of the colorful cloud," the man said.

Not that Harper needed any warning about that. Once they retreated to a safer distance, the man knelt down and touched the ground, uttering words Harper couldn't understand. A green circle shimmered along the dry leaves and other forest detritus, encircling them and extending out several yards. Harper recoiled from the shining green line, drawing up on her tiptoes with her hands clasped under her chin.

"The circle should protect us from prying eyes for a time. My name's Nuada. Pleasure to meet you at last."

"Harper." Her eyes focused on his silver hair. Not grey or white, but silver and almost as shiny as a coin. The last thing Selina told her was to trust the silver-haired man, and that was the only reason she wasn't running as fast as her legs could carry her.

Harper let her arms fall to her sides and stared at the dog.

"You're a talking dog." Her knees felt suddenly watery, so she leaned her back against a tree and met the man's bright blue eyes. "Did I wake up in freaking Narnia?"

"Animals can't talk." The dog spoke slowly, like he was explaining something to a moron. "Narnia is from a book, and you're welcome." The dog's shape rippled, became hazy, and then Harper stared slack jawed at the creature standing before her. He looked like a cobbled together mishmash of various animal parts.

The past few days had been a parade of the surreal, or the being's appearance would have pushed her over the edge. Plus, the alcohol lubricated her slide into fairy tales and horror stories, so instead of hitting the roof she went with the flow.

"What is that?" Harper asked Nuada while pointing at the Phooka.

Nuada smiled at the look of indignation from his Fae companion.

The Phooka drew himself fully upright on his hooves, almost at military attention. A top hat and monocle appeared, and he stared down his long, goat-like nose.

"This"—he swept his hand over his shiny black fur and turned a slow circle—"is the magnificent Phooka of infinite shapes and even more infinite heights of cleverness and charm. I've tricked gods with my silver tongue." He flicked out his very pink tongue to prove his point. "I assisted in the slaying of the mad dragon Griahle."

"After you drove him mad in the first place, forcing him to listen to your entire dubstep collection until he chose a favorite," Nuada said. And crossed his arms.

"I tamed the Great Yellow-Eyed Manticore of Ardennes for King Louis the Fourteenth."

"That one was actually all you. You pretended to be the manticore, attacked his castle, scammed him out of thousands, then faked your own death."

"I once made the Statue of Liberty disappear." The Phooka's hands framed his face with waggling fingers.

"That was David Copperfield," Harper said.

"Well, I've walked the earth tied to no Court for six hundred years, no minor feat." The Phooka stopped the recitation of his resume and looked out of the corner of his eye at Harper.

Harper rolled her eyes, a single eyebrow arched, and her mouth curled in a disbelieving smirk, much like the look a teenager gives an adult when faced with what they believe to be unbelievable hogwash.

The Phooka's top hat and monocle faded away. "You really should be more impressed."

"I live with an alcoholic. I know bullshit when I hear it."

"Philistine." The Phooka snorted and turned his back on both Harper and Nuada. He played with the tip of his tail and mumbled under his breath.

Harper hoped she hadn't hurt the Phooka's feelings. She wasn't sure if she should trust him or not, but he'd already saved her from worse Fae. "You two saved me in the alley yesterday. So far you're the least scary Fae I've met."

The Phooka jerked his thumb toward Nuada. "He's not Fae. Nuada's the former High King of the Tuatha de Danann. The ancient Celts thought he was a god. Morons."

Her eyes scanned Nuada from head to toe. He was beautiful, high cheekbones and all, but it was hard for her to see him as a god. That last drink was taking full effect. Her head swam. She brought a hand to the back of her neck and rubbed.

"I don't know what any of that means." Her head shot back up. She had allies now. "Nuada, Phooka. Please help me. I'm pretty sure the red-haired woman killed my father and my friend Emilio is—"

Nuada held up a hand to silence her. "One thing at a time. Your friend isn't going anywhere. For now."

He stood, tilted his head, and gestured back to the throng of dancers. "You seem to have some kind of ability to resist the glamours of the Fae or you would be pirouetting around the clearing with the rest of the humans. There are many Fae on this island—"

"I know. One of the vendors told me." She swayed a little as she spoke. The heat blooming through her body told her that last slush was too many. She was rounding the corner from moderately drunk to really drunk.

"How many Fae did you see?" the Phooka asked.

"I'm not sure, but I think the big trolls might be real. You think I'm not dancing because of this?" Harper pulled the rowan and iron amulet from beneath her shirt.

The Phooka motioned her to bend down to him. Harper leaned over so the pendant dangled at his eye level. His nose wrinkled. He snorted a few times and spat a wad of foamy white spit in her eye. "Yep. Iron and rowan. Explains why you aren't tripping the light fantastic."

"Ew! What the hell is wrong with you?!" She dug at her eyes with her sleeve. When she opened them again she gasped. Fae in all shapes and sizes clustered around the periphery of the crowd. Green creatures with leathery ears and wiry limbs surrounded the venue. Interspersed with them were wispy-winged women with gigantic lavender eyes. Indeed, the trolls were real.

"I have bestowed upon you the gift of my magical spittle." The Phooka tipped his nose in the air. "Now you can see Fae even when they wish to remain invisible from humans! You are most welcome."

"That was the most disgusting . . ." From the corner of her eye her new sight revealed something else. Her blood ran cold at the sheer number of black birds high in the trees. Now that she could really see them, they didn't look like birds at all. Most of them were too gaunt and tattered to be crows. One of them threw its head high and flapped its leathery bat wings.

Nuada followed her gaze. "Sluagh. Not quite fairies. Some of them were once, but now they are something far worse. You are seeing them as they truly are."

"Don't call them fairies. They don't like it," Harper corrected and clapped her hand over her mouth for an instant. With the horror show perched overhead, that was her response. "Crap! I said fairy."

The Phooka eyed her appreciatively. "Are you drunk?"

"No! Maybe. A little. I was freaking out and thought it would calm me down enough to think." She looked down at her shiny red shoes, the crazy thought to click her heels together three times came to her and she giggled. *Harper, you're cracking up.* "I didn't think they were that strong."

"We must get you out of here," Nuada said as he grabbed her elbow and started off deeper into the trees.

Harper wrenched her arm away, stumbling slightly. Her hazel eyes flashed. "I'm not leaving Emilio drugged out of his mind in this place. I'm not abandoning my only friend!"

The Phooka pranced over to her on his hooves. His golden eyes met hers. "Nuada and I will come back for him. It is critical we get you to safety immediately."

"Why? What makes me special enough that a goat thing and a god are trying to save my ass? What kind of god would leave all these people to whatever's happening here?"

"I had hoped to have more time to ease you into this, but necessity prevails. You, Harper, are the last living heir of Niall, the last High King of Ireland and probably the only person who can stop the coming war."

Harper waited for one of them to laugh. Lips parted, her eyes traveled from goat-rabbit face to chiseled features and back. But both of them looked dead serious, and they echoed what Selina said. The last great war or something like that.

"You two are crazy. I can barely keep my mom from killing herself or pay our mortgage. You think I'm equipped to deal with that?" She flung her hand toward the stage and stamped a foot.

"I know this is a lot to take in. We can talk about it once we get you safe."

"What, so I can go fight some hopeless war with you? Because I'm your damn Obi Wan Kenobi? I got news for you two weirdos. If I'm your only hope, you two are utterly and completely hosed! I want to rescue Emilio and get the hell out of here. You can help me do that or you can piss off! And once we get him to safety, you can piss off after that. I want no part of this."

"Technically, you're more like our Luke Skywalker, young, unskilled, impulsive, committed to a hopeless cause, a bit whiny . . . He's our Obi Wan." The Phooka jabbed a thumb at Nuada. His face melted into an expression of despair. "Oh no. That makes me the walking carpet. Nope. Not doing *Star Wars*."

Nuada ran his hand over his head. "Look, Harper. That red-haired woman is named Badb Catha. All of this is just the beginning. She wants to wipe humans from the face of this world. Only a new High King or Queen can unite forces against her. As soon as she finds you here, you will be dead. She's already murdered the rest."

Harper stalked toward the stage. Nuada caught her elbow and pulled her to a stop. She scowled at him, her arms tight across her chest. She still had questions, and she planned to get answers, after she rescued her friend. "Is that why I remember the Dark Boys and the red-haired woman in my house the night they killed my father? The alley wasn't the first time I'd seen them. And they knew my name. And why could I see them when I couldn't see other Fae until the Phooka spit in my eye?" Thoughts chased themselves around and around.

"Yes. No, it wasn't. The kelpies recognized your blood. Because they wanted the humans in the alley to see them." The Phooka ticked off the answer to each of her questions on his fingers. "No doubt they reported what they saw to their boss. Badb knows you're out there. She won't stop until she finds you."

A series of loud bangs sent them into a crouch. Harper looked between her fingers to see the ethereal band pushing the music to a furious crescendo while a curtain of shimmering powder rained down on the crowd. More Dust. None of the dancers noticed. Bodies whirled, stamped, and leapt with beatific smiles and glassy eyes. Harper's stomach sank when she heard the same harp music from the alley.

"Emilio!" she shouted and sprinted toward the stage, carving a serpentine line between the trees. She didn't make it more than ten yards when the sight before her stopped her dead in her tracks just short of the shimmering green protective border. High in the night sky, an undulating black cloud loomed closer with every passing second. Beating wings rumbled like thunder. Sluagh and crows alike took to the sky and flapped toward the approaching cloud. No. It couldn't be a cloud, because it moved impossibly fast and against the wind.

The cloud resolved into individual specks that she could see were many kinds of Fae and men riding flying horses. She clasped Nuada's arm.

"What is that?" Her voice quavered.

"That, Harper, is the Wild Hunt," Nuada replied as he reached his hand back to rest on his sword.

"We're doomed," the Phooka said in a reasonable impersonation of C3PO.

CHAPTER 22

The mournful strains of baying hounds accompanied the brass tone of a hunting horn. The familiarity of the sound stopped Harper's breath. She froze in place like her joints had turned to ice. Within seconds the white spectral shapes of five hunting dogs streaked across the sky. Every hair on their sleek glowing bodies gleamed purest white, except for the blood-red ears that matched their red glowing eyes. Snarling and howling, they met the cloud of crows and Sluagh, who swept in line behind them, weaving themselves between the multitude of the Hunt.

"Gabriel hounds." The Phooka melted into the shape of a massive black wolf. His hackles were up and strings of saliva dripped from razor-sharp teeth.

Behind the hounds, mounted on a shiny black horse with pale white eyes, rode the leader of the Wild Hunt. He was broad chested and clad in leather breeches. A deep brown longcoat swept out behind him as he rode. Flames rose from the eye holes of the horned deer skull mask that occluded much of his face. He was flanked by more mounted Fae that resembled the musicians on the stage. Elves, Harper supposed.

In between dragons and impossibly thin-winged Fae were huge wiry green-skinned trolls and creatures of every size and shape. A cold sweat broke out all over Harper's body at the sight of dozens of Dark Boys—kelpies—in their ranks. Her hands shook and her knees gave out, sending her crumpling to the ground. Directly overhead, the procession banked toward the crowd. Most of the Fae who had clustered around the edges of the stage rose into the sky to assist the Hunt, leaving a half dozen on each side of the crowd.

In Harper's mind, she was that terrified ten-year-old girl, hiding under the bed like a coward while her father died downstairs. Talons of guilt ripped her heart. No. Not guilt. Shame. She could have done something. Screamed, thrown something, distracted them, anything but run and hide. But she hadn't. She'd saved herself and doomed her father to death, and now Emilio would be the next victim of her cowardice.

She knelt, stuck fast by the ghosts of her past. The Wild Hunt plunged toward the crowd. Hand and claw seized people as they thundered past barely three feet from the ground. Everyone should be screaming and trying to escape, but they weren't. They were utterly silent. Every one of them stood eerily still with their eyes cast up at the mad cavalry. Some even held up their hands like they wanted to be taken. The abducted floated, intermingled with the Fae and Sluagh, limbs limp. The leader of the Hunt hovered high above the island and sounded his horn. The Gabriel hounds howled and gnashed their long teeth as the Hunt raced down for another pass, the taken tumbling and flailing in their wake.

Nuada knelt beside Harper and pushed a very long silver knife into her hand. "Get to the shore, that way." He motioned away from the dock through the trees. "The Phooka can fly us out of here safely."

Harper held the dagger in her hand limply and remained rooted in place. Faraway eyes met Nuada's, tears streaming down her face. At that moment, she caught sight of Emilio. He hadn't yet been taken. The Wild Hunt raged across the cloudy sky, more dangling prisoners swelling their ranks. Her cowardly inaction all those years ago had cost too much, and she couldn't make the same mistake again.

Something deep in her shifted like the tumbler in a lock. These monsters had shattered her life. She'd done nothing but try to put the pieces back together since. Now they hunted her. They already had Abraham, and they wanted Emilio. Fear evaporated under the simmering flames of rage. Her fist clenched around the dagger. Her heart became a war drum, no longer tapping out the quick tattoo of horror. Instead, it pounded out the fierce thrum of combat. She wanted as much Fae blood as she could draw, and she didn't care if she died trying to stop every last monster.

She launched herself to her feet and screamed. Her face contorted in rage, spittle flew from her trembling lip. Before Nuada or the Phooka could react, Harper raced for the stage, sweeping the flashing horn from her head and shrugging off her handbag.

"Harper!" Nuada yelled at her retreating back.

"You're going the wrong way," the Phooka shouted.

She turned and yelled over her shoulder as she ran. "If you want to protect me, you'll have to help me save Emilio."

Nuada cursed and sprinted after her. The Phooka changed shape into a tall black horse and galloped ahead.

In her rage, Harper was unfazed by the hideous shapes of Fae that she previously saw hovering at the edges of the dance area. They were the height of fifth graders with gray-green skin, long noses, and wiry hair.

They growled and brandished hammers and axes.

"Goblins!" the Phooka called.

Ahead of her, Emilio disappeared from sight in the mass of

bodies scattered by the Wild Hunt. If she had to fight every goblin on this island, she'd never get to him in time, so she swayed and twirled, slipping past the cluster of Fae.

"What are you—" the Phooka said.

But beside her, Nuada did the same, sword tucked into the folds of his flowing black coat. Harper tripped and bumped into him. Her head swam. She regretted the rum slushies.

The Phooka loped past the goblin line and cleared an easier path for Harper and Nuada by knocking dazed humans sprawling. None of the Fae seemed concerned by a massive black horse in their midst, likely seeing him as one of their own.

In his wake, Harper twirled her arms overhead and rotated a circle on her tiptoes in time to the lilting tune emanating from the stage. With a toss of her red-maned hair, she squinted up at the circling Wild Hunt, checking for Emilio in their ranks.

Nuada caught her about the waist and pulled her into a twirl. The alien faces of Fae wheeled around her. He pressed his lips near her ear and whispered, "Wise move we blend in, but we better find your friend fast. The Hunt is gearing up for another run."

Harper whispered back, "I don't see him up there. He has to be on the ground."

The Wild Hunt slashed the sky with their latest pass and more of the revelers now careened along with the movements of the Fae host. They tumbled along in their wake like rag dolls blown by a hurricane. The horn sounded again, signaling yet another dive for the ground for more prey.

Harper spied Emilio still in the crowd toward the edge of the stage, close enough that if she shouted he might hear her. Relief drove a rush of air from her lungs. "Emilio!" she screamed before she thought the action through. He didn't respond, only stared skyward with his hand reaching out to where the Wild Hunt banked for their next dive, but the bigger problem was that her outburst betrayed them as unglamoured.

A mob of jagged teeth and weapons surrounded the three of them. She lost sight of Nuada as her vision laser focused, leaving only a snarling clump of attackers in her sights. With the blood rushing like whitewater in her ears, she flicked the dagger up.

Nuada leapt between Harper and their attackers, drawing a black metal sword from a sheath on his back. The more ornate-looking silver blade still hung at his waist. Harper's jaw dropped at his efficiency dispatching the goblins. He moved with the grace and poise of a professional dancer. The blade swung a wide arc, separating the head of one goblin from its body. The skull hadn't even hit the ground, and he spun around and the sword continued its high, deadly sweep. He jabbed the blade down through the second goblin while kicking his leg back, knocking a third off balance. By the time the last Fae recovered, the sword was already impaling him through his heart.

The metallic smell of blood filled the air and Harper retched at the sight and reek of it. Nothing prepared her for the reality of death this close up.

One of the goblins lunged for her. She lashed out with the blade. The creature hopped out of the way and backhanded her on the shoulder. She crashed to the ground. Her training finally kicked in. When the goblin pulled his arm back to smash her with his hammer, she drew her knees to her chest and kicked him in the gut. He sailed backward, beady eyes circles of shock, his long fingers spread wide. His dropped hammer thudded into her shoulder and she yelped in pain.

Behind her, the horse-shaped Phooka trampled slightly smaller versions of the goblins that wore little red caps, keeping her free of attackers for the moment. "Yippee-Ki-Yay, motherfuckers!" he shouted as hooves crushed arms and legs.

Nuada hovered over her, deflecting blow after blow like he

was flicking away insects. His free hand reached toward the earth and he chanted in a language Harper didn't understand. Bright green tendrils of energy twined up from the earth, forming a ball while the wind howled overhead. The earth energy wound up around the sword and bent the winds into a vortex, the ebony blade the eye of the storm. Nuada's voice rose to a shout and whipped the winds faster and faster.

The Wild Hunt bent into the headwinds, the leader's coat flailing around his legs. His masked head turned toward Nuada and Harper saw the flaming eye sockets burn hotter. He banked and dove straight for Nuada.

Shit just got worse. Pinned in with Fae, Harper was no help for Emilio. *Please, I can't lose him, too.* One of the redcaps slipped past the Phooka's pulverizing hooves, twirling twin knives. He lashed a knife toward her leg. She brought the goblin's hammer down just in time to deflect the blow but caught the second blade on her forearm.

The sight of her own blood brought a wave of dizziness. The redcap rolled across his back and landed on his feet right next to her exposed side. The nasty bastard licked her bloody arm. His jaw dropped when she stepped in closer, threw her knee into his chin, and whacked him between the shoulder blades with the hammer.

The crunch of bone beneath the hammer turned her stomach and her mouth filled with the burning flavor of vomit. Still she was no closer to getting to Emilio.

Nuada's chanting brought the winds to a howl and their earthbound attackers to a temporary standstill, but for Harper not a breeze stirred. Nuada's chant ended when the crackling sphere of green fire grew to the size of a small car. He threw his head back in a sonorous yell, slicing his upraised hand down. The winds blew straight downward while the green energy ball exploded outward over the Fae on the dance floor, sweeping the Wild Hunt from the sky and smashing them into the dirt. The green blast flung the remaining Fae far into the trees.

Somehow, Nuada spared the humans from the blast. They dangled in the sky over the battlefield and others twirled their empty dance near the stage. The Hunt didn't fare that well. The first wave of them thudded into the ground, where they lay unmoving. When the remaining Fae recovered, they were scattered all over the field, no longer an organized host.

The Wild Hunt descended into chaos. The handful who avoided the magic remained aloft and pulled the enchanted people back into ranks. Nuada clutched the air with his hand and pulled down as though tearing something from the sky. A second wave of goblins and elves came crashing down, including the horned leader. He tumbled from his flying steed just before he slammed into the earth. Momentum rolled him right to where Harper and Nuada stood, his hand on the grip of his sheathed sword. This man had stood next to Badb the night she murdered Harper's father.

For a moment, battle paused, all eyes were riveted on their leader, awaiting orders.

The imposing rider was back on his feet in an instant, deep brown hair buffeted by the aftereffects of the magic. His body was coiled and ready to strike, a great broadsword in his hands. "Hello, Father," the leader snarled in a deep voice that reminded Harper of the sound of dried leaves scraping the sidewalk in the wind.

"Gwyn, this isn't you."

"You have no idea what I've had to do because of the role you cast me in. You'd best draw the sword at your hip if you hope to prevail."

Nuada stood tall and his eyes dropped into an expression of profound sadness. "I will not draw this sword against you, son."

"Then you will die." Gwyn rushed forward in a half crouch, his hands holding his sword to one side, ready to strike.

A swarm of Fae rushed Harper and the Phooka.

"Stay behind me," the Phooka shouted. He reared up and clobbered kelpies and redcaps with his broad hooves.

Kelpies attacked Harper from both sides. Her fingers closed around the cold wet hair of the nearest. She yanked him forward while she drove a shoulder low into his friend. When he doubled over, she brought the hammer up into his jaw, then stomped her boot into the back of his prone companion.

Too many injured and unconscious Fae piled up around her. When a goblin attacked, she lurched a step back, tripped, and landed sprawling over one of the kelpies, hammer loosed from her grip.

The goblin cackled and kicked his metal boot into her side. Sharp pain exploded across her stomach. Jagged goblin teeth sank into her leg; she screamed with the pain.

At the same instant, the Phooka leapt over the ring of short Fae and kicked the goblin aside with his front hoof. The Phooka's hooves were covered with the gore of his conquests. Harper appreciated his timing; the ring of goblins and redcaps had closed around her. She crouched in the center, hands balled into fists.

"We have to find Emilio. Black hair. Light-up horn like mine."

"Saddle up," he said in a perfect imitation of Mr. Ed. Harper grabbed hold of his neck and clambered up on his broad back. She gripped his sides with her legs and wound her free hand in his mane. Sharp claws and pointed teeth ringed them.

She caught sight of Nuada and Gwyn for just an instant. Sparks flew from their clashing blades as they battled. Nuada was fending off his son, barely. To Harper, it looked as though his heart wasn't in the fight. Gwyn was relentless, yet Nuada only defended.

Wave after wave of attacking Fae kept her attention on her own battle. It was useless fighting them one by one. There had to be a way to get to her friend now.

"Hold tight," the Phooka said.

Harper had just enough time to wind her hand through his long mane again before he took a small leap over the heads of the shorter Fae into a small clearing. Another leap carried them over the heads of some grounded Sluagh who had retaken their human-like forms. Sallow flesh sagged over bone. The folded wing membranes gave them the appearance of wearing tattered cloaks.

At that moment, a far more formidable foe rose before them. Five black-haired elves clad in shiny red-and-black jointed armor formed a wall between them and Emilio. Menacing black metal swords flashed from their scabbards. They attacked all at once.

Elegant, pale hands dragged Harper from the Phooka's back. She landed on her feet but toppled onto her side, catching a glimpse of Emilio swaying and twirling. The elf woman stood over her, black eyes glittering with hatred.

The Phooka changed shape back to a great black wolf almost as large as his horse shape. Snapping jaws crushed the arm bones of the nearest warrior. The fighter screamed and fled into the crowd, but the other three circled the Phooka. He kicked and snapped, but their swords and skill were much better than the goblin hoard. Deeper wounds soon peppered his flanks. He was losing.

Another elf woman lashed out at Harper with her sword. Harper scrambled out of the weapon's path, half on her side. She was too slow and the sword bit into her free arm. She sucked in a breath over her teeth. Sensing an easy victory, the elf sneered and kicked Harper in the sternum. The impact flattened her, and she lay helpless on her back. The elf was beside her, sword raised for the final blow. Harper was weaponless and out of moves. In the background, she heard Nuada shout her name and the Phooka scream "No!"

Time slowed. She saw her death in the eyes of the elven warrior. Images of Emilio slumping along behind watery kelpies alternated with visions of her mother run through by Badb. This would be their fate.

This can't be how my life ends, not like my dad at the hands of these demons.

Her vision turned red. If this actually was the end, she'd take out as many of them as she could, revenge for all they'd already taken. Fury contorted her face and her muscles surged to life.

From somewhere deep inside her, an unknown power stirred. Her body pulsed with electricity like the time she'd touched an electric fence. A well of burning, jagged energy percolated in her chest just looking for a path to travel. From some unknown unconscious place, she knew just what to do with the magic raging inside. Yes, that was what it was. Magic.

She screamed at the top of her lungs and struck out with the full force of that surging electricity, fists clenched at her side and her head curled toward her chest. She directed all of it at every damned Fae she could suddenly sense around her, like a hundred tiny lights in a dark room.

A blue fire laced with spiraling tendrils erupted from her body and expanded out like a supernova, tearing through the closest goblins and redcaps. They sizzled and screeched. It slammed into the more powerful Folk and drove them to the ground with the force of ocean surf.

The edges of her vision darkened but, through the falling shadow, she could still make out the remnants of the blue fire she somehow conjured and Gwyn clawing himself away from her. Nuada's gaping jaw made her smile.

The force of her knees hitting the dirt clacked her teeth together and sent sparkles across her almost black vision. She was delirious. As her head met the earth, a golden-eyed Toothless the black dragon bent over her.

"Emilio, I'm sorry," she whispered and sank into the abyss.

CHAPTER 23

Emilio Soliz plodded along behind one of the tulle-clad glitter fairies from the party. He barely noticed the chill in the night air or the moon trying to break through the clouds; he noticed little except for the most gorgeous woman he'd ever seen, glimpsed from the corner of his eye.

Wispy thin and draped in what looked like a diaphanous gown spun of spider silk, her pale triangular face was filled with enormous lavender eyes. White-feathered wings whispered with each languid flap. The vision of beauty struck Emilio with an ache in his heart. He'd do anything for her. That was why he was walking with the others in the middle of the night when he should have been in his bed sleeping. She wanted him to.

With each slow step his mind cleared from a soporific fog. He thought he might have done Dust; that might explain why he had no idea where he was right now. He was dimly aware of a line of people extending behind him and more plodding bodies in tattered costumes marching ahead, but none of that mattered.

On his other side strode a tall warrior with gleaming black hair and eyes to match. Long pointed ears knifed through his shining locks. Black armor with a beetle sheen plated his chest, and the clothing underneath the plates flowed in blood-red folds to his knees. He was perfect. Emilio would do anything this man's heart desired. He, too, wanted him to walk with the others, so Emilio obeyed. He hoped the winged lady and the dark warrior would take notice of his obedience and reward him. Just a smile from one of them, that's all he asked.

The unearthly parade wound through a dark wood. During the few moments Emilio could tear his eyes from the beautiful flying sylph or the otherworldly man, he noticed great broad-trunked trees with gnarled branches. Fall had stolen their leaves, making their limbs look like clawed hands straining to grab the people passing beneath. A low mist hung on the forest floor, reflecting the bright light of the moon.

This place is wrong. All of this is wrong. Wake up. The tiny voice called deep within himself. *Come to think of it, nowhere in Oregon has trees like this.* Maybe that squeaky voice was right. But once he beheld the winged woman again, the voice fell silent. Somehow, he knew listening to it would displease her, and all he ever wanted to do was make the winged woman and armored man happy.

He turned his face to drink in their beauty. The warrior met his gaze, and a slightly puzzled expression played across his chiseled face. Emilio followed his eyes as they swept down the line of marching humans. The rest of the company trudged along, their jaws slack and their eyes unfocused. No one else took heed of their guides. His pulse quickened. Disappointing them would be more than he could bear.

That tiny voice in Emilio's mind clamored for him to look straight ahead and act like the others. Avoid drawing attention. The sylph's lips drew into a pout and her eyes narrowed as she studied Emilio. Maybe the voice was right. They wanted him to act like the others. Above all else he desired to please them, and so he focused his gaze straight ahead and plopped one foot in front of the other.

He fervently hoped he hadn't angered them. The look of consternation he imagined on their faces at his poor behavior made him want to throw himself at their feet and beg for mercy. In his mind, he promised them he'd be good.

Emilio's heart smiled when the concern faded from his escorts' faces and they focused back on the winding trail ahead. The warrior, especially, looked pleased with his obedience, Emilio noted with glee.

Some time later, the group emerged from the forest into a large clearing. That tiny voice in Emilio's mind, the one at war with the creatures he so loved, grew stronger with each passing moment.

You're walking in the woods surrounded by elves and fairies. Wake up, Emilio. This is wronger than wrong. They drugged you or something. Wake up.

He took the risk of letting just his eyes sweep the area, just to prove that irritating voice wrong. An imposing grey stone building jutted up from the center of the clearing. Its central spire towered over a broad base and ended in a sweeping arch at the top. A small plaza nestled into the arch, almost like someone had built a band shell at the top of the building. Three long rows of dark windows ran in parallel up the center. Flanking each side were smaller buildings with about ten floors. The only windows on these were two horizontal rows near the top.

The beautiful creatures led them toward a flat plaza ringed with a flight of a few steps. The oversize sign in front of the plaza read Erimus Pharmaceutical.

Am I at work? At a satellite office... Deep in the woods... And that was perhaps the wrongest thing of all. Who plops a monolithic corporate building smack dab in the middle of the Forest of Nowhere?

As the procession approached the stairs, the cacophonous

prattle of crows filled the air. They crowded every branch of the trees and perched along the edge of the building. When his eyes followed the cawing, Emilio witnessed something that cut right through his hazy thoughts about how he could gain the gratitude of the beautiful ones.

His fear would have forced him to sprint for the relative safety of the trees were it not for the invisible force that locked him in sway to the gorgeous beings around him. Despite the magic, his throat clenched at what he could see from the tops of his eyes. He didn't dare turn his head. Suspended above the Fae and their victims were misty cocoons, like a string of macabre lanterns adorning the black trees. The moonlight filtering through the milky shells cast into relief the distorted shapes within. Shapes as wrong as the surrounding forest. Some had curved backs and legs with an extra joint. Others sprouted wings. *Jesus. It's a nest of these things. They're breeding more monsters.*

Movement caught his eye on the right. Just outside the building, a small group of short, greenish-tan figures with big leathery ears and wiry body hair grappled with the dead weight of someone and shoved him toward the tree line. Emilio's breath quickened as one goblin lifted a hand in the air. The person, a blissful expression on his face, drifted upward. His head drooped to one side. The man looked to be about fifty years of age and wore shabby clothes. In a time and place that felt like a hundred years ago, Emilio recalled his friend telling him *they* were stealing the homeless. Fae.

The Fae at the base of the tree guided the poor guy next to one of the oblong clumps of mist. Slow tendrils of fog caressed the man and pulled him inside. Satisfied with their work, the green things turned and walked back toward the entrance, their chain mail clinking. Emilio couldn't fully wrap his mind around what he had just seen, but it looked like the goblins had *fed* the poor man to whatever waited inside the constellation of fog.

Emilio wrenched his attention from the sight and jostled a dude in a vampire costume next to him. The guy didn't even register the contact. Black elven eyes flicked his way, drawn by his sudden movement. The voice of reason grew louder in his mind. *Don't look at him. God, he's beautiful, but don't look. You'll go back to sleep if you look.* Emilio lowered his head and peered at the green monsters and the vampire costume out of the corner of his eye.

His heart pounded, sending jittery bursts of adrenaline to every limb. The spell or Dust or whatever it was all but faded, the absence of its warm analgesic leaving him exposed to the unfolding nightmare. *Is this my fate? Fed to demons?*

His pulse roared in his ears as the group climbed the stairs to the plaza. That little voice, one he now recognized as his own, advised him to act like the others who were still spellbound.

He must not have been the only one whose spell had worn off, because in front of him he heard a scream and the thump, thump, thump of running feet. A guy dressed in a satyr costume pedaled back down the line toward where Emilio stood. His eyes were pulled wide with terror and he babbled as he ran.

The man made it a few feet from Emilio before the beautiful warrior and several green monsters swarmed him. The warrior drew a long black blade from its scabbard and drove it through the man's chest in a single fluid stroke.

The man's scream turned to gurgles when the green monsters closed in on top of him like piranha. Clawed hands tore out his throat and shredded his flesh. Emilio squeezed his eyes shut, but nothing blocked the wet smacking of the feeding monsters or the thrashing of the dying man. When the green demons scurried back to their work, all that remained of the man was an unrecognizable pile of shredded faux fur, blood, and guts.

The warrior wore the same bored expression as he examined the blood smeared along his weapon. Like all he had done was swat a fly. He dragged each side of the blade along a patch of grass and slid it into the sheath. The red X marked the place where the stranger died.

"Won't Breas be angry we killed one of the new subjects when we caught so many less than we thought?" The winged woman's voice was like the tinkle of wind chimes.

"I won't tell him we failed to glamour one if you don't." The elf smoothed his tunic and they resumed their walk to the building.

"I hope the Wild Hunt can catch the human spell caster who ended our harvest."

"She's probably already dead. No way one of these vermin could cast that kind of magic and live."

Emilio sucked in a breath before he could catch himself. He remembered a blue flash of light and then getting bowled over by flying bodies. That had to be Harper. That was probably why the Fae wanted her.

The warrior and the winged woman glanced over at him. He'd messed up. Caught their attention. He was sure they could hear his heart beating against its cage like it would have better luck escaping this horror show than the satyr costume did. He forced his eyes to look at the curly blond wig just in front of him.

Just stare ahead. Don't move and they'll pass by. Don't move. Don't move. Although he managed to stand statue still and keep his head down, his breath came in hitching gasps and his eyes were saucers. He did his best to unfocus them to hide his awareness.

The dark-haired man stepped toward him, his hand hovering over the grip of his sword. He leaned in to Emilio, his perfect face mere inches away. So close, Emilio's cheek felt the caress of his sweet breath. Every muscle fiber in his body screamed *run*, but his mind knew if he so much as twitched, he'd end up skewered monster food before he made it ten steps.

The elf was the most beautiful thing Emilio had ever seen. Those thoughts disturbed him. A man had died right in front of him at this Fae's hands and he was daydreaming about how pretty he was. The tickle of a wisp of stray hair from the warrior's braid brushed the skin of Emilio's neck. He was standing inches in front of him now. The black eyes of the elf searched Emilio's soft brown ones.

Adrenaline drove waves of fight-or-flight energy into every muscle. The urge to move was overpowering. Still Emilio stared forward over the heads of the people in front of him, fixed on the doors to the citadel. The seconds felt like minutes, but ultimately the beautiful face withdrew. Emilio noticed a line of leathery scarred flesh running down the cheek and neck of the warrior. His beauty was not the perfection that had melted Emilio's heart moments ago. How had he not noticed that before?

The elf waved his gloved hand over Emilio and the scar rippled, then faded. The gesture brought the return of that overwhelming desire to do anything this man wanted. Warm, fuzzy peace and love dripped through Emilio's mind and tired body, calming his thoughts and soothing his muscles. He didn't see the hideous scar anymore but the perfect beauty of the tall dark stranger before him. He would die for this man.

Emilio wore a dopey smile and plodded along behind his captors because that's what they wanted him to do.

CHAPTER 24

Clawing her way back to consciousness felt like swimming through dark, chill water. It took effort and her limbs felt like lead. Harper's eyes fluttered open, but her mind was still half in the dream world where, moments ago, she had been battling beauty and beast alike with blue fire.

Harper didn't remember coming home or exchanging red velour and fur for the white sweatpants and purple shirt she wore now. Truth be told, she didn't remember much except a lot of alcohol and that she might have ingested Dust. Hallucinogens would explain the monsters and the talking dog.

She rolled over and flopped her hand all over her nightstand, searching for her phone. Emilio should be able to fill in the missing gaps of her memory. Pain lanced through her left arm the instant her weight pressed on it. She sucked in a hissing breath and picked at the thick bandages over her lower arm. The fleeting image of a tussle flashed through her mind. That must be it. There was a fight, and she got injured somehow. Next time she went to a party, she promised herself she'd smuggle in at least one weapon. You never know who's at one of these rave-type events. She sat up and a wave of dizziness sent her halfway back to the mattress.

She hunched over her outstretched legs in the bed, noting dull pains sprouting up all over her body and more spots with bandages. What the hell happened last night? Did the festival end in a brawl? With bleary eyes she texted Emilio to make sure he got home OK and begin a conversation that would shed some light on the mysterious end to the party.

She dropped her feet over the edge of the bed and levered herself up, bracing herself with her hands against her thighs. Her muscles all over felt as weak as wet noodles. The room faded to an overexposed yellow, like it usually did before she fainted. Old advice of putting your head between your knees loaded like a computer program, so she let her head dangle next to her knees until the feeling passed. Then she rolled up her spine, vertebra by vertebra until she was vertical again, bracing herself on her bureau. Every muscle in her body throbbed in resistance to movement.

Emilio must be immobile if I'm this sore. He was dancing like a machine all night.

After a shower, she dragged her protesting body and foggy mind up the stairs. Light streaming into the living room made her wince. She turned away from it like a vampire in an old movie and looked down at her phone. Emilio hadn't texted her back yet.

'Hey, reanimate your corpse soon so you can tell me what happened last night,' she typed. She pressed 'send' and followed the mouthwatering nutty aroma of coffee to the kitchen.

Her mother slumped over the table. The posture told Harper it was safe to approach; her mother was still in the depressive trough of her illness, the peaks of mania at least days away. A fight was unlikely.

"Look what the cat dragged in. And somehow you also dragged in a cat."

Harper stared blankly at her mother for an instant while her head wrapped itself around the scene before her. Eileen cradled coffee in one hand, her other hovered over her Candy Crush game, and on her lap curled a black cat with intense yellow eyes.

Those amber eyes shone like lamps, burning away the brain fog obscuring last night's events. There had been Fae on the island. A silver-haired man and his yellow-eyed, shapeshifting friend had helped her win a fight. Nuada and the Phooka. They must have helped her get home when she passed out from the rum slushies. Just how did they know where she lived? She made a mental note to ask the Phooka about that right before she banished him from their home. They might have helped her out of a jam, but they were part of this crazy crap and she wanted all of it the hell out of her life.

"I didn't bring that mangy beast home with me."

The black cat laid its ears back and hissed. She returned the gesture by extending her middle finger.

"I don't think he likes you." Her mother ran her hand down the cat's back repeatedly.

"I'll take it to the pound as soon as I'm done with breakfast. Must have wandered in behind me when I came home last night. Probably riddled with diseases."

The cat growled and raised the hackles on its back. Mrs. O'Neill reached for her plate and offered the feline a bite of her eggs. The cat took the gift and purred. Harper's mother stroked the animal's back affectionately. "I don't know. I kind of like him. You always wanted a cat when you were little. What should we call him?"

"Phooka."

Eileen scratched the cat's ear. "Do you like that? Are you Phooka? My little Phooka?" she crooned in a sing-song voice. The feline purred and rubbed against her hand. Yellow eyes narrowed at Harper.

"Whatever, Mom. If you want him, he is most definitely yours, but you get to take care of him. I want nothing to do with the filthy animal."

Harper's mother scowled while the Phooka stuck out his pink tongue at her. Harper flipped off the cat again and busied herself making toast and coffee. She brought her breakfast over to the table and dropped into the chair opposite her mother. Her legs shook.

"God, Harper, you look horrid. How much did you drink last night?"

"All the rum slushies, I think." She reached for the sugar on the table. A bandage peeked out beneath the sleeve of Harper's shirt. She snapped the sleeve back down, but it was too late. Her mom's face creased.

"Harper, that looks huge! What happened?"

What had happened? There was a knife and a fight and . . . and . . .

"The dumbest thing. The wind caught the door of Emilio's goth golf cart just as I was reaching in for my coat. It's not that bad. I'm super sore from dancing, though." She hoped her fake smile was convincing.

Her mention of Emilio prompted a check of her phone for a reply. Nothing. "Just a sec, Mom. I'm checking in with Emilio. He's got to be worse off than me. He was a dancing machine all night." She dialed Emilio's number. It rang several times and went to voicemail. She glanced up at the time on the microwave. 11:24. He should be up. A cold stone took up residence in her stomach.

"Well. You know what the best thing for a hangover is." The flower-print nightgown fell in long folds when Eileen stood and deposited the black cat on the floor. She grabbed Harper's coffee cup. Pink fuzzy slippers whispered against the linoleum as she shuffled past. The Phooka twined his way around her legs with every step and uttered a convincing 'meow.' Harper's mom reached up into the top cabinet and withdrew a small bottle of Bailey's Irish Cream. She poured some into her daughter's coffee and smiled. "Hair of the dog."

"Mom! Alcohol doesn't solve every problem."

"It solves this one. Trust me, I'm a pro. I'm hitting the shower. Enjoy your breakfast and take it easy today. Leave the cat. Phooka here is making me feel better." With that, Harper's mother straggled off toward the bathroom to ready herself for a day that would most likely comprise going back to bed as its zenith. The black cat followed behind, tail high in the air.

"Here, kitty kitty." Harper beckoned the cat with a single finger.

The cat halted and Harper paused to take a sip of the spiked coffee. Creamy sweetness melted over her tongue. The hiss of the shower started, and she rounded on the Phooka.

"Just what the hell do you think you're doing?"

The cat's eyes widened in simulated innocence. "Meow." He hopped up on the table and faced Harper.

"Cut the act. I know you're not a cat."

"Au contraire. In this form I am quite literally a cat, albeit with a little *je nais sais quoi*."

Harper rolled her eyes. She felt the Irish coffee melting the hangover. Hair of the dog, indeed. Her hands were damp with sweat, but not from last night's drinking. Still no call from Emilio, and she remembered now a brawl had erupted and separated them. "Tell me what happened last night. I remember pieces. How did Emilio and I get home?"

"Well, I found you, we fought the Wild Hunt, you passed out, and we brought you here. That about sums it up."

"So was Emilio with us?"

"No." The Phooka lashed his shiny black tail back and forth.

"You left him there?" she said through gritted teeth.

"I don't think you fully recall how desperate the situation really was. It was a miracle the three of us escaped that island. Emilio was too far away—"

"Well why couldn't you turn into Godzilla, crush the Wild Hunt, and grab Emilio?"

The Phooka sighed. "First, because Mothra would be more effective against a flying army. Second, shapeshifting requires energy. The further my shape is from my true form, whether large or small, the more exhausting it is. Only enough juice for one flight away from the party. I had to choose. I chose you and Nuada."

"Thanks for nothing."

Harper's face flushed red. She snatched up the phone and tried Emilio again, as though it would give a different result. Maybe he lost his phone. That had to be it. She dialed Emilio's sister, Juana. He sometimes crashed there when life with his roommates irritated him. Juana picked up immediately and hadn't seen him. Not wanting to alarm her, Harper reassured her he was probably just sleeping still.

Tears threatened to pool in Harper's eyes. "Well, I'm going to look for him. He has to be OK. He has to."

The Phooka nodded sympathetically and held up a paw to end her train of thought. "Nuada is already out looking for him and I brought you here. It isn't safe for you out there. He told me to stay put, and that's just what we'll do."

"No. He told you to stay put. I'm not his lackey and I'm heading downtown to look for Emilio." She quaffed the last of her coffee and lurched to her feet, only slightly steadier than before.

"Yeah. Sure. That'll help." The black cat jumped down and positioned himself in her path. "You're in no condition to go anywhere. Your prodigious use of magic last night has left you weak." The Phooka clapped his paws over his mouth.

"My use of *magic*?"

The blue fire from her dream. It was real, and she had created it. Harper's head started buzzing again. This time it wasn't the hangover; it was the memory of casting the spell. Not just any spell, either. It was a fairy-frying ring of blue lightning. On the battlefield, the sensation of raw power roiling inside her had been delicious. In the wake of the released blast, she felt her life drain, like water leaving the bathtub, and then blackness. "Is that why I'm so weak?"

"Bloody noob. You drew on your own life force and nearly killed yourself. Miracle you're still alive." The Phooka snickered. When he saw Harper's downturned mouth and flashing eyes, he sat on his haunches and lifted a front foot. "On the other paw, it gave us the opening we needed to escape."

"How is this possible? I can't use magic."

"And yet there are several overcooked redcaps who would disagree with that statement." The black cat padded to the window. Standing on his back legs, he waved his paws in intricate patterns and muttered something under his breath in a language Harper couldn't understand. Gleaming spirals bloomed along the threshold, then faded. He repeated the patterns and hushed spell at every door and window.

"What're you doing?"

"Well, if we're leaving the house to go tilt at windmills, I want to make sure your delightful mother remains safe in case anyone followed us here last night. These are warding spells, should keep out the baddies."

Harper felt touched by the gesture. "Um. That's kind of you," she muttered, smoothing her messy hair from her face. She didn't ask what a warding spell was or how it worked. Her tolerance for magic and things out of legend was nearly full for the day already and she'd only just got up.

The Phooka beamed a feline smile and sauntered over to the next window. Harper's eyes narrowed. Nuada seemed like a high ranking whatever he was. He had told the Phooka to remain with her here, to protect her. And yet the Fae was all too eager to do exactly what she wanted and disobey Nuada. *Well, he seems like the rule-breaking type.* She dismissed her curiosity and raced downstairs to get dressed. Nothing from the past few days made any sense. Maybe this was just how shapeshifters were.

CHAPTER 25

"This is a terrible idea. I can't protect you as easily out here." The Phooka bounced along at Harper's heels, his canine tongue flapping with every step.

Harper refused to look at the Fae. His presence reminded her that the messed-up crap that happened over the last couple days was all too real. Acceptance of Fae and demigods wasn't in her near-term plans, even though magical creatures had taken Abraham and maybe Emilio. If she stepped into their world, she'd have to admit the situation was beyond her control and that she didn't know what to do to fix it.

The bus clattered up to the stop, squealing and grunting. The accordion doors clunked open.

"Can't bring a dog on the bus." The driver barely turned his face toward her as he spoke.

"It's a service animal."

"You don't look blind."

"I'm not. I'm crazy. Manic depression. The dog keeps me from flipping out and creating one hell of a scene." The driver eyed her. She must have looked haggard enough to pass for someone suffering from acute mental illness because he snorted and waved her on.

She dropped into the bright blue seat, plopped her rainbow unicorn backpack in the one next to her, and dialed Emilio's number. *He's OK, he just lost his phone.* The phone rang and rang while her fingers folded the seam of her jeans back and forth.

Voicemail. Again. She envisioned Emilio being led away by kelpies, and a tear trickled down her cheek. She'd failed, passed out, and left Emilio to face monsters all alone. What fools Nuada and the Phooka were to think she could help them fight a war with the Fae. She couldn't even save one of the few people in her life she cared about.

Seeing another tear roll down her cheek, the Phooka laid his head on her knee. His golden eyes looked up to Harper's tear-streaked face and he let out a whistling whine.

Harper only half glanced at him. *Oh god. Mom. I've been so focused on Emilio I left her all alone. Those spells the Phooka made. Will they keep her safe if the Fae tracked her home?* Panic launched her upright in her seat and drove some of the lingering heaviness from her body.

Eyes wide, she pressed her face up to the Phooka's canine ear. "You mentioned warding spells. Will they repel those demons and keep my mother safe?"

The Phooka growled. "Fae aren't demons."

"Will your spells protect my mom from the Fae?"

"All but the most powerful, yes."

"Will it keep out that monster with the horned skull mask? I can't believe he's Nuada's son." Harper's voice trembled. She stood to lose everyone she ever cared about in the same way she had lost her father, and to the same masked man, and Badb Catha, the evil holding his leash.

The Phooka's ears drooped and he shifted his weight to lift his face closer to hers. "Gwyn was a good man once. Being trapped in the Underworld changed a lot of us."

All Harper had seen of Gwyn was his cold, murderous side. She doubted anything else existed beneath. Her tears became a storm, her hitching breath the thunder. At her feet, the Phooka whined his canine pleas, but Harper turned her face toward the window and fought to regain control of her fears. She was thankful only a few people rode the bus today.

Emilio usually worked a shift at Powell's bookstore on Saturdays. It was close to his apartment, so she got off the bus two stops early to see if he'd gone to work.

Powell's was its usual crowded on a Saturday afternoon. The Phooka had somehow manifested a harness and handle so he looked like a real service animal. Harper slipped on her sunglasses and gripped the harness handle. The pair walked through the glass doors. Curious glances followed them, but none of the staff questioned her presence in the bookstore with a golden-eyed black dog.

Harper approached a sandy-haired employee next to the coffee shop. "Excuse me, do you work here?"

The Phooka turned his head toward the rows of bagged snacks below the register and his tongue lolled out, nose quivering inches from a bag of cheese curls.

"Heel," Harper commanded.

The Phooka chuffed but reluctantly returned to his role.

"Yes, how can I help you?" the clerk replied.

"My friend Emilio works here. Can you find him for me?"

The man shrugged. "He didn't show up this morning."

Harper's jaw clenched. "Did he call?" He was probably hungover. He was just asleep in his apartment. And yet, in the past, when he'd been in bad shape after a party, his pristine work ethic always forced him to his shift. On time, every time.

"Dunno." He shrugged again.

"Thanks."

Her stomach flipped. He was really missing. Stolen. Like Abraham. Her own hangover and emotional pain welled up. The back of her throat gave her that telltale crawling sensation that foretold she was about to lose her Irish coffee. She dropped her pack and raced her stomach to the bathroom, flinging open the stall door just in time as wave after wave of sickness wracked her.

When the moment passed, she sat on the grubby floor empty, shaking, and weeping softly. She loathed feeling powerless again. She flung her fist at the metal stall and instantly regretted it. It hurt, but at least physical pain gave her something to focus on other than helplessness.

What am I going to do? The tears slid into silent laughter. I've got to trust a shapeshifting goat thing and a strange pointy-eared man to keep my family safe. Emilio would tell me I woke up in Bizarro World.

Harper wiped her eyes on the sleeve of her black jacket and took several deep breaths. Splashing a little water on her face reduced some redness. She wiped her hands on her jeans, smoothed the purple sweatshirt, and perched the sunglasses on her nose, hoping they'd hide her puffy eyes.

She found the Phooka still in front of the wall of snacks, shoving the last little bag of cheese curls into an ornate grey satchel that had somehow appeared at his feet.

"Phooka!" she hissed. "That's stealing."

He returned an innocent look and popped a bag of potato chips inside. "I paid for them." He swung his nose to show a pile of gold coins on the counter. A wolfish grin spread over his face.

Harper rolled her eyes, snapped up his handle, and jerked him toward the door. He glared up at her and clawed a few more chocolate bars into the satchel before being dragged too far from the aisle to add any more to his junk food collection.

"Where are we going?" he asked.

"Emilio's apartment."

"And if he's not there?"

Harper hadn't allowed her thoughts to go that far. "Police station, now be—"

"Pffft." The Phooka flicked his ears. "I'm sure they'll fix everything. Definitely won't make matters worse."

Emilio's apartment was in a high-rise a few blocks from the bookstore. Harper turned and started up the street. Then she felt the Phooka pull against the harness. She gave it a little jerk to usher him forward.

"I gotta pull a Clark Kent," the Phooka said and herded her toward a dumpster.

"A what?"

"I'll need a better disguise if we're heading into an apartment building. No dogs allowed and all that. Gimme a second."

Harper sighed and dropped the harness. The Phooka sauntered behind the dumpster while a middle-aged woman with a severe-looking bob haircut sneered at Harper, no doubt disgusted she'd allow her dog to do his business behind the dumpster. Harper stuck her tongue out at the woman and she hurried away seconds before a tall black man with waist-length dreads and amber eyes stepped from behind the trash.

Under a yellow zippered hoodie, he sported a Hawaiian print shirt with red splashy flowers. Red cargo pants completed the ensemble. The Phooka slipped on a pair of yellow mirrored sunglasses. "Shall we?" His accent sounded Jamaican to Harper.

"You impersonate humans too? Why not just be human all the time in the city? A talking dog seems risky."

"I can be a human for a fairly long time, but it's still too much more mass than my natural state."

"You could just be a child, then."

"Ew."

The Phooka walked beside her in his human form, long

dreadlocks swaying with every step. Periodically, he scanned the skies and trees, fixating everywhere a crow perched.

"I have a bad feeling about this, and I don't like the look of those crows. Any one of them could be eyes for Badb Catha. We should go back to your house and wait for Nuada. Maybe he already found your friend."

Harper squinted at the black birds perched on awnings and treetops. There were an unusual number of the birds, but she had the sight now. If they were Sluagh or some kind of Fae crow, she thought that would be obvious. "I don't see any Sluagh, do you?"

"Badb's pets are far harder to pick out. They're actual crows, and if she's looking for you, she'll see us through their eyes."

His vigilance was infectious. Harper peered at every bird and child, looking for anything amiss, like rivulets of water or shiny red eyes. She was about to sigh with relief when she noticed an undulating black cloud wheel above.

Harper pointed into the sky. "Do you see that?"

The Phooka had already pulled his yellow hoodie over his face. "It's the Hunt."

Harper's jaw dropped as the Phooka's chocolate-brown hand pushed against the small of her back, propelling her forward. "Didn't Nuada say they only attacked at night?"

"Not exactly. They're weaker in daylight, but plenty strong against the two of us. Into the building." The Phooka clenched her arm right below the shoulder and yanked her toward the revolving glass doors of a corporate high-rise composed of steel and glass.

The Phooka's sneakers squeaked as he raced for the bank of elevators in the sparsely populated building, dragging Harper in his wake. She glanced over her shoulder. The Wild Hunt zoomed closer, so close she could pick out the shapes of the lead riders.

The next instant, a maelstrom of creatures swept over the river and right toward the almost transparent building. Five pale dogs slavered at the head of the oncoming storm.

The hazy memories of the battle at Mystic Island snapped into focus. Even at this distance, she recognized the Gabriel hounds. In moments the chilling tone of Gwyn's hunting horn would herald the Wild Hunt's arrival, and then they'd probably die.

The Phooka's magic satchel appeared at his side and he yanked out a long dagger and thrust it into Harper's hand. The same one Nuada had given her the night before. It promised to be more effective than her own armaments, which were mostly meant to incapacitate humans, not kill Fae. Shaking fingers curled around the grip. From out of nowhere, a sword appeared in the Phooka's hand, curved and black like a pirate scimitar.

The couple of people in the lobby gasped and scrambled away from the two people with blades in their hands. Or was it just one? Harper wasn't sure anyone else could see the Phooka right now. Outside on the drizzle-dampened street, people flowed past the building, chatting, looking at their phones, oblivious to the descending horde.

CHAPTER 26

The glamour from the warrior lasted only a few minutes this time. It had already begun to fade by the time Emilio waited just inside the building in a broad room with vaulted ceilings stretching several floors high. White marble covered the floors and interior columns. A pale gray wooden molding accented the shining stone. The group of people from the Mystic Island party clustered together in the center of the room, ringed by their captors, each with identical dreamy expressions Emilio did his best to emulate.

The winged woman sulked barely two feet from Emilio. He gazed lovingly at her and continued to pretend he was still fully under their spell lest he suffer the same fate as the poor guy in the satyr costume.

Beings of every shape and size milled about. The beautiful and the monstrous bustled through corridors and flitted in and out of rooms. More of the wiry green goblins waddled around almost everywhere he looked. He shuddered.

Thin-winged Fae like the woman guarding him glided by, their wings stirring the air above Emilio. In their wake, clouds of tiny winged pixies chattered. Glittering black eyes darted everywhere at once. A couple of them flitted over to a pair of red-and-black-clad elven knights and tugged on their hair. The elves swatted at them like they were annoying insects. Emilio caught glimpses of creatures that resembled an anthropomorphic forest floor striding down a long hallway that tucked under a dramatic double-sided stairway.

An enormous contraption at the end of the vestibule looked like something out of a steampunk movie blended seamlessly with the natural. Where a bank of elevators would have been in a normal building, loomed what looked like a gigantic round mirror. Only, the surface of the mirror didn't reflect images; instead, it shifted and shimmered in an everchanging kaleidoscope.

That mesmerizing circle was framed by a golden tree with silver foliage that someone had coaxed into a perfect circle. Branches of the tree split from the center but continued to follow the curvature of the trunk. Emilio couldn't identify it. He had never seen anything like it growing in the woods of Oregon.

His eyes followed the branches to where they tapered into silvery glowing filaments, hundreds of them leading away from the portal on either side. As they wound along the floor, they braided themselves together to form luminescent cords. Emilio followed the looping cords to where they split once more into smaller threads that formed a web of links feeding into rows and stacks of cages serviced by machinery bristling with levers and gears.

Emilio's stomach and jaw clenched. Inside cages large and small huddled Fae of every shape and size. More green monsters, tiny winged Fae, and a gorgeous male who looked like a chocolate-skinned but blond version of the dark-haired warrior all hunched in their prisons. The blond elf reached a hand through the bars to comfort something that looked like a woman crossed with a frog. He twined his fingers in her long green hair and she twisted her face to rest it in his palm.

Suddenly, the surface in the circular tree pulsed and

shimmered. The denizens of the cages turned their heads toward it, their wailing and moaning echoing off the marble walls. Cages rocked under the thrashing of limbs, either from a futile escape attempt or because the process that began hurt. Emilio couldn't be sure. The chorus of wails increased in pitch as pulses of light traveled from their bodies where the shining leads terminated, zipped along the filaments, and entered the tree.

Once the streams of energy reached its branches, the rippling surface in the center thinned and became transparent. Through it, a dimly lit wood stretched, populated with the same gnarled trees he'd seen outside. They wore similar cloaks of fog.

Something big emerged on the other side, lumbering toward the gateway. Three of them. Nine feet tall and ugly. Mossy beards stretched over long torsos. Arms that terminated in long branchlike claws dragged on the ground as they shambled on stumpy legs covered in mottled grey bark that also covered every part of their bodies. Step by plodding step brought them closer and closer to the glittering surface, that Emilio realized with a shock was the gateway to another world.

He recalled old fairy stories he'd read as a child. Tale after tale of unwitting souls stepping into their world, the very same world that had to be on the other side of that big round tree. If a mortal returned from that world, they crumbled to dust with their first footfall back in this world, for time passed differently in fairyland. They were the lucky ones. Most died or went mad in moments.

Other stories percolated up from childhood. Tales of people being forced to dance until they died. Others of their gentry forcing women to bear and foster fairy children. And some of fairies dining on their victims in the most gruesome ways. Emilio's feet were planted mere yards from that world now, where a pack of monsters that looked like the human-eating variety of Fae seemed ready to step through.

The trio stepped up to the glimmering membrane and pushed

against it. The surface bulged but didn't break. Undaunted, the group dug their feet into the ground and launched their shoulders at the gate. It bowed but held strong. The beings in the cages pounded on the bars and screamed. Why would these Fae imprison their own while opening the doors for others? None of this made any sense.

"Bloody spriggans. Gonna drain the lot to get them through. And for what? Slow. Stupid. Useless." A nasty looking little fellow with a bright red cap continued muttering at the gate, bolted across to the other side, and pushed a lever up another notch. He flipped switches, turned cranks, and spun gears. Wails of pain pitched higher, cages shook, and the trickle of light escaping the prisoners became so bright, Emilio was forced to drop his eyes.

Oh god. They're draining them for power. Emilio knew nothing about Fae culture, whether each species here had its own customs and leaders or whether they were all one people. They seemed to live in this building together somehow. His stomach clenched at the way they so casually tortured their own. Even though it was Fae who held him captive, nothing deserved this. Nothing. He wanted desperately to cover his ears with his hands to drown out the wailing, but that would alert his captors to the fact that he was, by some fluke, immune to their magic. And so he smoothed the wrinkles of disgust trying to form along the bridge of his nose, forced his eyebrows to drift apart, pulled the corners of his mouth into a half smile, and stood as still as a statue while he endured the sounds of torture.

The trio of wood monsters jostled and pushed against the portal. Passage through it must harm them too, because deep bellows escaped long, grimacing faces. With a final shove they broke through and the screeching of the prisoners reached a crescendo before tapering into whimpering. The little red-capped fellow beckoned to his near-identical little friends, who stomped over and opened several cages. Tiny hands dragged out motionless creatures and deposited them into piles next to the cages while the survivors wept.

The little amphibian woman was one of the dead. Her beautiful brown-skinned companion sobbed and screamed her name over and over. Rana. Her name had been Rana. Even though the pair were utterly alien to him and they bore no observable difference to the Fae that held him prisoner now, Emilio's heart ached for the couple.

He was only slightly relieved to see no humans in the cages. At least it didn't suggest being a battery for a gate to hell would be his fate. Nevertheless, his mind raced with the dark possibilities of what might be in store for him. Maybe he was food for these demons, like the man they'd sent into the misty cocoon thing. Or maybe they'd killed so many of the creatures in the cages, they needed human slave labor for essential tasks.

He forced a languor to his limbs with every breath, fighting against the knots of fear twisting his muscles. One twitch might betray his secret.

Emilio didn't have a lot of time to indulge in worry. A duo of the redcaps scuttled over to the winged lady and the warrior, motioning them to one of the large sweeping marble staircases that flanked the portal.

"That stinking doctor is ready for them now, head up," it said.

They were on the move again. Emilio feared what awaited them up those stairs would be worse than what he had just witnessed.

The group from the festival passed silently by the three spriggans. Each was crisscrossed in the same leathery scars his captors wore; one was missing an eye. Elves guided the spriggans out the front door to enjoy their new habitat in wherever the hell they were right now.

Emilio lost track of how many floors they ascended, but he

guessed when they finally turned down a long hallway, they must be at least ten floors up.

A meticulously dressed blond-haired man met them midway down the hall. Full lips smirked beneath large moody eyes. This man lacked any of the scars he had seen on the others, and Emilio swore he knew the guy.

Where have I seen this dude before? The knowledge hung just out of reach. Every swipe he took at the information sent it fluttering farther away. Only when the man spoke did the realization of who he was dawn on him.

Shit. It's my boss.

CHAPTER 27

"Into the elevator!" the Phooka shouted, furiously motioning Harper into the steel box.

"What? We'll be trapped!" The only thing she feared more than being attacked by the Wild Hunt was being trapped in a tiny box surrounded by the Wild Hunt.

The Phooka winced and edged into the elevator, lifting his feet high, hands glued to his sides. "Seriously. Don't you know anything at all about my people? It's steel. Iron can kill Fae if we touch it too long."

"What are we going to do, stay in the elevator until Nuada happens by to save us?"

"If you stop asking silly questions, we can try to get to one of the stairwells and escape from another exit."

"What about the people out there?"

The Phooka didn't answer and Harper didn't have a better plan, so she leapt into the elevator. Behind her, glass exploded and the Gabriel hounds' snarls echoed in the empty vestibule. God, they were fast. As the doors pulled closed, Harper marveled at the people surrounding the building. They gaped at the exploding glass yet were oblivious to the hell hounds and nightmare creatures reeling over their heads.

Wide eyed and panting, she hammered the button to the fifth floor over and over until the elevator lurched upward. The Wild Hunt had found them. Panic clawed at the edges of her mind.

Beside her, the Phooka closed his eyes and muttered under his breath. "Never figured you'd be religious," Harper said.

"I'm trying to call Nuada to us. It's a long shot. If he's on that island, he'll probably not hear me."

The elevator dinged and the door slid open. Harper held the dagger in front of her, the point of the weapon quivering. Beside her, the Phooka poised his sword across his body and covered their retreat. The fifth floor was empty as far as she could see. They ran.

"Coast is clear. I always wanted to say that," the Phooka said. Legs pumped and arms swung. The door at the end of the hallway felt very far away. The next one at the bottom of five flights of stairs seemed like another zip code.

The same ancient instinct that froze rabbits in their tracks when a hawk glided by yanked Harper to a halt. Her head revolved inch by inch toward a movement that flashed in the corner of her eye. Terror glued her feet to the floor while the Phooka sprinted ahead.

"Phooka!" she shouted and pointed. He careened around and his yellow eyes widened.

Through the glass windows, they could see the Hunt soaring up the side of the building, galloping toward the sky as though the vertical edge of the skyscraper were a paved road. Broad hooves churned the surrounding drizzle followed by flying elves, goblins, and more, all peering down through the tinted glass in their effort to locate their quarry.

Gwyn must have noticed their movement inside the hallway through the windows of the outermost offices because he pulled his mount to a halt and guided the beast into an upright position, parallel to the street below. The Gabriel hounds broke from their ascent and circled back to their master's side. The bone-white skull mask's fiery sockets bored right through Harper while its wearer hovered, his red-eared canine companions slavering and gnashing their teeth while the Wild Hunt Sidhe fanned out behind him. Harper could almost feel him smile as he lowered his sword, pointing it at her chest.

He swiveled and raced away from the building, his Fae host trailing behind him. Wait. He'd definitely seen her. Why were they retreating? Realization dawned on her just as Gwyn banked and barreled straight toward the building.

"Keep running!" the Phooka shouted.

Harper's body unfroze and she tore off toward the stairway door, feet pounding the floor. She hoped the stairs were the same industrial textured metal most buildings had. Their only hope now was that the iron would slow the enemy Fae down, which would leave only Gwyn, who was not Fae.

The crash and tinkle of broken glass exploded behind them. Harper couldn't resist checking over her shoulder as she sprinted. Gwyn burst into the hallway, turning the grisly mask toward her. The front hooves of his black horse flailed in the air. The animal completely filled the narrow hallway, forcing Gwyn to dismount to continue his pursuit.

He slid from the horse's back and swirled his broadsword in one fluid movement. The Gabriel hounds collected behind him. More and more of the Wild Hunt poured into the building through the gaping hole they'd blasted. Smaller and faster, the goblins loped ahead of Gwyn, filling the hallway, some of them racing along the vertical walls. Then their leader sprinted straight for Harper.

The Phooka grabbed her arm. "Everybody knows you never look back. That's when you fall and the guy with the chainsaw gets you."

"This is worse than the movies, Phooka. Movies can't kill."

"Really? I've seen plenty that made me want to die. *Zardoz*. *The Fifth Element . . . The—*"

"Phooka!" Harper yelled.

The pair scurried the last few steps to the stairwell. The Phooka drew back, unwilling to touch the metal door handle with his bare hands. Harper yanked the door open and they careened into the stairwell.

The tiny rectangular window framed the goblin hoard and the masked man striding toward his quarry with a loose swagger to his steps. They didn't even bother to hurry now. Gwyn's bearded face broke into a slow smile beneath the mask's edge. He pulled a horn to his lips and blasted a clarion call. Behind him, his army jeered and shouted, a sea of jagged yellow smiles and flailing claws.

Harper thundered down the stairs. The Phooka looked queasy and he pointed up. "High ground" was all he could manage.

"We stand a better chance under the cover of trees and buildings."

"The people here don't. Gwyn won't care about collateral damage." The Phooka gripped his stomach and doubled over. "I can fly us off the roof."

"Are you OK?" She needed him to fight if they had any chance at all of escape. Should he be too weak to take a shape big enough to carry her, getting trapped on a rooftop with the Wild Hunt didn't feel like much of a plan.

"Iron." *That's why he's woozy.* Harper's wish had come true. The doors, stairs, and railing were all steel.

The Phooka's human shape faded at the edges like a lens losing focus. In seconds a black wolf wearing bright yellow Wellington boots slavered in the stairwell.

"You really should be a bear if you're going to wear those. And you're missing the yellow hat."

"We're hopelessly outclassed, outnumbered, and about to die

and you pop off with snark." He and Harper dashed up the stairs, taking two at a time. "You're getting better at this!"

The goblins burst through the door below, hissing and gnashing their teeth. Harper risked a glance over the handrails. A chorus of bloodcurdling screams echoed through the building as the iron seared their skin. The acrid smell of burning hair and flesh saturated the air as goblins fell to the floor, writhing. Their bodies sizzled and popped, and then they were still. The horde was in a frenzy, the grisly deaths of their companions not slowing their assault; in fact, it only made them angrier and louder. They cackled and screeched. More and more pressed their way through the narrow door, followed by swarms of little blue pixies zigzagging forward, showing silvery needles for teeth.

The pixies hovered above the metal. The Phooka paused and used a paw to dig a bag of powder from his satchel. He tossed it to Harper. "Open this and blow it on the pixies. It'll freeze them."

Harper grabbed a handful of silvery dust and blew it down over the pixies. Their veined wings stopped beating, and they fell to the metal floor. For an instant the onslaught slowed as the tiny bodies and writhing goblins piled up so high they partially blocked the entrance. Then one of the elves placed a gloved hand on the doorframe and kicked the suffering goblins up the stairwell, making grisly stepping-stones for more of the Wild Hunt to pursue their quarry.

Harper and the Phooka used the time to scurry up another flight of stairs. A deep and resonant voice called up to them. "Bad move, little girl. You've just made every Fae in my Wild Hunt furious. No telling what they'll do now."

Something steely rose in Harper. She had had enough of goddamn fairies ruining her life. "Won't your boss be pissed if one of her idiot lackeys damages her prize?"

Beside her, the Phooka laughed.

Her reply was a howl of rage from Gwyn ap Nudd. He lunged

over his fallen goblins and into the stairwell, more elves pressing in behind him. The Sidhe coughed as the fumes of iron entered their lungs. Gwyn seemed unaffected. He charged up the stairs. The goblins and smaller Fae had given up, their mostly naked little bodies no match for the exposed steel in the stairway, but their alien faces peeked through the doorway. Harper and the Phooka turned and bolted up more floors.

They reached the last floor with a small head start on the Sidhe and their masked leader. Harper reached back to fling open the door to the roof. It didn't budge. Locked. They were trapped.

"Damn! Can we make it down a flight to the hallway?" Harper said.

"Our only hope is the iron bottleneck of these stairs. We get back out into a hallway, we're dead."

Slim hope. A black wolf and a woman whose only practice with a blade was in a dojo. And that one was made of wood. At least it'd be over fast. Harper gripped the dagger and tried to draw on the magic she had cast last night. She focused on building the storm of energy in her core. Not even a stir, likely still tapped out. Then she tried to feel magic in the air and envisioned it soaking into her. Still nothing.

Gwyn's laugh was wicked as the macabre mask tilted up at the pair. Only a single floor separated them now. The Phooka stepped in front of Harper, weapon directed at the Wild Hunt. She swallowed the lump in her throat.

"What are you waiting for, Skeletor? Or are you afraid I'll electrocute you like last night?" Her words suggested a bravado she didn't feel.

"Come with me now, and your friend, at least, won't be harmed."

The door below Gwyn blew open. Nuada crashed through the door on the landing Gwyn stood on, barreling him over and knocking an elf into the handrail. Harper could hear the hiss as the railing burned her face. She screamed.

Nuada had a pair of short swords drawn. The ornate scabbard at his hip still held the longer of his weapons. Harper sighed with relief. The Phooka's spell had worked. They were saved.

In the impact, Gwyn's blazing mask flew from his face, and Harper met the eyes of the man who probably murdered her father. She'd expected a demon, or at least the cold visage of a mercenary to whom life meant little. But instead she saw a bearded man with a blue spiral tattoo beneath his right eye, and he wore same bone-weary look as every broken, downtrodden soul she'd ever known. The same hollow hopelessness that whatever low state his life languished in now was all there was or would ever be.

"Your timing sucks," the Phooka shouted.

"I thought it was rather on point," Nuada replied. "You're still alive."

He began a whirling dance with his swords. Elven blades rose in defense. The clang of metal on metal reverberated in the stairwell. He was succeeding in holding them back until more goblins and redcaps pushed the hallway door open; they had strapped various items from the empty offices onto their feet. Some wore bits of cardboard box, others had wrapped their limbs in sweaters, and one had manila interoffice mail envelopes held to his feet with about fifty rubber bands. They forced Nuada several steps up the stairs toward Harper.

Some Sidhe fighters pushed past him to meet the Phooka's teeth, but avoiding the iron made them slow. Powerful jaws snapped around the leg of a tall elf.

No longer shocked at the sight of the Fae, Harper's self-defense training kicked in, emotions switched off, and she was on the autopilot made possible by years of practice. She engaged a shorter Sidhe woman, but she was still no match for Fae speed.

The woman's blade whirred around Harper. The sharp edge bit into her arm and once into her thigh. Adrenalin kept her from feeling much pain. Undaunted, Harper worked her blade under one of the warrior's strikes and gashed her side, but it cost her her dagger as the elf quickly recovered, wrapped an armored elbow over the blade, and jerked the weapon from her hand. Harper's dagger clanged down the stairs and out of her reach.

Gwyn slashed forward and drove his father back several steps. Nuada's double blades wove in and out of Gwyn's broadsword. Sparks flew from blades crashing against the tight walls.

While father locked son in combat, three elven warriors launched themselves over the heads of Nuada and Gwyn and landed in front of Harper, swords drawn. Goblins followed, sharp yellowed teeth bared. They were being overrun. Harper thought of what would happen to her mother and Emilio and people like Abraham if she died here in this stairwell. She was the only person who'd know what happened to them. It surprised her that her concern extended to Nuada and the Phooka. They were battling the strongest enemies, so it was up to her to save them somehow, but she was weaponless.

In front of her, Nuada's blades moved so fast they blurred. Her eyes fell to the sheathed sword at his hip. It was the only weapon in sight. Her hand shot around the fold of his coat, and her fingers found the grip.

The weapon sang a high pure note as it leapt from its sheath. Time slowed, like a movie scene in slow motion. Nuada glanced over his shoulder at her, jaw slack, eyebrows high. The Phooka's currently canine face mirrored the Tuatha's. But what bewildered Harper the most was the look of abject terror on the faces of the three elves before her.

A second ago they had been fierce, almost gloating. Did they think just because Harper drew a bigger sword, she was suddenly more skilled with a long blade? She soon had her answer.

Raw power surged into her palm from the sword. It blazed through her entire body like she drank lava. The weapon forced her into a fighting stance and positioned itself to do maximal damage as though it were the master and she merely its puppet. Its compulsion to cut them all down coursed through her blood. She fed it all her rage at her father's death, the kidnapping of her friend, and the shattering of her life. The blade drank in her fury and surged in her grip. It took all her strength to maintain her hold; it felt like it would leap out of her hand. The ancient weapon whispered in words she didn't understand, but she felt their meaning. Cool and satiny, the sword's voice called her to righteous battle, sang of sweet victory.

"You drew it. Surrender to it!" Nuada's voice called back at her. She remembered then. The Claimh Solias, Sword of Light. Once unsheathed, no foe could prevail against it. She had drawn it against these elves.

Harper surrendered to the desires of the sword, and the two of them became one being. She was the eyes of the blade, and it piloted her body through a deadly tango of destruction. The weapon drew strength from her and she gave it willingly. Her movements with it were efficient, not even a twitch wasted. And she was fast. Suddenly much faster than these elves. She parried and dodged effortlessly. A few quick strokes and all three elves sprawled dead at her feet in a tangled pile.

Gwyn faltered at the sight of his vanquished warriors, allowing Nuada to slice into his sword arm. He howled and his weapon clanked on the stairwell. His sword arm hung useless and dripping blood.

Nuada thrust out a hand toward the door to the roof of the building. It flew open with a blast of invisible force. "Go! Onto the roof," he shouted. The Phooka grabbed a goblin by the shoulder and flung it over the railing. The way clear, he bounded through the door.

Harper held the sword high over her head and shouted at Nuada. "No! We can destroy them. All of them!" Her hazel eyes gleamed with a smoldering fire. She wanted more than anything to use this sword to kill every last member of the Wild Hunt. Make them leave her family alone, exact her vengeance on them for kidnapping Emilio. Then she'd find the kelpies and Badb and make them pay too. After that, she'd hunt down all the rest of the evil Fae. None of them would hurt anyone else ever again. The sword wanted that too. It whispered that together they would raze any empire that stood against them and usher in a world of peace for all.

Power and fury coursed through her veins, hardening her heart to a dense stone. The surrounding air crackled with the same blue light she had somehow summoned the previous night. The blade amplified it, feeding on years of accumulated rage. Rage for her father. Rage at the inept police. Rage at her stolen dreams. Rage at everything that kept her trapped and failing everyone around her. Because of her union with the sword, she could feel the life force of the smaller Fae. She wouldn't make the mistake of using her own energy to lash out with her blue fire. Not this time. Oh no. She'd drain them. Sacrifice their wretched lives to strike down the rest of these elves and Gwyn. She reveled in the terror in their eyes. Those eyes told her they knew what she and the Claimh Solias were capable of.

A firm hand gripped her sword arm. Nuada, his pale eyes grave. "Harper. Return the sword to its sheath. You do not know what you are doing. It served its purpose. We can escape. If you use this weapon in anger, you'll be lost. Forever."

"I can save us," she shouted at Nuada, tears beginning to stream down her face. His touch had roused her from the stream of thought.

"You already have, but we need to go. Now. Before they

regroup. Even with that sword, one person cannot fight a war. Emilio needs you."

The mention of Emilio blunted her anger. She dropped the sword from over her head, her chest heaving with exertion and emotion. One last delicious look at the terrified eyes of her enemies and she passed the weapon to its rightful owner.

As Nuada sheathed the blade, he cupped her chin in his hand with a reassuring smile. Then both of them turned and sprinted for the roof. Gwyn and the remains of his Wild Hunt thundered behind them once the sword was in its sheath, but they couldn't catch them.

Nuada and Harper shot through the door onto the roof to come face to face with an enormous black dragon. A Night Fury. Harper smiled despite the recent horrors. "Really?"

"What? I love Toothless." The Phooka crouched for them to hop aboard his broad back.

"You really watch too many movies," Harper said. With a weary half smile, she scrambled onto his back.

The remnants of Gwyn's horde stood behind him. Injured elves leaned on each other for support. The Gabriel hounds circled their master. They made no effort at pursuit.

Emilio crowded into an exam room along with a couple dozen more victims from Mystic Island. He kept his eyes straight ahead and unfocused, staring right into the elaborate black breastplate of an elven guard. He kept his mind from dwelling on the horror show around him by counting the thorns on the roses carved into the thin armor. When the Fae's cold eyes found him, he slackened his jaw for good measure. These Sidhe elves hadn't noticed Emilio's wakeful state and Emilio planned to keep it that way. It was his only advantage.

He'd been only nine years old when his family crossed the El Salvador border, escaping the gangs and poverty that had gutted his town. His mother and grandmother had taught him the fine art of keeping his head down and not being noticed, even when fear screamed for you to do crazy things like run or try to reason with the people whose boots rested on your neck. When the wolves closed in, silence and stillness provided the space to assess the situation and locate your assets. It was the same now, except the oppressors had wings and claws, but abusers functioned much the same everywhere.

As much as he could manage, he sneaked glances around the room. Laboratory equipment of every kind packed shelves and cabinets. Completely unsecured. Maybe the Sidhe and their minions didn't realize that chemicals and equipment could be weapons. There had to be something in here he could use, but further plans would have to wait. Too much activity suddenly happened around him.

A human man in a lab coat rose from his desk at the back of the room and strode forward to meet Emilio's elven captor. He brushed a stray lock of salt and pepper hair out of his face and adjusted his glasses by pushing the center up the sweaty bridge of his nose. The man tried to steady his hands by gripping them tight in front of him.

"G-good evening, Callon, new subjects?" The man's voice almost squeaked at the end.

Callon sneered at the scientist like he had stepped in something vile. "Not the usual malodorous dregs, Doctor Jones. These cattle are younger and better fed."

"The beasts are still malodorous," the sylph said.

"Well they are human filth, Zalille. They're all disgusting." Callon's face pulled into an arrogant smirk and bored into the doctor. The sylph beside him nodded her agreement, pointed nose lifting to the ceiling.

Dr. Jones smiled the way you smile to calm a snarling dog. He clapped his hands together. "Very good, very good. And, um, these are the strongest from the Wild Hunt's harvest?" The doctor couldn't hide the quaver in his voice.

"Let us hope they fare better in your experiments. Zalille and I will miss you ever so much if you fail this time."

"This group meets all the requirements you set for us. We don't fail our mistress." Zalille hovered a few feet from the floor and glared down her shoulder at the doctor.

"Yes. Well, uh, uh, thank you." The doctor put on a wide smile that ended up looking more like a wince. "Let's get them prepared."

"I do hope you don't fail us again, Doctor." The owner and CEO of Erimus ambled into the room. Breas leaned for a moment in the door jamb and lowered his head so he was looking at Jones out of the tops of his eyes.

The doctor literally squirmed and fiddled with his identification badge.

I picked the wrong company to intern at. Human experiments. Elves. Secret labs. Emilio let one shoulder sag to tilt his head down and away from Breas. He doubted the lofty CEO even knew he existed, but better to be cautious.

"No, no, no. The homeless are far too weak for the Abraxas Project, even with a genetic match. These are much stronger, able to withstand the physical strain from my process. Once we extract some bone marrow, we'll be able to identify the best candidates for a new trial." Dr. Jones's shaking hand pushed his round glasses back up the bridge of his nose. He was quivering like a chihuahua.

The clip clop of hard-soled shoes approaching the room announced a new arrival. Gleaming black boots strode at the edge line of Emilio's sight. The woman wearing them came to a rest beside Breas. Emilio lifted his head ever so slightly to glimpse a woman with red hair cascading underneath a headdress with branching black horns.

Every Fae and human worker snapped upright at her approach, but Emilio didn't need their reaction to tell him she reigned here. She radiated power and authority. The woman stalked a slow path along the besotted people and then resumed her place next to Breas. A long transparent skirt cascaded over the skin-tight brocade black pants she wore.

A velvety voice oozed from ruby-red lips. "Doctor, your need for better stock has presented us with an additional problem. No one misses the indigent, so we had the luxury of all the failed experiments you could dream up. But these have family who will, no doubt, be searching for their lost treasures. There is no margin of error. We can't raise the mortals' suspicions again until we are ready for our first strike."

The doctor lowered his head and stammered. "Wi-wi-with much respect, it's not as risky as you think, Highness. A good many of our young guests are college kids and transient festival hoppers. No one will miss them or take reports of their disappearance seriously for weeks at least. We're close to a deal with the warden of Columbia Correctional to secure more young, healthy subjects than we dreamed. Subjects no one will search for."

"Even animals have more regard for their own. Disgusting." Callon wrinkled his nose and turned his back to the doctor.

Badb nodded. "Indeed."

"Don't forget the Tuatha defended humans to the point where they surrendered the entire Green World to them. It's no wonder your brethren cower in the Undying Lands now." Breas tilted his head to smirk at his partner.

"Come now, are you still nursing wounds of your failing as the Tuatha king?"

"And yet it was I who helped you keep your little secret from them for hundreds of years after your people cast me out."

"That was long ago. Today you have fulfilled your promise to me with the lab and staff, and now a continuous flow of subjects. Why do you remain?"

"I'm hurt." Breas placed the back of his hand on his forehead and slumped. "When your own people refused to see the warning in your prophecy and the wisdom of your solution, I was the sole person who supported you. Even your sisters did not."

Badb sighed. "Only because I helped you avoid a worse fate. As you pointed out, that was long ago. Today, the Fomorians work hand in glove with the humans, driving their *corporations* to new heights. Because of that, your people have profited the most from human crimes against land, air, and sea. You stand to lose all that if we succeed."

"But I stand to profit even more when our war makes me the ruler of my people. Fomorians will still prosper. I will merely prosper more. Getting my revenge on Nuada and the Tuatha for taking my throne from me is a delicious side benefit."

Badb raised an eyebrow. "That's a very human attitude."

Terror warred with curiosity and Emilio struggled to make sense of what he was hearing. These monsters were gearing up for a war with people. He'd never seen an elf or a goblin before today, and he certainly couldn't imagine why beings who chose to hide themselves would be on the warpath now. In any event, how would this handful of magical creatures overcome just this city much less all the nations of the world?

Realization jolted him. Dust. It made him want to do anything for his captors. If one of them had only asked, he would have torn someone apart limb from limb. He was their new soldier, along with everyone the Dust pulled under its sway. And the drug spread like wildfire through the streets of Portland. His knees felt suddenly weak.

Dr. Jones and Callon maneuvered their group along a back wall. A pair of the little redcaps moved along the line and handed out fresh clothes. Green scrubs and white tank tops. As each person received their clothes, they stripped and pulled on their new outfits under the direction of Callon. The leathery little redcap shoved Emilio's clothes into his hand. Emilio studiously imitated the actions of the others, fully aware of the cost should his acting slip.

On the other side of the room, Breas draped himself over a chair. Emilio hoped they'd keep talking. He wanted to overhear as much about their plans as possible, uncover some weakness in it he could use to escape.

"We share a common vision with the people of this human culture in particular. The United States accomplished what even the great Fomorian empire could not, albeit with a little guidance from us. In less than a hundred years, they have bent this land fully to their wishes and the strong profit from it. The weak, well, without the weak you wouldn't have so much chattel for your grand plans."

Badb rose to her feet and leaned over her companion. She pressed a slender finger between his eyes. "Even with Balor long dead along with his massive, scorching eye, its burning gaze merely migrated to a new home in humanity. Millions of tiny consuming eyes in place of the giant one, seeing a thing and immediately calculating how they can cut it down, rip it from the earth, and shape it to meet only their needs."

"Yes! Isn't it wonderful?" Breas said and laughed while spinning the wheeled chair in a circle. "We've put down our blades and become businessmen, and now a handful of Fomorians rule the world."

Badb fell silent and reached a long arm out to a crow gliding through the door. The bird landed on her outstretched wrist and sidled along her arm. Coming to rest on her shoulder, the bird muttered and clacked its beak. Badb reached out her other hand and stroked its neck, the warm smile on her face at odds with the casual cruelty of this secret place.

The crow croaked in Badb's ear, the series of rough squawks resembling a sentence. The avian words brought a storm over her porcelain features. Her teeth bared. Her brow creased. With her fist clenched at her side, she rounded on Breas, who was still talking.

"All the same, your concern about the other Fomorians is well placed. They may fight against us if they believe their position at the top of the economic food chain—" He tilted his head, a single brow arched.

"Fiach tells me we have a more immediate threat to deal with."

"Oh?" Breas rose and smoothed the wrinkles from his suit. "And what is that?"

Badb motioned the elf and his sylph friend to her side.

Emilio split his attention between the plotting of his enemies and the actions of the doctor and slipped into his drab new outfit. Nearby, the doctor prepared a series of very large hypodermic needles that made Emilio's insides clench. His attention flicked to the redcaps. They wheeled wooden gurneys with leather straps behind each of the prisoners. Emilio's breathing became fast and shallow. Whatever would happen to him was starting right now, and it would be terrible enough that they were strapping them all down.

The Fae joined Badb and Breas barely three feet from Emilio and inclined their heads.

Emilio wasn't sure how much longer he could feign stupor. Mounting panic set off a klaxon inside his skull broadcasting only a single message: Run. But his rational side argued he'd never make it out alive. His life narrowed to two choices. Obey his interior alarm system and make a suicide run or endure whatever hellish hybrid of magic and medicine waited. Aside from that one choice, he was powerless. The only card he had to play was to remain unnoticed.

"Callon. Zallile. I have an assignment of the utmost importance for you." The two bowed deeply before Badb.

"Anything, mistress." Zallile's voice rang high and pure.

"Gather as many elves, sylphs, and other gentry as we can spare. Rouse the kelpies from their pond. The Wild Hunt has sustained heavy casualties in pursuit of the girl who cast the spell last night. They're of no more help for now." A look of fury spread across her face and she ground out each word through gritted teeth. Her hand clenched and unclenched at her hip.

"Casualties? But how? A lower Fae and a human girl could never prevail against a single Sidhe warrior," Callon said.

"Fiach has been tracking the girl for a couple of days. Seems Nuada and his shapeshifter friend have found an heir. Harper O'Neill. It was she who interrupted the Wild Hunt last night, and moments ago, the three of them battled Gwyn's forces in the city. Fiach discovered the girl has a home where her mother also lives. She will, no doubt, go there soon, and you will be waiting when she does." Badb's eyes flashed.

Harper. Emilio's knees almost buckled. In hindsight, she'd been right about skipping Mystic Island.

A group of redcaps seized him with leathery hands, hoisted him onto a gurney, and strapped him down. Gnarled fingers wormed over copper buckles while breath reeking of rotting meat wafted over his face. In moments he lay immobile, lined up next to the other abductees.

The sylph bowed low to Badb. "Mistress, we will not fail you. We'll bring her broken body and cast it at your feet."

"No," Badb said. "Bring her to me alive. She has something that belongs to me. Fiach tells me she used a familiar magic—my sister's. This is the heir foolish Macha tried to hide from me with her geis and the remains of her power. She will die, but only after I tear it from her to stabilize our gateway below."

Breas and the two Fae rushed out into the hallway. Emilio clenched his teeth to hold back screams of fear and frustration. The cords in his neck bulged, but no one noticed.

Badb leaned down to examine the tray of needles and surgical tools then fixed the doctor with a glare. "It pains me that your progress has been so slow. You have everything you asked for. You'd better not fail this time."

Dr. Jones blinked rapidly and continued to study Badb's tall black boots. "Y-y-yes, Highness. I am confident some in this group will be perfect candidates for Project Abraxas."

The redcap grumbled and pulled the straps even tighter so that Emilio's arms and legs hurt. Emilio's body locked up. He couldn't move, his eyes were wide, and he was panting. Soon the monsters would notice he wasn't in la-la land anymore and probably slaughter him on the spot. Right now he'd welcome their spell just so he wouldn't have to be awake for this.

Several more human assistants appeared from the hallway and hooked up the others to an IV drip. Emilio's head rolled back and forth on his pillow like he could deny the reality of whatever invasive testing was about to occur. Fear took over and overrode his ability to pretend. His legs twisted against the straps, but the bonds bound him tight.

Just as a red-haired woman dressed in scrubs approached Emilio with a hypodermic that looked long enough to lance clean through his shoulder, his head dropped to the side. He met the gaze of a black man whose eyes rolled with terror. He was awake too. The man's screams pulled the attention from Emilio.

The needle slid into Emilio's arm.

CHAPTER 29

Late afternoon had faded into evening. The twinkling lights of Portland shone below through gaps in the clouds, betraying no sign of the supernatural war. The city looked peaceful and beautiful, like a faceted jewel set into the mountains. Harper imagined hipsters clustered inside bars sipping microbrews, and vegans deciding which of the plethora of meat-free restaurants they would go to for dinner. All of them blissfully unaware how much their world had changed.

A glance at the scaly cartoon dragon she rode shattered any illusion that her own world would ever be normal again. Toothless the Phooka glided high, only occasionally flapping his great wings to catch the next thermal, making the wind whip Harper's hair. They soared at an elevation allowing a view of the entire city below. Nothing held her on the dragon's back except her own grip. She should be freaking out right now, but her lack of fear surprised her.

Harper watched Nuada continually scan the skies and occasionally whispering in that strange language she didn't understand.

"Is something following us?" she asked.

"I do not sense any Fae, but Gwyn is far more difficult to locate. We can't land until I am sure he is not tracking us."

"Aren't we a flying target up here? Wouldn't it be better to find a place to hide down there?" Harper jerked her head toward the ground, unwilling to release her grip on the Phooka.

The Phooka rumbled an affirmative. "The Hunt tucked tail and ran. I think it's safe to land. Besides, holding this large a form is exhausting me."

"Gwyn rarely gives up so easily, and we stand a better chance of seeing him first up here. Give it a few more minutes," Nuada said.

Gwyn's face during the skirmish floated in Harper's mind. Without thinking she spoke out loud. "Gwyn wasn't what I expected, you know, for a guy in a skull mask on a murderous rampage."

Nuada scrunched around to face her as best he could. "You expected him to be more like the mask?" His voice was tinged with sadness.

Harper lifted her face to the night sky and caught the twinkle of a cluster of stars in a break in the clouds. "Something like that. But he looked . . . Well, he just looked tired." She looked into Nuada's icy blue eyes. "And sad."

"He's sad all right, a sad excu—"

Nuada thumped the Phooka on the flank with a dark gray boot.

"My son never understood why I cast him in the role I did. And he hated it, hated me. When the first humans arrived on Ireland, an opportunity presented itself to escape his fate, and he took it. The first human to die in Ireland became the new Lord of the Dead and later created the Sluagh."

"Those zombie bird things?" Harper wrinkled her nose.

Nuada nodded. "But why did you make him the Lord of the Dead if he didn't want the job?"

"The place the Tuatha came from is different in ways I can't easily explain to you. But when we arrived in the Green World, living here wasn't as easy as we thought. We struggled. Made mistakes. I had to create and maintain a certain order." His forehead creased and the corners of his mouth edged down. "I thought I knew best. Gwyn was the kindest of us. The first of us born in this wondrous new world. Who better to guide the souls of the dead back to the source? Or so I thought."

"And then daddy's little boy went all *Rebel Without a Cause*, got himself a scary mask, and went to the dark side," the Phooka said.

"Is that true?" Harper asked.

Nuada shook his head. "I don't know what happened after I returned to the Undying Lands. I have no clear grasp of the hold Badb has over him or why. But I have to hope he can one day be redeemed."

Nuada turned away from her then, apparently done talking about his son for now. That's why he didn't use his magical blade on the leader of the Wild Hunt, Harper thought. He held out hope for his son. The same son who along with his friend Badb had murdered her father.

Harper shivered, not just from the cold. Her eyes strayed to the silver sword dangling from Nuada's hip. When she held it, she'd become so much more than the frightened little girl she felt like now. She'd felt even stronger than when she'd used magic.

Memories of the luminous destructive energy spell she somehow cast at Mystic Island terrified her. She hadn't believed or wanted to believe anything Nuada told her. Until the moment magic ripped through her body, she'd convinced herself she could leave all the Dark Boys, harp-playing demons, and mumbo-jumbo about being some lost heir far behind. She'd sink back into the well-worn armchair of her dead-end job and the game of whack-a-mole she played, keeping her mother stable and a roof over their heads.

Not that she wanted to go gallivanting off with Nuada and the Phooka on their quixotic journey. Far from it. But drawing the Sword of Light had planted a seed—a life without fear. More than that, when she held the sword, she felt understood for the first time since her dad died. *That's ridiculous, Harper. A sword is just a hunk of metal. It can't understand anything at all.*

And yet it had.

Until the moment she and the blade joined, she hadn't realized how much fear lay coiled inside her. The white noise of free-floating anxiety in her day-to-day life was constant. It took a moment of its absence for her to realize its omnipresence. The sword had lifted the weight of angst from her, just for a second, and revealed what lived beneath. Anger. Rage. And the strength that came with it.

For those few moments, she hadn't feared the magic she'd manifested the previous night; she'd craved more. There was no enemy that could ever take away the people she loved or make her cower in an alleyway ever again. She was shocked to find both she and the sword had savored the terror in the eyes of their enemies. It felt good to be the powerful one for once.

"You should not have been able to draw my sword," Nuada said as though aware of her thoughts.

"Why not? It's just your boring old everyday magic sword."

"Oh, it is far from ordinary. And no ordinary person or even Fae could wield it. That it obeyed your wishes tells me you are no ordinary descendant of Niall."

She pressed a finger to her temple and scrunched up her face. "Oh, please do tell. Wait. No, let me guess. I'm the reincarnation of some Celtic battle goddess."

"You're not that far off, actually." Nuada scrunched back

around to talk face to face. A half smile softened his angular features.

Harper rolled her eyes. "You don't say."

Nuada reached into his pocket and withdrew what appeared to be a hunk of plain grey rock. Harper was just about to roll her eyes again when it emitted a glow. Just a little at first, and then the stone shone with a clear light.

"A piece of the Lia Fail." Nuada slipped it back in his pocket. "The Stone of Destiny responds to those fit to be the High King through blood and deed. After lying dormant for a thousand years, it glowed like that the night I saw you in the tent camp." Nuada quickly explained how the Lia Fail had cried out for the ancient Kings of Ireland if they were in right relation with land and people. No king could ascend without the test of the stone; a silent stone meant the candidate failed the test.

Harper laughed. "Old swords and a glowing rock—"

"Are the reason Badb is after you. The last prophecy of my wife, Macha, foretold the Stone of Destiny would cry out one last time for a descendant of the last great human High King, Niall of the Nine Hostages."

Niall. The Dark Boy in the alley had whispered that name to her. Needles prickled every inch of her skin and her eyes shifted to the sword. "Taking hostages doesn't sound very great."

"The taking of hostages meant something very different in ancient Ireland, but that's not important. Macha's dying words told of Niall's descendant leading a great army of Tuatha, Fae, and other races against Badb in the third and final Battle of Moytura. And so Badb silenced the Lia Fail by shattering it. Then she devoted decades to hunting and killing the descendants of Niall."

"She murdered my father over a fairytale."

Nuada narrowed his eyes. "A true tale. And now she knows you exist, and she will not stop until you are dead by her hand. But there is more you must know. When you battled Gwyn's Hunt with magic last night, I recognized something precious to me. My wife's final act of defiance against her sister's betrayal was to send the heir the rest of her magical power. I recognized that power last night. It lies in you. You carry within you my wife's legacy. It is the energy you used to turn the tide of battle. Macha would have been proud."

Harper's throat constricted. All this threatened to overwhelm her already threadbare coping mechanisms, but she may as well take in the full sweep of the crazy story driving a homicidal maniac. "So who was Niall?"

The Phooka snorted. "Oh, here we go. Nuada loves to tell musty old stories."

Nuada scowled at his Fae friend. "Niall was the youngest son of the High King Eochaid. It was growing late in his reign and he had yet to choose a successor to take the test of the stone and become king."

"And so the land picked Niall, and he was your great, great, great, great, so on and so forth, grand—" the Phooka said.

"And so it was that one day Eochaid's five sons were out hunting very far from home. A great thirst came upon them, and they sent one of their brothers looking for water. He eventually located a well, but a hideous hag guarded the water."

"Hideous is an understatement. She had a big fleshy back hump. Greasy hair that hung in long clumps almost to the ground. Huge, nasty warts, one of them right on the end of her nose. A unibrow!" The Phooka shuddered, rattling Harper's teeth.

Nuada shook his head. "Her appearance repulsed the king's son, but he and his brothers were withering with thirst. He plucked up his courage and asked the hag for a drink. She smiled."

"Oh, and her teeth were covered in brown goo and green moss. They erupted from her gums, all crooked like gravestones after an earthquake. Her breath reeked like a thousand rotting corpses on a sunny battlefield."

Harper wrinkled her nose.

"Yes, as the Phooka has so graphically illustrated, she was quite possibly the ugliest thing ever to walk the land. The hag agreed to let the king's son drink, but only if she kissed him. Repulsed, he refused her request, returning to his siblings empty handed. One by one the king's sons approached the hag, and each made the same choice."

"The wise choice," the Phooka said.

"Only Niall remained. Fearing for his brothers, he sought the well and met the hag. When she named her price, Niall drew close to her and said, 'Not only will I kiss you, but I will lie with you too.' And he took her into his arms. Niall kissed the hag deeply and laid her down on the grass to make love to her."

"Everybody's got a kink." The Phooka stuck out his tongue.

Nuada ignored him and continued. "Beneath Niall's hands, she transformed into the most beautiful woman he had ever seen. Long golden hair framed an alabaster face with full, rosy lips. They made love on the grass by the well. The woman gave him enough water for himself and his brothers, and told him she was Eriu, Ireland herself. Because he had been willing to lie with her when her appearance was unsavory, he would be accepted by the Lia Fail and become High King of Ireland over his brothers. And that is how your ancestor, Niall, became the High King of Ireland."

"Cool story," Harper said, "but what does that have to do with me and drawing your magic sword?"

"Niall had many children by his later human queen, but none of them are your ancestors. Only someone with the blood of my people can draw the Claimh Solais and wield Macha's magic. You are a descendant of Eriu. Badb herself could not find you because Macha's geis, a curse of sorts, prevented it. Eriu's blood and Macha's magic have been protecting you ever since. The Tuatha will rally behind you, because you are part of us."

"That's impossible." Harper shook her head and ran a shaking hand through her brown hair.

"I know it is a lot for you to process, but it is true. But if you still cannot believe me, then tell me how you cast such potent battle magic last night and at exactly the moment you most needed it."

Ah. That. Harper had no explanation. Until she had drawn the sword she had refused to think about it because that kept her world like it was. Magic free. Predictable. She didn't want to believe Nuada's words, but like it or not, it did explain what was going on around her. Any hope of returning to her old life sputtered out . . . but she could run. Find Emilio, get her mother, and flee somewhere. Brazil, maybe. Or New Zealand. Somewhere none of this could follow.

"Gwyn saw your little light show last night and your Sword-in-the-Stone act in the stairwell. He'll confirm what Badb no doubt suspects, and she'll send everything she has against us," the Phooka said as if reading her thoughts.

The color drained from Harper's face. These monsters would never stop coming after her. Guilt muscled its way into the already crowded lobby of emotion. Her mother. In her quest to find out what had happened to Emilio, she hadn't even thought about her mom sitting at home with only the Phooka's spells to protect her. Spells she knew powerful Fae like the elves she fought today could break.

What was she going to do? Regardless of her pedigree, she was in way over her head. The safety of her mother and Emilio was her main concern right now. Once they were safe, she'd resume her plan of running. Flee this place and never look back. She just needed to figure out how to be in two places at once.

In her heart she knew the Wild Hunt had stolen Emilio. Her eyes squeezed shut and she stifled a sob as she realized he was beyond her reach for now. Her mother, on the other hand, was not.

They had to find her mother and make sure she was safe before she could resume her search for her best friend.

"I have to go home. We've got to protect my mom. Then we have to save Emilio. Oh god, my mom is going to freak when she sees you two."

"Harper—" Nuada said.

"Phooka, can the Wild Hunt break your protective spells? Does Badb know where I live?"

"They—"

Nuada interrupted, speech fast and pressured. "Most likely. The Wild Hunt knew where to find you. Her crows and the Sluagh have probably been keeping eyes on you since the alley. Harper, this won't be easy to hear, but you are the last hope, and we have to get you safe. Now. Nothing else matters. The Phooka and I can return for your mother. Then we collect any allies who will join us and go to Sauvie Island, where Badb has reopened the gate to the Underworld and—"

"Wait. What? The Underworld? I don't want to hear about any more about any of this until the people I love are safe."

"The Underworld is where most of my kind live," the Phooka said like he hadn't heard her.

"If we do not act now, put a stop to the war Badb is planning, your loved ones will die anyway, and millions more with them. Badb wants a genocide. We need to get through that portal and travel to the Undying Lands where you can take the throne and lead the Tuatha against Badb. The longer we wait, the lower our chance for success."

"Hell no. I don't want to be a queen." Harper was shouting now. "I'm going to save my mother from these monsters and then I need to find Emilio. After that I'm running far away from here."

"Emilio is probably on Sauvie Island where Badb is holding the abducted and where the gate to the Underworld is. If you come with me, we can both save your friend and find my people."

Harper's heart felt like it was being torn in two. Both people she cared about were in mortal danger on opposite sides of the city.

She leaned over the Phooka. "Answer my previous question. Will the wards you set protect my mother from all harm?"

"They are powerful protection spells." The Phooka's clawed foot made tiny circles in the air.

"That's not what I asked. I remember from stories Fae can't lie, but you can avoid telling me anything. The only answer I want from you right now is a yes or a no. I repeat. Is my mother fully protected from harm against the Wild Hunt by the spells you cast?"

"No. It would take time, but they'd get through."

"Phooka, take me home." To her shock, he obeyed and banked toward the suburbs. Why was he doing what she wanted and not following Nuada's commands? Wasn't he the grand pooh-bah of this freak show? Maybe he thought crunching the spines of more goblin things would be more fun than anything Nuada had planned.

"Harper." Nuada leaned back so close she could feel his breath.

"You can either follow us and help me get my mother to safety, or you can piss off." She wrenched herself around, facing away from Nuada on the Phooka's scaly back. Nuada placed his silver hand on her shoulder.

"Wait," he said. "If I can get your mother to a place where she will be safe from Badb, will you help me close the portal on Sauvie Island?"

"I'll go with you to Sauvie to save Emilio. The rest of this fight still isn't mine."

"I ask you once more, how long will either of them be safe if Badb wins?"

Harper closed her eyes and didn't reply.

CHAPTER 30

A quavering, high-pitched scream jolted Emilio from his chemical sleep. He tried to sit up, but pressure across his shoulders, waist, and legs prevented any large motion. He turned to the direction of the scream just as a woman, also strapped to a cot, let out another wail. Several abductees from the festival were alone in the room without Fae, so he risked calling out.

"Hello? Are you OK?" he said in a harsh whisper. Only silence returned. "Hello," he said again. No answer. Either she dreamed or he did.

Light from the hallway and a desk lamp provided just enough illumination for him to make out the contents of the room. The most disturbing sight was the pair of IV bags connecting to his arm though a looping tube. One contained a transparent solution he hoped was just to prevent dehydration. The other contained a pale blue liquid that reminded him of Windex. That one worried him the most. His hand became a claw, trying to curl back to work the needle free. It was no use. He was powerless to stop whatever brew of Fae magic and modern pharmaceuticals in those bags from oozing into his veins.

He tilted his head back and scanned the room, panting. Similar wooden gurneys stood in three neat rows, all holding people strapped down tight. They occasionally jerked and twitched in their restraints. *Why are these all wood? Come to think of it, there isn't much metal in here at all.*

He let his chin fall back to his chest and rotated his head left and right. He didn't recognize anyone from the last time he was awake. They must have moved them. Not just moved, *sorted* by whatever biological metric Dr. Jones spoke about earlier. Whatever diabolical experiment his biology qualified him for.

Only about eleven people lay in the room. Half had their eyes open, staring up with identical blissed-out expressions. Emilio envied their lack of awareness for a moment. Spaced-out happy, they weren't trying to assimilate the existence of fairytale beings into their worldview. Nor were any of them white-knuckling their grip on their sanity as those fairytales murdered and did heaven knows what to them. Instead, his immunity to the spells the elves cast left him wide awake, bearing witness to every needle prick, each discussion of the mysterious ways they planned to experiment on him.

He rolled his head back again, bending his neck to scan the room for a weapon. A way out. Anything that would help him. Aside from the probably well-guarded door, there seemed no other means of egress. No windows. No other doors. Dull cabinets contained the glass and potions of a chemistry lab. The sight would have been comforting if the place wasn't swarming with Tolkein's elves and other creatures he had no names for. Maybe the cabinets housed what he would need to make chlorine gas or something even more toxic. If these creatures avoided metal, there was a good chance they were weak to noxious chemicals too. Then again, so was he. Things were really looking up.

Voices drifted up the hall and he heard the doorknob turn. Emilio pressed his head back down on his pillow and unfocused his eyes a second before the salt-and-pepper-haired doctor and his tall elf companion swung the door open.

Under the lab coat, Emilio could tell the doctor was fashion challenged. Brown shoes never went well with black pants. His pointy-eared escort, though, was beautiful, a trait of his kind. His shiny black hair gleamed as bright as the black chest plate. The flowing red tunics they all wore underneath were the perfect choice to set off their pale skin and dark eyes. If Emilio wasn't being tortured by them, he'd be swooning at the elf's feet even now.

Pretending to be glamoured was coming more easily to him, despite the gnawing fear circling the edges of his awareness like a pack of wolves. Practice made perfect. He stared at the ceiling with unfocused eyes.

"These have the most overlap with your sample. This one, in particular, seems to respond the fastest to the repressor proteins. Let's make sure he has what he needs to complete the process. You'll tell your mistress we're on track, won't you?" Dr. Jones wheedled while his dry hands mashed at Emilio's stomach, beginning a wave of nausea and a burning sensation in his torso. The doctor drew out a syringe. Emilio felt the bite of the needle and the cold rush of its contents into his arm. He fought back tears.

"This one looks quite dead, Doctor." The tall elf sounded bored, toying with the long hair sweeping over his shoulder beneath the braid at his crown.

"Ah, yes. Yes. To be expected. It's not a failure. Even with better stock, there is a rather high rate of rejection. At this stage, about half, so I expect more casualties from this batch." He clapped his hands and a pair of wiry-looking creatures with huge ears and red caps skittered over to the gurney, unstrapped the dead girl, and dragged her behind them by a bare foot.

Emilio closed his eyes to block the sight of her lifeless body, but the squeal of her flesh sliding over the marble and the slapping of bare feet conjured the mental picture anyway. Fifty-fifty shot he'd be following the poor girl soon if he couldn't get out of here. Emilio didn't like those odds. Heads you live in this fantasy movie from hell. Tails, horrible death.

The doctor and his companions moved on to inspect the subjects on the other side of the room. Emilio let his head drift to one side and inadvertently met the eyes of a plump woman with long black curls on the next gurney. Her deep brown eyes met his, and in an instant he knew she was aware, like him. Both of them moved their faces back toward the ceiling and lay perfectly still until the doctor and his friends left them alone once more.

The door to the lab closed with a snick. Emilio's energy level surged like they'd mainlined him with crystal meth. He felt suddenly strong. Strong enough to bust right through the straps like the Incredible Hulk. He flexed arms and legs against the restraints. The doctor and his companions had shut off the light when they left, but Emilio could now make out every detail in the dimly lit room.

The black-haired woman turned her head back to him and their eyes met again. She looked familiar. Recognition flashed in his mind. The Romani woman who gave Harper the necklace.

"Hey. I saw you on at Mystic Island," he whispered.

"Yes. You're Harper's friend. My name is Selina. Selina Leanabel." She gave him a weak smile.

"Emilio Soliz. Do you know what's happening to us, why they brought us here?"

"No more than you do. This is some lab run by the Fae, but someone even more powerful is pulling their strings."

"Fae, you call them. I get it. Like fairytale? I think they're working with my boss. Blond guy. Owns Erimus. He's partnered with some goth chick. Badb."

Emilio watched a frown play across Selina's face. Just then her body spasmed with pain and she tried to stifle a scream through gritted teeth. It took her a few seconds to recover.

"That is very bad news, my sweet. My ex-husband suspected a new threat had emerged in the city. I'd hoped he was wrong."

"Are you OK?" Emilio wanted to ask why her ex-husband would know anything about this place, but concern took precedence over curiosity.

"I'm afraid my body isn't coping as well as yours to whatever they're doing to us."

"Well, we're both better off than that poor girl they dragged out. We need to escape. Fast."

"That is a tall order surrounded by hundreds of Fae."

"Are all these things Fae? They all look so different."

Selina took several minutes to give Emilio a quick primer on the Underworld, Tuatha, and Fae. Emilio shuddered. He'd believed Harper and had always half-believed his grandmother, but his love of science had cast doubt on myth. Science told him sorcery didn't exist. And yet here he was. The victim of some unholy alliance between his beloved biochemistry and magic. All the more reason to kick his escape efforts up a notch.

"We're on some kind of island. Toward the west side of the building. If we ran straight, we'd be on the side of the island with the least amount of river to swim. I could see traffic and land just across. Do you know a way out of this building?"

"I don't, my sweet, but if you can slide over a little closer to me, I may be able to work your straps loose and you can try to find one." Her body spasmed again, her face turning red at the effort to hold back the wail. In a few seconds it passed. "I'm afraid I'm in no condition to assist you."

Emilio wasn't so sure the best plan was to venture out and try to, what, blend in? There had to be another way. He was a scientist. He thought enumerating the facts of the situation would suggest the best course of action.

"Fact one: We're being held against our will, poked, prodded, and injected with who-the-hell-knows-what by things from fairytales. And my boss."

"Mmm. Hmm, your boss is a Fomorian asshat, by the way."

Emilio hadn't been aware he was speaking out loud, but he continued anyway. "Fact two: The Fae are crazy strong. And vicious. Fact three: We'll probably die from whatever they're giving us, and whatever it's doing to us will probably be far worse than death."

"No doubt. Back to my asshat point." Selina groaned with another wave of pain.

"Fact four: We have no idea where we are."

"Yet."

"So we need to find a way out of the building, through some scary woods, across an icy river, and fast enough to evade creatures who have plenty of wings and fins to go around."

"Would you believe me if I told you I'd been in worse situations?"

The cynical part of Emilio enjoyed the irony of being killed by fairies. People had called him one often enough. All the same, their odds of success were low. Then again, he really didn't want to complete whatever course of 'treatment' they were being subjected to.

"At least I'll die fabulous, and off this gurney."

"That's the spirit, my sweet."

He rocked his bed back and forth, slowly inching next to Selina. The rubber wheels squalled against the floor. Their stupefied roommates paid no heed, remaining eerily silent. On the other hand, some of those monsters outside the doors had big ears. All the better to hear him with. And big teeth. All the better to shred him with. His heart raced with each scrape and his eyes darted to the door, expecting elves to rush in with every scronk and whine.

With a last push, his cart crunched into hers. He felt Selina's fingers crawl over his wrist and work at the strap. The pain from her reaction to the IV drip slowed her down, yet she undid the buckle holding the leather manacle around Emilio's wrist. He slid his hand out and went to work on the other side.

"Thanks. I'm free." Emilio sat up and swung his legs over the edge of the gurney. Waves of dizziness accompanied a burning sensation in his back. His hands wrapped themselves around his stomach and he doubled over. With a deep breath, he forced himself to push past the stabs of pain. *That's new. I hope I don't end up writhing in agony like Selina.*

He staggered to her side. Footsteps announced premature company. Selina's manacles would have to wait. His palms sweated and his heart pounded.

"Leave me. You've got to find a way out of here, Emilio, and get help. Quick. Grab that cloak." She jerked her head toward the desk by the door.

Emilio's eyes zipped around the room in the direction Selina was waggling her chin. Draped over the back of a wheeled chair lay a dark grey cloak left behind by an elf. He raced over and snatched it, swinging it across his shoulders in one faltering motion. Trembling hands lifted the voluminous hood over his head.

"Got it. Now what?"

"Get ready to sneak out the door." Selina waved her head toward the wooden desk that flanked the entrance. Emilio gave her a puzzled look. That was all he had time for. Selina wailed and shouted about thieving goblins. She shrieked and thrashed about on her gurney. Emilio cringed. Slapping footfalls and guttural shouts from the hallway outside announced company within seconds.

His eyes strayed to the two empty gurneys. They'd know someone was out if they bothered to keep count. He pushed the dead girl's bed around behind a tall cabinet. Not perfectly hidden, but it would have to do. He hunched his torso over and loped back across the room.

He dropped behind the desk just as the door burst open. In raced Dr. Jones, Callon, and a trio of redcaps. Selina rattled her gurney and railed about monsters and nightmares. The doctor and his companions raced to her side and pressed her shoulders down. Emilio took his opening to slip quietly out the door before it slammed shut. He glanced back over his shoulder to see the tall elf wave a hand across Selina's face. Her face went slack, and she sagged back against her pillow.

At least she'll have some peace from the pain for a while.

Another stab of pain lanced from Emilio's abdomen. His pulse rushed in his ears. Adrenalin masked some of the jabbing sensations in his body, but it still took some force of will to draw himself up straight and peer out from beneath the hood. His intestines throbbed in waves, but he felt stronger than he ever had.

Huge green-skinned giants lumbered up the hallways, their greasy black hair swinging in time with their stride. Elves milled about, elegantly gesturing to each other as they conversed in small groups near what Emilio hoped was the main stairway leading the hell out of here. He willed his feet to move and forced himself to look down at his bare feet so the hood fell forward to occlude his very human face.

He inched forward one footfall at a time, hugging the side of the wall. The greasy giant turned its long-nosed face toward him. He was close enough to smell the stench of rotting fish on its breath.

Sweet Virgin Mary tell me how to get out of here and what to do with Stinkybreath the troll there, and I swear I'll go back to church with my grandmother. His prayer went unanswered. He was on his own, so he lifted his hand and waved. The troll snorted. Its mouth turned up in a sneer, revealing yellowing teeth.

That was smooth, Emilio. Wave to the nice monster. His mind raced with a hundred scenarios of him being discovered. In some of them he was unmasked by the haughty elves at the end of the hallway. In others, the troll, having realized that waving was a very human thing to do, grabbed him by the leg and bit him in two.

He forced his back upright and his legs began their rubbery march up the hallway. He was halfway to the central stairs when the group of elves cast furtive glances toward him. *Stay cool. Don't look human. Don't do human stuff. Be a fabulous elf and keep it moving.* It took all his willpower to not turn tail and sprint in the opposite direction, but Emilio kept one foot treading in front of the other.

His heart turned to ice when one of them waved him over, calling, "Greetings, Jian, what news?"

Shit. Shit. Shit.

CHAPTER 31

Harper and Nuada leapt from the Phooka's broad scaly back while he circled a few feet from touchdown in the O'Neill backyard. The Phooka's claws tore up divots in the brown grass when his feet slammed to the earth.

"They're almost through." The Phooka's voice was a wolf's growl when he loped past Harper.

Harper's knees felt watery when she saw three of the black-haired Sidhe elves, palms against a pale glimmering border covered in the symbols the Phooka had made across the doors and windows. The magic already flickered and gaps appeared in the membrane of sorcery protecting Eileen O'Neill inside.

"Mom!" Harper screamed.

Her mother moved her face close to the window, cast-iron frying pan in hand. Cooking dinner while magical beings intent on killing them all attempted to force their way in through the sliding glass doors. Harper remembered then that her mother probably couldn't see her attackers because night had fallen outside.

Kelpies and goblins swung around to charge Harper and her friends while their masters worked to break the protective spell.

"Behind me," Nuada shouted.

Harper obeyed and kept close to his back. Nuada's blade clanged off the daggers of two kelpies at once, while one of the goblins cocked a wiry-haired arm and lobbed a fireball at him. Both he and Harper ducked and the fireball smacked into the damp lawn and fizzled out.

A hissing redcap skittered at Harper and attacked low at her feet. She dropped the tip of the sword to the ground to block him, took a step and punted him, screeching, into the siding.

Both the short sword and her legs felt heavy. She was still exhausted from their last fight a couple hours ago and from her magical blast at Mystic Island.

The Phooka sailed overhead and knocked two of the elves from their spell casting, but his effort was too late. The last shreds of the wards splintered and the sigils burst into glittering shards. The elf shattered the glass door with the grip of his sword and rushed into the O'Neill family's dining room.

Eileen screamed.

"Mom! Hide!" Harper screamed from the lowest of three concrete steps.

"Stay here, I'll get her," Nuada said as he dispatched a human-shape kelpie with a backward thrust of his blade. He leapt through the glass after the elf.

"No wait, she'll freak," Harper called uselessly behind him.

"Better freaked than dead." The Phooka bounded to her side, snapping and kicking at the goblins and redcaps. Their enemy hissed and bared pointed teeth. Goblins swung their hammers over their heads and advanced.

Harper ducked behind a hedge. The redcaps followed, slowed to a crawl by the unkempt bramble. Harper slid along the edge of the siding, emerged behind them, and sliced into the backs of their legs. As much as she hated the little bastards, she didn't want to kill anything. She just wanted to keep them from her mother.

"Who the fuck are you? Get out of my fucking house!"

"I think your mum just met Nuada," the Phooka said.

The Phooka charged the enemy's makeshift line, teeth bared and hackles raised. A ring of white light zipped outward from his lupine shape, stunning the smaller Fae for a second. The magic leveled the field in seconds, and the Phooka tore into their line. A redcap tumbled end-over end into the air to meet the Phooka's open maw on his way down. One snap and the Fae was dead and his friends were running for cover into the overgrown juniper bushes flanking the sliding doors. Harper winced at the metallic scent of blood.

"Go after her, I can fend off the rest."

"Awesome." Harper sprinted into her home, heart pounding either in fear for her mother or from exertion, she couldn't tell.

Harper's shoulder crashed into the remnants of the glass door as she rounded a tight corner toward the kitchen. Her mother's back was pressed against the stove on the other side of the kitchen island, cast-iron pan held in front of her like a shield, her eyes and mouth wide.

In the attached dining room, Nuada spun and wove a deadly dance with a goblin, two redcaps, and the remaining elf. He parried a magical blast of white flame from the elf while side kicking a goblin. The green-skinned Fae slammed into the shelf, sending dozens of sappy figurines flying.

"Harper, what the hell is happening?" Her mother's voice cracked.

Harper paused at the island. With the Phooka preventing any more waves of Fae from entering, and Nuada keeping the ones in the house at bay, she had a moment with her mom. She thought of how it must look to her mother to see just Nuada and Harper while her home exploded in battle. She almost hoped her mother was already intoxicated, because some alcohol might make this easier.

"Mom, the man over there is a friend. He's saved me twice from . . ." She paused. How to explain this was a challenge. "From some bad people."

"Honey, what's—"

"I'll explain later, but it has to do with Dad."

"What?!" Eileen O'Neill yelped and fumbled the metal pan.

Harper smiled and reached a hand toward her. "Whatever you do, don't drop that pan. It's keeping you safe. It's iron."

Just then a swarthy little redcap escaped Nuada's onslaught and raced right for Harper's mom. With the island in the way, Harper couldn't intercept it in time.

"Mom, *right now*, swing that pan low, aim for the bottom of the fridge."

Her mother hesitated.

"Do it now!" Harper shrieked, already clamoring around the edge of the island, sending plates crashing to the floor and a bottle of vodka sailing.

Eileen's shoulders drew high around her ears and she swept the frying pan toward the bottom of the fridge. A loud clang emanated from the pan followed by a thud that shook the fridge. Eileen screamed and hopped to the far corner of the kitchen, but she did not drop the pan.

"Harper! What the hell was that?" Harper recognized the edge of hysteria that marked Eileen's descent into borderline psychosis.

"Guys, we got reinforcements incoming!" The Phooka leapt into the house, hackles up, bloody drool dripping from his jaws. He stationed himself at the threshold.

"Harper, what the hell? A talking wolf?"

"Mom, he's my friend, he's protecting us."

"Oh hell, we don't have time for this." The Phooka reared up on his haunches and spat straight at Eileen's eyes. A wad of gelatinous Fae spit flipped end over end and landed true.

Harper's mother dropped over at the waist, making a gagging noise. She swept the sleeve of her sweatshirt over her eye. When she drew herself back up, she screamed, dropping the pan.

Eileen's hands framed her gaping mouth as she surveyed the dead and bleeding Fae in her ruined dining room. Her eyes rolled in panic.

"Mom, deep breaths. We got this. We're getting you out of here, OK?"

Nuada had eliminated all his opponents except the elf. Between graceful strikes with his blade, he stretched a hand out, whispered a word, and a thread of soft light zipped out and entered Eileen's forehead. Her posture softened and the fear faded from her eyes. Whatever he did gave her enough calm to be rational again.

"Harper . . ."

"I'll explain everything, but we have to get out of here."

The reinforcements the Phooka warned about swarmed the broken doorway. More elves, Sluagh, goblins, and winged creatures that would be beautiful if they weren't trying to kill her. Last to enter was a tall lithe elf with gleaming black armor and a single braid keeping back most of his long black hair.

"Perfect. All of you in one place. Badb will be pleased." The elf spoke in a matter-of-fact tone. Shifting his eyes between Nuada and Harper, he called over his shoulder. "Capture the girl. Kill the rest."

"No!" Harper yelled and slashed out with her dagger, impaling the shoulder of a winged Fae the size of a toddler. No way these monsters were hurting her mother. Or her new friends.

Across the room, the Phooka leapt in behind a group of approaching goblins. Weaving around hammers and daggers, he sank his teeth into their necks one after another. His black head whipped side to side and shook the last one to death, raining goblin bits all over the dining room table.

Squelching footfalls behind Harper warned of an attack. She pivoted. Three dark-haired kelpies sprinted toward her, hugging the wall. Their deliberate movements were a counterpoint to the swirling chaos of the battle, and black eyes glittered with malice while they bared pointed teeth.

"O'Neill," the lead hissed and slithered its tongue across yellow teeth.

In a split second she closed the distance between them. "Yeah. I'm the last O'Neill you'll ever see."

The element of surprise let her bury her dagger in the chest of the nearest one. She froze for a second, just staring at the body. She'd killed it. Meting out death felt different without the Cliamh Solais whispering about the righteousness of their cause. A wave of nausea made her gag, and her whole body trembled. The loss of focus meant she didn't see the other kelpie.

Harper's head jerked back from the grip the Dark Boy had on her hair. She pulled against the Fae's clutches, wheeling around to come face to face with him. The moment of shock dissipated when she peered into the dull silver glint of its eyes. The tension drained from her body. Limbs instantly felt like lead. She was dazed, defenseless, under an enchantment she couldn't resist.

"Phooka!" Harper called with the last of her will. The kelpie reached up a fist to punch her in the face. Just as she squeezed her eyes shut, the grip on her hair released.

"Oh, no you don't, you filthy swamp pony." The Phooka had the monster by the ankle. With a jerk of his gore-covered black head, the kelpie flew backward. The last thing he saw was the jaws of a great black wolf heading right for him.

Immediately, Sluagh swarmed the Phooka. He bled from several wounds. Harper shook off the last of the enchantment and started toward her friend when she caught sight of Eileen out of the corner of her eye. Her mother wore a dreamy expression and was drifting toward another Sidhe beckoning her to the sliding glass door. The frying pan was still on the floor beside her.

"Mom! Snap out of it!"

Her cry roused Nuada's attention. He sliced through a goblin and lunged for the lithe elf casting the spell. Nuada's icy-blue gaze locked on his deep black eyes. A whispered spell fell from Nuada's lips, breaking the magical hold on Harper's mother. With his sword arm he fended off a winged sylph. Eileen shook off the fading glamour, but she was in front of the cover the kitchen island provided and the sylph fell right next to her.

"Jian!" the sylph screamed as Nuada dispatched the spell caster. Losing her friend caused the sylph to underestimate the bleach-blonde human stepping up, frying pan poised in her hands like a baseball bat.

"You creepy bitch."

It was the last thing the delicate Fae heard before Eileen swung the frying pan in an arc. It smashed into the perfect face, causing a satisfying sizzle. Nuada leapt the island and whisked Eileen to the safety of the emptying dining room.

Their leaders routed, the remaining Sluagh and smaller Fae fled before the slavering Phooka. Harper couldn't tell how much of the blood soaking his fur was from his own wounds.

The last Sidhe in the fight was an elven man with a long braid holding back his gleaming hair. Black eyes flashed; all his rage focused on Harper.

"The Wild Hunt is coming for you. Don't think you have won the day, little heir. There is nowhere you can hide from us, and when we catch you, oh how Badb will make you beg for death."

"Bring it on, Legolas. I'll fry some more of your Wild Hunt with my crackly blue fire," Harper called at the elf's retreating back. "And tell your boss the deer skull for a face costume looks really amateur!" Actually, Gwyn terrified her, but it felt good to piss off the Fae that had upended her life.

Eileen stood next to the toppled table in black yoga pants and an oversized sweatshirt, now more red than pink. The words 'Keep Calm and Sparkle On' composed of gold sequins splashed across the front. Her ponytail had pulled half free and stuck out from the side of her head. Gashes and bite marks covered her arms, but she appeared to be in one piece. A trembling hand gripped the cast-iron pan defensively in front of her.

"Harper? Who are these . . . people?" Her eyes jumped back and forth between Nuada and the wolf.

"Mom, it's OK. They're both my, um, friends." Harper was glad for whatever magic Nuada had cast that was keeping her mother sane.

The Phooka's shape faded and shimmered while he leapt for the only upright chair. As he landed, he coalesced into a sleek black cat, tail waving upright behind him.

"We've met, sweet Eileen. It is I, your cat!" The Phooka leapt to the kitchen island and sauntered to the edge.

"The cat from this morning . . ." Eileen pointed at the Phooka but looked at Harper.

"Mom. Put down the pan. This is Nuada, and the cat is the Phooka. He's a shapeshifter." A newfound respect for her mother flowered in Harper's heart. She was taking all of this far better than Harper had, calming spell or not.

Harper's mom stared in blank shock at the cat, but she did lower the pan.

"He was a wolf and now he's a cat. There were monsters invisible and then not . . ."

"Mrs. O'Neill, there is no time to explain. Trust your daughter. We are here to help you, but we need to leave quickly. The entire Wild Hunt will be on its way here. Now." Nuada held out a hand to Eileen, beckoning her out of the kitchen.

"What the hell is a Wild Hunt?" Eileen seemed to recover

even more of her composure. She set the pan down and crossed her arms over her chest.

"Pretty much more of these, some phantom dogs, and a scary dude with an antlered skull mask. We don't have time to explain, but Fae like these were what killed Dad."

Harper's mother nodded and raced for the back bedroom.

"Mom, where are you going?"

"I'm packing."

"Mom, we don't have time—"

"I may not have taught you much, but I taught you to be prepared." Eileen didn't slow her sprint.

Harper started down the hallway after her mother while Nuada and the Phooka shrugged their shoulders and waited.

Harper entered her mom's 'war room' and stopped, gaping in wonder. She avoided this room much of the time because of the paranoid layers of photos and clippings littering every wall. As she took in the array of guns and drawers of ammunition that lined the walk-in closet, Harper realized her father's murder had affected her mother more profoundly than she ever dreamed. She had a minor armory right in their house. It was lucky for the Fae they had cut Eileen off from accessing this room.

"What the hell is all this?"

"Protection. I wasn't going to let anything happen to you." Her mother jammed boxes of ammunition into a large blue backpack. She took a small handgun off the wall and what looked to be a snub-nosed shotgun. She shoved the weapons into the pack, then piled protein bars and items of clothing on top. Harper marveled at the survivalist's paradise her mother had amassed over the years. Her mom had not only soothed her pain by abusing alcohol, she had coped by arming herself to the teeth.

"Mom, how did you get all this stuff?"

"Bought most of it between hospital admissions the year after your dad died. Kept in storage." She finished stuffing the two bags, zipped them closed, and tossed a navy blue one to Harper who moved the essentials from her damaged unicorn pack to the new one. It felt heavy. Of course her mom had bugout bags to accessorize her shotgun collection. No prepper weapon stash would be complete without them.

"Do you even know how to shoot these things?"

"You bet I do. I'm from Idaho." She shrugged into her pack and motioned Harper into the hallway.

Their footfalls thudded against the thick tan carpet as they raced back into the kitchen. Careening around the corner, Harper found Nuada watching the back door. His eyes swept over the darkened yard, then he motioned them outside. Eileen staggered to a halt and gasped when she saw the golden-eyed dragon in the backyard. She pointed at the Phooka and her eyelids fluttered.

"Oh my god, is that—"

Harper nodded. "Toothless. Yeah. He watches too many movies."

The Phooka narrowed his eyes at her while he lowered his neck in welcome of his passengers. Nuada swung onto the Phooka's back and held out a hand to Mrs. O'Neill. She stepped beside the Phooka. Nuada clasped her hand and pulled her into place behind him.

"Mom, you better take the pack off. I'll hang on to both of them." Harper clambered up behind her mother just as the Phooka lifted off.

Broad wings unfurled and beat the air. The ground dropped away below them. Eileen let out a yelp and threw her arms around Nuada.

"Hold on tight, Mom."

"Yeah, sure." Eileen's voice was shaky.

"You can relax, Mrs. O'Neill. I've never lost a passenger. Except that one time. But, in fairness, he jumped," the Phooka said. He raised his voice and spoke in the tone actors used in an infomercial. "Thank you for choosing Fantabulous Phooka Airways to fly the unfriendly skies. Please follow the safety information printed on the card in the seat pocket in front of you. Emergency exits are literally three-hundred-sixty degrees around you. In the unlikely event of a water landing, place your head firmly between your knees and kiss your ass goodbye."

"Funny." Eileen gripped Nuada's waist tighter.

"He thinks he's hilarious," Harper said.

Great leathery wings flapped frequently as they gained altitude. Speed drove the chill autumn mist all the way to the bone. Harper scanned the skies around and above them for signs of pursuit. No crows or evidence of the Hunt.

"Where are we going?" Harper's mother called above the rushing wind.

The Phooka glanced back at her, his yellow eyes sparkling. "To some friends of mine. The Wild Hunt won't be able to find us there."

Harper snorted. "You have friends?"

"They sheltered me after an unfortunate incident. They're dull as marbles, but they're experts at remaining hidden. And, for the record, I am beloved by all."

Nuada turned to smile reassuringly at the remaining O'Neill family. "I think I know where he is taking us. We should be safe there for a while."

CHAPTER 32

Emilio raced through several possible outcomes, none of them good. An elf with his hair bound in a ponytail squinted at him. His lithe female companion paused in conversation and shifted her black eyes to Emilio. His progress toward them slowed to a crawl.

"Jian? Is there something wrong?"

The third Sidhe, somewhat shorter than the rest, also fixed his eyes on Emilio. Every nerve in Emilio's body pulsed in alert. His blood felt like ice in his veins.

This is it. I'm going to be a pincushion for those thin blades.

The word 'wrong' ricocheted back and forth through his mind. *Something wrong.* The idea coalescing in his mind had about as much chance at working as he did becoming Miss America.

He paused and held up a hand as if to ward off his supposed Fae friends. His other hand slid over to the wall to steady himself. He snapped forward at the waist, letting the hood cover as much of his face as it could. Emilio pretended to say something to the trio but started coughing loudly. He hacked and gurgled, forcing all the air out of his lungs. He drew in a hitching half breath and unleashed a round of coughs worse than the last. A dry hacking gag bent him over his knees.

The trio recoiled several steps. The female's hand flew to her mouth, black eyes wide. The other two wrinkled their noses and averted their faces. They peered at him through the sides of their eyes. All three had flattened themselves against the opposite wall in a second, their black-and-red armor clanking against the white marble.

"By the Dark Lady, Jian, what happened?" the elf woman said.

"I knew these stinking humans were riddled with wretched sickness," another chimed in.

Emilio wagged his head up and down in agreement. He raised his head and hand as if to speak to them, only to fake an even louder volley of hacking and gagging. He spat a great big wad of spit on the floor at the end of his display. He rested his hands on his knees and gasped for breath before raising himself to a hunched-over stance, leaning against the wall.

I can't believe this is working. They look petrified.

He was on a roll at this point. He wanted to make certain none of them would try to follow him out into the stairwell. Noting their anxious stares at the splatter of his phlegm, he drew himself up slowly and took a half step toward them. They jostled into each other in their haste to scramble backward along the hallway as far as they could get from him.

The elf with the long ponytail wrinkled his nose again, marring for a second those stunning features more than the jagged scar along his cheek already did. His chin drew back, and he placed a protective arm across his female companion. "Uh. We'll check on you later, Jian. You'd better get up to the healer."

The three elves slid by him single file, shoulders pressed tight against the hallway like they could become one with it. All to avoid the airspace around Emilio. He coughed deep in the hood, making them jump and quicken their pace. Even the redcaps and trolls were avoiding him now. This might be just the opening he needed to get out of the building.

Emilio didn't look back at the Fae in the hallway. He rounded the corner that led to a great sweeping stairway. He paused with his shaking hand on the railing, looked down to the bottom floor, and then risked a glance up. He estimated about thirty floors total and he was more than halfway down. Below him Fae of every shape and size bustled about in the stairway and in the ground floor plaza beneath, some bustling other slack-jawed human experiments between rooms. Emilio's eyes flashed beneath the hood when he saw other people who weren't prisoners. No, these people wore lab coats or other Erimus Pharmaceutical insignia. They conversed freely with these monsters as though they were allies. *How could they do this? Why would anyone be part of the nightmarish things happening to their own people in this building?*

Emilio hugged the elaborately sculpted handrail and began his descent toward what he hoped would show him a way out of this place. Now he had to do more than merely escape himself. There were others up there that he felt obligated to save. They probably stood a better chance of success if there were several of them, anyway. Emilio realized with a falling heart that right here on this stairwell was as far as his plans had taken him. He had no idea what to do once he learned the best exit. Plans would have to wait, though, because right now he was still surrounded by creatures that would cut him down like swatting a fly.

Even with damp palms and his heart hammering out an allegro in his chest, he adopted a steady gait and focused his eyes straight ahead. He'd observed the elves when he was conscious. They didn't waver. They wasted no movement. Every one of the Sidhe he'd seen epitomized confidence, and most of the other races either averted their eyes or paid them no heed, probably assuming they were on their way to more important tasks within the building.

He reached the landing one floor beneath the floor of his room. He looked up the hallway to his left and wondered if Harper had escaped Badb's minions.

A beautiful creature fluttered through the air enclosed by the spiraling stairs, wispy thin body carried steadily aloft on feather wings. Emilio resumed his descent. When she passed his level, he could see her beauty marred by crisscrossing scars all along her exposed skin. Whatever caused it must have been agony. He felt a pang of compassion until he reminded himself that these creatures had abducted him and were torturing hundreds of humans.

He made it down to the bottom floor where he could once again see the giant circular tree. It pulsed with life and the portal simmered within its center. He pitied the creatures languishing in their cages. Small pulses of light traveled from the glowing fibers that left their cages and ended at the portal tree. Each pulse brought a shudder from the creature housed within.

This was not the best way to escape. Far too many Fae bustled between the gateway and the gigantic doors to the outside. A small band of humans without escort would definitely be noticed. It was the west entrance that gave the most cover and had the benefit of being closest to the water's edge. He'd seen side doors flanking the building during his march into the building. There had to be a hallway that led to one of those.

A familiar voice carried over the hum of activity. He froze in his tracks. Badb. Seated in an elaborately carved chair in front of a thick marble table flanking the portal but positioned to give her a continual view of the tree. Fae large and small scuttled around shuffling papers and refilling glasses. Breas sat to her side with his feet up on the table.

Emilio's hands shook, so he tucked them inside his voluminous sleeves. A group of Fae on the other side of the stairs tended the imprisoned Fae, reaffixing the leads and removing the dead. Some shoved plates of dull food between the bars. He walked over toward the cages to pretend to do the same.

"I'm sick and tired of sacrificing our own to keep the gate to the Underworld open. Our people are dying every day in there, or have you forgotten that? The longer we delay, the more our army dwindles. I need Abraxas to work and now." Eyes aflame, Badb slammed her hand down on the table. Several glasses of red liquid toppled over.

A Fae about the size of a toddler ambled through the shimmering gateway while the pair spoke. It appeared composed entirely of bramble and sticks with a head full of long mossy hair. Badb rose and met the creature with a brief caress before the cloud of pixies guided it toward the door and into its new island home. From the look of it, the Fae's passage was bought with the life of something that looked like an animated mushroom. The poor thing lay motionless in its cage.

"We've been through this repeatedly. We're so close to a steady stream of prisoners. Without patience, all our work and your own noble sacrifice will be for naught when the human authorities come before we're ready." Breas kept his voice casual like he was discussing what was for dinner or who won the last playoff game.

"Let them come. We'll cut them down and revel in their blood. I grow tired of biding our time. Every day this mewling pack of self-absorbed animals drives Fae from their homes, slices down another forest, or poisons another stream. Every moment the web of life frays with the loss of another species. They breed indiscriminately, more and more mouths mindlessly consuming the earth. There has never been a race more deserving of complete annihilation than humanity." Badb beckoned a pair of kelpies to her side. "Bring me one of the oldest ones. I need something to calm me."

"And I agree with all that," Breas continued in a measured

voice. "I want them dead as much as you do. But if we move too quickly, we will fail. Like it or not, sheer numbers make humans strong. Let the mist do its work, let it expand. Spread the Dust to more cities. It's already reached the suburbs, even the Seattle Metro. We're winning, Badb."

Emilio leaned against a column like he was lounging there, a posture he had seen elves adopt. Across the plaza, a pair of kelpies approached, dragging an elderly Hispanic man behind them. The man didn't resist when the kelpies flung him at Badb's feet.

A cruel smile spread across her face. She passed a pale hand across the man's mustached face. The change was instantaneous. His body tensed while his wide eyes took in the ring of Fae in every shape and size that had formed a circle three rows deep around Badb. Emilio recognized that look of shock and horror because he had worn it a short time ago. It was the look of a man learning for the first time that the stuff of his nightmares was real. He whimpered and pleaded with her in Spanish.

Breas sighed, rolled his eyes, and propped his face up with his hand.

The circle of Fae laughed, some of them parroting the poor soul's babble back at him. The man's eyes rolled in his head and his breath came in hitching gulps. He threw himself at Badb's feet, sobbing so hard Emilio couldn't make out his words.

Badb stretched over the man, fingers closing around his neck one by one. With a heave, she jerked him into the air and looked straight into his eyes. His feet flailed uselessly in the air.

Emilio wanted to help him, but there was nothing he could do. If he tried, they'd both be dead. He scanned the area for a diversion. Maybe he could make a noise, give the man an opening to flee. But even if that succeeded, the horde of Fae would make a quick end to any escape. He hated feeling so powerless. *I'm sorry. I'm so sorry.*

The man pounded uselessly against Badb's arm as the life drained out of him little by little.

"What do you say, my people? Shall I kill this man or let him go?" Badb called to her adoring crowd.

"Let him go! Let him go!" The chant rose in voices, airy and guttural.

"It's your lucky day. My people have decided to grant you more life." She lowered him to the floor but kept the grip on his neck.

"Gracias," the man croaked.

"You are so welcome." Badb snatched her sword from its scabbard and jammed it into the man's side.

He screamed, and she released her grip on him. He fell to the floor in a fetal position, blood streaming from his wound.

Badb bent down and pressed her faces inches from his. "Well. Run."

He rolled back to his feet, and run he did, clutching his side. The throng of Fae let him get almost to the door before closing over him. Emilio wanted to clap his hands over his ears to drown out the man's screaming, but that would only give him away. He pressed his eyes closed and tried to push the grisly scene out of his mind. He had to remain focused, or they'd catch him.

"Was that necessary? We work so hard to get subjects only to have you waste them like this." Breas picked absently at his fingernails.

"Hardly a waste. My people are dining, and I feel much more at ease."

Badb's avian minion soared over the carnage and landed on her outstretched forearm, followed by a trio of smaller creatures with leathery wings. And an oily-looking man appeared, dressed in flowing dark robes and with a greedy set to his features. Thick eyeliner ringed each eye like the thin mustache and beard ringed his mouth. He leaned on a black staff set with a shimmering grey stone.

Emilio battled the urge to get to safety or make a run for it, but he guessed by Badb's reaction, the bird would likely share information about what was happening outside. He hoped it would not tell her Harper was dead. Badb smiled at the bird and passed a hand gently over its feathers.

"Welcome home, my pet." The crow turned its head into her affectionate stroking. It muttered and squawked for several seconds and gestured to the east with its black beak.

Badb's hand flew to the air like she was picking up an invisible object. At the same time, one of the empty cages rose into the air. When she flung her hand back down to her side, the cage smashed into the ground.

"Bad news?" Breas asked, smoothing a wrinkle out of his aqua tie.

"Harper and the failed king have escaped and disappeared." Every word a growl.

"What do you mean disappeared?"

"We can't track them." She threw her horned head back and screamed at the ceiling.

The thin man bowed and ran a hand through stringy hair. "My Sluagh are far stronger than the Fae in the city. Send us. We won't fail you like Gwyn ap Nudd does time and again."

Badb rounded on the man, her nose wrinkled and her teeth bared. "Donn, I thought I made clear you and your soul-sucking scavengers are not welcome in my halls, or even on my island."

Donn bowed and laughed a high, tittering laugh. "My only wish is to serve your majesty. My Sluagh can scatter, search the city, the forests, the waters, even in places the Fae cannot tolerate. Is this not of value to you?"

"Go. If you find her, bring her to me."

"And if it is I who deliver her to you instead of Gwyn, will you give me a seat at the table?"

All eyes turned to their furious leader. She shoved past her assembled Fae and headed right for where Emilio crouched beside some cages. He didn't hear what happened next; he was too busy slinking up a hallway behind the stairs to avoid Badb's line of sight. Every muscle had locked tight during the spectacle, and forcing movement took effort.

When he was safe for the moment, his heart skipped a beat. She had escaped. Harper was OK for now. He didn't mind he'd missed the end of Badb's exchange with her leadership team.

He rounded a corner, and at the end of the hallway a door was drifting closed. The exiting goblin slouched down the hallway opposite Emilio, who took two bounding steps and jammed a hand in just in time to open the door farther and slide into the room.

He pulled himself up tall and adjusted his sleeve while his eyes flicked over his new surroundings, ready to fake another coughing spell.

He exhaled. Aside from a row of large cages containing more blissed-out people, he was alone. He tossed the hood back and cracked the door, waiting for the hallway to clear so he could resume his search for a path of escape.

"You're not one of the doctors. How are you here?" The nasal voice droned in that irritating sorority girl drawl he despised.

Emilio's entire body jerked, and he spun to face a thin blonde girl, maybe nineteen, huddled in the back corner of her cage.

"You're not affected either?" Emilio crept close to the bars while keeping one eye on the door.

The girl's shoulders shook and her breath hitched. Tears coursed down her face. "No. The things they're doing . . . I need to get out of here. Please help me."

The edge of hysteria crept into her grating voice. Emilio needed to calm her down and fast.

"I'm Emilio, what's your name?" He extended a hand through the bars.

"Ashley." She sniffed and shook his hand.

"Well, Ashley, if we try to go right now, they'll just capture us. We'll be right back where we started. If we're lucky and they don't kill us right then, they'll know their magic works poorly on us, and I don't want to think about what they'd do about that."

"No, you have to. There's keys in the lab coat, maybe they unlock the cages." She pointed behind Emilio to a coat on the back of the door. "We need to run. If you help me, my dad will pay you. He makes a lot of money. Just please, please get me out of here." She was sobbing now.

"I know you're scared. I am too. Has anyone noticed you're resistant to their spells or whatever they do to make us go all dopey?"

"Yes." Her breath hitched. "They just. Keep. Doing it to me." She slumped forward and her body shook.

"Ashley. Ashley. Look at me. I need you to do something for me. Something that'll help us get out of here." Emilio looked over his shoulder. The snuffling moaning of her tears was too loud for his comfort. "You need to pretend their magic works on you as much as you can without arousing their suspicion and, if they move you, reach out to others who are aware. Find out where they're kept. Can you do that?"

"Why can't we leave now?"

"I've already explained that." Emilio levered himself up and walked to the lab coat. Right next to the door were also a pair of rubber clogs. He smiled. This would be a disguise he would be much better at pulling off. A brief search revealed a drawstring bag he could use to stuff the elven cloak. He might still need it.

He slipped out of the cloak and shoved it into the duffel bag while he looked around. Not that he was any good at fighting, that was more Harper's thing, but he could use a weapon in a pinch.

He stepped over to the cabinet filled with lab equipment. Rows of glass beakers and metal stands packed the shelves. Metal. Stainless steel meant iron and Selina's primer on the Fae mentioned they were weak against it. So little of this place showed any metal, but the human scientists needed equipment.

Emilio took a few seconds to disassemble a stand used for suspending beakers over flame. When he finished, he had a metal stick that just fit into the bag. He remembered Selina and grabbed another one for good measure.

"What are you doing? Get me out," Ashley whined.

"We may have to fight some of these things. We need weapons."

His only answer was a whimper. Now that he was ready to step into the hallway decked out in the lab coat, his pulse quickened. It was a long way back to his floor. One thing he was sure of, the longer he delayed, the likelier he'd be discovered, and he already knew what these monsters did to escapees.

Emilio rested his hand on the door handle and pressed his face against the chilly glass of the tiny window. He strained to see into the hallway. For now, it was empty. He turned the knob and waited another second.

"What the hell are you doing? Get me out of here." Ashley was screaming and bashing the doors of her cage. Her protestations threatened to draw attention.

"Ashley. Stop it," he hissed. "I'll come back for you. I promise. You'll get us both killed."

"Let me out. Let me the fuck out! You don't know who the fuck I am!" She was screaming at the top of her lungs, her face pinched with fury and fear.

Their captors definitely heard that. An elf and a pair of redcaps rounded the corner, heading their way fast. Thundering footsteps shook the door. Emilio risked a glance out the thin window. Trolls. Two of them. He was caught.

<h1 style="text-align: center">CHAPTER 33</h1>

The Fae burst into the room just as Emilio yanked open one of the filing cabinets. A pair of trolls and a male elf. Trembling fingers rifled through files. He half-registered photos of tiny winged things being scraped for something and another thing he recognized: drawings of a chemical compound.

"What the hell?" he yelled and pressed his back to the file drawer.

"He promised to get me out of here, he has the keys. He's planning to escape." Ashley's words ran together between sobs.

"What is this filth babbling about?" A pale elf bent down in front of Ashley's cage, his face wrinkled with disgust.

"Quiet," one troll rumbled and covered his ears.

Sweat beaded on his brow, but Emilio forced himself to stride confidently toward the Sidhe and his troll companions, shocked his disguise had worked well so far. They actually thought he worked here. "This one woke up when I came in and has been raving about me letting her out the whole time. Can't you do that Jedi mind trick thing and shut her up?"

"Liar!" Ashley shrieked.

Emilio widened his eyes at her from over the elf's shoulder, attempting to signal he was on her side but playing a role. He still planned to come back for her.

"Human quiet." Both trolls covered their ears again and shook their heads as though that would block out the sound.

"Jedi what? I don't take orders from you, human."

"Whatever. Let her scream then. The process works the same whether they're quiet or wailing their heads off. But I think the screaming is hurting your friends' ears."

"Hurt." Both trolls nodded.

The elf waved a hand across the cage and Ashley went quiet.

"Thank you. I'd had about enough of that." Emilio turned and walked back to the cabinets, drawing his spine straight and lifting his chin up.

"What are you doing in here?" The Sidhe had narrowed eyes and a hand on his weapon.

"My job. Just like you. And now I can do it in peace. Thanks again for your help."

Emilio pulled out a file and opened it on the desk. He leaned over it with his hands flat on the wood to quell the tremor in his fingertips.

"I've not seen you before. What are you doing with that?" The elf beckoned to the trolls, who lumbered toward their commander.

"I didn't know elves were interested in biochemistry. I think you'll find it just as riveting as I do. This molecule is really very fascinating. See how these carbon—"

The elf held up a hand and shook his head. "I don't care about your human science. Carry on." He turned his back on Emilio before he finished his sentence. The redcaps and trolls fell in line behind him, and Emilio was alone in the lab once more. *I used the same tactics in bars to ward off unwanted dates.* The thought made him smile. Even amid hell, he hadn't lost his sense of humor.

Free from Fae supervision, Emilio let himself slump into a chair. His legs quaked and he felt weaker, like his old, unathletic self. He was uncertain whether the injection had worn off, or hypervigilance had tired him out. Images of Badb running the old guy through and feeding him to her followers threatened to reduce him to a gibbering mess. He slapped his face with his palms. *Snap out of it, Emilio. You still gotta get yourself back to your room without being ripped apart. You came this far. And your dad told you those theater classes were a waste.*

Curiosity about what the drawers contained warred with the fear of being discovered missing from his gurney and suffering a fate like the poor soul below. He decided he'd better get back to Selina. He told himself things were looking up now there were three of them who were magic resistant. Not that Ashley promised to be much help. Still, there was strength in numbers. Perhaps if he could slip out again he could find more information and recruits.

Emilio returned the file to its drawer, slung his bag over his shoulder, and pushed the door open. To his right loomed the grand staircase flanking the portal. To the left a long hallway ended in a door he hoped led both to the outside and to a more secluded set of stairs.

Rows of nearly identical rooms lined the hallway, each with their narrow glass windows. He caught glimpses of more cages or rows of prisoners on gurneys in every room he passed. How many people did they kidnap? If the other floors contained a similar setup, there could be a couple hundred.

A trio of people in similar lab coats rounded the corner behind him. Emilio's spine pulled ramrod straight like a marionette and his pulse quickened. If his heart beat much faster, he swore he'd have a heart attack at the ripe old age of twenty-four. The group paid him no mind and scuttled past him, studying a clipboard the leader held. Why hadn't Emilio grabbed one of those to complement his disguise? Everyone avoided a guy with a clipboard. Plus, flipping the pages made you look important and too busy to disturb. He vowed to nick one for his growing bag of disguises.

He arrived at the stairwell door just as it swung shut. With a furtive look over his shoulder, he pulled the handle. It turned, but the door didn't open. He tried again like he expected a different result, but the door didn't budge. The little black box to the right was familiar. Magnetic lock, they were all over downtown Erimus to protect their precious trade secrets from their own employees. He needed a fob to open it. Crap. He most certainly didn't want to go back up the main stairs. Luck had smiled on him so far, but he didn't want to tempt fate.

"Hey you. What're you doing?"

Emilio's legs shook like they did after gym class in college. Part of him demanded he think of something, yet the other part drew a blank. He pivoted on his heel and swung around to find a tall, hunched man with messy brown hair and his own Erimus lab coat exiting an adjacent room.

"I don't exactly know." *Brilliant response. Very smooth.*

The man's eyes narrowed, and he started toward him.

"What project are you attached to? Where's your badge?" The man fired questions one after the other.

"I was with Dr. Jones. I think he's on the tenth floor." The only name he could think of would be recognized and frankly the only name he knew.

"Project Abraxas. Nasty stuff." The man's horse-like face looked down at him.

"Wouldn't know. It's my first day. I was an intern at the downtown office. They hired me on last week and sent me here."

The man's posture loosened and a knowing smile spread across his face. "Damned HR. It's a coin toss whether newbies get the right equipment." He thrust out his hand. "Dr. Bobby Zimmerman. I work in genetics." The doctor nodded his head toward the other hallway.

"Emilio. Soliz. Lowly lab tech. I work in the zoo." He grasped the man's hand and then pointed over his head.

The sound of someone strangling a goose forced Emilio to duck. It took a second before he realized the doctor was laughing. A ridiculous sound that threatened to draw unwanted attention.

"The zoo! Ain't that the truth." Dr. Zimmerman actually slapped his knee. When he regained his composure, he lowered his head and dropped his voice to a whisper. "Between you and me, these things creep me out."

Emilio nodded. "Yeah. Good old-fashioned nightmare fuel."

"You'll fit in around here, Emilio. Here. Take this." Bobby pressed a badge that had a glimmering button on it into Emilio's hand. The doctor noticed him peering at the shiny dot. "That sparkly bit gets you past the glamour spells. The rest works like any key fob and lets the door open." He reached around and pushed the door open behind Emilio to demonstrate.

"Thanks, Dr. Zimmerman."

"No worries. Just bring it back when HR gets you your photo badge. I only have the one extra. And my friends call me Bobby."

"Thanks, Bobby. I owe you."

"I said my friends call me Bobby." The doctor elbowed Emilio and honked out more impossibly loud laughter.

Emilio forced a single laugh. "Good one, Bobby. Say, can I borrow that clipboard too?" Bobby removed his papers and plopped it into Emilio's outstretched hand. "Sure. See you around."

Bobby turned and started up the hallway. He waved over his shoulder. Emilio was already in the stairwell. Just as he thought, there was a door to the outside right beside him. The same little box that kept the door behind him closed hovered to the left of the exit. Emilio turned the badge over in his hands. Things were looking up.

He bounded up the stairs two at a time. Although his body constricted with anxiety, strangely he didn't feel the slightest bit winded. He was in fair shape, but ten flights of stairs should make him at least huff and puff a little. And come to think of it, the pain from the injection had subsided somewhere along his journey through the building.

Emilio took a deep breath at the door to the tenth floor. He wasn't entirely sure which room was his, and humans, elves, and a handful of goblins lined the length of the hallway. He fished around in his pocket and found the keys and a pen. He took a second to slide the fob onto the cluster of keys and held the pen ready. He held the fob to the black box and pushed through the door.

The instant he was through, he whipped the clipboard up, hunched over it, and strolled up the hall. He thought his door was toward the middle and would be on his right. He sidled up to a room and peered inside over the clipboard. It held cages. Not gurneys. Not his. He pretended to check something off an imaginary list and went to the next room. He was right about the clipboard. No one paid him any mind. Two doors later, he found his room. Locked.

Great. Most of the people and Fae in the hallway were clustered right here. He tried a key that looked like the right size. Nothing. He tried another. The lock remained stubbornly in place. Then he saw Callon coming up the hallway. He would definitely recognize him if he didn't get into the room quickly.

Emilio's hands trembled so badly he couldn't get the key near the lock. He squinted at the fob and remembered the countless times he had locked himself out of his dorm room in college. They charged you twenty-five bucks to let you back in, and so Emilio became the master of the credit card lock pick. He never thought he would use those same skills to run from supernatural demons bent on experimenting on him.

He jammed the fob against the tongue of the door and wiggled. A low snick told him he was in. He pulled the clipboard in front of his face and stepped inside just as Callon walked past behind him.

Selina pulled her head up off her pillow and smiled. "So. How was your field trip?"

"Bladder-draining."

Emilio looked around the room for the best place to stow the bag containing his makeshift weapons and the elven cloak. He decided on the cabinets across the room from the desk where he'd discovered the cloak. He pulled out some boxes and nestled the bag all the way to the back. Once he was satisfied the bag was secure, he perched the boxes back in front. No one casually opening the cabinet would see his stash.

He kept the fob and keys out in case they moved him or he needed to make a fast getaway or they moved him out of this room. Plus, he just felt better knowing he could open some doors around here.

"Well. What did you find?"

Emilio dangled his treasures in front of Selina. "Keys to almost everything. And I know the way out. Did anyone notice I was gone?" He lay back down on the gurney and pulled the leg strap tight.

"Some goblins came to check on us. They didn't seem to notice your absence." She flicked her head behind Emilio. "They took away another one."

Emilio sighed. At least they died blissfully unaware. The terrified face of the old man Badb murdered flashed in front of his eyes. He took another deep breath and focused on his new friend.

Selina worked to tighten and buckle the straps at Emilio's

wrist. He told her about what he had seen on his little walkabout and about the girl, Ashley. When he finished his story, she had redone the buckle holding his hands.

"You'll need to go out again," Selina said, her dark eyes serious. "If we're going to stop this thing once we're out of here, we need those files."

CHAPTER 34

Harper twisted and turned in her bed in the grip of some nightmare where she was flying low through dense trees on the back of a winged monster. Then the sensation of falling. She woke with a start and sprang upright in bed. Definitely not her bed. Her bed had a downy microfiber comforter. This blanket felt like burlap. Her bed had fluffy pillows. These felt like stone. But most of all, her bed most definitely did not contain white filaments covering her arms and legs like food left too long in the refrigerator.

"Eew."

She reached her un-moldy hand over and started to tear the filaments off. Long bundles of them, like cords, cascaded over the bed. She peered over the side. They appeared rooted in the floor.

"It's alive!" The voice was a decent imitation of Dr. Frankenstein.

Harper turned to see the Phooka crouched by a fireplace poking at a bed of hot coals. "Phooka?"

The Phooka's hooves clicked and clacked across the wooden

floor as he sauntered to her bedside. Grabbing his tail in his hands, he plopped down on the end of the bed.

"Don't touch it."

Harper's uninjured hand hovered over the filaments. "What the hell is it?"

"It's a mushroom. It's healing your wounds. I'll go fetch the healer."

Harper grimaced and turned her face from the stuff. "My arm looks moldy. I want it off."

"Just don't touch it until I get back."

"Where are we? I don't remember getting here."

"Well, Sleeping Beauty, we're in the Fir Bolg village."

"And where is Fir Bolg?"

"Not a where. A who. I'll explain that too. Just lie back down, and don't you touch that stuff." The Phooka spiraled his long finger at her and scuttled from the room.

Harper soaked in her accommodations. The room was silent except for the whisper of the wind, which told her she wasn't in the city. She wondered if the Phooka had brought her to one of those boutique AirBnB places where you stayed in a treehouse or a hobbit hole, because the owner had built this round room around the trunk of a thick tree. But the sandpaper linens suggested this was no fancy glamping experience. And expensive places certainly didn't cover you with mushrooms. Harper wrinkled her nose at her arm and resisted the urge to claw all of it from her body.

The architecture of the room was simple, wooden plank floor and walls covered in lamps, at least that's what she guessed they were. Each one was shaped like a shelf mushroom but emitted a faint glow. One section of the wall was covered in thick plants to the ceiling; the other walls were adorned with paintings of a forest, abstract spirals, and sculptures of even more mushrooms carved in wood. Rustic tables and chairs of varying sizes perched on handwoven rugs with geometric patterns and muted earth colors. It was actually quite beautiful.

Daylight peeked between thick fabric curtains over the windows. Might be morning or afternoon, no telling how long she'd slept.

The white filaments itched. Harper shifted on the bed, resting her back against the wall, wondering if something bad would happen if she disobeyed the Phooka and scraped the stuff off her arm. She scowled at it and shrugged. The aches and pains from the wounds she had sustained over the past few days felt much better, so maybe this nasty junk wasn't so bad. *Cotton candy. Just think of it as cotton candy, that's way less gross.*

The haze of waking up melted away and she lurched to the edge of the bed. "Mom!" she called out to no one. Bare feet met the smooth coolness of the floor. Details of rescuing her mother snapped into focus, followed by a stab of guilt. *You abandoned your best friend and Abraham.*

"I thought I told you to lie down and not touch anything." The Phooka's hooves scraped as he stuck his head through the entrance.

"Where's my—"

But Harper's question froze on her lips. What she could only describe as a gigantic half woman, half other primate strode around the tree trunk toward her. She was stout and stood at least eight feet tall. A simple dress fashioned of light brown cloth swept around her calves and revealed thick, hairy bare feet. Harper flattened herself against the wall, her breath stuck in her chest. The Phooka had betrayed her. This must be a Fae.

The heavily muscled woman set down the wooden tray she carried and spread her hands wide. "Be at ease, little one, I mean you no harm." Her voice was sonorous, each word enunciated.

Harper guessed if the creature had wanted to attack her, she would have already. She swallowed hard and nodded slowly. The woman picked up her tray again. Powders, herbs, and bowls filled with crystals covered the entire surface. The Phooka placed a hand on Harper's knee. Yellow eyes met hers reassuringly.

"This is Glani. She is the Fir Bolg shaman. She's been taking care of your mother."

At her introduction, Glani grinned, revealing a mouthful of broad flat teeth. Pieces of colorful glass, shells, and feathers were woven into her waist-length brown hair. They tinkled together when she moved.

"Glad to meet you, little one. I'm just going to check you over, make sure the mycelium has completed its work, and see where else you need balancing before you can join us in the village." She pulled a bench over next to the bed and sat her tray on the floor next to the Phooka's hooves.

"I'm Harper. And my mom, is she all right? Fae attacked us." *And Emilio. I have to find Nuada so we can get out of here and save him.*

Glani regarded her with soft, compassionate eyes and a small smile played across her face. "Your mother is fine. She was desperately ill a few hours after her arrival, but we are tending to her physical needs."

"Physical needs?" Harper's voice wavered.

"I believe they call it withdrawal," the Phooka said. "Maybe even delirium tremens. Great beer, by the way. The pink elephant on the bottle is a nice touch."

"I need to see her right now." Harper slid back to the edge of the bed again, her mind painting pictures of her mother violently ill. "She has to be so scared."

"She's adjusted to Fir Bolg and Fae better than you have so far," the Phooka said, picking at the long fur ruff around his neck.

"Our healers are tending to her. Harper, your mother has been poisoning herself for many years. Trying to fill a hole in her soul."

"Her drinking."

"Yes. The poison has only widened the hole and now it threatens to consume her."

Harper's heart felt squeezed in a vice, and a tear slid down her cheek. The night Fae took her father from them had broken their family so profoundly, neither of them had ever healed. She remembered her mother had been a vibrant woman once. Warm, filled with laughter. She'd had a lucrative career in pharmaceutical marketing. The Phooka handed her a bit of cloth. She accepted the makeshift tissue and lifted her face to Glani.

"The same trauma also eats at you, Harper. Sit back, little one, we shall begin."

The Phooka slid over next to Glani's tray, pressed his goat-like face down, and sniffed the contents. A long black hand reached toward a bowl-shaped shell. Glani pursed her full lips and slapped his hand away, the only quick movement she'd made since entering. He flicked his rabbit ears with a scowl and returned to sitting on the end of Harper's bed.

Harper side-eyed the tray. "What are you going to do with all that?" She drew her knees to her chest and hugged them with her arms.

"You need rebalancing before you join the rest of the village. Everything here lives in perfect harmony. You and your mother's fear and trauma bring anger and pain to our community, disrupt the energy of peace. And your friend here brings something else entirely." Glani arched a thick eyebrow at the Phooka.

"Yeah. Excitement. Fun. Culture. And you need—"

"Phooka, I thought you said these people were your friends. So far they don't seem too happy to see you." Harper wiped away her tears and smiled.

"Oh they are. Not all of my friends are as swashbuckling and exciting as you and Nuada. A few are downright dull." The Phooka curled up and laid his face on his hands. His ears flopped down over the sides of his cheeks, and he closed his eyes. "Well, Glani, as usual, you guys have bored me to sleep."

"How is all that stuff going to rebalance me?" Harper was wary of all New Age woo-woo stuff, and everything on that tray looked decidedly woo-woo.

"Put your heart at ease. I promise no harm will come to you here." Glani took a pinch of several powders and tossed them into a large seashell. She placed some dried herbs on top and struck a flint to light them. Once they smoldered, she grasped a small bough cut from a fir tree and wafted the smoke around Harper. She hummed and swayed a little while fanning the smoke over every inch of Harper's body. Harper decided that some smoke and mirrors were unlikely to hurt her. If it made her giant, furry benefactor happy, she'd play along.

Smoke drifted under her face and saturated her hair. It smelled slightly of pine with a sweet vanilla undertone and an acrid tinge she couldn't quite place. The Phooka made a grand gesture of coughing and sitting up. Rolling his eyes, he manifested an old 1940s gas mask.

"Are you my mummy?" the Phooka said. Harper ignored him.

Glani leaned forward so her face was inches from Harper's. She scanned along Harper's body and wafted the smoke back toward her own face, breathing deeply. She took the shell from Harper's hands and set it on the tray. The tendrils of smoke slowed. The healer sat for several moments with her breathing suspended, her eyes unfocused. Harper, fearing something was wrong with her, reached out a tentative hand. Before she could touch her, Glani exhaled suddenly and mixed more herbs together in a small clay cup. She poured steaming water over them and placed a small blue stone in the cup's bottom.

"Drink this, little one."

"Um, what is it exactly?"

"Medicine for the body and mind. Just drink. Quickly and all at once. The stone too."

"You want me to drink a rock?" One side of Harper's face scrunched up.

"It will pass through and make the needed adjustments on its way. I'm not trying to harm you, little one. Drink."

It looked harmless enough to Harper, so she grabbed the cup and quaffed the mixture like she was doing whiskey shots. The taste was vile. If a basement had a flavor, it tasted like that with a twist of lemon. Harper grimaced and stuck out her tongue.

"Gah! That's wretched, what the hell's in that?"

Glani smiled her slow grin. "Dried honey mushroom, rosemary, lemon balm, motherwort, hawthorn, and a blue opal."

The healer motioned her to lie back. As Harper shifted downward in the bed, a warming sensation radiated out from her stomach. As it tingled along her extremities, a pleasant heat spread through her veins. When it reached her heart, it brought with it a dull ache that came in pulses. She could feel tears coming unbidden to her eyes. Glani smiled another reassuring smile and supported her head as she lay back on the pillow.

"I feel strange," Harper said.

"That means the medicine is working. It will pass quickly. The mycelium has healed your superficial wounds. I'll remove it now and you can join your friends for some lunch whenever you're ready."

Harper's stomach growled. "Lunch sounds wonderful."

The Fir Bolg woman sang softly as she worked, a deep guttural sound but soothing. She wove her fingers through the white strands and closed her eyes. The filaments itched as they disconnected from her skin and melted into the floor, leaving no trace. A little of the pain came back, but it was negligible.

"How do you feel, Harper?" Glani asked.

Harper stretched and twisted her head from side to side to

work out a kinked muscle in her shoulder, but she had to admit she felt better than she had as far back as she could recall.

"I feel different. Lighter, I guess."

"The tea has cleansed the polluted life energy you carried with you into our home. Your body has more resources to finish healing your physical wounds. In a day's time, no trace of them will remain."

Polluted energy? "What does that mean?" If the woman had not been so kind, Harper would take offense.

"Humans so often hold on to things that no longer serve them. Things that fester, cause anger and despair and ultimately sickness in mind and body."

Harper nodded, but she wasn't sure she fully believed what she was being told. She felt just fine physically before today, and even if she hadn't, harboring a grudge against the Fae was hardly a health problem. On the other hand, she had watched her mother descend slowly into alcoholism and mental illness, all because her grief process stalled out in its earliest stages, a living example of illness of the body stemming from mental anguish. She'd held tightly on to her denial as though it were a life raft when actually it was the deluge drowning them both.

After the horrible rock tea, Harper felt amazing. Stronger. Brighter. Like she could run a marathon. She would give Glani's medicine the benefit of the doubt if it could heal her mother. She supposed that might be worth a day's delay looking for Emilio. And she'd need her strength for more encounters with the Fae. She soothed her own guilt by reminding herself Nuada had said they wanted their prisoners for something. That gave her hope Emilio still lived.

"I guess that makes sense," Harper said.

"In this moment you are free of anger and despair. The earth has received that energy from the fungal network. Now our earth mother will break it down and transform it into something that nourishes once again. It is your choice whether you pick your pain back up and create more rage, or live in the here and now with your freedom, where you can cultivate healthier emotions."

"And my mom is being healed in the same way?"

"Yes. However, she needs more time connected to the network."

"I can't believe she's not flipping out."

"Eileen has surprised us in her openness to our teachings. She has committed fully to her healing." Glani rose and ambled to the door. "You are free to go anywhere in the village now. Your friend can show you where you can get some food. Your mother is two huts over to the left. Feel free to visit her."

"Thank you," Harper said. Glani inclined her head, smiled, and stepped out into the early afternoon sun.

As soon as the Fir Bolg healer departed, the Phooka hopped to his feet and peered up at her.

"Well, that was fun." He rolled his eyes. "Not."

"I'm starving. You know the way to the kitchen?"

"Unfortunately, yes."

Harper raised her eyebrows. "Unfortunately?"

"The Fir Bolg are vegan." He mimed vomiting on the floor.

"What happened last night? I remember flying and then waking up here."

The Phooka looked down at his hooves. "Nuada, uh, had to put you to sleep to come here."

"Phooka! You guys glamoured me against my will?" Harper's forehead creased and her hands were on her hips.

"It was the only way. It's how they remain hidden from the outside world. They would have never let either of you in here otherwise."

Harper supposed he was right. It wasn't worth being angry over, although the Fae ability to manipulate her so easily made her deeply uncomfortable.

She stepped out of the broad wooden door. The soft murmur of village life hummed in the distance. Harper's jaw dropped. Before her was a scene out of a storybook.

The hut she emerged from was a circular tree house built twenty feet up around the trunk of a massive fir tree. Dozens and dozens of similar houses stretched out as far as she could see, suspended both above and below her, all of similar construction, roughly round with stunning thatched roofs and circular boardwalks winding around the perimeter of each hut. Rope and slat bridges and other walkways connected the buildings. The hirsute Fir Bolg moved back and forth among the buildings about their daily business.

As she regarded the arboreal city, the Phooka stepped up next to her.

"It's like the bloody Ewok village, isn't it?"

CHAPTER 35

Harper snorted with laughter. "Yeah, if the Ewoks were friggin' huge."

The Phooka giggled beside her. His laugh was ridiculous, like a high-pitched braying donkey. Each time Harper's eyes met his, whoops and chortles erupted, ending only when her throbbing stomach muscles made another giggle too painful.

When she regained her composure, she soaked in the crisp smell of fir trees and the sunlight-dappled boards. The natural beauty soaked into her like water into parched soil and she felt a deep peace take root in her soul. Despite all the upheaval and terror of the past few days, being here was the best time she'd had since she lost her father, and she fell instantly in love with the village.

"It's far more beautiful than the Ewok village," Harper said and drank in more of the beauty. The buildings were exquisitely crafted with fine architectural flourishes incorporating branches and the shape of the trees they encompassed. All of it melded in total harmony with the forest as though the woods themselves had simply grown this place.

"Well." The Phooka clapped and rubbed his hands together. "Let's eat."

"I want to visit my mom first."

The Phooka groaned and smacked a hand on his forehead. "I'm wasting away from starvation. The tearjerker after-school special can wait for an hour."

"Why don't you eat and then come back for me in an hour." Harper continued toward the building Glani had said housed her mom.

The Phooka slumped as he beckoned Harper to follow. "If I pass out, it's your fault."

"I'll take the risk." She raised an eyebrow and glanced sidelong at him. He seemed oddly unwilling to leave her side. Nuada probably told him to guard her.

A drizzle accompanied them on their walk to Eileen's room. The Fir Bolg they passed all wore the same brown clothing, same as the simple pants and tunic they'd dressed Harper in, but each had some individual flourish. Blue embroidered spirals. Shells sewn into the neckline. One bore a painting of a deer across the back. Everyone moved like they were underwater. Slow, deliberate, and unhurried, every citizen took the time to acknowledge their guests with a gentle nod or a soft smile as they passed. Harper found them calming, in the same way watching fish swim in a tank soothed jagged nerves.

The Phooka motioned to an arched door with a branching tree carved on it. Harper pulled the door open a crack and glanced inside. The room was nearly identical to her own arboreal accommodations.

"Mom?"

"Harper?"

Harper didn't wait for an invitation. She whammed the door open and rushed into the room. At her feet a black cat zipped past and leapt up on her mom's bed.

"Hi, Phooka." Eileen patted the amber-eyed cat on the head.

"You're looking better, Eileen," the cat said.

Eileen nodded. "Still trying to get used to cats that become dragons and a treehouse city run by giants."

"Stick with us, it'll all feel normal in a day or two." The Phooka purred and waved his long tail high.

Harper settled on the edge of the bed and wrapped her arms around her mom's shoulders. She squeezed her eyes shut to hold back tears. That didn't work. Seeing her only family with the mycelium strands sprinkled over her sealed the deal. She wept while her mother smoothed her loose hair, something she hadn't done since her father died.

"Oh sweetheart, don't cry. It's OK. I'm OK. Better than OK. Somehow these people have lifted a decade of pain and darkness from my heart in a single day."

But that moment of long-craved tenderness from her mom only opened the floodgate and Harper sobbed, welcoming the gentle touch and soft voice that melted fears away. In this moment, she wasn't the one having to hold everything together, so she fell apart. After a couple minutes, she dried her nose and eyes with the cloth the Phooka had given her earlier and grasped her mother's hands in her own.

"Mom, I'm so sorry. I didn't mean to get you involved in all this."

"Technically, you didn't. The Fae came to you," the Phooka said.

"The cat's right." Eileen placed her hands on Harper's shoulders and looked her daughter in the eyes. "You saved me. From the Fae and from myself. My strong, brave girl. I wish I could take credit for how you turned out." A tear slid down her mother's cheek. "But I think we both know you raised yourself, and I'm so, so sorry for that."

"Mom, don't, I—"

"Besides, in a way, I'm thankful those Fae showed up. There are some things I need to tell you about that night. Things I told myself I only imagined because of my breakdown. Glani says the Fae used a glamour spell to keep me from remembering. Maybe that's why I always felt like we never had the full story. Somewhere under there, not quite conscious, I knew Gerald didn't die in a random home invasion. But the mycelium is clearing the cobwebs, making it all clear little by little."

"Fae killed Dad."

Eileen nodded. "I keep seeing a red-haired woman surrounded by things I can't name and a man in an antlered mask. I remember now. He led her to us, and then she killed your dad."

"Badb and Gwyn." Harper's voice had an edge.

"The red-haired woman, Badb, left, I think. Even now, I don't remember seeing her again, so she must have. She told the man to search the house, leave no survivors. I remember him laying a hand on my forehead and I collapsed. After that I could never put the pieces together. All those therapists said it was a reaction to the trauma, but I knew in my heart it was something more than that. All these years, bits and pieces of that night would bubble up and then some invisible hand wiped the board clean again."

"That was glamour. A kind of spell that lets us control what you see and feel," the Phooka said.

"You weren't crazy, Mom. They did search the house. The teenagers that always look wet came upstairs. I hid under the bed. One of them bent down and looked right at me. Well, more like through me."

Harper then told her about the alley and the Dark Boys she recognized from her dream. The Phooka filled Eileen in on Nuada's theory that Harper was the last heir of the High Kings of Ireland. They both shared the tale of Macha's magical power passing to her. Eileen listened with occasional exclamations of wonder.

"It had to be Macha's power that protected me that night," Harper finished.

"Two days ago, I would have checked myself into the psychiatric hospital if I suddenly believed all this, but . . ." She gestured around the wooden yurt. "That's why they left me alive. It was your father who had the blood. And you. Thank god they didn't find you." Eileen pulled her daughter into another embrace. "And I left you to face it all alone. You had to grow up so fast, I stole your childhood." The corners of her mother's mouth pulled down, her face reddened, and she buried her face in her daughter's hair.

"No, Mom. Fae stole my father and my childhood." Harper's own throat tightened. It dawned on her just then that they had both done the best they could. She pulled her mother closer.

"They got Emilio. I don't know how I'm going to save him." Fresh tears trickled from her eyes.

The sound of the door opening interrupted the reunion and Harper drew away from her mother. They both swept tears from their eyes with the backs of their hands. Glani and a shorter Fir Bolg entered with broad wooden trays of their medicine.

"Hello Glani. Paegrinn," Eileen said.

Harper's mother smiled at the alien species like they'd been friends for decades. Harper was suddenly jealous of her mom's ability to adjust to the high weirdness their life had become. Eileen went with the flow, whereas Harper tried to paddle upstream.

"Good afternoon, Eileen. It is time for more medicine." The shorter of the pair worked at laying a ring of crystals around her mom's bed.

"Ready as always."

"Harper, why don't you and your friend explore our village and find some lunch. I will be a while. Paegrinn can show you the way," Glani said.

"But I want to stay here. When am I ever going to get to help heal a human again?" Paegrinn stamped an enormous, impatient foot against the floor, causing the walls to shake.

Glani inclined her head to Harper. "There's more to healing than herbs and chants. Go on, finish the ring, then attend to our guests."

The almost whine in Paegrinn's voice marked him as a Fir Bolg teenager. The way he slouched and rolled his eyes at Glani wouldn't have been out of place in any high school in America. Harper rose from her mom's bed and stuck out a hand to him.

"I'm Harper. This is the Phooka."

Paegrinn dusted his hand off on his pants and looked down at Harper's hand. She reached for his hand and gripped it and shook it gently. The embroidered bag at his side swung back and forth. His deep brown eyes met hers with a look of confusion as Harper let his hand drop.

"It's how we greet each other," Harper said.

A smile spread ear to ear and he seized Harper's hand again with an iron grip. He shook her arm with enough force to jostle her neck and make her teeth clack together.

"I'm Paegrinn, Glani's apprentice and the son of our leader. Am I doing it right?"

The Phooka brayed his ridiculous laugh. "Yeah, if you want to dislocate her shoulder." He leapt from Eileen's bed, melted into his authentic form on the way down, and landed with a clack on his hooves.

Paegrinn dropped her hand with a sheepish grin. "Sorry. This is how we greet each other." He reached out his fingertips and rested them just below Harper's collarbone. She lifted a hand and did the same.

"Nice to meet you, Paegrinn."

Paegrinn reached a hand down to the Phooka who skittered away on his hands and hooves. "Well met, Paegrinn. I'll skip the handshake. I like my head where it is."

Harper turned to Glani. "When can I come back to see my mom?"

"If this treatment goes as well as the last, your mother will be well enough to move about the village in a few hours, but she will still require several weeks of healing from the mycelium."

"I'll find you, sweetheart," Eileen called as she lay back down on her bed.

The Phooka was already at the door. He rubbed his hands together. "Right then. Let's find us some grub."

CHAPTER 36

Paegrinn led them on a winding path along the footbridges and walkways that edged each building. As they strolled, he pointed out the finer points of Fir Bolg architecture and asked Harper a million questions about life in a human city. Questions of her own rose with every meandering turn along the walkway. Like how an entire civilization remained hidden in the woods, and how the mycelium worked to erase years of mental anguish from her mother and heal wounds in just a few hours that should take weeks to mend.

"I want to come visit you in the city someday," Paegrinn said.

The Phooka snorted. "Oh yes. That's a fantastic idea. We'll get you a cage all prepped in the Portland bloody Zoo right next to the giraffes. Or better yet, in the primate area."

"The Phooka's right. People would be terrified of you. You'd end up in a lab or a zoo or shot dead."

"But he's been to the city, and he's fine." Paegrinn gestured to the Phooka.

"But I am a master of disguise." The Phooka shifted into his human form and sported a black mask and cape. "I can be

282

anything." A black dog with the same mask pranced a tight circle. "I can even be unseen, slipping through the masses totally unnoticed until it's too late." He disappeared and then popped into sight a few paces to their left, Paegrinn's bag dangling from his hand.

Paegrinn snatched the bag back. "Well, someday I want to see the human city."

"Wait a second, maybe you can. Sort of." Harper felt for her phone in the pocket of the grey Multnomah Community College sweatshirt she'd thrown over the brown Fir Bolg clothes. She knew there would probably be no signal this far into the wilderness, but she had some videos of Emilio and her in the city. The thought of him pushed her shoulders down with sadness and guilt. Here she was enjoying the natural beauty and the gentleness of their hosts while he was dead or enduring the unspeakable. She pushed her feelings deep within and refocused on her new friend.

Harper held the device in front of Paegrinn, showed him how to turn it on, and then touched the photos. His eyes widened with wonder and a yelp escaped his lips. "What is that?"

"It's a thing we use to talk to each other when we're apart. It also takes pictures. See?" She swept her finger across the screen, scrolling various photos in the city she had snapped. "Just sweep your finger on the glass."

Paegrinn brought the phone up to his face and studied the picture of a squirrel hauling a bagel up a tree with skyscrapers in the background. His jaw hung slack with wonder. His finger almost covered the screen when he swept it to the next picture. He yelped again and nearly dropped the phone.

"It's moving!"

"That's a video. Captures movement. Here." Harper held out her hand and Paegrinn passed her the phone. She turned the camera toward him. "Wave to me, Paegrinn." Harper waved her hand in the air.

The Fir Bolg pulled one side of his face into a quirky frown but brought his hand up and waved. The Phooka leapt up and down like a pogo stick waving into the camera.

"That's called a photo bomb. And this video would be worth a fortune in the human world." The Phooka stuck out his tongue on his last bounce.

Harper handed the phone back to Paegrinn and pressed play.

"That's us! Just now." His mouth hung open.

"That's video. Captures a moment forever, or until you delete it."

"Video." Paegrinn whispered the word like it was sacred.

The trio continued their walk toward what Harper hoped would be a very large lunch. Paegrinn fell silent and focused on Harper's phone, occasionally indicating where they should turn with an absent wave, but his face never budged from the miraculous phone.

The arboreal houses lined the trees both above and below their path. Eventually they came to the biggest building in the village. The great dining hall of the Fir Bolg was an enormous oval supported by a trio of giant fir trees. The smell of exotically spiced cooking wafted from the open windows. Harper's stomach growled and her mouth watered.

The dining hall was a much larger version of her room except filled with long wooden tables and benches. From the high ceilings dangled what looked like metal bowls that would be lit to provide additional lighting at night to supplement the gently glowing shelf mushrooms growing up the vertical supports. The Phooka motioned for Harper to sit down at the end of one of the long tables. He scampered back to the kitchen while Harper made herself comfortable.

The Phooka returned in a few moments followed by a lanky Fir Bolg man with a large tray of food. He smiled that warm Fir Bolg half-smile as he slid the tray in front of Harper. It smelled delicious, like Indian food. Smooth orange-colored soup, a grain dish with nuts and small fungus, large grilled mushroom caps, and more spread out over the rustic slab tray.

"Thank you," Harper said.

"My pleasure." The Fir Bolg poured three cups of tea and placed them before his guests. With a nod, he returned to his kitchen.

Harper reached for the wooden spoon to dig into her meal but Paegrinn laid a hand on her wrist.

"It's tradition to drink the tea first. It brings the body in harmony with the forest so that the meal benefits you most."

"What's in it?" Harper swirled the light green liquid in the ceramic cup. "Please tell me it's not another rock."

The Phooka stuck out his tongue and pulled his chin back. "It's like drinking Pine Sol. I swear these tree-hugging throwbacks just scrape this crap off the forest floor."

Paegrinn focused on Harper, ignoring the Phooka. "Pine needles, mint, and dried berries." The Fir Bolg teen cupped the round mug in his great hands and sipped.

Harper smelled the crisp, sweet scent of the tea and took a gulp. The flavor tasted crisp and bright. "It's not so bad, Phooka." Tea finished, Harper shoved spoonfuls of food into her mouth. The meal was as tasty as it smelled.

The Phooka's ears fell flat as he regarded the spread in front of him. He rummaged in the satchel that always seemed to appear at his side just when he needed it. "How do you Fir Bolg get so big eating the food that real food eats?"

"I like it." Harper moved on to the mushroom cap. The only utensils provided were the wooden spoon and something that resembled a single chopstick. She shrugged, skewered the shroom with it, and munched away, rich juice from the fungus trickling down her chin. She swept it away with her fingers, then licked the juices from the tips. The mushroom was simple and earthy, but delicious. She paused with her wooden stick halfway to her mouth and stared at the Phooka. From his magic bag he pulled a small pack of cheese puffs. He hummed to himself as his long black fingers teased open the bag. He scooped them out onto his palm and crushed them over his plate like bright orange croutons.

Paegrinn cocked his head to the side and leaned in to more closely examine the Phooka's snack. "What is that?"

"This"—the Phooka made a dramatic sweeping gesture across his plate—"is the peak of culinary invention. The food of the gods. The divine ambrosia." He spread his hands wide, palms up, and looked to the sky like a priest praying for a holy message from on high. "These are cheese puffs, and they'll make this dreadful slop edible."

Paegrinn raised his eyebrows and looked over at Harper.

"It's junk food."

"Why would you eat junk?"

"Try one. You'll see." The Phooka took one of the remaining whole pieces out of the bag and handed it across the table to Paegrinn. Harper and the Phooka watched him as he gingerly took the cheesy cylinder and brought it to his face for inspection. He turned it this way and that before bringing it to his nose and giving a light sniff. His head jerked back a little, and he grimaced.

"Just eat it." The Phooka leaned forward. His eyes locked on Paegrinn's face and his lips curled up. Furry black hands drummed the edge of the table and he sat up a little taller.

Paegrinn brought the snack to his lips and bit off a minute piece. His face contracted. He turned his head to the side and spat half-chewed cheese puff onto the floor. He quickly grabbed for his drink and gulped the entire contents down in one swallow. "Blech. It's just salt and air."

Harper laughed as the Phooka threw his hand over his heart and doubled over like he'd been shot. "Now I understand why your people's cultural development stopped at this." He waved a hand around the room. "I guess cheese puffs are for a far more refined palate." He turned his back to Harper and began munching away at his improved meal.

She had nearly finished her own lunch when Nuada stepped through the doorway followed by an imposing Fir Bolg man. The man wore a richly embroidered sash across his tan tunic and pants, and the fur on his face and arms was tinged with grey.

Harper's delight in seeing Nuada surprised her. His presence in her life had coincided with a deluge of nightmare creatures and the disappearance of her best friend, and yet he'd risked his life to defend her more than once now. If not for him, her mother would have died in the Fae attack on their house. Deep gratitude flowered in her heart. He'd done more than just save Eileen's life; he'd helped bring her back from the half-life she'd been living.

Harper sprang to her feet, sprinted to him, and threw her arms around his waist. He drew back from her embrace for an instant. A bewildered look crossed his face, but he wrapped his arms around her shoulders and returned her embrace.

"Thank you for saving my mom," Harper mumbled into his chest. Nuada stepped back from her and gave her a warm smile.

"Your mother did a lot of the saving herself. She is a formidable woman."

"And downright deadly with that iron pan." The Phooka shuddered.

"Harper, this is Aeld, the leader of this village."

Paegrinn looked up from the device. "That's my father."

"Hello," Harper said, unsure how to greet the leader of anything. "Thank you for welcoming us and helping my mom."

"They are disconnecting your mother from the fungal network as we speak. Her healing is progressing well." Aeld lowered himself onto the bench across from Harper and his son.

"The white mold stuff." Harper's face must have registered the weirdness she felt when she thought of how the mold had healed her wounds. Aeld reached a reassuring hand to her shoulder while Nuada seated himself across the table.

"The mycelium is fungus—our medicine. It healed your arms and legs and has restored much of your mother's physical well-being. And now the much longer path of spiritual healing can begin for her." Aeld glanced toward his son. "What is that thing?" He gestured to the phone in Paegrinn's hands.

"It's pictures of the city," Paegrinn said. His father scowled.

"Give the thing back to Harper. You need not feed your obsession with humans. Your fascination with them has caused enough trouble already." His voice was stern. Paegrinn slid the phone back to Harper and hung his head.

Aeld motioned Harper to return to her meal. Even more food had appeared in the scant time her attention wandered from the table. A bowl of sweet fruits and a tea that smelled of jasmine flowers steamed next to the few spoonfuls of soup on her tray.

Harper's curiosity got the better of her. "So Fir Bolg aren't Fae. Are they Tuatha?"

"Not Tuatha. You call us Bigfoot. They draw me on shirts in your world. I see hikers wearing them sometimes." Paegrinn stood and adopted a mid-stride stance and turned his head toward the table. He had an impish grin on his face, which disappeared when his father glowered at him and jabbed a hand back toward his son's seat.

"That's you in that picture?" The Phooka was mashing handfuls of cheese puffs between his palms over his food. His smile stretched from ear to ear. "Bravo, my young friend. You just became my favorite Sasquatch."

Aeld shook his head. "Despite our best efforts, humans sometimes glimpse us when they are in our woods. Sightings have increased as your cities press deeper into our homeland. A problem compounded when some of our more impetuous youth stray too close to your kind in the forest." Aeld turned his head to his son. Paegrinn studied his hands.

"How long have you lived here?" Harper asked.

"Long before humans came to this land. This village is well over twenty thousand years old. New by our standards. Isolated pockets of us still live on every continent, living much the same way you see here."

The idea that entire civilizations, older than any human culture, were tucked away from prying eyes boggled her mind. How did they avoid detection?

"Not Fae. Not Tuatha," Harper said almost to herself.

"No, but we are your cousins. I believe your scientists call us Neanderthals. In other lands your kind refer to us by more names than I can count, but Nuada's people call us the Fir Bolg, the name we chose for ourselves."

Harper took a sip of the flowery tea, which she decided she liked more than the pine flavored one. She recalled a bit about humans coexisting with Neanderthals and the latter disappearing. What she had just learned would completely change the anthropology department at any university. Their ancient cousins hadn't died out at all; they merely hid. Just like the Fae and the Tuatha.

"Why hide from us?"

"Our people followed the teachings of the Tuatha. Good stewardship of the land, learning, and magic. Your people listened to their own counsel and that of the Fomorians, and that made you dangerous."

Harper tried to focus on what Aeld was saying, but her mind wandered back to Emilio. If her world wasn't disintegrating, Harper could happily stay here, listening and learning for weeks. Her dream had always been to travel to meet new people and learn new worldviews. This village was as new as it got, and so far she loved everything about this culture and its people. But every second they remained here lowered the chances of finding Emilio alive.

Aeld leaned across the table where Harper sat with her eyes unfocused. Nuada reached out a hand to her.

"I think your thoughts drift elsewhere," Nuada said.

"I'm sorry. I'm terrified for Emilio. Every moment we're here, something terrible might be happening. When are we going to go rescue him?"

Nuada sighed and shook his head. "It's not that simple, Harper—"

"We need more than a former king, a magic sword, and a wet-behind-the ears mortal. Even with my astounding cunning and prodigious shapeshifting, we three cannot hope to win," the Phooka said.

"What about the Fir Bolg? Aeld, will you help us rescue my friend and maybe a lot of other innocent people?" Harper's eyes pleaded with the chieftain.

"Nuada and I have been discussing the threat to your people at length. We have agreed to pass no judgment until we convene a Council with the solitary Fae and the Green World Fae Courts. The decision would affect all the hidden races, so we must decide together."

"You can't be serious. The Fae are the ones stealing people away and doing god knows what to them. And they're trying to kill—"

"Speciesist."

"What?"

"Ahem. I am Fae. Am I stealing people? I may liberate some snacks here and there . . ."

"I'm sorry, Phooka, I didn't mean you."

"The solitaries and the Fae topside are the lesser Courts. They chose to remain in this world and not retreat to the Underworld," the Phooka said.

"So they are friends to humanity?"

"Not exactly. But they hate you a lot less. Some of them even enjoy your company slightly." He smoothed the long fur of his neck ruff.

Harper didn't have time to wait for some supernatural committee meeting to find Emilio. But she couldn't just think of him. He wasn't the only person in danger. Perhaps Nuada was right. If they had an assault team, saving everyone became an option. The Fir Bolg seemed like huge hairy peaceniks, but she bet they could be deadly in a fight when provoked. Some muscle might be just what they need, but if it cost too much time to get, Emilio might die anyway.

"So when is the meeting?"

"The solitary Fae representative will arrive by nightfall. I am leaving within the hour to visit the Court of Dusk and the Court of Dawn and ask for their attendance. When they arrive, in a day or two, the deliberations will last several—"

"Days? Plural? Deliberations?" Harper's voice rose. The bench made a low moan as it slid across the floor. "Every day we wait, they take more people. What if they're killing them? We can't just sit around in paradise and talk. We have to do something!" Row after row of deep brown eyes turned and stared at her. Waves of anxiety crashed up from deep within, and she felt the walls closing in.

"This is bigger than just your friend. It is the way they do things and it cannot be rushed. There are rules—"

"To hell with your rules." Harper kicked the bench over and raced for the exit.

CHAPTER 37

Emilio thought a day had passed. Two at the most. Knowing how much time passed inside the building proved difficult since there were no clocks or windows. Instead, he estimated time by the periodic injections that had replaced the drips. They seemed about four hours apart. Every time the needle slid into his vein, his stomach flipped, filling his mouth with the burn of acid. An hour after that, every muscle in his body throbbed along with his beating heart. Once those symptoms passed, with each dose, he felt stronger. Sharper. Like the chemicals were honing a blade.

Shortly after his illicit tour of the building, his little group of abductees graduated from being strapped to gurneys to being locked in cages, like Ashley had been. This was simultaneously a relief and a curse. The gurney was difficult to break out of and get back into. The cage, however, was torture. A four-foot cube of agony furnished with a blanket and tiny pillow. He couldn't stretch out. Or stand up. The best he could do to relieve the pains in his lower back and neck was to lie in almost an 'L' shape around the perimeter of the cage. For once he was thankful to be short. Selina was tall.

Selina groaned. "Let me out again, Emilio. I don't even care if they catch me anymore." Emilio could hear her shifting again and again in her cage.

"Once they give us our injection, I'll go back to Ashley's room. Pass me your blanket."

"How many like us have you found so far?"

"Just three more. That makes six with you, me, and Ashley. We're up here on the tenth floor. There's a guy at the west end of this hallway named Alan. Tamika and Jerome are on the sixth floor, one at either end."

"Damn. That's pretty spread out." Selina let out a long breath.

"I can make it through all the rooms in just a few minutes. I tried to count it out to myself when I came back last night."

"We need to find a way for all six of us to get to the west door without being caught. You think your lab coat will cover you moving so many prisoners?"

"No." Emilio rested his chin on his knee. "Only the Fae seem to move the prisoners. Using the cloak is riskier. I'm short for an elf. I only made it last time because I doubled over and faked a nasty cough that scared the bejesus out of them."

"Hmm. Maybe the tallest of our new friends wears the cloak?"

It would be asking a lot. Emilio had practiced his impersonations for several nights, increasingly managing his fear and playing the part. He wasn't too sure about the others.

"Maybe. Regardless of any disguise, we've got to be fast. The Fae don't seem to sleep much, but I only saw a few human staff the last time I went out, which probably means it was night. Fewer people in the halls gives us the best chance."

The door swung open and florescent lighting flooded the room. Emilio quickly slumped over in his cage and unfocused his eyes.

"How long will this take? I want to get to the revels." Zallile's musical voice made Emilio relax despite himself.

"Um. Of course. Would you check to see if they're all still glamoured? I can handle the injections." Dr. Jones pushed his glasses back up his nose and dropped his eyes to the floor.

The sylph fluttered over to the row of cages, coming to rest with her hands clasped behind her back. She meandered along the line, bending down to peer into each tiny prison. She stepped in front of Emilio's cage. He faked a dopey grin, letting his tongue hang out and reaching up a hand toward her.

"The cattle are all hopelessly glamoured, doctor." She wafted out of the room, and they were alone with the doctor.

Emilio dreaded this part. His wakefulness gave him a slim hope of escape, but it was a gift with a price. The liquid in the fat syringe burned like fire when it entered his veins. He'd rather not be aware for that bit. But he had to keep the stupefied look on his face while this evil douche pumped who knows what into his body.

"Arm." Dr. Jones's tone was flat.

Emilio obediently stuck his arm out of the cage and froze his face in an expression of oblivion. His stomach muscles clenched at the pain, but his facade never slipped. The doctor was on to the next cell in moments. He finished his work, flipped the lights off, and disappeared into the hallway.

"Ugh." Emilio dropped to the floor of his cage.

"That's an understatement." He could hear Selina's bulk hit the floor.

"I gotta find out what's in this stuff tonight. There's no way this shit's organic."

Selina laughed a little. "Whatever happens, Emilio, I'm glad to share this nightmare with you."

"I'm glad to *escape* this hell with you too, Selina."

Emilio waited until the waves of nausea passed and the muscle pain faded, then he fished the keys and fob from his waistband. He unlocked his cage and then Selina's. She crawled out of the opening, slowly stood, and placed her hands on her lower back, leaning backward.

"I never thought standing up would be the thing I looked forward to most in the world. Don't get old, my friend."

"Just keep an eye on that door and don't get caught. I'll be back as soon as I can." Emilio had already slipped the lab coat over his tank top and scrubs. He plunged his feet into the clogs, pinned the badge backward to his lapel, and emerged into the hallway.

Despite the danger of being skewered by an elf and eaten raw by goblins, the *Mission Impossible* theme served as his internal soundtrack when he snuck out of his cage. *Your mission, Emilio, should you choose to accept it, is to visit the first-floor room where hysterical Ashley is being held against her will, snag some intel, and get the hell back to your room before you turn into a goblin snack. Should you or any of your team be caught or killed, they'll be torn apart and eaten by monsters.* He couldn't remember the rest of the schtick from the old show, but pretending he was on a secret mission felt less desperate.

He hoped he'd get a lot of time with those files he'd stumbled onto his first night. The contents might shed some light on what the Fae were doing to him and his new friends. He frowned, thinking of Ashley. Her hysteria could get them all captured. She was definitely the weak link.

He missed Harper. She'd know what to do to calm the girl down and take command of the situation. All that experience managing her mother made her the hysteria whisperer.

Only a slouching troll and a winged woman with blue skin and ram's horns lingered in the hallway. Many more often hung out by the double staircase in the middle of the building. Even though it made his walk longer, Emilio decided it would be safer to use the stairs at the end of the hall.

Even though he had made a couple more trips like this since his first sojourn, his heart still hammered and his hands shook.

As he nudged the first-floor door open, lively music blended with the hum of a crowd. A party in this hell struck him as out of place as a clown at a funeral. He clutched his clipboard and started up the hallway toward the stairs.

"Your kind are not welcome at the revels," a raspy voice hissed.

CHAPTER 38

Emilio spun on his heel and cringed inwardly at the brownish goblin glaring at him up his long, crooked nose. Short legs carried him toward Emilio faster than he thought possible. When the goblin drew near, he noticed the black scars crisscrossing over an empty eye socket.

"I, uh . . . Injections for them. Not trying to crash your party." He pointed to the room across from his target.

The goblin's eye followed the gesture and narrowed to slits.

Emilio's muscles were like rocks while watching the goblin internally debate whether to ignore him or slay him.

"Finish your business and leave."

"Yes, sir. Hey, are these a regular occurrence?" Emilio winced. Probably an awful idea to press his luck, but this might be the opening they needed for their escape if the Fae were all distracted by some grand party. The goblin stepped closer and growled. Emilio pressed his back to the wall and turned his face from the goblin's rancid breath. "You know, so I can finish my work beforehand and not be underfoot again."

The creature harrumphed but backed off a step. "Midnight. Always."

"Um. Awesome." Emilio managed an awkward smile.

The goblin grunted and walked away, muttering to himself. No doubt complaining about human idiocy. Or how bad they smelled. Emilio's shoulders fell and he smoothed his lab coat, taking a second to collect himself before letting himself into Ashley's room.

"Emilio?" Ashley whispered.

"Yeah. It's me."

"Are we getting out of here now?"

Emilio sucked a breath over his bottom teeth, bracing himself for the tsunami of screaming and sobs that would follow when he revealed he was just here to read. He needed to see those files. With the human staff no doubt home asleep and the Fae at their party, this was the best chance he had to read through them, but not if the girl threw another hissy fit and got them both discovered.

"I have one more piece to fit into place to figure out why these creatures are pumping us full of god knows what, and then, yes. You, me, and a handful of others are out of here."

"You promise?"

Emilio squatted in front of her cage. She was curled up in the corner. Her blonde hair was matted to her head. Streaks of tears striped the filth caked on her face. He reached a hand through and she grasped it.

"Yeah. I promise. How are you holding up? Have they done anything new to you?"

Ashley pulled herself upright and hugged her knees to her chest. "Just the injections. They hurt, and then I feel all buzzy and strong."

"Same here."

"Do you know what they are?"

"That's what I'm trying to find out. Maybe we can get help after we escape if I can discover what's in those syringes."

"When're we leaving? I want out of this cage."

Her calmness surprised him. Maybe the treatments had a sedating effect, or she'd just been enchanted and the spell still provided some emotional analgesic. He supposed he should use the keys and let her out to stretch; he knew how painful sitting in his little box was. All the same, the girl seemed completely unstable. If she freaked when she was out, she'd get herself killed panicking and running through the hallways or something. So he lied.

"I need to find the keys to the cages on this level before I can get you out. Don't worry, I'm not leaving you behind." That was true, at least. His grandmother would haunt him forever when she passed if he didn't save as many people as he could.

Her smile was eager, like a starving man getting a bit of bread. "My dad will give you anything you want. Cars. Money. Name it."

"Ashley, I'm not helping you to get something out of it. We have to stick together so everyone can make it out of this hell." That was how his family and friends had banded together to flee the gangs in El Salvador. You escaped together because you needed everyone if you hoped to survive the journey. And because it was the right moral choice.

"No one does something for nothing."

Emilio drew his hand back. Ashley pressed her face to the bars of her cage as he stood.

"OK. If it makes you feel better, your dad can get me a nice Versace coat or something."

"Done." She smiled. "Talk to me some more before you go?"

"Sure. But I need to read these files now." Emilio gave her his most reassuring smile and turned to the wood cabinet. Everyone goes through stages of acceptance. Maybe he'd met Ashley in the shock and denial phase. He was thankful for her relative calm, because it left him with one less potential catastrophe to cope with.

Emilio settled into the cheap plastic office chair and flicked on the desk lamp. He folded it down to shine on the wall to avoid anyone stopping in to turn off lights.

Where to start. He couldn't quite remember the drawer he had opened the last time he was here, so he started with the top one. He flipped through file after file, looking for anything that might tell him what they designed this lab to do. He glanced through files on Fae glamour; the vast majority of the prisoners fell under the glamour merely in the proximity of the Sidhe, so why were some, like him, resistant?

He hit the jackpot in the middle drawer. Dust. He pulled out a couple stacks of files and piled them on the desk. Settling in the chair, he bent forward. An hour slipped by while he pored over data.

"Did you find anything yet?" Ashley called from her cage.

"I think so. Have you heard of the drug Dust?"

"Yeah. It's all over the news. Makes you see things."

"And brings euphoria. What does that sound like to you?"

"I don't know."

"Glamour. It's just like the spell the Fae cast on us. Apparently, if they choose, they can make us see whatever they want us to see . . ." Emilio trailed off as he flipped through pages. It was fascinating. Right here, on the topmost floor, were hundreds of tiny Fae in little cages stacked floor to ceiling. Pixies. An ancient sub-type of that particular Fae species used a powder they produced like a dander to glamour their victims, whereas younger Fae races could produce the effect with magic—literal fairy dust. The drug Dust used a chemical binding agent that made the gross Fae dandruff both a consumable powder and extended the release. "What I don't know is how well they can control us with this."

"I saw some ugly ones ordering people who were under the spell. They did whatever the monsters said," Ashley said.

Emilio glanced through pictures of a winged pixie about the size of a field mouse. Humans in lab coats immobilized the Fae with an apparatus that bound its tiny neck to a small stand. Men in surgical gear scraped a device that looked like a wire brush along the poor thing's wings and body while its face contorted in agony. The dander had the same sheen as Dust.

He rehearsed his discoveries so far. A human company—his employer incidentally—worked with magical creatures who had taken over this place. Together they made a highly addictive drug amplifying the powers of pixie dander and created novel ways to dose masses of people. Dust put anyone addicted to it under Fae control.

But why? He was missing something. What was the point of drugging so many people? Control? Most people didn't experiment with mood-altering chemicals; generally traumatized people and party types did. Not exactly key members of society you'd want to take out of the action if you were planning something like the war they spoke of. Better to focus on dusting the military or the police.

"There has to be something else. Maybe Dust is just the lure." Emilio didn't realize he spoke out loud. Even in this hell, his scientific mind loved a good puzzle and his mental gears ground away despite his terrifying reality. He knew they'd taken samples of his blood and swabbed his cheek, and now they were poking him with syringes Dr. Jones had hinted were to strengthen and prepare them for something.

"How are you going to get us out of here?"

Emilio frowned. The girl was again derailing his train of thought. "On the way in, I saw the shortest path to the water. We're going to swim." He smiled to himself. The second time in his life he was planning to swim across a river to freedom.

"We'll never make it. Not all of us have a disguise. They'll catch us." Ashley's voice was steady. Still nasal and whiney, but no hint of hysteria. He hoped that meant she could hold herself together during what promised to be a grueling journey.

"Apparently, the Fae party every night at midnight. They're all down there by the main entrance having a blast. We can slip out of here unnoticed while they rock out."

"I'm scared, Emilio. How much longer till we get out?"

"I'm scared, too. Hang in there just a day or two more. I need to gather a couple more things."

"You promise you won't leave me behind?"

"I already prom—" Emilio's jaw hung open as he stared at a file full of information on something named Abraxas. He thought he'd heard the doctor mention it. A genetic profile taped to the inside cover with several genes highlighted piqued Emilio's curiosity enough to delay his departure. The profile itself was labeled 'Abraxas.' Did it belong to a person, or was it merely the name of the experiment? He scanned through page after page of genetic workups, his tongue clamped between his lips. All of them had notations and a file number at the top.

Emilio flipped another profile into the stack and his blood ran cold. 942 A1. That was his cage number. Sweet mother of god, this was his genetic scan. Notations filled the margins and were scrawled between the lines of text in glaring red ink. He shoved it next to the sample code taped to the cover. For the highlighted genes, he was a ninety percent match.

Emilio shoved the chair back hard and rocketed to his feet. It rolled back and collided with another cabinet, the noise loud enough to arouse unwanted attention. Emilio ignored it. The discovery brought both the thrill of discovery and the creeping dread of what it meant. He scrambled, half sliding across the floor to Ashley's cage. 173 B3.

The girl started. "Emilio! What—"

Emilio held up his hand and shook his head, already on his way back to the desk. The pages crinkled under flying fingers, but soon enough he found what he was looking for. 173 B3. Ashley's genetic analysis. She was a seventy-four percent match to the Abraxas profile.

This time, he had the presence of mind to just bring the folder with him. He stood in front of the cages, matching cage numbers to genetic profiles. Everyone in this room was over a fifty percent match. Ashley was the highest. It was just a theory, but he'd bet he and Selina were the highest in their room. Something about these genes made them valuable, and, it seemed, very high concordance with the Abraxas profile might explain why the three of them were resistant to the glamour.

"I found something." Emilio was breathless.

"What?"

"Maybe some answers. I need more time." Emilio opened a drawer, shoving post-it pads, boxes of staples, and other desk detritus aside searching for a pencil to jot down some more cage numbers. Next to the pencil he found, a watch with a broken band announced it was a sliver away from three in the morning. He didn't know how long Fae revels went on, but he guessed stragglers at least would start leaving soon. He had to get back, but he also wanted more time with those files.

He grabbed the file containing his genetics and scanned the room. He'd left the duffel bag hidden in his room on the tenth floor. Nothing like the fabric bag was here. Maybe he could use the trash can lining. No. If he encountered anyone, a lab tech carrying a transparent bag of files would raise too many eyebrows.

But what rested in the can's bottom would work. A plastic shopping bag at least was opaque. He whisked out the white bag and shook the receipt into the trashcan before racing back to the file drawer. He scrambled for more files on Abraxas and stuffed a handful into the bag, hoping in his rush he'd nabbed something worthwhile. Once he felt there wasn't more he could accomplish, he jotted down the cage numbers of this room and did his best to return the desk and the remaining files to the state they were in before his espionage.

The watch was too valuable to leave behind. The revels, the injections, timing their escape would be everything. Bag packed, he was ready to creep back to his own room.

"I'll be back for you, Ashley," he whispered as he opened the door a crack to scan the hallway.

"You'd better."

Emilio smiled at her over his shoulder and stepped out into the empty hallway.

CHAPTER 39

Whatever the Fir Bolg decided, Harper felt enduring gratitude to them for doing in a single day what she'd spent ten years attempting: fixing her mom. While not a magical cure for the unresolved grief Eileen O'Neill carried, at least with the enchantment gone and her dependence on alcohol broken, she could heal. Once Harper had Emilio back, maybe she really could travel to India or New Zealand knowing her mother could manage herself.

Emissaries from the Green World Courts passed in and out of the Great Hall, refreshing themselves after their journey. So many shapes and sizes. Some beautiful, some grotesque. Most of the time she avoided them. They made her nervous. None had tried to kill her yet, but they all looked at her like she was something vile they'd stepped in. Regardless of their icy reception, she tried to think of them as more like the Phooka and less like the kelpies, so she wouldn't offend them by recoiling.

Still, avoidance seemed prudent. She didn't understand what to say to the elite of the Fae crowd or their entourages. What if she set off a war with the wrong salutation? Or inadvertently sold herself into slavery with a simple 'thanks'? Diplomacy was a job better suited to Nuada and Aeld. She threw herself into her work, keeping a respectful distance between herself and the dignitaries.

Paegrinn had told her the Green World Fae Courts hadn't met all in one place in over a hundred years. No pressure there. In her heart, she still believed asking Fae for help was a fool's errand and a waste of time Emilio might not afford. If it were up to her, she'd charge in, race to Sauvie Island, and then . . . Well, there's where the plan ended.

Truth is, Nuada was right. They needed muscle and lots of it. She scurried up the ladder she'd just placed beneath one of the beams in the ceiling, looped the rope holding the luminous mushroom lantern she hung, and retreated back down the ladder.

She scowled up at her handiwork. Crooked. Again. She blasted a puff of air from flared nostrils and stomped up the ladder. With a jerk she righted the lantern, but her forceful movement damaged the edge of the mushroom.

"Ugh. I'm no decorator," she grumbled.

"Helps if you don't manhandle the thing." The Phooka's ears twitched.

"I'm just frustrated."

"It's just a lantern." He shrugged and grabbed a box of flowers, heading to the massive table in the middle of the room.

Frustration threatened to blow the lid off her ability to keep her cool, but it wasn't at her questionable decorating skill. She felt utterly powerless. Emilio's hopes rested on the outcome of this council, not on anything she could do. Her stomach responded accordingly, growling and churning so violently and so frequently she hadn't been able to eat since the previous night.

Thankfully, she had a lot more lanterns to hang. Busy hands calmed her racing thoughts. Over and over, she climbed a small ladder and hung her lights. She'd never seen lighted fungus before; they glowed surprisingly bright.

The entire Fir Bolg culture seemed to revolve around fungus. They ate it, used it in medicine, and Paegrinn alluded to somehow using the same network of mycelium that had healed her wounds for long distance communication and other magic.

The ladder scraped across the floor as she dragged it a couple of feet over for the next light. *Always keep your word with the Fae. Never lie.* She rehearsed Nuada and the Phooka's primer on Fae etiquette. Her best friend's life depended on how well she navigated this meeting. A place at the table was reserved for her, and that made her nervous.

Her fingers crawled over the rough twine while the fungus swung back and forth beneath her elbow. *Don't ask them for anything but be ready to give them aid if they ask you. Don't accept any gifts but be conciliatory if you must turn them down.* She craned her neck to the side to check she'd placed the lantern at the same level as the last one. With a nod, she dusted her hands against her tan pants and backed down the ladder.

Don't eat any food they offer. Never say thank you because it implies a debt and they will collect, with interest.

She dragged the ladder to the last place she could fit a light. *Never speak to outsiders about encounters with the Fair Folk. They take swift vengeance if they believe their confidence is broken.* The Phooka had added they liked sincere flattery and, above all, always be hospitable. Harper recalled the rules perfectly. Still, she wasn't optimistic. This was not her world.

"It looks beautiful." Harper's mother finished planting the last blue flower on the living wall framing the entrance and joined her daughter.

"Just like a Sasquatch prom." Harper and Eileen giggled while Harper smiled at the natural beauty of Fir Bolg decor.

In the center of the room, the Phooka scuttled around the table arranging a spray of flowers just so. Stepping back and strolling past the table, he scratched his chin and squinted, tilting his head this way and that.

"More goldenrod, Paegrinn, then it's perfect." Paegrinn handed him a handful of yellow flowers and watched as he wove them into the bouquet.

"Take this chair out of here. The back is far too high. Lord Ezrynivhar's horns sweep very far back. Bashing his head into the back of this chair all day will piss him off mightily." The Phooka shoved the chair toward Paegrinn. The young Fir Bolg hefted it onto his hairy shoulder and slumped toward the kitchen.

"You're worse than a Bridezilla," Harper said.

"Keep talking like that and I'll have Nuada ship you off for cultural sensitivity training."

"No one is this particular about the ratio of gold to red in a bouquet."

"Au contraire. We Fae are exacting in our standards. It is late mid-fall. Were it but a few days later, yellow flowers would be a faux pas in a centerpiece and might cost us the negotiation. But on this day, precisely ten percent of this arrangement should be yellow. Though why I am going to all this trouble for second-string Green World Courts is beyond me. Bloody proletariats, the lot of them."

Harper opened her mouth to reply, but the Phooka was already scrambling back toward the table. His ears drooped against his face and he waved his long arms in the air like he was landing an airplane.

"No, no, no. This won't work. Queen Serotina is a dryad. It's bad enough they made this entire town from wood, but making her sit on the dead flesh of a tree is an insult that would have caused a war in the old days."

"Phooka, it's not like these people have any plastic chairs lying around," Eileen said.

The Phooka plopped his forehead in his palm, head waggling

from side to side. "I can't work under these conditions." He fluttered his hand in front of his face and keeled over to the floor like an old time Southern Belle.

"I got an idea that just might work." Paegrinn disappeared into the back kitchen for several minutes while Harper and her mother worked under the exacting direction of the Phooka, setting cutlery on the table.

Paegrinn returned with a single wide brown mushroom. He smiled. "Dryad's saddle."

The Phooka looked from the fungus to Paegrinn and back to the fungus with pursed lips and wide eyes. "What the actual hell? How is the Queen of the Dawn Court supposed to sit on a three-inch fungus?"

Paegrinn held up a finger, set the dryad's saddle in the opening for the queen's chair, and crouched down next to it. Furry hands hovered just over the top of the mushroom while a low humming rumbled in his chest, cresting and falling. The dryad's saddle ballooned out and shook like a marshmallow in a microwave. Bigger and bigger it grew. Paegrinn whisked his hand straight up and the brown top elongated into a high back. Palms down, he made a gentle curving motion with both hands outward from his body and the sides pulled up into arm rests. White gills feathered up the back and beneath the arms of what became a majestic dryad's saddle throne. His spell was complete. He stood up and smiled with his hands on his hips.

"My giant friend, you may have just saved the day." The Phooka beamed at the mushroom throne. "Dryad's saddle, indeed."

"It's gorgeous, Paegrinn." Eileen ran her hand over the top of the chair. "Looks comfy, too."

Nuada strode into the Grand Hall. Harper started at the sight of him. The former king of the Tuatha had exchanged his long black coat and knee-high boots ensemble for something far more regal. Head to toe, his clothes shone in iridescent midnight blue and silver brocade. Spiral patterns wove in and out of swords and symbols Harper didn't recognize. A gleaming silver breastplate peeked out from under the knee-length coat. His shining hair was loose but held back by a torque made of metallic vines.

She had never seen him reveal the silver arm, but today he flaunted it openly. The appendage was a steampunk fan's dream. Tiny plates and gears meshed together seamlessly. Constantly spinning and sliding, the machinery was capable of the same dexterity as his flesh and blood hand that rested on the Claimh Solais strapped to his hip. Every head in the room swiveled to behold him.

Nuada motioned Harper to his side. She finished placing the last glass on the thick table, wiped her hands again on her tan pants, and hurried to his side.

"The time for the council draws close. I need to prepare you for what is coming since you will join us at the negotiating table as the representative of humanity."

Harper's jaw hung slack. She knew she had a seat at the table, but her plan was to observe and try not to screw up. She was perfectly happy to assist in the preparations and honored that she would get to listen in on the deliberations, but no way was she prepared to interact with kings and queens. Royalty that hated her kind. Nope. This was a horrid idea.

"You can do the negotiating for me." She swept her hand over his regal clothing. "This is clearly more in your wheelhouse than mine."

"You have every right to sit at the table and speak for your people. You are—"

"Yeah. Yeah. Some lost heir to a dead throne, and a glowing rock thinks I'm pretty neat."

"The blood of Eriu is within you, and the magic of Macha is in your veins. Do not make light of this. Every person at that table honors that power and takes the possibility of a High Kingship seriously. Whether or not you recognize it, you have authority. Once you stand on the Stone of Destiny, you will be their queen, too."

"Couple glitches in your master plan. First, even if I wanted to be a queen, I have absolutely no idea what to do. Second, your fancy boulder seems irreparable if you're carrying around a chunk in your pocket."

"The right person can heal the stone, and you will learn all that you need to lead your people. But now is not the time for this discussion. We have to get you ready to take part in this council meeting. Walk with me." He turned and held out his hand for her to join him on the boardwalk.

Overcast skies greeted her when Harper stepped outside the hall. Ominous black clouds drifted in. She hoped they weren't a sign of things to come. It was cold, and incoming rain would make it colder. The afternoon chanting of the Fir Bolg surrounded her, just a few now, but in minutes every member of the village would join the chant. It was a part of Fir Bolg life that calmed her heart and brought with it a rare sense of well-being. She longed to join them rather than cram for this council meeting.

"It is important for you to know how the political lines will flow in this meeting."

Harper had no stomach for politics. Even the posturing for class president in school was too much for her to tolerate.

"The solitary Fae do not recognize any Court, but they have a leader elected to represent them. Heironymous is an ogre. He and I have an extensive history."

"A good history?"

"We have helped each other from time to time. He runs a lodge close by. Magical beings from all over pass through. He will be the one among the gathering with the most knowledge of what is coming. He is not the concern, today. Heironymous will remain neutral for as long as he can to protect his business prospects, but he will chose right in the end. The solitary Fae have lived among humanity and have a less adversarial view of your kind."

"Got it. And the Dusk and Dawn Fae?"

"Far more complicated. Dusk and Dawn both benefitted when the Veil thickened."

"I thought the pathways to the Underworld closing was like the end of the world to the Fae." Harper ran her hand along the smooth wood bannister as they walked. The chanting was in full swing and the forest rang with deep, throaty voices.

"For the Underworld Courts it was, but for the Fae who always preferred to live in the Green World, their power increased. No longer were they merely territories under the Seelie and Unseelie. Here and now, they rule unchallenged. They will not want the gateways open again, for it will erode their power."

"Then they should be against Badb opening the gateways again. They should join us, right?"

"They will also not want to be under the rule of a new High Queen either. Dusk especially will object to your less-than-Sidhe heritage. They dislike humans. Dawn merely distrusts you. The important thing is neither will want to give up their power so easily, and they will back whichever side gives them the most of it."

"It sounds like the choice they have is who they'll give up their power to." Possibilities unwound in Harper's mind. She had no intention of being on a throne, but if Badb already had the Underworld sworn to her and if she could convince the Dawn and Dusk Courts to join her, she would have unchecked power. No one was safe.

"Exactly. They will be slow to choose a side because they will wait to see which side affords them the most sovereignty. Dawn and Dusk are not who we need to convince today. They will wait until the boot is on their neck to choose a side. It is Aeld and his people we need to bring into the fold."

"But Aeld said he'd go with what the council decides, so don't we need to convince Dawn and Dusk now?"

Nuada smiled. "You are not as bad at politics as you think. Yes, and no. Aeld is fully aware of the attitudes of the Courts. He may be swayed even if they are reluctant to join us right now. He fully expects the Dusk Court to be last to join with humans, if they join them at all. And even then, there are elements in that Court who would act as double agents to the Underworld Courts because of their hatred of humans. If the Dawn Court ends this negotiation by offering help in even the smallest way, that is the best solution. Aeld will take his cue from the Dawn Queen."

Harper had absolutely no idea how she could help sway the Fae leaders. All the same, she couldn't fail Emilio. Or the others the dark Fae had taken. How many more would they steal? Worse, how many would die if this became a war? The Fae with their magic clashing with human weapons of mass destruction would lay waste to everything. Her stomach answered her racing thoughts with more gurgling, an acid taste spreading up the back of her throat.

Nuada halted outside Harper's room and motioned her inside. "The Phooka found a change of clothes for you in his bag. Once you are dressed, meet me back at the Hall. The council convenes in under an hour."

"Um, ok." Harper swallowed the sour taste.

Nuada's silver arm came to rest on her shoulder and his other hand tilted her face to meet his. "You are not alone in this meeting. Follow my lead and we may yet prevail." With that, he turned and strode back toward the Hall.

Nuada's presence comforted her the way family should, and that surprised her. In their short few days together he'd protected her, taught her, and soothed her. Much like she imagined her father would have, had he been here. A part of her would miss him once she got Emilio back and got far away from magic and Fae.

A golden dress lay draped across her bed. She held it up to look at the subtle needlework around the neckline, bottom, and waist of the gown. The embroidery depicted the flight of many magical birds tumbling after one another. Tiny jewels blinked from every inch of sheer sleeves. But the most gorgeous thing of all gleamed on the bed. A golden circlet of vines similar to Nuada's silver one.

She wriggled into the dress and worked her hair into a low bun. With sweaty palms she arranged the folds of the golden gown before slipping on the matching flats.

Well, I'm as ready as I'll ever be. She stepped out of her hut. The Phooka was waiting for her with an umbrella to shelter her fancy dress from the steady rain.

"Well, don't you look like a Disney princess." The Phooka morphed into a black and gray version of The Beast and bowed as he held the umbrella for her. "Tale as old as time . . ." he sang in an exaggerated Frank Sinatra voice.

Harper rolled her eyes. "Don't you have to pay Disney royalties every time you sing that? Let's get this over with." She gathered up the hem and started walking back toward the Great Hall.

CHAPTER 40

The Phooka scrambled in front of Harper to push the door open. He waited there in an awkward half curtsy while she stepped inside. Still in his Disney form, he held out his arm for her. She raised her eyebrows but looped a hand around his elbow and the pair strode into the Hall.

"Since you are formally representing your people, I will serve as your herald," the Phooka said.

"Herald?"

"As the council members arrive, I will make your formal introductions. Follow my lead, for I am also your advisor regarding Fae manners and customs."

For many reasons, the thought of the Phooka making introductions made her nervous. Nevertheless, this was not her world, so probably best she obeyed their customs if she wanted a hope of receiving their help.

Across the room, Nuada conversed with a tall, barrel-chested Fae covered in rich brown fur. This must be the ogre. The label ogre conjured up images of smelly gross brutes, but this one was the opposite of all that. Rich red velvet and white lace clashed with horns and claws. Then again, this was her first ogre. Perhaps they all dressed like they lived on the set of a musty PBS television show only the elderly watched.

The Phooka led her to Nuada and his friend. With a flourish of his other hand, he bowed low.

"May I present Harper O'Neill, High Ambassador for the Human Realms."

Harper dropped a quick curtsy she hoped wasn't horribly awkward. "Pleased to meet—" The Phooka stamped on her foot.

"Don't speak to the ogre until his herald makes his introduction," he hissed in her ear through a fake toothy grin.

A wiry goblin with a near-spherical mass of curly black hair was dressed in matching red velvet and lace. He stepped forward from the ogre's side, bowing so low his long, pointy nose scraped the floor. "Before you stands the elected emissary of the solitary Fae and esteemed proprietor of the Fogradh Lodge, Master Heironymous."

"Pleased to meet you, Ambassador O'Neill. Nuada has told me much about you."

Harper inclined her head. "Likewise pleased to meet you, Master Heironymous."

"Just Heironymous will suffice."

"And you can call me Harper."

They were just in time. Aeld rose from his seated position. Paegrinn gently tapped on a small hand drum and the Hall fell silent. Harper missed entirely Paegrinn's introduction of his father while she tugged on the bodice of her dress to keep it from digging into her side. The Phooka melted into his true form and introduced Harper the same way he had to Aeld.

Just then Harper's mother emerged next to Nuada wearing a midnight blue and silver dress that matched Nuada's clothing. One of the Fir Bolg had braided her hair in a crown around her head and laced it with tiny white blooms, a style many of the Fir Bolg women wore.

"Please welcome Nuada Silver Hand, Master of the Elements, and former High King of the Tuatha de Danann."

Harper stared wide-eyed at her mother. She was Nuada's herald? The flow of introductions prevented her from asking how her mother had been drafted into the job.

A pure-white satyr clopped forward on shiny brown hooves to introduce his queen. "Queen Serotina of the Dawn Court, Defender of the Northern Woods is honored to make your acquaintance."

Her beauty was wild and alien, like the forest itself. Twigs jutted from a cascade of moss green hair tumbling over a pale green chiffon gown that contrasted with her deep brown skin. Long fingers resembled tree branches. When she spoke, her voice was the whisper of the wind through branches.

As the last to appear, the Dusk Court King's arrival marked the end of the formal introductions. The king cut an imposing figure. He was as tall as Nuada and clad in glittering black from head to toe. Vast horns swept forward over his forehead and then dramatically back over a fall of shiny obsidian hair. His piercing red eyes were the only splash of color and contrasted with his dusky grey complexion.

Harper felt a rush of warmth spread over her face when the Dusk King flashed a dashing smile. Despite the row of pointed teeth, he was beautiful. Her mind started spinning a litany of excuses she could make to get near him, even if only to peer more closely into his ruby-red eyes. He was so perfect, not even the long black tail sweeping behind him bothered her.

"He's amazing. What is he?" Harper bent down and whispered to the Phooka without allowing her gaze to stray, even for a second, from the Dusk King.

"An incubus. Be wary, he has a profound effect on mortal

women. He'll bewitch you, drain you of life force, and leave you a husk."

"Uh-huh." She licked her lips while pivoting her body toward him. Unbidden, her short fingers smoothed the wisps of hair that had escaped her bun.

"Oh, for crap's sake." The Phooka grasped her hand and tugged her to his level. He pushed a fuzzy face into hers and studied her. His bag appeared at his side. Flipping it open, he reached inside and drew out a tiny bottle of amber liquid. "Stick out your tongue."

Harper obeyed, and he squeezed several drops of a sweet mixture onto her tongue. Her attraction to the Dusk King melted away, and she noticed with a shudder the cape he wore wasn't actually a cape. Floor-length leathery wings folded over his back.

A loud clap from Aeld silenced the chatter of the assembled Fae guests. A dozen Fir Bolg strode forward with cups of the same pine and herb tea they served at the beginning of every healing, meal, visit, or anything, really.

"My friends, welcome to our humble village. You honor us with your presence. If you would please make your way to the table, some refreshments await you and we can begin."

The assembled leaders meandered toward the table. Harper noted the eyes of all the Fae drifting frequently to her. It made her skin crawl.

The Dawn Queen arrived at the table first. She ran her hands lovingly over the fungal chair Paegrinn made for her and smiled.

"Aeld, you honor me with this dryad's saddle chair. How very thoughtful."

"Your Majesty, I cannot take the credit for it. My son, Paegrinn, made it especially for you."

The adolescent Fir Bolg studied his squirming feet. If a Sasquatch could blush, he'd be red all over.

The queen gracefully lowered herself into her seat. The little white satyr pushed the chair containing Serotina to the table. "Paegrinn, you honor me with your thoughtfulness."

Paegrinn dropped an awkward bow and muttered, "My pleasure, Your Majesty." At a nod from his father, he brought out the flat drum and tapped on it again to bring the meeting to order.

Aeld stepped up to the head of the long table. His wide, shaggy head scanned the room, meeting each representative's eyes in turn. "Honored guests, some of you have traveled far to be present with us. If there is anything we can offer you for your comfort, please do not hesitate to ask. My son, Paegrinn, will ensure we meet your every need."

Harper's shoulders hovered around her ears and under the table her foot tapped out a nervous rhythm against her calf. She felt like she was drowning. Despite Nuada's pep talk, she only wanted to stay silent. The less she said, the less chance of the ignorant human handing Badb more allies. Her mom caught her eye and smiled a warm smile. That long-sought support bolstered her.

"Your hospitality is sufficient, but I, for one, am wondering why you have called us all here. The sooner we can dispense with the matter the sooner I can return to more, shall we say, civilized shores." Ezrynhivar wore a bored expression and sat draped across his chair sideways. He picked up the plate of rustic-looking cakes, sniffed them, and wrinkled his nose before returning them to the table and sliding the plate away.

The Phooka pushed his face forward next to Harper's ear. The fur tickled a bit, and she resisted the urge to scratch. "He knows very well why he's here. His *Majesty* wouldn't know civilized if it jammed a hot poker—"

"Phooka!" Harper hissed and held a hand to his muzzle.

But the Phooka refused to be deterred. He swatted her hand away and pushed his lips right up to her ear. "Pale imitation of his father's Court in the Underworld even if he is right about the food." He flopped back in his chair and crossed his arms over his chest like a chastised toddler.

"Don't be such a snob, Ez. I find this place delightfully rustic." Queen Serotina smiled at Paegrinn and leaned back against her dryad's saddle seat. It would appear Paegrinn's handiwork had scored brownie points with the Dawn Queen. Harper was proud of her friend.

Nuada pushed himself to his feet. With his fingertips resting on the table, he leaned forward, head swiveling first to the right to regard the Dusk King and to the left to tip his head to the Dawn Queen. "His Majesty is correct. We have much to discuss and the threat to us all grows greater by the moment."

"Oh, please do enlighten us about this phantom threat. I, for one, have seen nothing ominous in my lands." The Dusk King flicked his hand at Nuada as though dismissing a servant. "And please, have the courtesy to make this tall tale an entertaining one."

Nuada ignored Ezrynhivar's jabs. "Doubtful the cancer growing here has yet spread to the city of New Orleans. Regardless, I will have you on the edge of your seat, Ez."

The Dusk King rolled his eyes and opened his mouth to offer a rejoinder, but Nuada held up a hand.

"Now that passage to the Underworld is again possible, I am sure it would delight your father to have you returned to his side." Nuada looked at the Dusk King from the tops of his eyes and a slow smile spread across his lips.

Ezrynhivar sneered and waved for Nuada to continue. His reddened face and narrowed eyes were at odds with the nonchalant gesture. Black wings crumpled against the floorboards when he tilted his chair back so it rested on two legs.

"That's impossible," Queen Serotina said with a tilt of her head that sent her green hair tumbling forward over her shoulder. "The devastation to the Green World made the Veil impassable, completely destroyed all the gateways. No one has come or gone from that place in over fifty Earth years."

"And yet spriggans have been spotted at the edges of Portland city. None of that race remained here before the last gate fell." Heironymous swirled his mead in the wooden goblet and took a long pull.

"Heironymous is right. Someone has opened a single gateway, and I can prove it." Nuada swiveled his head back to Ezrynhivar. The Dusk King had gone pale. His throat bulged with a string of hard swallows like he was trying not to retch.

"Daddy's coming to take your toy throne away, you usurping whelp," the Phooka whispered in Harper's ear with his eyes trained on Ezrynhivar. "That will be what the Dusk *King* fears above all." He made air quotes at the word 'king.'

"Though it is not the portal we should fear the most." Nuada stalked the outside edges of the circle. Harper stifled a grin. Every alien-looking eye followed his slow revolution, riveted. "Other things are stirring in the mist that now perpetually surrounds Sauvie Island. Things even I do not yet understand." Nuada told them of the streams of indigent humans being shepherded into the tower on the island and about the peculiar transformation taking place there. To dropping jaws, he told them of the return of Badb Catha and he ended by describing the burgeoning ranks of the Sluagh.

"Venerable Nuada, with no disrespect, I fail to see how missing humans is much of a problem." Queen Serotina's green eyes drifted to Harper and Eileen as she spoke. "We have always taken a few to be midwives or servants."

"But never in these numbers," the Phooka chimed in.

"The human . . . whatever-she-is allows her vassal speak for her?" The Dusk King narrowed his eyes at the Phooka.

"I-I gave him permission." Harper stammered and looked at her hands.

Horns scraped the back of his chair as Ezrynhivar threw his head back and laughed. "Your choice of servants is poor, human girl. Not even my father tolerated this whelp's presence for long." He jabbed a finger at the Phooka.

"Enough. Petty bickering gets us nowhere." Nuada had circled to stand behind the Dusk King.

Harper felt her indignation rise. These monsters spoke of kidnapping and forcing people to work for them with nonchalance. Like they were entitled to it. Her skin flushed and she smacked her hand on the tabletop, sending her empty teacup toppling over. The hushed whispers abruptly stopped while every strange new face rotated to stare at the upstart human.

"What's wrong with you? You speak of abducting people and using them as you please like it's some god-given right. It's monstrous."

All around the room, the jaws of royal Fae and herald alike hung open. Even Harper's mother looked at her daughter like she was a stranger. The Dusk King's features knitted together, his eyes narrowed, and he leaned over the table in Harper's direction, about to speak or do something far worse. Aeld rising to his feet denied him the chance.

"It's really no different from how your people treat the non-human beings you share this world with, and for the same reasons. Because you can." The Fir Bolg chieftain's voice rang over the gathering. Aeld's face held a tinge of sadness, and he looked only at Harper as he spoke.

Chastised, Harper smoothed invisible wrinkles out of her dress and lowered herself to her seat. Across the table, the Dusk King laughed again as though watching an amusing play.

"Regardless of the morality, this would seem to be a human problem. As always down the millennia, they will have to find ways to prevent Fae abducting them. This is like any predator-prey relationship. It is not a reason to begin a war to stop it," Aeld added.

"I agree with the Fir Bolg Chieftain. This doesn't concern us. Even if Ez is not looking forward to his family reunion." Queen Serotina placed a deep brown hand over the lower part of her face, but Harper saw the smile she hid.

It was just as Nuada had warned. None of them wanted to be involved. She was beginning to agree with the Dark Douche King. This entire council was a waste of time. Besides, she was more and more uncomfortable around creatures who would enslave her without a passing thought. The sooner they left, the better. This charade was keeping her from saving Emilio. They'd just have to figure out another way to get to him.

"All of you are missing the point," Nuada said. "The only reason Badb opened the gateway to the Underworld is to build an army to attack the human world. War is on our doorstep."

"Fae can't attack humans directly, for all are still bound by the ancient laws. And most of us can't tolerate being in their cities for more than a handful of hours. An open gateway is mixed news to us, but only slightly dire news for humans," the Dawn Queen said.

"That is where this comes in." Heironymous beckoned to the goblin. The wiry creature pulled a vial full of iridescent purple powder from his pocket and tossed it onto the table where it spun to a halt. Harper recognized it immediately as Dust. "Go on, pass it around and see if you can guess what it is."

Aeld picked the vial up first and uncorked it. He sniffed at it a bit, shook his head, and passed it to the Dawn Queen.

Her branchlike fingers looked to Harper like someone attempting to grasp a test tube with chop sticks. The little white satyr scuttled to her side and held it up in front of her eyes. He turned it this way and that for her to see. Her lips pursed and brow wrinkled in thought. "This is of Fae origin. But how . . ."

She looked at Heironymous and passed the vial to Harper.

Harper knew full well what Dust looked like and she hastily handed it to her mother with barely a glance. Her mom passed it like a hot potato to King Ezrynhivar.

The Dusk King dipped his little finger into the vial and brought the shimmery powder closer to his eyes to examine it. "It can't be," he whispered, then sniffed gingerly at the rim. "Human drugs and something else," he muttered like no one else was watching, then dipped his finger into his mouth. A storm passed over his features and he leapt to his feet. "It's glamour. Humans making glamour. How is this possible?"

"The king is correct." The soft, deep voice of the ogre oozed into the Hall. "Specifically, the glamour of older races who secrete it rather than cast it like a spell. Harvested and bonded to a human pharmacological substrate."

"But how?" Serotina asked.

"How do humans do anything? They probably have hundreds of the poor things locked in a lab somewhere." Heironymous shrugged. "But they couldn't do it alone. Tuatha, Fomorian, or Fae helped them create this, and for a very specific purpose. Control."

Ezrynhivar's face became a storm fixed on Harper. "And the little human wonders why we hate them."

Harper's heart pounded half in anger and half in fear of the imposing dark Fae. The desire to knock his arrogant ass down a few pegs fought a pitched battle with her fear of being zapped to a pile of dust. Anger was the tiebreaker and she opened her mouth.

"With respect, venerable King, what I heard from Nuada's story is that making this drug would require Fae and humans working together. Your own kind are just as deserving of your anger. If it matters, the thought of Fae locked in cages being harvested is offensive to me as well." Her last words surprised her. So far Fae had only caused her pain, yet the thought of something like the Phooka tortured in a lab somewhere turned her stomach.

The Dusk King loomed, statue still, his eyes locked on Harper, expression unreadable. He inclined his head and lowered himself into his seat. Harper caught sight of Nuada out of the corner of her eye. A half smile played across his lips. His approval brought a wave of warmth.

"Heironymous, you said control was the reason this substance is being made. To what end?" Aeld asked.

Understanding unfolded in Harper's mind in a blinding flash. Her mind raced through the implications. The cold stone was back in her stomach again and she felt a brief wave of dizziness. Emilio was in bigger trouble than she thought. The room was silent as each leader pondered the implications of Aeld's question.

"Soldiers," Harper said in a small voice.

"What did you say, child?" Serotina's voice was high and soft.

"It's like you said, Your Majesty. Fae can't attack humans directly. The next best thing is to make them puppets to fight other humans." Harper eyes never left her hands as they twisted in her lap.

"A disposable army where every soldier lost to either side is a victory for Badb. That is brilliant." Ezrynhivar's smile stretched across his face. "You, my dear, are fucked." The king looked positively delighted.

Heironymous stroked his furry chin and tilted his head to the rafters.

Nuada spoke up. "Harper may be right. I fear there is more going on with Dust and the human population of Portland than even we know. But I am certain these events point to the dawn of the Third Battle of Moytura."

A hush fell over the room and every eye rested on the former king. Seconds ticking past felt like an eternity.

"That's not—" Ezrynhivar began before Nuada cut him off.

"All great events resolve in threes. The world changed when my people came to Ireland from the Undying Lands. Our arrival caused the First Battle of Moytura with Aeld's people. The betrayal by our own King Breas caused the Second Battle of Moytura against the Fomorians. Both times, the balance of power in this world endured a seismic shift." Nuada paused and raised his silver arm to the warm light where it seemed to glow like embers. "The great powers of this world gather again, and Badb Catha prepares for the annihilation of all who oppose her. You must see this. She opened the portal in the Veil and is bringing Underworld Fae to this world by the dozens, and now a new drug gives her potentially tens of thousands of human pawns resilient to all Fae weaknesses. Here, right now, we stand on the cusp of a final war to decide control of this Green World."

"That cannot be true." Serotina wore an incredulous expression. "If this is the leadup to some final war between the three Noble Races, where are the Fomorians, and why is Badb targeting humanity, not Fomorians or Fir Bolg?"

"The Fomorians are here. Who do you think own all but a few of the major corporations of this land? The company that makes the Dust is owned by Breas himself," Heironymous said.

"This isn't Ireland. We fought both previous Battles of Moytura at Inisfáil. It would seem any last war would occur there, very far from our concerns." The Dusk King looked like he was trying more to convince himself than anyone else.

"Oooh-oooh! I can answer that one." The Phooka stood on his hooves, hopping up and down with a hand waving high in the air like a know-it-all desperate for the teacher to call on him. "That is, if milady wishes it." He snatched the waving hand back down with the other like it had a mind of its own.

Harper nodded. She didn't have a better reply.

"The treaty negotiated with the Milesians. You know, the one that sent you lot to the Underworld. That treaty forbade war between Tuatha, Sidhe, and humans on Ireland forever, but it did not forbid it elsewhere. That is why Badb is here and not there."

The Phooka made a dramatic bow and sat back, perching on the edge of his seat with his chest thrust out and beaming ear to ear.

"And before any of you say there is no High King to lead such a war . . ." Nuada reached into his breast pocket and placed the stone shard in front of Harper's place at the table where it immediately glowed a blinding blue. "Let me introduce you to Harper O'Neill, last descendant of Niall of the Nine Hostages and the Tuatha Eriu, gifted the magical essence of Macha, and chosen by the Lia Fail to be the High Queen."

CHAPTER 41

Harper felt an elbow in her side. "Stop slouching and look regal," the Phooka hissed in her ear.

Jaws hung on all sides of Harper, but the council members recovered fast. The initial shock of seeing the shard of the Lia Fail wore off and the room hummed with muttering. The Dawn Queen sat up straighter in her mushroom chair, her face taking on an air of superiority.

"But the stone—"

"Can be mended." Nuada cut Serotina off. "You must see what I say is true. All the signs are there, and a new High Queen is here to lead us despite Badb's purge of the line. I call an initial vote. Will we stand against a coming war as one against Badb Catha to save this Green World? My vote is yes. Harper?"

She suddenly realized Nuada was right. Whether or not she believed all this crap about her supposed lineage, the Fae did. And they'd pursue her to the ends of the earth, some to recruit her, others to kill her.

A short, private laugh bubbled up. Hadn't she been hunted her entire life, fought her whole life? Child protection services, bill collectors, or people on the street when they were homeless. Now she was hunted by Fae. At least most of those monsters looked the part. They were far more powerful than anything she'd faced before, and her life as she knew it was over.

Like always, her life boiled down to two choices: fight or run. God knew she was tired of fighting. Once she made sure the people she cared about were safe, she still planned to run. Last heir and magical powers or not, she was outclassed. One person couldn't stand against armies of demigods and Fae. But if her actions today could bring in those more prepared to battle than she was, it was her duty to speak her mind and do her part, hoping their help could save Emilio and the other abductees.

Not that it mattered. Harper could tell by the stony faces around her what the outcome would be. Nuada had played his hand too early. She'd find no help to save her friend here, but she agreed that someone needed to stop what was coming. Countless people would die if Nuada was right.

"I vote yes."

Eyes fell to Queen Serotina. "I have heard nothing here today that makes this anything more than a human's problem. My vote is no." Her gaze never left the Lia Fail shard.

The expected neutrality came from Heironymous. The ogre shook his shaggy head and said, "I abstain until we know more. If this is, as Nuada says, the Final Battle of Moytura we will, of course, side with the Tuatha." Interesting, Harper thought. He signaled more willingness to join their side than Nuada initially guessed. But, she supposed, his people likely had the most to lose should a war break out.

Aeld was next. He got to his feet and smoothed the chieftain's sash he wore. "Our time of making war has passed. No Fir Bolg has harmed another being in battle since the Tuatha first came to Ireland and we lost our Northern lands to them. Our only goal is to protect our villages from intrusion by humans or Fae. Our vote is no."

The final vote was that of the Dusk King. Harper knew already what his answer would be. Ezrynhivar swiveled his head to stare right at Harper. "This untested child couldn't lead a fly to shit. The Dusk Court is an emphatic no."

Something snapped inside Harper. That familiar iron core of anger galvanized her, giving her the audacity she needed to speak her truth to the monsters that stalked her dreams.

She was unaware that the room had gone silent. Every eye turned to the shard of the Stone of Destiny that flared so brightly even Nuada brought up a hand to shield his eyes. Before common sense could take hold of her again, Harper shot to her feet, kicked her chair tumbling into the back wall, and slammed her fist down on the thick table hard enough to cause dishes to clunk together.

"No! No. This is not how this ends." The blinding light of the shard lit her features with a brilliant glow. "I have sat here and had my people be the subject of scorn, ridicule, and sanctimonious judgment. And yet I am the one surrounded by hypocrites and fools."

Ezrynivhar's wings fanned out behind him and his hands curled into claws. "How dare—"

"You are the worst of the lot. Sitting here looking down your nose at me while you stand to lose the most. Humans have a saying: Better to be a big fish in a small pond. When your daddy returns and takes your little gothy Dusk Court back into the Unseelie Court, who's the loser then? You should be the first to rally to our side. But you're terrified that if we lose, your big bad father will destroy his upstart son for opposing him."

Her words angered him. He rose, hands shaking, breath hissing in and out of flared nostrils. Smug delight bloomed in Harper's chest, but she wasn't finished. This would either goad some of the Fae into joining them or lose them completely. But they were, mostly, lost anyway, so Harper pressed on.

"I imagine the same would happen to your Court, Queen Serotina." Her focus swept past her to the Fir Bolg Chieftan. "Aeld, you are right to fear and avoid most humans. We destroy the natural places around us, mostly for profit." Harper paused and pulled her spine ramrod straight. "None of you understand the danger. When someone pokes human nations with a stick, especially this one, we don't turn the other cheek. We lash out. Hard. In war we hold nothing sacred. Not all of us are this way, but the ones in power are. What do you suppose will happen when the United States government figures out the West Coast has become the battlefront in a war with monsters? We have weapons of destruction so stupid strong it makes your glamour and magic spells look like quaint little parlor tricks. And when the warmongers in our capital city decide to strike on domestic soil against invaders, they won't care about collateral damage. Pretty forests and a bunch of people won't stop the bombing. We've completely leveled a lot more for a lot less."

Harper checked the temperature of the room. Every face wore the same expression of sobering fear. *Good, they needed to pull their heads out of fairyland and wake the hell up.*

"I thought all your races were supposed to be older and wiser than us puny, pathetic humans, but from what I can see you merely aged. Wisdom passed you all by. Nuada's told you we can band together right now to stop this thing before Badb completes her army and picks a fight everyone will lose. We can end this now before it even starts, and all you can do is stick your heads in the sand."

Nuada stood between Aeld and Heironymous across the table. He nodded encouragement. She had their attention. Now she needed to drive the point home, but she was fresh out of ideas because she'd said all she wanted to say. Critique came easily, problem solving was more difficult. Nuada's preparation and her own observation meant she knew the members of this council were dead wrong. But how could she do more than reduce their defenses to rubble? If she was planning to sway them to Nuada's cause, they needed something to rally behind. Something to inspire them. Something to make them see the common goal. It took a genuine leader to do more than obliterate the enemy's argument, and, predictably, she drew a blank.

She wasn't really a queen; she was playing the role Nuada had cast her in. Her eyes fell once more to the blinding bright stone. The magic rock felt otherwise. Then it hit her. Emilio had started all this by getting himself abducted at a party. It was only fitting that something he loved would finish it. He was always quoting the Dalai Lama about oneness and how it dovetailed with the astronomy class they'd taken together. Harper couldn't recall any good quotes exactly, but she thought she remembered the gist. She took a deep breath and changed her tone for the final plea.

"You know, my friend Emilio is an armchair Buddhist. He says all separation is an illusion. Everything is really one thing. I could never wrap my head around that until this moment. He was so excited to tell me he learned in his college classes that the entire universe started out as one tiny little particle that grew and changed, forming stars and planets and the endless beautiful things surrounding us now. Don't you see? If you go back in time far enough, we're all that one tiny speck. We should fight together to save as much of the world as possible from whatever seeks to destroy it, because it's really ourselves we're saving. I'm going to that island to rescue the taken, even if I have to do it alone. If I find any of your people that need my help, I'll free them, too, if I can. Because if Emilio were here now, he'd tell me if I looked back far enough, they're my family, too."

Harper sank back down at the table and cradled her head in her hands, not willing to show the hot tears that splashed on the wood. Memories of her father and Emilio flooded her mind even though she didn't want them to. She felt the Phooka place a paw on the center of her back so that no one would see. The stone shard gleamed brightly before her as though it, at least, cheered her on.

"A more perfect description of the Great Song I've not heard in a century," Heironymous said.

"I think young Harper has given us more to think about. I suggest you enjoy our hospitality and we reconvene tomorrow morning for another vote. For now, our home is your home. Dinner will be served for us shortly." The Fir Bolg Chieftain moved toward the door to assist in the preparations for dinner.

"You surprise me, Harper." Serotina's silky voice cut through the murmur that erupted.

"Yeah, well, I surprised me, too. I just hope I changed your minds." Harper looked up at the Dawn Queen. She merely smiled and stood.

"We shall see."

Harper's mother yanked her into an embrace. "I always knew you'd accomplish amazing things someday. You were incredible," she whispered into her hair. They stayed like that for a moment. Tears returned to Harper's eyes. Before their time in the village, she couldn't remember the last time her mom had really seen her or said the kind of words she needed to hear. Whatever their vote tomorrow, at least she had that. Eileen O'Neill released her daughter and held her at arm's length, an expression of wonder on her face. "I think there are others who wish to speak with you. We'll talk later."

Nuada stood conversing with the Phooka. When they saw the family moment had ended, both of them stepped over to her. Harper caught the Dusk King out of the corner of her eye chatting with Heironymous while fixing his eyes on her. He turned away quickly when he saw her glance in his direction.

Nuada rested his flesh hand on Harper's shoulder. "You performed better here than I could have hoped."

"It was basic reasoning. No one here is seeing the big picture. I merely called them out for it. Not like it made much of a difference, anyway, but it felt good to unload on them."

"I can't tell if you made an enemy or a devotee out of Ezrynhivar. He hasn't stopped staring at you since you called him the worst of the lot. I thought his head would explode!" The Phooka's donkey laugh echoed in the room, and he slapped his furry knees with each whoop.

"You spoke wisdom and it shocked them. They will not forget that," Nuada said.

"Yeah, the great wisdom of Introductory Astronomy at the Mount Hood Community College. I just told them about the Big Bang and some of Emilio's Buddhist ideas."

"Let's go get changed for dinner. We can talk more later, and then it's time to begin your lessons in swordplay." Nuada turned and guided Harper out of the Hall. She glanced back over her shoulder.

Ezrynhivar was still staring at her.

CHAPTER 42

Harper felt much more at home in the brown tunic and pants the Fir Bolg had left draped across her bed than the fancy outfit she'd worn to the negotiations. Both the dress and the role she had played pinched in all the wrong places. The rain had stopped for now, but the moisture dripping from the pine needles tapped out a gentle rhythm against the wooden roof. The sound harmonized with the voices of the Fir Bolg chanting, creating a symphony that soothed Harper's jangled nerves. The sonorous tones ebbed and flowed as voices joined and fell away. It was a lot like the chanting of monks, only deeper and less structured.

Her brows knitted together, and she twisted her fingers back and forth in front of her as she leaned on the railing of the walkway just outside the entrance to her room. Emilio hated sleeping in the woods, but she was sure he'd love it here for the food and the Fir Bolg's forest mysticism.

If Nuada was right, she wasn't sure if it was better if Emilio was alive. The Fae were doing something horrible to their stolen people. She shouldn't be lounging around enjoying her vacation from the city. Her fist clenched. Fae. Fir Bolg. None of them seemed to care about the suffering taking place on that island. Nuada and his magic rock were definitely wrong. She was useless here.

Nuada had felt it best she channeled her anger by learning to use a blade. Harper wanted to spend time with her mom instead, but her mother's current round of mycelial healing wouldn't end for a few more hours. She supposed waiting around with no distractions would just lead to rumination. Still, what did Nuada think a few lessons with a blade was going to accomplish? Swordsmanship wasn't learned in a day or two. It had taken her five years of classes to become a decent fighter. They had a day or two here at most before those skills would be tested. *What did Gran always say? Every little bit helps.*

But there was a far simpler answer. The thought of it brought a quickening of her pulse. Wielding Nuada's sword again promised the answer to her problems. No training needed. Echoes of its whispers caressed her mind. She could almost feel the cool metal against her palm. Freed from its scabbard, the magical blade would make her powerful, tell her what to do to save her friend. Together she and the Cliamh Solais would end this war before it began, just like they did against Gwyn's forces.

The clip-clop of hooves announced the Phooka's arrival.

"Back in this hideous frock again?" He wrinkled his nose at her Fir Bolg outfit.

"I don't know. I kind of like it. Surprisingly warm and freeing." She turned her head back toward the singing. "Why do they sing like this for so much of the day?"

"Don't tell me you want to start rumbling and crooning too." Harper shot him an eye roll. He sighed. "It's a way they pray to the ebb and flow of the Great Song or something like that."

"It's beautiful."

"I prefer Bowie."

The Phooka led her to a stairway that spiraled down the trunk of a tree. As soon as they reached the bottom and stepped away from the trunk, the entire treetop city vanished from sight. Harper twisted her head this way and that, trying to glimpse the arboreal city, but it had faded from sight.

"What the—"

"I told you the Fir Bolg remained hidden."

"But invisible? I hope you know the way back. Where are we anyway?"

"I do. And we are smack dab in the middle of bloody nowhere."

"And where on a map can I find this bloody nowhere?"

"We are deep in the Mount Hood National Forest. Somewhat north and a little west of the actual mountain."

Knowing that didn't really help her feel less dislocated. They walked the forest floor for a few minutes. Harper's mind chattered on and on inside her head. Second-guessing whether she could have done more at the meeting to secure some allies. Worrying about what would happen to her mom when they left for Sauvie. Her thoughts turned to the Fae of the Green World Courts and their reaction to learning a gateway between the worlds had opened. She grasped little of their response. They seemed to dislike humans yet chose to live here.

"Why wouldn't the Fae be perfectly happy to live in the Underworld, cut off from the humans they so dislike?" she said out loud before realizing she was verbalizing her thoughts.

"As much as we hate the very idea, the Fae depend on you humans. Without the exchange both our people suffer."

"Exchange of what?"

"Our people call it foyson. It roughly means vital essence. Foyson is the nourishment of a thing, the spark of creativity, the breath of inspiration. It is the oxygen of the Underworld. Starved of it, the Underworld decays. Not dies, but decays."

"I still don't get it. You take the inspiration of a thing and what? Leave the rest?"

"Exactly. It's why butter spoils too soon and stolen children who return are more like a husk than the person they were before they met the Fae."

Harper shuddered. "How beastly. You're like vampires or something?"

"Not exactly, and don't forget the exchange is a two-way street. Fae differ from humans. Our physical forms are more fluid, yet the rules we must live by more rigid. The Underworld is much like its people, a half life."

"Half life?"

The Phooka scratched his head and tilted his chin up for a few moments before continuing. "Imagine a perfect golden summer day."

"Sunny, for once, no rain." Those days were few in Portland.

"Now imagine that same day forever. And add people who either never die or live for many hundreds of years."

Harper's grandma had read stories to her where a wayward soul ended up in the dazzling lands of the fairies, where their every desire was met and beauty surrounded them. She'd always wondered why people always came back. It sounded much better than having to go to school or do chores. As a child she'd vowed if the fairies ever took her away, she'd never return to her boring life, she'd stay in the land of wonder and magic forever.

Then she thought of how excited she was when she got that job at City Pizza. All the pizza she could eat, and tips! After a week of stuffing her face with every kind of pie, the sight of pizza ruined her appetite. What would it be like to feel that way about literally everything. Forever. "Now that you mention it, that sounds horrible."

"It's worse than horrible. Our secret is that the entire Underworld is a kind of living death. Without the bright fire your people and the Green World brings, our gorgeous clockwork realm winds down."

Harper scrunched up her face, lost again. The Phooka paused before continuing, giving her a chance to take in the soaring pine trees towering over them and draw in the tangy air of the deep woods.

"We excel at perfecting a thing. Fae music, food, art, all honed to their ultimate transcendence, yet merely copies," the Phooka said. "Like a music box playing a pretty tune. It does it impeccably, but there is never a variation. To us, humans wink out of existence as quickly as a flower wilts, but in that short time your mortality drives you to make symphonies, start companies, create something new. To really live."

"I never thought of it that way."

"Without the spark of life brought by the specter of death, our world becomes a waking nightmare."

Harper's forehead creased. "The destruction of the gateways meant there was nothing to wind the clock again."

"And it traps the beings who live there in an unending, decaying hell. They can't even escape by dying."

Harper tried to imagine what that might be like, but couldn't. The thought of her new friend trapped in the Underworld like most of the other Fae brought a wave of sadness. "Can't we save them too?"

"Why Harper O'Neill, I didn't know you cared." The Phooka batted his eyes up at her, his eyelashes suddenly several inches long. He paused and added, "I hope so, but first we need to save your friend from Badb, as we promised."

The deer trail they had been following opened out into a small clearing in the dense pine trees where Nuada waited. His back turned to Harper, he moved with sword in hand through a series of battle postures. He flowed from one pose to the next with no movement wasted, like the tai chi classes she remembered from the beach when she was a child. At the sound of their approach, Nuada stopped and faced Harper.

"Good morning," Harper said.

"Good morning, Harper."

"It's the eye of the tiger, the thrill of the fight. Risin' up—" the Phooka sang while he pumped his hips and swept an extended arm in a slow half circle.

Harper smiled. "Really?"

"This is the part in the movie where the training montage happens backed with heart-pumping, inspirational music."

"Skip the soundtrack, Phooka."

The Phooka stuck out his tongue at Nuada, simultaneously melting into the form of a black and grey tiger. He bounded up a tree and stretched out along a branch, still singing, "And he's watchin' us all with the eye"—he thrust a paw in the air and tossed his head to the side and down his opposite shoulder—"of the tiger."

Nuada guided Harper to the center of the clearing while the feline Phooka hummed the rest of the song, head bobbing to an invisible beat.

"So wouldn't learning how to summon up that big energy blast I somehow made at Mystic Island be a better way to prepare for this mission?" Harper asked.

Nuada's expression was unreadable. A mix of worry, kindness, and that blank face people adopted when they didn't really want to tell you something.

"I mean, I've used a wooden katana at the dojo I went to, but it wasn't real combat. Magic seems a lot more powerful." She traced circles in the brown pine needles with her soft brown boot.

"You nearly killed yourself back there. You need to learn to focus and shape your power, and that takes far more time than learning a few tricks with a blade. Those skills might keep you alive long enough to train in magic."

"We could just use your magic sword."

Nuada's face melted into a soft half smile. "When you held the Cliamh Solais, what did it feel like? What did the blade urge you to do?"

Harper let her weight fall back against a towering Douglas fir and rested the back of her head against the scratchy bark. Overhead the pines swayed a slow dance that made her a little dizzy. "I don't know. I felt powerful. At first when I drew it to save you and the Phooka that was all I thought about. But then it changed, and I wanted to keep fighting, right other wrongs. More than that I felt . . ." She rubbed a temple with her fingers. "Like it understood my anger. Understood me. Together we could burn the evil from the world."

The third of the Great Wars is upon us and you are the fulcrum on which all will turn. Selina's words from the Mystic Island festival echoed in her mind. She dropped her head forward.

Nuada unbuckled the Cliamh Solais and lowered himself to sit cross-legged in front of Harper. His handsome features were grave while he turned the weapon over in his hands. He swept a silvery strand of hair out of his face and met Harper's eyes. "This sword was made for me on the Island of Findias. It is not a weapon to be trifled with or wielded on impulse. Drawing this sword has serious consequences and has to occur for the purest of reasons. It reacts to what is in the heart of the one who drew it."

"I didn't have any consequences, and I just felt like I could end this all right now."

"The sword doesn't make you invincible," the Phooka said. He sat on a low branch with his arms crossed over his chest, ears drooped. If she didn't know better, Harper thought his face showed concern.

"The Phooka speaks truth." Nuada picked up the sheathed blade and held it across his lap. Harper's gaze traveled along the intricate knot design that wound its way up the silvery scabbard. For the first time, she noticed it was an elongated tree with several apples worked through it. At its tip was an end cap adorned with interlacing spirals.

"I still think drawing the sword on Badb solves all our problems. It's yours, you should do it."

"Does it? The power of this blade is that, once drawn, it will prevail. Badb has equally powerful magic and an entire army waiting in that tower. If you were to draw the sword on Badb and fail, you would either be dead, or the sword would drive you in pursuit of her death until it completed its task. Your terrible quest would continue even if it meant you had to crawl on your stomach across flame, sacrifice everything you loved, and lose your very soul. When you unsheathed it in the city you drew it to save us, and you did. You were very lucky."

Harper dropped her head into her hands, recalling the battle with the Wild Hunt in the stairwell. Once she held the weapon, the solution to this whole mess had seemed so easy. She and the blade would cut a glorious swath all the way to Badb and free all she had taken. What was she supposed to do now? It would take her years to master either the sword skills or the magical ones. Years to convince the Green World Courts or Fir Bolg to lift a finger. Emilio didn't have years.

"Then what good is it? Just a musty old relic unless you use it." Her heart was heavy. Hope seemed to recede with every moment.

"This blade is much more than a weapon to slay your enemies. Do you know what Claimh Solias translates to?"

Harper shook her head without taking her eyes off the ground.

"The Sword of Light. It is a force for illumination and should only be used for the highest of purposes. At all times in its history, unsheathing it meant a glorious change for our people. We built a new world in its shining light. It may very well come to pass that the blade is drawn again in this battle, but it is not the solution to our problem. You got lucky when you wielded it. Had you focused on your fear, not on your intent, you may have been lost."

Harper let out a long breath and her shoulders slumped. A hand drifted up to rest on her heart. "Back at the island I met a Romani woman, Selina. She was psychic or something. She said I was the fulcrum of this fight, and to win, I had to keep my heart soft."

Nuada's smile was like the sun bursting through a cloudy day. Radiant and complete. "That, my dear Harper, may be your greatest power. After all you endured, you could have become hard, selfish. But you didn't. Your first instinct is always to aid those less fortunate. Even now you offer help to suffering Fae despite their role in your family's tragic past. That is the mark of a High King. Not a sword, a torque, or magical power. But it's harder than you think to keep that trait alive." He slipped off the black glove from his silver hand and lifted it between himself and Harper, flexing his fingers several times. "I should know. I've failed that test myself. Twice."

Harper gulped. Nuada was so powerful, he seemed almost godlike to her. If he failed, what hope did she have? Before she could respond, the former Tuatha king had moved to the opposite side of the clearing and crouched.

The Phooka's ears perked up and a slow smile spread across his face when Nuada retrieved a pair of wooden practice swords from their resting place at the base of another tree. Nuada handed one to Harper and twirled his own practice blade in an intricate dance.

"Try to get a feel for the balance of the weapon." He nodded at Harper's hand.

Harper swung the thing from side to side with none of the smooth arcs Nuada made. The pattern looked as awkward and clumsy as she felt.

The Phooka's ears and smile both fell. "This is battle practice. You're not bushwhacking a trail."

"Bite me," Harper said and flipped him off.

"We begin with proper grip." Nuada stepped toward Harper with his sword held in front of him, gripping it with both hands.

Harper bobbed a little in place, keeping her body loose and ready to react. She thought about the elves she had fought in the stairwell. They were deadly fast and likely had years of practice. Hundreds of years. This whole exercise seemed fruitless in the face of their overwhelming skill.

"Let us focus on learning a bit about how to shield yourself with a sword. You will have more control and less chance of being disarmed if you hold it like this." He placed her right hand just below the hilt and the left just above the pommel. It extended away from her body. He reached over and bent her elbows. "You are stronger closer to your core."

Nuada demonstrated a ready stance and showed Harper how to stand with her sword in front of her body. Her knees were bent slightly and she could more easily move the sword in multiple directions. Harper learned some basic strikes and defensive movements and the two of them practiced forms side by side for the better part of two hours.

"So am I ready to fend off an attack?"

"If you think you are ready. Defend yourself." Nuada came at her at half his usual speed.

Harper barely got her sword up in time. Their wooden blades crossed with a dull clack. He pressed an attack from above; she swung her sword up in a low arc to parry below. She was too slow and the edge of his weapon clunked into her thigh. A dull ache flowered. The Phooka whooped from his vantage high in the tree and slapped his hand on his knee. Harper glared at him.

"Again."

Harper dropped into the ready stance with the sword in front. This time she tried to fake him out and feint left, then dive to the right. Nuada lazily stepped out of the way of her attack and swept her leg from under her. The tip of the wood was pointing at her neck before she recovered. Harper smacked his blade out of the way with hers and levered herself to her feet. She had a sharp pain in her back to match the throb in her leg.

Several more attempts ended both quickly and with Harper picking herself up from the ground. Nuada's expression remained neutral. He reached down a hand to help her up. Harper smacked it away, pulled herself to her feet, and chose an enemy in the clearing she thought she could beat. With a scream she battered a pine tree with blows, screamed again at the top of her lungs, flung the sword into a bush, and then kicked the tree. Colossal mistake. Her foot screamed in pain. Harper stalked back across the clearing and dropped onto a big rock, legs folded in front of her. She pushed up her sleeve to check the light brown oval bruises dappling her arms and legs. She looked like an overripe banana.

"This is useless. I'm just a receptionist, not goddamn Conan the Barbarian."

"You're right there! You're not even Samurai Cop good!"

Harper rolled her eyes and offered the Phooka her middle finger again. "I'm not strong enough for this." She rubbed her throbbing foot with both hands.

"You are doing rather well. We have a long road before us to win this fight. What you learn now may save you, keep you alive for us to heal the Lia Fail. Then you can fulfill your destiny and rouse the Tuatha from their long complacency."

Harper rubbed the flat of her hand down her face and focused on massaging her aching legs.

Nuada's lips pulled into a thin line. He reached out a hand and rested it gently on her knee. Harper tilted her head and looked at him askance. Her father used to look at her like that when he was about to tell her something she didn't want to hear. It was one of her clearest memories of how he was. Her back stiffened slightly as if to brace for unwelcome news. Nuada drew in a lengthy breath.

"Once we free your friend, you need to come with me through the gateway to the Undying Lands. The talented magician Morfesa can better teach you to control your anger and your magic." He flexed his silver hand again with a hint of sadness in his eyes.

There it was. So Nuada was planning to abandon her too. Her dad died, her mom left her to climb into a bottle, and now Nuada seemed to think she was too much to handle.

"You don't have to worry about passing your problem to a tutor. Once we save Emilio and the others, I'm done with this crazy shit." A tear splashed onto a rock at her feet.

"Harper, you mistake my meaning. Your education should be from the best of us. I only want you to learn from the man who taught me."

Harper bit her tongue to hold back the emotional storm that simmered.

The Phooka slid from his branch, catching himself with his tail. He hung upside down for a second before dropping to the forest floor, skittering past Nuada to sit next to Harper. His yellow eyes sparkled and a slow grin spread across his face, revealing pointed white teeth. He looked from Harper to Nuada. "Watching Silver Hand bash you around like a piñata has made me hungry enough to eat the Fir Bolg's nasty vegan food. Let's head back for lunch."

The Phooka's diversion gave her something else to focus on and helped strengthen the levy holding back her tears. She nodded and fell in behind him.

CHAPTER 43

Cold vegetables rolled around the plate, prodded by Harper's wooden spoon. The Phooka munched on cheese puffs at the opposite side of the massive room, his ears flopped low along the sides of his head like a lop rabbit. Harper had told him she wanted to be alone for a while to spend some time with her mom. Across the table, brow creased, Eileen tracked the path of the mushroom along her daughter's plate.

Harper shifted in her seat, searching for a position that didn't ache. Every move pushed against a bruise or sore spot and reminded her how dreadful she was with a sword. And her craptastic performance with the weapon reminded her she performed equally poorly at controlling magic. Sure, she had accidentally blasted the Wild Hunt to oblivion a few nights ago, but she didn't know how to summon it again or keep it from killing her. *This is absurd. I should be more worried about getting fired for not showing up at work for days.*

Harper had informed her mom she planned to go with Nuada to rescue Emilio, even if the council refused help. Nuada must have spoken to Eileen already because she didn't attempt to talk her daughter out of it. The fact remained the Fae would keep coming for Harper. She probably wasn't safe to be around. Better for her mom to be as far from her as she could get. It wasn't fair. The Fae had already taken one life from her already; now they'd destroyed hope for another.

"Mom, once I get Emilio back, I have to leave."

"Leave? Where?"

"I don't know, but you can't come with me. You heard what Nuada said. Even if I don't believe I'm some last heir, all these Fae, Sluagh, and Badb do, and they'll come for me. I'm not safe company."

"Oh, sweetheart." Eileen slid around to the same side of the table and wrapped her arm around her daughter's shoulders. "Why don't you come back here and stay with me? They can't find you here. I'm sure Aeld would allow it."

"You're staying with the Fir Bolg?"

"I have a lot to work through. But even more than that, this way of life. It's such a beautiful way to live in the world."

Harper realized in a lot of ways her mother was a stranger to her. She had been very young when tragedy changed them. Who Eileen O'Neill was before the Fae took everything from her was a mystery.

"Never figured you for a crystal-waving hippy. I'll ask Aeld if he thinks it's safe for them to have me here." The arboreal village was well hidden and there was a lot of muscle lumbering around to protect them if things went south. A tiny ray of hope broke through her despair at the thought of living here with her mom. In this place of serenity in the forest, she could just be a daughter and all the weight of scrambling to hold their lives together would evaporate in the slow simplicity of the Fir Bolg way of life.

"There's a lot you don't know about me. A lot I lost track of." Eileen's face tilted up like she watched something from long ago replay. "Did I ever tell you how I met your father?"

Harper smiled. "No, you never shared that with me."

"We met at a silent retreat at a Buddhist temple."

"Dad was at a *silent* retreat?" One thing Harper recalled about her father was not a tendency to be quiet. He was constantly talking to her. Reading to her, teaching her about almost everything they encountered, or staging the elaborate plays they made up together. Gerald O'Neill had been like lightning and he was never still. "I can't imagine him sitting on a cushion meditating."

Her mother laughed and leaned her bleach-blonde head on her hands. Her brown roots were already showing. "He was terrible at it. Both the meditating and the silence. Never saw someone fidget on that cushion more than Gerald. And he was even worse at the silence part. He whispered to me all the time when we were on kitchen duty." Eileen's smile stretched across her face.

Harper giggled. "He hated cooking. Why did he volunteer for that?"

"He had a crush on me, and I'd signed up to cook. Meditation and spiritual pursuits were never his thing. But they were always mine. Before I met him, there was a time when I considered becoming a Buddhist nun."

"A nun?" The image of her mom shaved bald and in orange robes refused to come fully into focus.

"My entire life I ached for a more authentic, connected way to live. I felt most at home when I spent weekends in the temple. Being here is just like that for me." Her mother grasped her hands. Her eyes were shining. "Honey, thank you."

"For what?"

"Bringing me here. You saved me in more ways than one. Please come back here when this is over. We've lost so much time."

Harper soaked in the chandeliers of softly glowing mushrooms, the east wall planted with sweet greens like a living, vertical carpet. The gentle, slow ways of the giants who lived here wrapped everyone in their serenity. The Fir Bolg village was as close to utopia as Harper could imagine. Even if her mother wasn't planning to be a resident, she'd want to protect this place from harm. But Nuada had intimated it was so much more than that.

"Nuada says all hope for our side winning against this coming battle are here, now, inside this village." Harper dropped her forehead into her open palm, elbow resting on the table. "Who am I kidding. I'm no diplomat, and I'm certainly no hero. No one here is going to help us."

"Honey, you don't know that. Don't underestimate yourself. You're the most amazing person I've ever known." The corners of her mother's mouth trembled as she spoke.

Harper managed a weak smile. "You have to say that, you're my mom. You even used to put my crappy drawings on the fridge."

Eileen seized Harper's hand and clutched it between her own. "No, honey, listen to me. Your dad's murder shattered me, but it didn't break you. What fourteen-year-old goes to school, holds down a job, manages a household alone?"

"I did what I had to do for us."

"Yes, you did. I failed you, but you have never, ever failed me. I am both deeply grateful and ashamed."

A fat tear slid down Harper's cheek. "Mom, I don't think—"

Eileen held up a hand. "I need to tell you this. I should have been the strong one, the one saving you. Please know, as the years slid by, how much I wanted to express my gratitude, to become a real mother to you. Every day that desire burned in my soul, but it all got smothered under the weight of my suffering. But know, even in that darkness, honey, you were my bright light. The reason I'm still alive and here, now. Your dad's death forged you into a fierce, kind, powerful young woman. That's what the world needs now, the bright light of compassion."

Harper pulled her mother into an embrace. Her chest felt

tight. Nuada, Selina, even her mother saw this strength in her. Perhaps they were right and she did have the power to save her friend, after all.

After a few moments, she drew back. Her mother lifted a pale hand, fingernails speckled with half-worn pink nail polish, and swept the tears from Harper's cheek.

"Mom—"

Nuada interrupted their conversation by clearing his throat in the doorway. He was back in the blue ensemble he wore at the council meeting. That meant it must be time.

"Eileen. Harper. Time to get changed. The Fae courts wish to render their final vote within the hour."

CHAPTER 44

Nuada's news was like cold water dumped on her moment of happiness. Reality coiled around her again like a snake, clenching tighter and tighter. She wished she could feel optimistic about the council's outcome.

"Well. Let's go get prettied up," Eileen said, sweeping a hand across her cheeks to clear away her own tears.

"I can't breathe in that dress." *Or around all those Fae.*

Harper retired to her room and then slipped into what she thought of as her costume. It was beautiful, but it wasn't her. She peered more closely at the shining birds along the trim. They didn't seem to be any species she recognized. She reminded herself to ask the Phooka about it later. All dressed up, she ran her hands along her hair to check her bun was straight. The Fir Bolg didn't believe in mirrors, so she relied solely on feel. Satisfied it was as neat as it could be, she smoothed the wrinkles out of the fabric, drew her chin high, and hustled out into the crisp air.

Normally the Phooka hovered close to her. Even in the village he never strayed far. Kind of like a puppy. Was he avoiding her because it still hurt him that she wanted some space from Fae for a few hours? She thought she could find her way to the Hall alone, even though the buildings all looked much the same.

Her dress kept catching between the slats that lined the walkways. She bent, tugging the hem from a snag yet again when a pair of shiny black hooves slid next to her. Far too big to be the Phooka. Hazel eyes tracked up the tall, muscular form before her. Lord Ezrynhivar loomed, his hip canted casually to the side and a hand half-covering a devious smile.

The color drained from her face and she studied her shimmering gold shoes, suddenly regretting sending the Phooka away earlier. The magic juice he gave her must have worn off by now. She might be at the dark Fae's mercy in a few more seconds. *Just don't make eye contact. Don't look at him. Keep walking and count floor slats or something.*

"Relax, Ambassador." He said the word in a mocking tone. "I am not trying to bewitch you."

His horns made a graceful sweep along his head. Fine hands clasped behind his back, he waited for Harper to collect herself. It terrified her to be alone with the Dusk King.

"That's good. You're not really my type." She winced internally. *That was lame.*

"Nor are you mine, yet you interest me all the same." He offered her his arm. Harper drew back and placed her hand behind her back. "I'm not trying to harm you. Your herald seems to be otherwise occupied, and arriving with you on my arm will produce an amusing amount of shock and awe. Free lesson, would-be queen: Keeping your political opponents off balance gives you power."

Harper inclined her head and slipped her hand through his arm, resting it on his elbow. She remembered not to thank the Fae and trigger some mysterious debt.

Ezrynhivar paused and drew her arm up to his face, examining the bruises. "Have you been in a fight, Ambassador?"

"You should see the other guy." The Dusk King didn't smile at her dad joke. Harper felt a heat flower in her face. "Sword training with Nuada didn't go too well." She gave him a half smile, never meeting his crimson eyes.

"Indeed not."

"It was my first day." Harper shrugged. The smile spreading across the Dusk King's face looked genuine. For a moment, he was just a man and not a supernatural lord of the Fae, but the line of pointed teeth he revealed reminded Harper she walked arm in arm with something from her darkest night terrors.

"You are really planning on going to that island without an army behind you?"

"What choice do I have? They took my best friend and a lot of other people." She risked a glance into his chiseled face. "And Fae."

"You don't consider us people?" The dark Fae's half smile, she hoped, meant he was playing with her.

"That's not what I meant. It just seems your kind should be a lot more upset that Badb is also killing them."

"There's a lot you don't know about Fae culture."

"I know next to nothing. But I do know people. Humanity is divided too. When we should stand as one, we fight each other. We don't help people if they're from another country or race. From what I see, the Fae aren't much different. I just don't know where the ideological lines are."

"So your promise to free any suffering Fae you find wasn't just a political statement? Or one of the lies your kind tell so easily?"

"In case you hadn't noticed, I suck at politics. Fae or otherwise." Harper tilted her face to the king. His expression grew pensive as he studied her. Red eyes flicked over her features while razor-thin brows knitted together. For a moment the intense scrutiny made no sense until she remembered she could lie and he could not. Perhaps he believed he could sense her veracity by staring at her. Whatever his agenda, gone was the derision he'd heaped on her the last time they met. She found this more disconcerting than the hatred he projected before.

"You know, I could make you instantly a swordsman of great renown. A simple bit of magic and I can transfer every skill and trick of my best warrior into you. You'd be powerful enough to beat all but the Tuatha."

"And just what would that cost me?" Harper remembered the Phooka's little tutorial on accepting gifts from the Fae, even though the offer did tempt her. How much easier would her journey be with that kind of skill? "I'm not interested in a Fae bargain."

Ezrynhivar smiled like a wolf. So this was why his attitude had shifted. He wanted something.

"Don't say I didn't offer to help."

"Never dream of it. But what would you have asked of me?" Was that sadness flickering across his face? Lord Ezrynhivar pulled her to a halt beside him and lifted his chin to gaze at the canopy of fir trees. His chest rose in a long breath, and when he spoke, he seemed to speak to the sky.

"I think Badb may have someone. The only person in the world truly important to me."

Harper laid her hands on his shoulders and swiveled him to face her. She could feel the tendons of his wings flex beneath her fingers. "Then join me. We can both save the ones we love. You don't have to try to trick me into working with you."

The king sighed and pulled her back into stride again. "Little human, it's not that easy for us. My kingdom is not exactly human friendly. Even though I admire your convictions, I cannot openly support you. Even this conversation, should you speak of it to the wrong person, would be enough to mark me for death. I would be assassinated and someone worse might take over my Court."

"Not even to save someone you care about?"

"Not even then."

"I fear I'll never understand your world."

"There are days I don't either." Lord Ezyrhnivar flicked the bottoms of his leathery wings.

"Look. I know Fae have all kinds of complicated rules and regulations about gifts and bargains. So what I offer you, I offer freely. I want nothing in return. If I make it across that island alive, I'll do my best to save your friend too. Who am I looking for?"

"After what Fae have done to your family, you would help one of us?"

"Did anyone from the Dusk Court kill my father?"

"No."

"Then my fight isn't with you and your people. So, yes. I'll treat finding your loved one the same as I will finding Emilio."

"Her name is Alphine, and she is my sister. She is a succubus and looks mostly like me. She has hair of deep blue and eyes of aqua. Her horns spiral around her ears and her skin is palest lavender." He reached into his pocket and drew out a silver ring with filigree oak leaves all over it. He pressed it into Harper's hand and closed her fingers around it. "Show her this and she will know to trust you."

Harper gripped the ring in her palm. "I'll do my very best to find her."

For a moment he turned, his pale hand hovering over the doorknob to the Great Hall. "I don't want to blindside you in there. I cannot vote in your favor, but I am helping you, nonetheless. You are right about us. We cannot help but repay a gift even if freely offered." Then he cupped Harper's chin in his hand and lifted her eyes to his. "I can sense the raw magical power in you, stronger than anything I've felt in human or Fae. But it is unruly, and if you can't control it, it will kill you."

"You're not the first person to tell me that, but the most unexpected."

"And you are the most surprising human I have met. Wear the

ring. It will help you focus your power so it doesn't burn you up from the inside."

"A thoughtful gesture, Your Majesty." Harper slipped it on her left middle finger. "So will me wearing this raise a few eyebrows in there?"

Ezrynhivar regarded her from the tops of his sparkling eyes with a wide smile. "Oh, indeed it will. Let's go enjoy the show."

The Phooka clip-clopped up beside her, festooned in a shimmering waistcoat that matched Harper's gown.

"Whaaaaaaa?" His goat-like jaw dropped and his head whipped back and forth between the Dusk King and Harper like a spectator at a tennis match. "If you've bewitched her, Ez, I swear—"

"It's all right, Phooka. He hasn't."

"That's just what you would say if you were bewitched!" The Phooka manifested a pair of black insect wings and hovered next to her ear. "Do not trust him. You are not prepared to wade into the kind of games he plays. This is not your world," he whispered.

"I can hear you, shapeshifter. We entered no bargains. You have my word that tonight I bear Harper no ill will." Ezrynhivar swept a pale hand to the door, jerking his head at the Phooka. "Shall we?" The Phooka grumbled under his breath but stepped up to open it.

The low murmur of conversation halted the instant Harper stepped through the door alongside her dark escort. The white satyr serving Queen Serotina froze with his cup halfway to his lips. Her mother stood next to Nuada, her hand frozen in midair like she was trying to make a point. Slack jaws ringed the room.

The Phooka stepped in front of them before Ezrynhivar's herald arrived. "I present Ambassador Harper O'Neill and the King of the Dusk Court, Lord Ezrynhivar."

They didn't have too long to wonder at Harper's grand entrance before Paegrinn sounded the drum that called the meeting to order. The guests drifted to the table and took their seats. Ezrynhivar pulled her seat out for her before moving off to his own. Harper smiled up at him and smoothed her dress underneath before settling into the seat.

Nuada leaned over and spoke into her ear. "What was that all about?"

"Apparently His Majesty believes his sister may be on the same island as Emilio. I told him I would save her if I could."

"You entered into a Fae bargain?" he said through gritted teeth.

"No. I offered my help freely. But in return he lent me this to focus my magic and to get the cooperation of his sister." Harper waggled the finger with the ring.

"Curious. I will need to inspect that trinket later. Does this mean Dusk will back us?"

"He made clear he would not."

"Then why—"

"Because it's the right thing to do. And, well, because maybe he'll back you later once he gets his sister back."

Nuada was looking at her like he was seeing her for the first time. Aeld's rise to his feet to begin the meeting cut off any further conversation.

"My guests, I am pleased you have joined us here again. I will not waste much of your time since we have already discussed the issue before us at some length. Rather, let us render our decision. Lord Ezrynhivar, how votes the Dusk Court."

"The Dusk Court will not assist at this time." The incubus held his horned head straight ahead, lacking the normal arrogant tilt to his chin. He glanced sideways at Harper as he finished his sentence. At least he'd warned her.

Nuada and Harper voted in favor of storming the island, even though between them they had a total of three people in their army.

Aeld turned toward the ogre. "Master Heironymous, will the solitary Fae engage in this battle?"

"Our position remains unchanged. There exist too many unknowns. To act rashly now might bring about a war instead of avoiding one."

Harper felt her pulse quicken and a jolt of adrenaline sharpened her tongue. She rose to her feet. "But you do know—"

A hand on her shoulder and a paw on her arm pushed her back to the chair and silenced her.

"I am sorry my decision disappoints you, Ambassador. I offer you the considerable resources of my lodge. You are welcome there any time. If Nuada discovers that a battle is imminent, we will reconsider our position."

The Phooka pressed his whiskered face to her ear. "Take a deep breath. That is not the worst outcome. We have resources we didn't have before and an opening." Harper failed to see his optimism. Her concern was not whatever war was or wasn't brewing here. They could fight that or not, all on their own. Her concern was saving her friend, and a bar and some empty promises were no help at all.

"Queen Serotina, what is the decision of the Dawn Court?"

"The Dawn Court concurs with Master Heironymous. We need more proof of the gateway being opened before we decide how we will act. Despite the venerable Tuatha king's assurances, we lack total proof this portal exists."

That was it, then. Harper dropped her head into her hands and waited for Aeld to announce he, too, would stay out of it. Nuada had said if they could sway even one to join or offer conditional support, it could move Aeld to act. But they offered no support but 'resources.' Essentially nothing. Back where she started, and she had wasted days. Emilio might already be dead.

She didn't have long to wait. Aeld rose slowly to his feet. "The Fir Bolg will also not enter this conflict at this time. We have not gone to war in thousands of years. We will take no side in this battle."

Harper didn't look up from her arms. She didn't want any of these monsters to see her cry.

"Nuada, do you and the human still plan to make your journey?" Queen Serotina said.

"Yes, Your Majesty, we do."

"Then we will send an emissary with you to help you. If she returns having seen this new gateway, we will have much to discuss."

"We are honored by your offer and open-mindedness." Nuada bowed his head toward the Dawn Queen.

Shuddering scrapes and the slow rise of murmuring voices announced the end of the council. One Fae didn't seem to be much help given what they were likely to face on that island. Harper's throat ached. Biting the inside of her cheek didn't hold back the tears.

"Harper, I'm so sorry." Her mom draped an arm around her shoulder. "We'll find another way."

"Still think fucking Bigfoot is so spiritually advanced?" Harper sobbed into her arms.

"I'm still going with you to find your friend." The Phooka's voice was uncharacteristically devoid of snark and playfulness. Harper could only nod into her arms.

"Just like a human to be so short-sighted." The snark was most definitely back in Ezrynhivar's voice. Harper's sorrow hardened to fury in an instant, sending a jolt of electricity through her limbs. This must be how her mother felt when she drank, the alcohol like an old friend coming to erase all the fear and loss. And god, it felt good to feel strong again and not just sad. She reveled in the surge of energy sharpening her tongue.

"Just like an immortal to think there's all the time in the world while we little people die." She was on her feet, inches from the incubus. Out of the corner of her eye, she noticed her hands shimmering blue. They tingled with a familiar current. Power. Just like that night at the festival. She was fed up to her eyebrows with Fae.

Nuada stepped up beside them, his lips a narrow line at the sight of her now brightly glowing hands. He gently grasped her forearm. She jerked her arm back so hard it sent her staggering forward a step. Nuada remained standing at her side, icy blue eyes locked on the Dusk King.

Ezrynhivar held up his hands in surrender. "You act as though this is all over and it hasn't really even begun. Did you even listen to what Heironymous and Serotina truly said?"

"He may have a point," the Phooka said from beside her.

"All they want is proof. I last saw my sister in the Underworld before my father betrayed us. She will most definitely wish to know I am alive and thriving in New Orleans. She is your proof. You have everything you need."

"I have a single Fae from the Dawn Court as additional help to face swarms of Fae intent on killing me. You'll excuse me if I disagree with your assessment."

The entire room was staring at her now. Her eyes flashed. The glow in her hands was so bright no one could look at them directly. She felt it feeding on her anger like flame consumes wood. And like a wildfire, it threatened to burn everything.

She looked down at Ezrynhivar's ring and pulled her hand up before her face. The sigils flashed and glowed; she felt them wrapping around her, containing and focusing the power. She let the ring do its work.

Harper inhaled and tried to pull some current from the earth and sky. Nothing. Despite that, her hands glowed like twin suns. Visions of blasting every monster who refused to help brought warmth to her heart while her face contorted in rage.

"Harper, what are you doing, honey?"

She turned to see fear on her mother's face. She was afraid of her own daughter. Guilt dampened the burning fire, making the glow washing over her hands flicker.

"Mom, I—"

The desire to lash out and destroy the Fae receded, but she still needed to blast something. Harper sprinted for the door. Her legs pumped under the diaphanous golden gown. She raced along the bridges and walkways, past her hut and down the staircase leading away from the village. Muffled voices trailed behind her and still she ran along the deer trail, hands aflame with magic all the way.

She burst into the clearing where she and Nuada practiced swordplay. Harper's knees crashed into the earth, pine needles poking through the layers of her dress. She howled at the sky and focused the fire in her hands toward an innocent fir tree. The tree exploded into splinters that rained down and stuck in her hair.

Able at last to channel her power where she wished, she felt like a god. With the remaining magical energy, she blasted another tree to shrapnel. Her magical and emotional power spent, she slumped over her knees and wept, fingers clasping handfuls of her gown. Despite what Ezrynhivar said, she had failed.

The muted sounds of conversation drifted to her ears. Footsteps crunched loose stone. She wasn't ready to deal with anyone else. The rage, guilt, and embarrassment she felt were more than enough to handle.

"Leave me the hell alone!" she bellowed, spittle flying from her trembling lips. She meant it. She desperately wanted to avoid everyone right now. So she hitched up the layers of shimmering fabric and ran as fast as her feet could carry her away from the voices, without thought of how she'd find her way back.

CHAPTER 45

It was relatively easy for Emilio to keep the digital watch hidden in his waistband along with the keys and fob because the Fae never bothered to search them during the rounds of injections. The trickier part had been finding the time to slip out of his cage and read his pilfered files.

He and Selina made an effective team. They'd created a system that minimized the chances of discovery. Like many corporate offices, this covert branch of Erimus operated on a traditional eight-to-four work schedule. After that, both Fae and human populations in the building were halved. By the time Portland sat down to dinner, the hallways were nearly empty. Selina kept watch out of the tiny window above the door handle while Emilio perched by the cabinet and read. He was close to a basic grasp of what this was all about. All the same, he couldn't shake the nagging feeling they were running out of time.

Something about the biochemical process they were enduring had killed nearly all previous candidates last time. They were probably the lucky ones. The failure rate explained both why the Fae wanted younger subjects and why they were all receiving injections every four hours. Emilio felt more powerful in the wake of each dose. Both the files and his degree gave him enough to make an educated guess. The Fae were building up their frail human bodies to live through whatever experimental process had killed so many human subjects.

The sense of violation and the anticipation of what was to come at the end of the current rounds of injections brought the threat of panic and a desire to make a run for it. But someone had to put a stop to this, and he needed information. He couldn't bring himself to flee without first making sure he didn't need another batch of files to assemble a complete account. This would all be for nothing if bigger brains than his lacked what they needed for a cure or some way to reverse whatever was happening here.

He'd come up with the best possible escape plan under the circumstances. The glamour resistant group—that Jerome decided should be called "the woke"—were ready to follow Emilio. He'd located no more people who weren't grinning zombies. But he hadn't expected to. His hunch had been correct. He didn't believe the Fae had figured it out yet, because the surviving members of the woke learned real fast how to fake them out, but every member of the woke most closely matched the Abraxas profile. And there were exactly six of them. The same six Emilio had already found.

He'd noticed no one but Fae ever moved groups of multiple prisoners; they probably didn't trust humans to do it. During their grand escape, Emilio would have to wear the elf cloak, but he planned to wear the lab coat underneath. With only paper and whatever else he could grab, hopefully a sample of some kind, the bag would be thin enough to lie flat against him and not be noticed. He'd proceed floor by floor, unlocking the cages. Once he released Ashley, they would slip to the western exit, out into the night, and try to make it to the river and swim across.

It was time to begin his nightly studies. He swung his cage door open and moved down to Selina. She stepped out and bent backward with her hands on her lower back, a gesture Emilio already associated with her.

"Between you and me, they always creep me out." Selina looked at the row of cages. Each person inside sat with slack jaws and empty eyes.

"I wish we could get them out with us." Emilio felt the yoke of guilt around his neck. He was saving his own skin and leaving these people to their fate. It must have shown on his face.

"You're doing the right thing. No one has a chance if we fail." Selina pressed her face to the window. "Coast is clear, sweetheart."

Even at the low tide of staffing, Emilio only ever got a few minutes at a time with his collection before someone or something presented the risk of discovery and they had to scuttle back into their cages. Progress was at a snail's pace.

"Most of what I grabbed was about Dust. I've got a couple left on the rest of this freak show." He dropped to sit in front of the cabinet containing his stash. He spread the papers out in front of him and settled into a hunched posture over them, crossed legs, elbows on knees, chin resting on one hand.

He'd only been reading for two minutes when his blood ran cold and he snatched a page to his face. "Selina. The injections are about every four hours, right?"

"Yeah? You find something?"

He had indeed found something. Saying it wasn't good would be the understatement of the year. "Did you keep count of how many you've had?" He was already adding them up in his mind.

"I don't know. Twelve? Fourteen?" Her brow creased.

"I'm sure I had the fourteenth about an hour ago. We've got seven hours until the experiments really begin. I was right. The shots were just to make us strong enough to give us a chance to live through what comes next."

"And what's that?"

"I can't quite tell. The molecule in here is like nothing I've seen. There's talk of a catalyst and stem cells, which would make sense given they're looking for specific genetic markers. We've all got them, people like you and me have the most. That's why we're in this room together." Emilio was babbling, his mind racing to put the puzzle together, but if he was honest, what he was reading now was over his head.

"Sweetheart, I barely finished high school. I don't understand a single thing you're saying."

"I think we have something in our genes that makes us candidates for some kind of gene therapy that kills almost everyone they've tried it on. Even with the serum we've been getting to strengthen us, they project less than twenty percent will survive. The serum series is sixteen doses. We have to go. Now."

Emilio was already stuffing the files into the bag and pulling on the lab coat.

"Now? As in right now?" Selina scanned the hallway.

"If we're not the hell out of here in seven hours, most of us are dead." Emilio tied the bag around his waist with the handles and swept the cloak over his rather odd ensemble.

"Butter my butt and call me toast. I guess it's as good a time as any." Selina motioned him to the door then stood back, adopting the blank yet blissful expression the others wore.

Emilio glanced over his shoulder at the cages. He was leaving them to die. When they fled El Salvador, his grandmother made sure they left no one behind. Yet here he was running away, abandoning nearly everyone in this room to perish. Or worse. Visions of the guy in the satyr costume cut down by elves and eaten by redcaps on that first night played unbidden on a fast loop. He was leaving them all to that. What would his grandmother think of him now? A single sob shook his body.

Hands on his shoulders shook him gently. "Oh sweetheart, don't feel guilty. The handful of us are no match for what lives in this place. Our only hope, their only hope, is for us to escape and rally help."

Selina was right, but that fact didn't release the claws of guilt tearing at his heart. He was going to hell now, he was sure of it. "I'm so sorry," he whispered. He took one last look at the people he was dooming and pushed the door open.

Emilio pulled the hood as far as it would go over his head. Selina trailed behind him, wearing the face of the glamoured. A pair of redcaps whisked past, little feet slapping the tiles. He desperately hoped not to encounter any elves. They may have discovered Jian was not, in fact, sick like Emilio pretended, and that it was warm enough in here to not wear mythic winter wear.

He stepped up to Alan's door, unlocked it, and slipped inside. A human lab assistant inside started. Emilio hadn't thought of what he'd do if he encountered people in the rooms, only in the hallways. The Fae radiated nothing but disdain for their human partners, so Emilio merely jerked his thumb toward the door. The black-haired man nodded and practically ran from the room.

"Alan. It's me. This is Selina. Time to go." He was already unlocking the cage. Alan had dark brown hair and a beard and looked to be in his midforties. He crawled out of his cage and stood.

"About time. One more day in that pen and I'm going to tip my hand so they kill me."

"You know what to do. We're off to the sixth floor. Two more there." Emilio waited for an elf to enter one of the other rooms then guided his group into the hall and to the small stairs at the end. It was empty, so they wasted no time racing down the stairs, taking two at a time. Emilio couldn't tell if his heart fluttered from exertion or abject terror.

The sixth floor held several goblins, an elf, and a smattering of smaller blue-skinned winged creatures. This was risky. He needed to avoid that elf and not draw attention to himself. "There's too many out there. It's probably safer for you two to stay here until I get Tamika and Jerome."

Alan's eyes went wide. "What if someone finds us? We'll be done for."

Selina rested a comforting hand on Alan's arm. The man was visibly shaking and leaned on the wall to support himself. "We'd be done for if we raise any alarms in that hallway. Emilio is right. We should stay here."

"I'll be back as fast as I can." Emilio's own muscles felt like water, and he was sweating profusely.

Tamika's room was closest, just two doors from the stairs, but he decided to make the long trek to Jerome in the east wing, past the double staircases. Easier to get one back to the west wing than two. And probably easier, at least on the walk across, to hide the cloak. He quickly stuffed it into the bag, smoothed the coat, and slung the bag over his shoulder.

"I'll be as fast as I can. If you hear anyone coming from above, break for the door on the first floor and take your chances outside."

Emilio grabbed some papers to rifle through on his walk and stepped into what looked like the longest hallway he'd ever seen. His gamble paid off. The Fae ignored him because they didn't like to talk to the scientists, and the other lab coats ignored him because he looked engrossed in his paperwork. The sound of music drifted up the hallway. He pulled the watch out of his pocket. Late afternoon. Odd that so few Fae were in the hallways. Maybe the boss lady was out of town and the Fae were tying one on down there. He'd take any advantage he could get.

Emilio approached the twin spiraling staircases that flanked the central plaza and the gateway. A small band played music while clusters of elves danced or lounged about. He was thankful the gate and the monsters in cages were directly below him so he couldn't see them. They might be Fae, but their suffering was still hard to look at.

He quickened his pace across the plaza. Even six floors up, he didn't like feeling so exposed.

"Hey Emilio!"

The cheery voice froze him in his tracks. He turned slowly to see his acquaintance from a few nights ago waving jovially.

"Bobby. Hey."

"Still no ID badge, eh?"

"No, I see what you mean about HR. Incompetent."

"You're not wrong." Bobby laughed and clapped him on his back. "What are you doing in this wing?"

"Um. Well. You know." Emilio's mind was a blank. "Yeah, there's a super good Abraxas candidate down here I need to get some tests on since we're almost ready."

"Damn. The poor soul. Well, all for the mission, I suppose."

"Yeah. The mission." Emilio forced a smile. "Well, Dr. Jones will have my head on a pole if I don't prepare the guy. Talk to you later."

"Good luck!"

Emilio nodded and pushed his face back into the papers. He waited until Bobby disappeared around a corner, then, once he was satisfied he was alone, he adopted his absent-minded scientist face and pushed into the room. He found Jerome asleep in his cage. He was young, like Ashley, but with deep chocolate skin and a runner's muscle tone.

"Jerome. Wake up." Emilio shook the man.

Jerome snapped awake and impacted the back of the cage with a wham. They both froze, listening for the flap and clip-clop of Fae feet. Several seconds later, they both exhaled.

"Sorry, Emilio."

"It's OK. Jerome, we gotta go. Now. I'll explain later. Follow me just like we talked about."

"I don't know, man. I be crawling out my skin."

"Jerome, dude. Our time's up here. Seven hours from now something worse happens."

"What if they catch us?"

"Stick to the plan and they won't." Emilio had no way to guarantee that, but Jerome looked buttressed by his certainty.

"I'm scared, Emilio."

"Me too, but we got this. You can do it. Just focus on the back of my head and walk. Think of getting out. Don't look at the Fae."

Jerome nodded and stepped up behind him, nostrils flaring with every breath.

Emilio swung the cloak on and led his prisoner back to the hallway. He arrived without incident at Tamika's room near the stairwell. Jerome was shaking so badly he had trouble walking. He'd break any moment if Emilio didn't do something. He didn't relish the thought of adding to his time in the corridor, but he had to get Jerome to the others now. So he went first to the stairwell and moved Jerome inside. He'd have to go back out for Tamika.

"Jerome, this is Alan and Selina. You're safe with them. Take some long, deep breaths. We're so close to being out of here, but you gotta hold it together, dude."

Tears rolled down the tall man's eyes, and he took a long shuddering inhale. Selina wrapped her arm around his shoulder and Alan rubbed the middle of his back.

"That's good, big man. Again." She nodded to Emilio.

The coast was clear, so he ran the few steps to Tamika's room. He was getting close to breaking himself. The sooner they were all running through the woods the better. He'd been extremely lucky so far. The only close call was that Bobby guy. His grandmother believed in miracles. Maybe she was right because their success so far qualified. Just two more. Ashley was the wild card though. She and Jerome might feed off each other, panic, start screaming, and get them all killed.

He found Tamika wide-eyed and sitting upright in her cage.

"Emilio. We gotta get out of here. Something big is happening." She gripped the bars of her cage and stared up at him.

Emilio knelt and unlocked the door. "I know. We're leaving now. Just one more stop on the first floor and we make a break for the forest."

They stood by the door. Tamika's eyes darted back and forth and her hands fidgeted with the drawstring on her scrubs.

"Tamika. You gotta put on the glamour face. Like them." Emilio motioned to the row of stupefied faces in the room.

She tried, but tension in her shoulders and lips made her look hyperalert. Emilio shook his entire body and massaged his face. "Come on. Shake it out like me." He let his body hunch and his limbs swing like a puppet with a string cut. Tamika imitated his movements. When Emilio was satisfied with her approximation, they stepped outside.

Tamika did reasonably well drifting along behind him passively, but Emilio was glad the redcaps were at the other end of the hall and the trip to the door was mercifully short.

Once in the stairwell he didn't waste time with introductions. The group raced down the stairs to the first floor. Just Ashley left.

Emilio took the cloak off again and let it fall to the floor. He rifled through the duffel bag and pulled out the makeshift weapons he'd collected. Steel equipment stands and a single scalpel. He gave the blade to Jerome, who had the longest reach, and gave everyone else a weapon.

"What are we supposed to do with these?" Alan asked in a whisper, turning over the bunsen burner stand in his hands.

"Iron both damages and repels the Fae," Selina whispered. "One gets close, whap them with it."

"You never said we gonna have to fight our way out." Jerome gripped his weapon like he'd never held one before.

"I'd rather be armed than not. And these were what I could

find," Emilio whispered and stepped out into the hallway for what he hoped was the last time.

Goblin and redcap heads turned to him. They sneered and kept moving, but Emilio's heart beat even faster, anyway. He'd forgotten his decoy clipboard. Mercifully, he was already in front of Ashley's door.

He let himself in, braced for whichever Ashley he'd find. The hysterical privileged daughter of a wealthy man or the calmer version he'd met last time.

Fortune smiled on him. She was sitting cross-legged at the back of her cage, blonde hair bound in a single braid.

"Is it time to go?"

"You've calmed down a lot since the first time we met," Emilio remarked as he unlocked her prison.

"You said you wouldn't leave me behind."

Emilio's brows knitted together. She was the calmest one of them right now, the polar opposite of the howling privileged mess of a few nights ago. Maybe they gave her a different treatment than he got. That or she was having mood swings like Harper's mom.

Emilio glanced over at the cabinet. Last chance to get information. He bounded over to the drawers and pulled out the bottom one. Empty. He pulled out two more, both empty.

"They took the files?"

"Yeah, yesterday. Can we go now?"

Emilio's mind raced. If they took the files, they probably knew some were missing. And if some were missing, they knew someone was moving freely about the lab. Alarm bells screamed in his mind.

Don't psych yourself out. You don't know why they moved them. The experiment was entering a new phase, anyway. They probably moved them somewhere else because of that. Besides, he had no time to ponder; they were so close.

He stepped to the door and looked at Ashley. "You need to look spellbound."

"Like this?" Ashley tossed her braid over her shoulder and adopted a perfect slack-jawed look.

"Exactly. Follow me."

The six of them crouched in the stairwell facing the door to the outside. Emilio pressed his ear to the door to listen for any sounds that might betray the presence of Fae. It was quiet, but he wasn't too sure that meant anything.

"Here we go. I think if we keep going straight we should be at the river in about ten minutes. Run. As fast as you can and don't stop. Keep your weapons ready."

The five faces looking back at him were wide eyed and scared. "We've come this far. We got this." They nodded, held their makeshift weapons out in front of them, and Emilio flung open the door.

Six terrified humans rushed into the bitterly cold night air and right into a waiting ring of elves, trolls, goblins, and redcaps.

CHAPTER 46

Harper didn't stop running until her legs turned to lead and a stitch in her side pulled her into a low hunch. She staggered to a stop with her hands resting on her thighs and lungs bellowing despite the stabbing pain that accompanied every inhale.

Even though her sprint had hurt, it felt good. Her body told her she'd accomplished something instead of helplessly listening to everyone dither and debate. Even if that something was getting herself royally lost in the woods while wearing a ballgown.

She staggered over to a fir tree and dropped to the ground. The bark felt rough but solid at her back. White clouds against grey sky wheeled overhead. As the pain in her side receded, reason returned. Her rage felt powerful, but it didn't help anyone. Now she was exhausted and still in the same boat she was in an hour ago.

The sound of footsteps crunching along the pine needles stilled her breathing. It wasn't an animal. She slowly rose and took cover behind the tree trunk, eyes straining to peer deep enough into the woods to see whether whatever approached was friend or foe. She cursed silently. She was weaponless.

Agonizing seconds passed before she saw a familiar Fir Bolg and the canine Phooka walking toward the clearing.

"This way," Paegrinn called and pointed right at her location. It shouldn't have surprised her the Fir Bolg would be excellent trackers.

Harper emerged from behind the tree to face her friends, fully expecting Nuada and her mother right behind them, ready to chastise her for her little display. But it was only the Phooka and Paegrinn who hurried to her side.

"Harper! Thank the Underworld we found you." The Phooka melted back to his natural state.

"Where's Nuada and Mom?" Harper asked.

"Your mom is back in the village. Nuada promised her he'd find you," Paegrinn said.

"Nuada wanted to circle round and make sure nothing followed you. He'll be here soon," the Phooka added.

Harper watched her fingers twist and roll the fabric of the dress. The Phooka sat down in front of her and leaned so far to the side his ear brushed the pine needles, all to make some eye contact. Harper swiveled to the side to avoid his eyes. Still not trusting she wouldn't start crying, she poked at her bruised arm to distract herself from the feeling of failure. The move was effective; with the adrenaline fading, the aches and pains from sword practice throbbed. When she finally looked up, she noticed Paegrinn studying her wounds.

"Sword practice looks rough."

"Yeah. I suck."

The Phooka snorted. "Understatement of the year."

"I bet I could make a salve that would heal those bruises right up."

"If you have something that would help, I'll take you up on it."

Paegrinn's mouth grew into a broad smile and he listed herbs they would need, ticking each off on a thick, furred finger. "We can fan out and find some mullein, witch hazel, and I think I know where we planted some comfrey a few years ago."

It probably couldn't hurt. Harper didn't really want to go back to the village and face everyone just yet. Besides, Nuada would find them soon enough.

They quickly found the mullein and hazel within a few steps of where they were. Paegrinn guided them along a deer trail toward where he recalled the comfrey grew.

They were about to crest a small hill carpeted with bramble when Paegrinn stopped short. Harper nearly ran into him. He held a hand to his lips and waved for them to crouch. Her Fir Bolg friend didn't seem alarmed so Harper didn't worry.

They picked their way through the bramble, keeping their backs low. With each step, a shimmering lake came into focus. Both Paegrinn and the Phooka snapped their heads toward the shoreline. The Phooka's ears twitched, and he leaned his head toward a sound Harper couldn't hear. A broad smile spread slowly across Paegrinn's face.

"Want to have a little fun?"

"Sure, but what do you guys hear over there?" Harper glanced in the direction her friends were looking but saw nothing.

"Sounds like campers." The Phooka looked up at Paegrinn out of the corner of his eye. "I love a good bit of fun. Just what do you have in mind, my young friend?"

Paegrinn laid the brown satchel and the knife he was carrying down. His grin covered his entire face. "My dad would be very mad if this ever got back to him. You have to swear not to talk to anyone about what we're going to do."

"OK." Harper had a few reservations, but whatever Paegrinn was planning was a welcome distraction. Some harmless fun would let her blow off some steam and avoid Nuada a little longer. After her outburst, she wasn't ready to face him just yet.

"I solemnly swear I am up to no good." The Phooka's spine

was military straight. He raised his right hand in affirmation and his eyes glittered.

Paegrinn giggled and swept his long arms around the shoulders of his new friends. "Phooka, can you shapeshift into a Fir Bolg?"

"Of course." His shape faded. It became a black cloud before coalescing into the shape of a jet-black Fir Bolg. Paegrinn nodded and turned his attention to Harper, smile never dimming.

"What are you two up to?" Harper said.

"Squatching."

The Phooka's Fir Bolg features pulled into a grin as wide as the one Paegrinn wore. "I think I see where you're going with this. Bigfoot sighting." He jumped up and down and clapped his hands together.

"Guys, I don't think this is a good idea." A pang of guilt hit her at having fun when Emilio languished as a Fae prisoner.

"You've been through a lot. Trust me. A little fun is just what you need to soothe your jangled nerves. Besides, all you need to do is stay here and keep a watch out for the Five-O." The Phooka's voice was smooth, and he spread his hand, then formed it into an 'O.'

"The Five-O?"

"Nuada. Just make sure Nuada and Aeld don't catch us." The Phooka spoke slowly, like he would a small child.

Paegrinn and the Bigfoot Phooka were almost ready to make a run down the hill when a cloud of black birds wheeled overhead. Raucous cries wrenched Harper's gaze to the sky. Her stomach fell to her ankles when she saw the tattered leathery wings of Sluagh and the glint of red avian eyes. She was just trying to convince herself her nerves were causing her to see things that weren't there, when the all-too-familiar sound of baying hounds drained the last strength from her legs.

"Phooka! The Wild Hunt! They found us," she called after her friends.

The Phooka snapped into his wolf form and raced for Harper, Paegrinn hot on his heels. Harper caught a blur of white from the corner of her eye. Two spectral dogs trotted snarling out from the hillside behind her with their hackles up. Red eyes gleamed and teeth snapped. The two threw their heads back and flattened their red ears tight against their skulls, and then an unearthly wavering howl pierced the sky, answered by another. And another.

Then her nightmare strode out of the bramble. Gwyn. Eyes aflame in the antlered skull mask and flanked by dripping kelpies. Paegrinn and the Phooka arrived by her side. The three formed a ring facing the group of corpse-like Sluagh, elves, and more kelpies that emerged out of the tree line. They were surrounded and totally outnumbered.

Paegrinn held the little knife in front of him. The Phooka growled, sending strings of drool flapping. Harper merely stood. Her other hand grasped Ezrynhivar's ring, and she tried to summon the blue energy to her hands again. Nothing. Her magic had a mind of its own and cosmically bad timing.

Gwyn strode down the hill, coming to a stop just a couple feet from Harper. He leaned forward until the grisly mask was inches from her face.

"Want to know how I found you, little girl?"

"Dumb luck?" Even in the face of danger, the Phooka was as flippant as always.

"Or was it betrayal?" Gwyn shifted his eyes down to stare at the Phooka.

Harper drew back from the wolf by her side. So many had warned her about him. Not to trust him. Here they were alone in the woods, Nuada was nowhere to be found, and the Wild Hunt just happened upon them in the middle of some of the largest swaths of wilderness anywhere. If the Phooka was betraying her, he was doing a splendid job of keeping up the friend act. His legs splayed wide in a half crouch like he was coiled to attack, and a low growl constantly rumbled in his throat.

Gwyn laughed, a sound as mirthless as death itself. A gloved hand swept a brown cape to the side, and he paced in front of Harper, keeping those smoldering, empty eyes trained on her. "Oh, this is far too good. You don't even know, do you? I didn't need the shapeshifter's help. It was you, little heir. Did you burn the Fir Bolg settlement with your raw magic like you did my Wild Hunt?"

"No," was all Harper could manage with a throat as dry as the desert.

"Pity. A much worse fate is in store for them now."

"Worse fate?" Paegrinn's eyes were saucers.

Gwyn ambled toward the adolescent Fir Bolg and scanned his furred features. "We haven't seen your kind in centuries. Seems doubtful you'd join Badb's cause, but creatures as strong as you have other uses."

"You monster!" Harper screamed at Gwyn.

"Perhaps Badb Catha will go easy on you, little girl. Especially if I tell her we would have never found their village if not for your magic tricks."

The Phooka barked and growled.

"You won't take us down so easily," Paegrinn said.

Harper's throat tightened and her heart was in a vice. This was her fault. All her fault. She'd acted like a spoiled child and blasted those trees with her magic outside the barrier. She'd doomed the entire village and her mother along with it. Not just them. Everyone she loved was condemned now because of her, including Emilio, because no one was coming for him anymore. Teeth clamped down on the inside of her cheek, filling her mouth with the taste of iron, but it kept the tears at bay.

She staggered back into the tree, suddenly needing support.

Her head shook from side to side, like that impotent motion could magically negate the destruction she had wrought.

"There is a possibility the Fir Bolg could still be deadly in battle." Gwyn drifted back to Harper with his hands clasped behind his back, all while the ring of elves, hounds, and kelpies hovered at the crest of the hill, ready to pour down and slaughter Harper and her friends. "Tell you what. Let's make a deal, little heir. Badb isn't really interested in the Fir Bolg. If you come with me right now, I won't tell her you led us to them, and their pathetic lives can go on as they have for centuries."

"Don't listen to him, Harper. He might keep his word, but he'll order one of the others to tell her," The Phooka said.

"Have it your way then."

Despair had weakened her. He was on her before she could react. Muscular arms circled her and pinned her arms to her sides. Harper tried to kick off the ground and slam him backward into the tree, but he merely picked her up. Her legs pedaled uselessly in the air.

The ring of elves and other Fae advanced on them, swords drawn, and marched down the hillside. The Phooka leapt into the approaching throng with his jaws open while Paegrinn slashed at a kelpie with his knife. The creature hissed and danced out of the way, inky eyes glittering.

"Son!" Nuada's voice rang out over the approaching circle from the other side. A line of Fir Bolg dotted the hillside behind him. Nuada raced for Harper and the furry giants thundered toward the Fae.

CHAPTER 47

Emilio's heart plummeted. Wails of despair and surprise rose from the others behind him. His eyes darted from side to side, desperately searching for an opening that promised a path to freedom, but there were too many Fae. None of them would make it.

A ring of swords pointed at their chests, accompanied by jeering faces filled with sharp teeth. Emilio brandished his makeshift weapon in front of him, dropped it to the ground, and held up his arms in surrender. It was over. They had failed, and he had failed them. He heard the other metal bits clunking to the ground around him.

How did they know to catch them here? He'd never noticed cameras inside the building, and he'd been looking. No one had tailed them, unless some of these creatures could turn invisible. Wait. They probably all could, they were magic and all that. He kicked himself for not listening to that niggling little voice inside him that told him tonight had been too easy. They knew. Somehow they knew. But Emilio hadn't planned on making the escape tonight until a few minutes before it began. Had they stationed guards here night after night, just waiting?

"So tell me. Which one of you thought you could outsmart us?"

Emilio recognized that cold, mocking voice. A tall woman dressed head to toe in black pushed through the line of Fae to stand in front of the refugees. Her red hair caught the orange evening light and looked like flame. A long black dress flowed beneath plates of jet armor on her chest and shoulders.

Emilio forced himself to take a wavering step toward her.

The woman walked a slow circle around him as though trying to determine what made him so special. Emilio pulled his spine ramrod straight and stared ahead, making his face as expressionless as he could. He pressed his lips hard together to stop the trembling in his chin.

Once Badb completed her revolution, she reached out an alabaster hand to Emilio's chin and tilted his face up to her own.

"And why aren't you six helplessly glamoured like the others?"

Emilio felt a hand from behind reach into his waistband and pull out the keys.

"He used these to get them out of their rooms any time he wanted," Ashley said and presented her prize to the dark lady.

"You bitch," Emilio hissed. That was why she was suddenly so calm. Why she asked so many questions. She must have made a deal with them.

"You were never going to save me." Her voice had that nasally whine again.

"I tried. I got you out, just like I promised. And now you've doomed us all. You selfish, back-stabbing—"

"It doesn't matter. We'd have been caught out here, anyway. I had to. I had to." Ashley twisted her fingers together and pleaded with Emilio with her eyes like he would just forgive her.

Badb's lip curled in a sneer when she turned toward the

blonde girl. Ashley chewed her bottom lip and hunched her shoulders. Sidling toward Badb, she adopted a plaintive wheedling tone, one that probably worked on her father.

"I did good, right? I told you their plans, even gave you back the keys. I can go, right? You promised to release me." Her voice quavered and madness crept into her azure eyes, flicking around the circle of Fae. They tittered and squawked, continuing to point claws and blades at her.

"Yes, little traitor, you can go." Badb held up a hand toward the woods, and the line of Fae parted. Some of them bowed low and swept outstretched arms toward the forest.

Ashley's mouth curved down and tears streamed from her eyes. "But . . . but you have to take me home. You promised to let me go. How am I supposed to get home?" Her entire body shook and her voice rose an octave with every desperate sentence.

"But that wasn't our bargain, pathetic whelp." Badb's smile was predatory as she loomed over the sobbing girl. Around her a chorus of Fae laughter rose.

"But you promised." Ashley's voice was a shriek.

"I promised to let you leave my tower unharmed by any of my forces in exchange for bringing this little plot to my attention and assisting in their capture. And that is precisely what I am doing. Nothing more. Nothing less. You are unharmed and, as you can see, very much out of my tower. Our deal is complete."

"You dizzy bitch. You sold us out for nothing. They're going to kill you anyway." Emilio spat the words at Ashley, who was sniveling and groveling in front of the dark lady. Snot clumped on her top lip and her pale face was beet red from weeping.

"And if anyone deserves it, it's you." Selina finished his thought perfectly.

Ashley spun and grabbed Emilio by the shoulders. The madness fully flowered in her eyes. "Emilio. You have to help me." She hung on him and cried.

The Fae erupted again with laughter, entertained by the mortal spectacle. Emilio jerked away from her and shoved her staggering backward. "You seem pretty good at helping only yourself. Best of luck."

"Oh, little whelp, don't cry. We'll give you a full day's head start. If you can make it off the island, you are free to go," Callon said.

Beside Emilio, Badb bent down and conversed in low tones with a small winged Fae with lavender skin. Emilio strained to overhear what the little Fae said, but it was no use. Whatever it was made Badb's red lips pull into a wide smile.

The little Fae departed and Emilio's attention focused back on the elves taunting Ashley.

"I- I just have to find my way to the water and swim away?" Ashley's face showed a glimmer of hope, but more howls of laughter arose around her.

"This isn't a human island anymore. The trails fold and twist in on themselves. You'll exhaust yourself walking in circles all day and then we're coming for you!" one of the feather-winged sylphs called.

"Liars! Cheats!" Ashley shrieked. Her eyes rolled and her fingernails drew lines of blood from her cheeks. "This isn't fair."

"Oh, just get runnin' or I'll kill you myself," Jerome said from behind Emilio. That made the Fae howl with more laughter than ever.

Finding only hard stares from her fellow escapees and the jeering faces of the surrounding Fae, Ashley turned and sprinted toward the trees. Emilio watched her careen into the mist and then she was gone.

Badb stepped in front of Emilio once more. "Shall we all go back inside? I'd like to hear what the doctor has to say about your apparent immunity to our glamour."

The escapees shuffled back to the stairwell with their heads hung low. Emilio knew each of them must be running through the same nightmare scenarios of what would happen to them now.

Badb walked right behind Emilio, the elf Callon beside her.

"You look positively delighted, my queen," Callon said.

"Today has been a magnificent day. We thwarted an escape plan, had some fun with the little betrayer, and messengers just told me Gwyn has found the last heir. He will bring her to me shortly."

"Then nothing can stand in our way."

Emilio heard the glee in Callon's voice. They'd found Harper. The last tiny flame of hope flickered out. Surrender to the inevitable draped across his back like a blanket of lead.

Dr. Jones met them just inside the first-floor hallway. His eyes widened when he saw the small band, unaffected by the allure of the Fae.

"Doctor. Do you have any explanation why these five are walking about?"

"Yes, yes. I, um. I was just coming to tell Breas about the last round of tests. Without looking at their cell numbers, I, uh, can't be sure, but it's a safe bet, these six—"

"Five now," Callon said, his head swiveling in the direction of Ashley's flight.

"Right. Five. These five are the best candidates for Project Abraxas. I feel confident they will all survive both the catalyst and rewriting their genetic code. In fact, their immunity may hold the missing keys to some gene therap—"

Badb shook her head and glowered. "Yes, yes. I care little for your science. In all the humans we have here, you are telling me only these five are guaranteed to survive? That's not nearly enough."

Emilio's head swam. Of course. Catalysts. Stem cells. The match to the Abraxas profile. They were trying to revise their genetics, but it required the right genes to tinker with. He doubted anything too complicated could be reliably spliced in, so the raw material needed to be present beforehand. As for what they planned to change, he drew a blank. He looked into the wide eyes of the rest of his little band. Their fear reflected his own.

"We can still try Abraxas on others, although we will just continue to see the same high mortality rate. With people obsessed with having their own genes sequenced to discover their lands of origin, I believe there is a way to better screen potentials with the ancestry databases—"

Badb waved a hand to silence the doctor. "Take our intrepid batch of escapees and prepare them."

Panic tore at Emilio's mind. He shoved the nearest elf out of the way. She staggered aside, taken by surprise that one of them would try to flee when surrounded. Better to make a run for it and be cut down than the torture that awaited them. Beside him, he felt the others jostle and try to join him.

And then he was floating on a warm, effervescent cloud. His last thought was the recognition of the glamour spell descending and the certainty it would wear off all too soon, leaving him to face the full force of his terror.

CHAPTER 48

The moment Harper left the protection of the village, magic raging inside her, Nuada knew the Wild Hunt would sense her and descend. That kind of power would be like a searchlight guiding anything with magical blood right to them. After her performance at the Mystic Island festival, they knew the shape and feel of that mix of Eriu's blood and Macha's sorcery that flowed through her, just as he did. The Wild Hunt had simply followed the beacon. All the same, the speed of their arrival surprised him. They must have already been nearby to arrive so soon. He couldn't rule out a betrayer in their midst.

At least they had a fighting chance to prevail against the Wild Hunt. In his caution, he'd convinced Aeld to send out an armed party to search for any signs of unwelcome Fae the instant Harper ran. Trees blurred past as Nuada tore through the woods as fast as his enchanted feet could carry him. His Fir Bolg friends would catch up to him in moments, but by then it might be too late.

He wheeled around a massive stone at the crest of a hill. The scene below brought him skidding to a halt. At the hill's bottom,

Gwyn gripped Harper, dragging her from where Paegrinn and the wolf Phooka fought back to back surrounded by mostly smaller although no less deadly Fae. The Fir Bolg teenager backhanded one of the Gabriel hounds. His hairy arm sent the beast yelping and tumbling into the underbrush.

"Son!" Nuada called. He knew Gwyn was unlikely to release Harper, but if he stalled long enough, there might still be hope. A few minutes longer and Aeld's reinforcements would battle their way to them through the minions of the Hunt. A cool tingle spread through his hand as he gathered power from the earth for the fight ahead.

"Nuada!" Harper screamed.

The flames in Gwyn's antlered mask flared so forcefully they licked the edge of the antlers. Nuada flung out his hand, sending a wave of earth cresting toward his son. Fibrous roots torn from the deep flung clods in every direction behind the rumbling mound lancing for his son. Gwyn tried to react, but the wave seized him and smacked him against a boulder. Harper fell from his grip and she raced for the tree line, the tattered hem of the golden dress trailing behind.

Gwyn staggered to his feet just as a pair of rugged Fir Bolg thudded down the hill straight for him. Nuada exhaled a sigh of relief. Help had arrived. His son turned and fled for the underbrush, unwilling to face the sturdy reinforcements without cover.

Nuada wanted to get to Harper's side, but elves and other Fae closed in at the bottom of the hill. Now the real battle began. He bounded down the hill, double swords poised defensively before him. A sizable group of Fir Bolg engaged the lines of Fae flanking the trio below. The gigantic fighters jabbed and swung with their thick spears. The Fir Bolg were formidable warriors, but the sheer number of enemy forces threatened to overrun them quickly.

Nuada watched the Phooka let out a howl and zig zag through blade and claw toward Harper. He stopped in the middle of a cluster of goblins that had Paegrinn pinned. Blood spattered everywhere from the Phooka's whirling body. He bounded in tight circles, grabbing the small goblins and shaking them to death in his powerful jaws. The smaller Fae fell back to regroup.

Nuada tossed Harper the hammer from a deceased goblin and she backed up the Phooka's rescue of Paegrinn. The goblins had recovered fast. Jagged teeth bared, they hissed at her approach. In a flash they skittered toward her, all teeth and claws.

Nuada kicked pine needles and dirt into their eyes an instant before they assaulted her. Nuada's weapon cut a wide arc and all but two of the goblins fell. The survivors' gravely voices howled with rage.

"Harper!" Nuada screamed. One of the goblins had grabbed her hair and pulled her to the ground. Kelpies and redcaps closed in fast.

Nuada slashed the last goblin and crouched to close the gap between himself and Harper before she was overrun, but an attack from a more serious foe halted his advance. A tall Sidhe warrior. "Run!" he shouted at a Fir Bolg warrior who had taken down an elf with her bare hands. "Get back to the village! We need reinforcements!"

They were losing. Nuada hoped Aeld would send warriors and make sure both the village and Harper remained safe. Whether they knew it or not, she was their last hope.

A Fir Bolg woman grabbed her spear and raced for the hill to help him. She didn't make it very far before the whoosh and thud of an arrow landed her face down on the forest floor. Nuada let out a savage yell and lashed out with his blade. His elven foe parried easily and their deadly dance continued.

He couldn't see Harper. Panic tore at his mind. *Please don't let her fall.* The elf's lips pulled into a sneer as he launched himself at Nuada with a flurry of blows, but Nuada was faster. The tip of his blade caught the hilt of his foe's sword. With a flick, he tore the blade from his hand. Before the weapon hit the ground, Nuada slammed his own sword through the elf's chest. The Sidhe fell forward, staring at the blood pouring from between his fingers, futilely trying to hold it all in.

Nuada quickly scanned for Harper again. He saw Paegrinn and the Phooka fighting a group of goblins and redcaps. The broad sweeps of Paegrinn's spear sent smaller Fae flying, and the Phooka's jaws shredded countless enemies. Nuada's stomach twisted. *Where is she?*

He bounded across to his friends but a focused wind blasted him backward. He landed with a thud and nearly lost his grip on his sword. He shook his head rapidly to recover from the impact. He made out a pair of winged sylphs hovering in the air, directing the winds onto the battlefield. Redcaps poured in around him. He swiped at them as he scrambled to his feet.

As he fought, Nuada pulled energy up from the earth and channeled it toward a cluster of tall fir trees. Spell complete, his left hand flew forward and directed the tree roots below the sylphs to whip out of the ground, coil around the Fae, and drive them to the surface. The sylphs screamed as the roots hurtled back into the earth. Nuada heard the snapping bones that marked their end.

Searing pain snapped his focus back to the redcaps. One of them had taken advantage of his divided concentration and slipped past his blade. He tore a dagger from his thigh and brought his weapon down, cleaving the skull of his tiny attacker.

The wound cut through several layers of muscle, severe enough to slow him down. Nuada needed to get the redcaps away from him or they'd overrun him fast. His hand flew, fingers outstretched, into the air, tendrils of spinning power swirled around it. With a cry he crashed his hand into the earth, creating a circular shock wave. Redcaps and goblins crashed into the surrounding stones and trees, the life crushed from them. Free from immediate attackers, he frantically scanned the area for Harper. No sign of her or his son. His throat constricted. Gwyn might already be on his way back to Badb with her while he and the Phooka battled his Wild Hunt.

Then he saw her. The golden dress filthy and bloodstained, she crouched with the goblin hammer in her hand, chest heaving. A tall elf loomed behind her before Nuada could call out a warning. Ignoring the pain from his wound, he raced toward her. His feet couldn't get him there in time.

"Duck!" he yelled. And she did.

His sword sailed over her shoulder and buried itself into the elf's chest with a thud.

"Thanks for the assist," Harper said while Nuada pulled his blade free of the man's chest.

"Harper." Nuada let out a breath. "Stay close to me." He picked up a sword from a fallen elf and thrust it toward her. The weapon had a longer reach than the short goblin hammer she held.

"There's so many of them. We can't let them get to the village. This is all my fault."

He heard the strain in her voice.

All around them, the remaining Fir Bolg and the Phooka fought off wave after wave of the Wild Hunt and Sluagh. The handful of Fir Bolg were on the verge of exhaustion. Their movements slowed. They could only hope that one of the furred giants managed to bring reinforcements. Nuada took a step forward and his wounded leg sent a jolt of pain up his spine. The gash smoldered and was becoming impossible to ignore. Poisoned.

Harper stabbed a pair of approaching redcaps. "Oh my god, your leg."

Nuada looked down. His shiny blue pants glistened with

blood. "I'll make it. Focus on the battle. If you get an opening, run and don't come back for me. I'll find you."

"No. I'm done losing people I care about to Fae."

Nuada favored his leg as he cut down a pair of attacking goblins. Any hope of winning this battle faded from his mind when a tall, antlered figure stepped out of the tree line. Gwyn had recovered from whatever foe had pushed him so far from his target. Sword in hand and eyes smoldering within the skull mask, Gwyn ap Nudd strode right for his father.

"Oh, no." Harper's voice came from beside him. "Draw the sword, Nuada."

The muscles on Nuada's neck corded. His breath came in jagged gasps. "I can't," he whispered between clenched teeth. "He's my son." Nuada's chest constricted and ached. He shifted his weight to his uninjured leg and brought his weapon slowly up in front of him.

"He's already tried to kill you. You can't let him, I need you."

Nuada squeezed his eyes shut for an instant. Memories of Gwyn from before he joined Badb pushed at his mind and misted his eyes. So bright was the light within his heart, so full of gusto for hunting and revelry. For those reasons he'd chosen him for the most sacred role of guiding the dead. For mortals, crossing the threshold between life and death was terrifying. Who better to ease that terror than a being of light and joy.

Guilt. Love. Regret. All swirled in his heart. He shoved them back down. He had no choice. Gwyn had made his long ago. Nuada had lost him then. If his son captured or killed Harper, this world would be lost. Still, he couldn't bring himself to draw the Claimh Solias. Maybe he could incapacitate him. Maybe he wouldn't have to kill him. "Get the Phooka and flee. Right now. This fight isn't yours," he growled.

"You made it mine the day you pulled me into this war!"

"We don't have time for this. Just go. Now."

Gwyn ambled down the hill. His forces had left Harper and Nuada alone so their master could be the one to capture them. The Wild Hunt engaged the snarling Phooka and the cluster of Fir Bolg. Gwyn paused midstride. His antlered head tilted and turned to focus over Nuada's shoulder to where Harper had just cut down a kelpie who disobeyed his master's unspoken order to not attack.

"Very good, would-be-queen. The blood of your grandmother sings in your veins."

Gwyn threw his head back and his hands in the air. The ground behind Nuada rumbled, and Nuada dared to take his eyes from his son. Behind him, stones and roots jutted up out of the ground, ringing Harper. She screamed, her nut-brown hair flying back from her face and her green eyes drawn in agony as tree roots rocketed for the sky and then snaked in coils around her arms and torso. Rocks erupted in a small circle at her feet, pinning her legs. Root and stone bound her in place. "Nuada." She croaked his name. Her head lolled forward.

Nuada rounded on Gwyn. "Release her or I will cut you down where you stand." Nuada's silver sword arm trembled. His usually pale complexion was bright red. His chest heaved as his eyes bored into his son.

A low laugh escaped from Gwyn and his mouth turned up in a half smile under his mask. He held his hands wide and inclined his head. "Oh, come now, Father. If you had the courage to kill me, you'd have a different sword drawn." He flicked his chin at the ornate scabbard at Nuada's hip. Gwyn circled Nuada, stepping sideways, never dropping his gaze from his father. He scraped the tip of his blade along the forest floor in a wide arc as he drifted closer and closer to where Nuada hunched, waiting.

Pinecones crunched underfoot as Nuada and his son spiraled toward their inevitable clash. Nuada's entire body felt heavy. "Son. You ruled the dead with compassion and grace. This isn't you. You protect the souls of humanity and Fae alike. This war is not the way. Gwyn. I don't want to kill you." The corners of Nuada's mouth pulled down, eyes pleaded with his son.

Gwyn paused. His hand grasped his antlered mask and he removed it, pulling aside the coffee-brown tunic and leather breastplate to reveal long barbed scars running along his neck and disappearing beneath his sleeve. Even without the mask, his eyes still smoldered like dying embers. "Take a good look, Father. This is all humans are good for. This is what they do, who they are. They breed like flies and crawl over the earth like bloated maggots, blindly taking all they can." He spat the words out like they were poison. He swiped his blade into a young tree that toppled away from him as he tore the blade free once more. "They are empty. How many beings must fall to fill the pit that is their soul? Badb will wipe them from the earth, and the world will be the better for it."

"Those are Badb's words. Not yours. It's not too late, son. Come back to the light. Join me, or if you cannot, at least walk away."

Gwyn's left foot crossed over his right as he sidestepped Nuada, looking for an opening. He jerked his head to the ring of tattered avian Sluagh in the ring of trees. "She lets Donn send them with every mission I undertake for her. To remind me how powerless I am now that the human souls are trapped, wandering in the Green World, unable to return to the source."

"This is why you must join—"

"No!" "Gwyn barked so loudly it echoed off every hillside. "You failed. The Tuatha failed. And now I'm compelled to do my queen's bidding."

"No matter how lost you are, Gwyn, I will never stop believing the good man that is my son is in there somewhere."

"Then you are a fool." Gwyn ap Nudd let the mask drop from his hand and launched himself toward Nuada, his blade before him.

Nuada brought his blade up just in time to parry the blow, but the force of Gwyn's strike knocked him back onto his injured leg. His free hand instinctively flew to the wound and came away streaked with red. Gwyn used the opening to lunge forward with another attack, which Nuada escaped only by dropping and rolling out of range. Momentum carried him back to his feet and he stood facing his son once more, both swords ready to strike.

Nuada feinted to one side. Gwyn took the bait and stepped in to cut him with his sword. His lips pulled back and his forehead was creased in a mask of fury. Anger led Gwyn to overstep, and Nuada's sword bit into his side. Gwyn howled and spun around, spittle flying from his lips. Blood seeped through his leather tunic.

Nuada took the precious second he'd earned and whispered a spell. A crackling ball of white fire materialized and shot forward. The force of the collision with Gwyn's chest knocked him back several feet, and he landed with a thud. Nuada allowed himself to glance at Harper watching the battle unfold, suspended in her prison. Her eyes were drawn with worry.

Nuada was already sailing through the air toward his son. He landed just as Gwyn scrambled to his feet. Nuada brought the hilt of his sword up to smash Gwyn in the jaw. He heard a sickening crunch and Gwyn's head whipped to the side. Blood coursed down his jaw and he spat out a tooth. His head revolved slowly back, and he glared at Nuada from the tops of his eyes.

"Son. Please. Let's put aside this ridiculous conflict."

Nuada's answer was a flurry of blows from Gwyn's sword. Dull clangs and high-pitched rings filled the surrounding forest. The combatant's swords moved so fast they were nearly a blur. Then it happened. Nuada's injured leg buckled after catching the edge of a jutting stone. The falter was just enough to give Gwyn an opening and his sword flashed up, slicing into the silver arm. Sparks flew as the blade slid loose. Nuada's hand clenched involuntarily around the sword. Gwyn's blow had damaged the intricate mechanical workings inside the arm. He could barely bend his elbow. Gwyn's flat laugh revealed no joy. Nuada's breath heaved, and he pulled his sword free from the spasming grip of his metal hand.

"It's over, Father. Draw the Claimh Solias and strike me down, or say goodbye to your would-be-queen."

Gwyn flew at Nuada with his blade held high. Nuada saw his mistake instantly. His arrogant victory slash had exposed his chest. Nuada dropped onto his back and drew his legs to his midsection. Another instant later, his feet slammed into Gwyn's chest, sending him shooting backward with a whoosh of forced exhalation. He heard Harper's sharp breath and saw her relief from the corner of his eye. Her body shook with silent sobs. He watched his son gasping to catch his breath beneath him. He stood over Gwyn with his sword at his throat. Nuada's uninjured foot sent Gwyn's sword clattering across the rocks and out of his reach.

"You are correct. It is over, Gwyn. Call off your Hunt and leave this forest." Nuada's voice was calm and matter of fact.

Gwyn spat at his father. He shook his head slowly. "You have no idea what's coming. This is very far from over."

"Nuada, watch out, he's got a knife!" Harper's cry was shrill in his ear. But the warning was too late. Gwyn's hand had drawn a dagger from the laces and folds of his pants. He jammed the dagger up and into Nuada's uninjured leg, severing the hamstring. His leg was useless. Nuada fell forward and met Gwyn's knife a second time in the chest. Hot blood gushed from the wound.

He heard Harper screaming. Gwyn's face lacked the triumph Nuada expected to find there. Instead, his son just looked tired. Nuada felt his heart flutter. The blade had gone too deep.

"Son—"

Gwyn's face contorted in rage. "Don't call me that."

Pain wrenched his torn heart, and a cry escaped Nuada's lips.

Gwyn's jaw relaxed and his eyes softened.

"You don't know what it's been like in the Underworld. Trapped. Tortured. Badb freed us from our prison and she'll preserve this world too." Gwyn's voice was strained. He spoke the words, but Nuada heard no conviction in them.

"Badb was driven mad by her own prophecy thousands of years ago. Son. There's still time. Become the man I know you to be. Help her." Nuada glanced up at Harper. Her mouth hung open in a face drawn with pain.

Gwyn narrowed his eyes at the girl.

Grief constricted Nuada's wildly beating heart seeing what his child had become. Blood poured from his mouth and he tilted his head back to Harper. She dangled in her prison of root and stone. The golden dress hung in bloody tatters. Tears streaked the dirt on her cheeks and her breath came in ragged sobs. Because he could not bring himself to kill his son, she'd suffer. His mind raced with thoughts of what Badb and her followers would do to her.

His strength was ebbing. For the third time, Nuada was dying. The reviving cauldron of the Dagdha was very far from here, so this time might be the last. Nuada unbuckled the Claimh Solias and held it toward Harper. "This sword is yours now. Remember our lesson. Draw it only for the light."

Harper sobbed and shook her head. "Phooka!" she screamed, "he's dying. Help him!" Her cry for help trailed off in heaving tears. The others were deep in battles of their own; Nuada knew no one would come.

"Your protector has failed you, just like he failed me, little girl." Gwyn's soft voice lacked the arrogant tone of triumph Nuada expected to find there.

Nuada wanted desperately to hope somehow, someday his son would see the error of his ways and come back to the light. He ignored Gwyn's taunt. A smile played across his lips as he heard the thunder of dozens of approaching feet. More Fir Bolg, and he could hear the much higher voices of some Green World Fae. At least some of the council delegation had agreed to fight to protect the Fir Bolg village. Perhaps there was hope yet. He focused on Harper's face, searching her green eyes as his vision darkened.

"Take the stone shard to the Undying Lands, heal the Lia Fail. Find Manannan Mac Lir. He can help you. And Harper, I am so proud of you. My queen."

The last thing Nuada heard was Harper screaming his name.

CHAPTER 49

Searing liquid raged through every blood vessel in his body. A violent, whole-body spasm shattered the remaining dregs of blissful glamour. Emilio screamed. And he wasn't alone. Wails and shrieks from the other four escapees echoed off the empty walls.

His eyes snapped into focus but squeezed shut as soon as the scene in the room registered. His eyelids alone failed to shield him from what was happening.

"Emilio. What is this stuff?" Selina asked through gritted teeth. A low scream followed the question through her clenched jaw.

"Can't be sure. But it's bad." If Emilio was right, bad was an understatement. His best guess clouded his thoughts with terror. The last stage of Abraxas had begun, and the liquid oozing into their veins was the catalyst that would begin rewriting their genes. He wanted to protect the others from his revelation.

"Oh, my intrepid intern, don't sell yourself short." Breas bent over Emilio, hands clasped behind his back. "You stole enough files to piece it all together."

Emilio panted and bit back another scream. He turned his

head to see an IV connected to his left arm. The contents were as bright green as antifreeze. "I won't be seeking employment with Erimus Pharmaceutical once my internship is over."

Breas laughed. "I'm afraid I can't accept your resignation. You'll soon be employed in one of our more secret divisions. The pay is terrible, but we offer free room and board."

If not for the straps binding him to the bed, he would have flopped onto the floor from writhing. A wave of sharp pains lanced through every muscle, and when those subsided, his spine felt like it contained scalding water. But that wasn't the worst part. Beneath his skin and deep in his organs, he felt his flesh crawling and roiling like his body parts had become unmoored and were migrating to different areas of his body. Whatever this green crap was, it felt like he was liquefying from the inside. *Don't caterpillars dissolve once they make their cocoons?*

"Sir, the treatment is almost finished. Once the IV is complete, they're ready to go into the mist." Dr. Jones scribbled notes on his clipboard.

"What are you doing to us, you Fomorian bastard?" Selina hissed.

Similar questions called from around the room. Breas ignored them all and focused his attention on Emilio as though he were the only one worthy of a reply. "You've had a moment, have you figured it out yet?"

"This shiny garbage in the IV is changing our genes by using a catalyst derived from something I couldn't identify. But I'm certain its purpose is to reactivate stem cells, switch on some of our dormant genes. But for what? Why would you do this?" Emilio noticed his bag of shiny liquid was draining fast, like hourglass sand pouring out.

"Not quite right." Breas tapped the IV bag. "The catalyst is merely making you, shall we say, malleable? Reverting you to a state of genetic flux. The mist outside is what will sculpt you into something powerful."

Moans of despair rose like a chorus behind him. Emilio clenched his fists and slammed his body back and forth in his restraints. "You have no right—" The rest of his sentence was cut off by his own howl of agony as a fresh wave of white-hot fire engulfed his muscles.

"Why us?" Selina asked what Emilio, for the moment, couldn't before descending into her own bout of wailing.

"We have the most correct genes," Emilio said.

"Exactly! Erimus always hires the best and brightest interns. Long ago Fae intermingled with humans. You five are even more special. Dr. Jones here thinks your resistance to Fae magic is due to a high concentration of magical genes and that will cause something wondrous to bloom in the mist."

Emilio retched as his stomach rippled. It felt like the organ moved higher into his throat. It had to be anxiety. His conscious mind grasped at straws to deny what he knew was happening deep down.

"Oh look. Out of time." Breas flipped the empty IV bag between his fingers. "Time to go." With a wave, he summoned Callon and Zallile from their posts near the door.

The Fae went from bedside to bedside, glamouring the five of them. When Callon arrived at Emilio's bedside, Breas halted him before he could cast the magic.

"Silence him but leave his awareness intact. He's a budding young scientist, after all. Let him collect some observational data."

Emilio opened his mouth to curse out the arrogant prick dooming him, but his lips moved with no sound. He kicked at the end of the bed as much as he was able. His nostrils flared with every breath while he tried to burn Breas with his eyes.

More of the little black-eyed gothic boys, redcaps, and trolls scuttled around the gurneys. As the doctor unbuckled the restraints, rough hands seized the captives and manhandled them out of the room. The pain in Emilio's stomach intensified when a troll slung him over his shoulder in a fireman's carry. Scream after soundless scream tore from his lips.

Ahead of him, Selina bobbed along, borne by a small group of redcaps. Callon and the delicate sylph Zallile brought up the rear of the macabre parade.

Emilio thought of all the people he'd left behind in their failed escape plan. A similar fate awaited the ones who survived. "I'm so sorry," he mouthed.

The five prisoners ended their brief journey about fifty feet from the tower at a row of trees with corkscrew branches. The thick mist clung to the ground but surged at their approach. Foggy cocoons hovered in the trees around the perimeter. Not Fae larvae being fed humans like he thought his first night in this cursed place. They would have been pretty if Emilio didn't know what was inside. Soon, he'd be one of them.

His Fae escorts lifted their hands and he and his friends levitated. Emilio's head sagged forward, watching coils of the mist reach toward him like tentacles. Paralysis kept him from shrinking away as trickles of mist snaked up his legs, winding their way around his torso. More and more wisps climbed up from the earth and added layer after layer like cotton candy.

Everywhere the mist touched bare skin brought an electric tingle. He tried to hold his breath instinctively to avoid breathing in whatever lived in the miasma. It failed, and he sucked in a gasping breath. His lungs felt the same tingling sensation that quickly joined the searing pain and migrating organs.

With each passing moment, Emilio felt heavier and heavier. Mercifully, the mist seemed to put him to sleep. As his consciousness faded like the fall of a stage curtain, he thought of Harper. He still had hope she'd find him and either save him or put him out of his misery.

CHAPTER 50

"Nuada! No!" *Please no, he can't be dead. He just can't.* But in her heart, she knew that he was. A jagged cry wavered on her lips, building in fury until it became a bellow.

"I'll fucking kill you, you monster," she screamed at Gwyn.

"Unlikely."

Gwyn's brown cloak hung to midthigh. He reached up a gloved hand and unfastened a brass knotwork clasp. With a flourish he draped it over his father's body.

On the ridge, the clang of blades and shouting reverberated off the craggy mountains. The Fir Bolg and their guests were being overrun. The discovery of the village, her mother tucked away inside it, all but certain.

"Time to go, girl." With a casual wave, the stones and roots creaked and loosened their grip just enough so Gwyn could bind Harper's wrists behind her back. She squeezed her eyes shut and tried to ignite the spark of magic within. Nothing.

Gwyn retrieved his mask and lowered it over his face, becoming once more the monster on the outside he was on the inside. He swept the Cliamh Solais from where it lay and prodded Harper forward.

"You killed your own father. Demon." Her mouth was dry. So were her eyes. She felt empty, desiccated. Icy fingers of dread for her mother and her new friends tore at her insides.

"Yes, I did." Gwyn gripped her arm.

Once, Emilio had convinced her to go to a protest for gay rights. When the police came, the organizers had told them not to fight but to go limp like a ragdoll. She used the same tactic now. Gwyn's arrival would be bad news for the Fir Bolg. If the only card she had left was to slow him down, she would by any means necessary. She let all the tension drain from her legs and back and slumped, dragging Gwyn halfway down with her.

"Get up, foolish girl." His hand tightened like a vice around her arm and he shook her while hoisting her up.

He took a couple of steps before her weight dragged him staggering backward. "Stop this silliness now, or—"

"What? You'll kill me before your owner does?"

He growled through gritted teeth and the flames in the sockets of the skull mask crackled. "If this is how you want it to go." The leader of the Wild Hunt lurched forward, digging his heels deep into the earth with every step he dragged her along the forest floor. He was stronger than Harper expected and very probably fueled by rage. Her passive resistance barely slowed his advance toward her mother.

An image of the village burning, her mom and the Fir Bolg all dead, bubbled up and she cried out.

She flung her legs around a bush and gripped as tight as she could. As a result, Gwyn lost his hold on her arm, and she dropped face first into the pointy pine needles. With a triumphant harrumph, she looped her hands over her feet so they hung in front of her. Next she whipped around so her body was parallel to the bank of the hill and rolled back down as fast as she could.

Her captor leapt after her, landing on her other side so that she rolled into his legs.

"Enough! This is pointless," he bellowed. He bent down, grabbed her at the waist, and hoisted her over his shoulder so her head dangled down his back. So she flailed her legs and pounded his back as hard as she could, over and over. He was unmoved and loped even faster toward the skirmish.

Once they entered the part of the woods where the invisible village rested, Harper's chest tightened. Small clusters of Fir Bolg warriors battled the elves and other Fae of the Wild Hunt. Several lay dead. Lord Ezrynhivar and Queen Serotina led their entourages in a clash with some elves to rescue a pair of Fir Bolg pinned against a massive boulder by Sluagh and goblins.

Her friends were badly outnumbered. She craned her head to try to catch sight of the Phooka and Paegrinn. Her limited vantage didn't reveal whether they were there or not.

"You monster," Harper said.

Gwyn ignored her and intercepted an elven woman.

"Report."

The elf bowed. "We've not located their city, but we are trying to keep as many of the Fir Bolg alive as we can."

"They'll never join us," Gwyn said.

"Yes, but they can power the gateway. And that grisly human doctor may find them useful for his . . . experiments."

"Very good. Do your best to incapacitate them, but if you can't, use lethal force. We cannot afford the Fir Bolg to be roused to war against us."

"Understood."

One of Harper's punches must have hit a soft spot, because Gwyn let out an oomph and dumped her on the ground.

She shook all over, hating herself for showing such weakness. Gwyn rested barely six feet from the occluded entrance to the village. Six feet from finding and killing her mother just like he had his own father. A strangled moan tore itself from her throat.

Gwyn turned his fiery eyes to her. "It would be easier on all of us if you just told me where the entrance is."

Harper spat at him. "Fuck you." Empty defiance was all she had left.

"No matter. The Fae may not be able to sense the earth magic that hides this village, but I do, and it's close." He tilted his head and ambled a winding path around the entryway Harper knew was there. She focused on the tattered hem of her dress to avoid giving away its location herself.

"It's so close, but evasive. No matter. In a few moments I'll pinpoint it and tear the magic away."

Harper heard the smile in his voice and felt the surge of magic bubble deep in his core. Sensing another's power was new. She twisted Ez's ring around her finger, thinking it must be the reason. Gwyn ap Nudd reached a hand right toward the village and started a low chant similar to the magic she heard Nuada cast before.

Mom. No. Damned if she'd let this monster find and kill her friends and family. With a shriek she lurched to her feet and body-slammed Gwyn, sending the skull mask tumbling from his face. He staggered forward, pivoted on his heel, and backhanded her. She spun a half circle before slamming into the dirt.

Fury turned her vision red. Her breath rushed in and out of her chest and something flared to life deep within like someone struck a match. There it was, her magic at last. Fury was its pilot light. She closed her eyes and opened herself to its scintillating sear. As she rose, nostrils flaring, Ezrynhivar's ring blazed, focusing that bubbling, unruly power, and she surged it to a blaze, aiming it at Gwyn's magic, like an opposing wave crashing into another and canceling each other out.

She felt his magic dissipate. He rounded on her, eyes and

mouth open in shock. His brown eyes bored into her as he raised a fist high overhead.

Harper felt the crashing force of his power smash into hers. Her hand flared with that gleaming blue plasma. The entire clearing blazed with the same glow. She fed it all the fear and rage she had, and the light surrounding her gleamed so bright, Gwyn brought a hand across his face to shield his eyes.

Every cell in her body boiled, and it was agony. She howled, a sound half scream, half keening. The ground listed beneath her, and she allowed her shoulder to find a tree trunk to support her weight. She was losing consciousness, but the cloaking spell around the village remained intact, bolstered by her magic, so she dug even deeper and pushed more power through her hand and through the clearing, making many paths to confuse Gwyn so he could not discover the true one leading to the village above. Each time Gwyn's magic sliced at the fabric of the invisibility sorcery, her magic sewed it back together.

The Fir Bolg cloak was huge, and Gwyn was powerful. Harper's vision darkened around the edges and her head swam.

Gwyn's face burst out in beads of sweat, and she felt a tsunami of his power swelling within him, far more than she could hold back. But she'd die trying.

I'm sorry, Emilio. I have to save my mom, and this place of peace. I'll probably die here, never knowing what happened to you. Guilt wracked her. But in that moment, Nuada's pragmatic voice echoed in her mind. It told her that her friend was far from here, nothing she could do about that now, but she could save her remaining family, and the Fir Bolg.

"Harper, this is hopeless. I will find the village."

"Over. My. Dead. Body." The last word ended in a tortured scream and she slid farther down the tree trunk. He was so strong, and all that remained of her eyesight was a small disk, Gwyn ap Nudd at the center of it.

"You're using your own life force. I'm using the land's limitless power. You can't win. You'll only drain yourself and die."

The shove of his magic eased off while he spoke, giving her a moment to gulp in several gasps of air.

"Then I die protecting what I love. And you go home empty handed." *Maybe they're escaping through some other entry to the village even now. I have to hold on.*

Gwyn whipped a tendril of magic at her. Not enough to overpower, but enough to let her know he could, and would, destroy her.

Harper screamed. She felt as bright as the sun but was burning out like a candle. She had no idea how to draw on the energy of others, but it did seem her power responded to her emotion. Her anger, her best friend all these years, faded, because no feeling that intense could last and she was afraid for her family. She felt her power flicker. *No. Not now. Please not now.*

Gwyn sent another whip of liquid power and she fell back and slid the rest of the way down the trunk of the tree, coming to rest slumped on her side at the roots.

"It's over, little girl. Release your hold on the cloaking magic."

"Never." Her voice all but a whisper.

If this was it, she wanted to go out remembering her mother as she was then. Whole. The life back in her eyes. *I love you, Mom.* She couldn't recall if she'd told her that in their short time with the Fir Bolg, but she did. Fiercely. Love for her mother and her lost father opened in her heart like a flower, easing the agony of maintaining her grip on the cloaking magic.

New strength flowed into her legs and she slid back up the tree, standing, but wavering on her feet. Gwyn flicked another wisp of his power at her, but this time something different happened.

The magic roiling in her center felt less jagged, less searing. Only the light of it remained and she knew this power flowed from love, not anger. Both of her hands blazed with pure white light. She swung them around, both fists clenched, and aimed a blast right at Gwyn's chest. He toppled back on his backside on impact.

He responded by releasing the hurricane of magic he'd been building and hurled it toward the cloaking spell. But Harper's bright power met it like a wall of light surrounding what she loved, and it dissipated like droplets of rain.

Harper smiled and dropped to one knee, chest resting on her leg, lungs heaving. She lacked the strength to stand. The world around her appeared almost black, mere shadows remaining. The best she could hope for was that she'd bought her loved ones time to escape.

Her grip on the cloaking power was now tenuous at best, but she fed the last shreds of her fading life to her hands and stared into the eyes of Gwyn ap Nudd while her fists blazed brighter.

"You can't win. I can literally do this all night, but you barely cling to life even now. Give up before you kill yourself."

That resigned sadness edged back onto Gwyn's face. He stood his ground but did not test her again.

"I was pretty clear about my not caring about that. Wonder what your master will do when you bring back my corpse. I thought she wanted to kill me herself."

"Everyone you ever loved will fall to Badb's war anyway. This is pointless. Why fight?"

"Because it's all I have left." Harper hated the tear that rolled down her face.

Gwyn shook his head and barked a mirthless laugh. "You make a good Tuatha. Fighting hopeless battles. Except, unlike them, you haven't given up."

Harper heard the battle still raging behind her. She hoped the Phooka, Paegrinn, and the rest had survived. In front of her, Gwyn stroked his short beard, like he was mulling a puzzle, not slaughtering innocents. She felt his magic recede just a little and he crouched next to her.

"Tell you what, I repeat my earlier offer. You release your hold on the cloaking spell. Come with me willingly, and I will let this place remain hidden."

"Liar. You'll just knock me out and kill them all anyway. That's what demons do."

"My people do not lie. I'm offering you what you want. You can save this place, at least until Badb's war begins. All you have to do is come with me." He held out a hand to her.

Harper didn't believe him, but she had nothing left to give. Gwyn's next blast of magic would lower the invisibility spell and reveal the Fir Bolg's little utopia along with her mother. What surprised her was that he hadn't directed a lot of his power directly at her. Probably afraid of ruining his mistress's prize.

Stay safe, Mom. I love you. If it was a ruse, she hoped the additional time this one last move bought them was enough. If it wasn't, heck, she was planning on going to that island anyway. She'd try to escape Gwyn somewhere between here and there.

"Fine. I accept." The white light faded from her fists and she let her hold on the cloaking spell fade. Gwyn's magic also subsided. So far, he kept his word.

"A wise choice." The leader of the Wild Hunt drew himself tall and strode to her side. As he crouched next to her, he called over his shoulder. "We're done here. Break off the attack. I have what we came for."

"But what of the Fir Bolg? Badb would be pleased if we brought them to her alive." The Sidhe who spoke was a wiry, tall man with a single braid.

Gwyn met Harper's eyes, then lifted his chin over his shoulder. "If they are, even my magic cannot find them. The longer we delay, the more chance others may come for the heir."

Harper hadn't expected him to spare the others, but she was

relieved he did. At least she'd saved someone. Yet the cost had been steep. Her breath caught as she envisioned Nuada lying dead, alone in the forest, and Emilio, still a prisoner somewhere on that cursed island. Hell, she was on her way there, courtesy of the Wild Hunt. That might be a small advantage, but she'd need to figure out how to escape and find him once she had the strength to stand.

With a final, lingering glance above where the hidden village still existed, thanks to her magic, she resigned herself to being Gwyn's prisoner.

"And now, little girl, we can't have you making trouble and trying to escape." He passed a hand over Harper's face, and she slept.

BEFORE THE LAST BATTLE OF MOYTURA, THE BOUNDARY between the Fae and human world had closed. Discover how the Fae invasion of Portland began.

A missing father. A mind-bending mist. An island where two worlds collide.

Selina Leanabel survives by staying in the shadows, running a quiet apothecary far from the reach of the Fae. But when teen Charlotte Holloway arrives saying she can't go home...literally, with a story of a father lost behind a wall of unnatural fog, Selina's boundaries begin to crumble.

On Sauvie Island, the air is thick with a warding spell that breaks the mind and hungers for the soul. Entering the mist means risking the very stability Selina has fought so hard to reclaim.

Click below and claim your copy.

https://dl.bookfunnel.com/l4xleonwpi

AN ISLAND FULL OF ENEMY FAE LIE BETWEEN HARPER AND Emilio. Some want to deliver her to Badb Catha. And some have darker appetites. Will she make it across the cursed land in time to save him?

Find out in *The Cursed Land, The Last Battle of Moytura Book 2*

Get your special illustrated edition copy at MollyJStanton.com

ACKNOWLEDGMENTS

The book you are about to read would have never have crossed the finish line to publication without the critique and encouragement from my beta readers. Their insights helped make this book even better. A thousand thanks to: Renee Scattolini, Becca Bogin, Diane Gonzalez, Patti Van Brederode, and Jackie Loson Rago.

When I was a child, my family trekked annually from our home in Idaho to the Oregon coast. Those trips cultivated a love of Portland in all its weird splendor, and a sense of connection to the old forests surrounding the city. They winnowed their way into this story. So I owe thanks to my parents, Michael and Rebecca Stanton for bringing me to those magical places.

ABOUT THE AUTHOR

Molly J Stanton grew up in rural Idaho where cows outnumber humans fifty-to-one, and tipping them was an Olympic sport. Fed a steady diet of terrifying old Celtic fairy stories and the local firsthand tales of harrowing Sasquatch encounters, she cultivated a lifelong passion for unseen worlds.

While she loves rocks, trees, and water, she craved more excitement than Idaho could offer. So a couple short months after graduation, she up and left to attend Smith College in quaint Northampton, Massachusetts. After four years, she failed to develop a snazzy Massachusetts accent, not dropping even a single 'r'.

Graduate school in the Lehigh Valley of Pennsylvania shoved her into professional writing. Dull, pedantic scientific papers for academic journals that literally two people in the world read. During her subsequent career as an addictions therapist, Molly, for mysterious reasons, hoarded books on writing, yet never wrote a word other than snappy e-mails and clinical case notes.

Somewhere deep in her unconscious mind, Cerridwen stirred her great cauldron, brewing vicarious experiences as a counselor, Celtic myths, fairy abduction stories, and those Bigfoot tall tales into the inspiration and drive to finally write that Urban Fantasy series.

When she's not writing, Molly farms and sings off-key songs to her cat. To find out when her next book is released, or to watch the farm take shape and see pictures of her crazy cat, sign up for her newsletter at MollyJStanton-dot-com.

facebook.com/mollyjstantonauthor

instagram.com/mollyjstantonauthor

pinterest.com/mollyjstantonauthor

Hunted by Fae, The Last Battle of Moytura Book 1, by Molly J Stanton, published by Molly J Stanton Fogelsville, PA 18051.

www.MollyJStanton.com